Acclaim for Pepper Basham

LOYALLY, LUKE

"Readers, you are in for a pure delight! Luke Edgewood is, in a word, dreamy. At once tough and tender, guarded and vulnerable, he is a book boyfriend to rival all book boyfriends. And despite being a princess, readers will absolutely relate to Ellie's struggle to overcome her past, prove herself to her family, and make the noble choice—even if it means breaking her own heart in the process. Luke and Ellie's love story has the perfect amount of tension, chemistry, and tugging-at-your-heartstrings moments. Simply unputdownable! Even if this is your first trip to Skymar, you'll feel right at home in this funny, cozy absolute gem of a royal romance! To quote Luke Edgewood, 'I reckon the best kind of love is simple in one way . . . Choosing each other over and over and over again.' When it comes to this book (and the series), these will be stories readers choose to read over and over and over again."

—Emma St. Clair, *USA TODAY* bestselling author

"With a hero who's better at texting and a princess who can wield a hammer, *Loyally, Luke* is 'peppered' with Ms. Basham's signature style of swoony romance and charming characters. She's also added a message we all need to hear and believe for ourselves as two unlikely people wonder if worlds can really merge and not merely collide. This will definitely be another fan favorite."

—Toni Shiloh, Christy Award–winning author

"Fans of Pepper Basham's Skymar series will be thrilled and delighted with this much-anticipated third and final installment to the series. In pure Basham fashion, every page oozes with the magic of romance and characters you won't easily forget. *Loyally, Luke* is an escape many readers look for."

—Sarah Monzon, bestselling author of *All's Fair in Love and Christmas*

"Pepper Basham has done it again! The author's sly wit and enduring tenderness make Luke and Ellie's story a (literal) love letter to the power of authenticity, hope, and redemption. *Loyally, Luke* is sure to hook new readers and delight those who already adore the one-of-a-kind Edgewood family. Prepare to fall head over heels for flannel and fishing!"

—Julie Christianson, author of the Apple Valley Love Stories series

POSITIVELY, PENELOPE

"Basham is a rising star. *Positively, Penelope* is humorous and touching, and everything you want in the perfect summer read. Don't miss this one."

—Rachel Hauck, *New York Times* bestselling author of *The Wedding Dress*

"What do you get when you combine a lovable heroine with characters who have mastered the art of witty banter? A charming read. And that is what *Positively, Penelope* is."

—Sheila Roberts, *USA TODAY* bestselling author

"This book is a positive delight from the first line to the last. I adored Penelope in Izzy's book, and she screamed for her own book, so I couldn't wait to dive into the pages of this novel. Oh my goodness, it was a true, laugh-out-loud joy to read this book. The story was filled with twists and hiccups, but there was also such delight and fun. And fairy tales. And princesses. And Julie Andrews. And Gene Kelly. All the things I adore. In one place. And the kissing. Pepper does enjoy writing kissing books. I highly recommend this sweet, fun, romantic romp of a book. It was wonderful!"

—Cara Putman, award-winning author of more than 35 novels, including *Flight Risk*

"Like the character Penelope herself, this entire book radiates sunshine and magic. The banter between Penelope and her siblings kept me smiling. The theatrical references kept me humming and tapping my toes. And the overall joy that Pepper Basham exudes with her unique writing style and voice kept me engaged in a story I never wanted to leave. Simply put, this book is supercalifragilisticexpialidocious."

—Becca Kinzer, author of *Dear Henry, Love Edith*

"You won't want to put this book down! Pepper has a way of creating characters who are disarming and charismatic in all the best ways, while still reflecting our inner selves. Her stories are charming and witty, and I've never laughed so much while reading! You'll walk away with more joy than you came with and a heart full of assurance and encouragement about the power of our heavenly Father's heart for your love story."

—Victoria Lynn, author of *The Chronicles of Elira*, *Bound*, and *London in the Dark*

AUTHENTICALLY, IZZY

"A long-distance romance anchors this cute contemporary from Basham (*The Heart of the Mountains*) . . . Basham primarily tells her story through emails, texts, and dating app messages, a quirky approach that complements the adorable leads. Filled with humor and grace, this is perfect for fans of Denise Hunter."

—*Publishers Weekly*

"*Authentically, Izzy* is an absolutely adorable, charming, sweet romance that genuinely made me laugh out loud. A wonderful escape you're sure to fall in love with!"

—Courtney Walsh, *New York Times* bestselling author

"*Authentically, Izzy* is witty, endearing, and full of literary charm. Grab your favorite blanket and get ready to snuggle into this sweet book that will make you believe your dreams will find you."

—Jennifer Peel, *USA TODAY* bestselling author

"You don't see enough epistolary novels these days, so the format of this being told almost entirely through emails appealed to me straightaway, and I wasn't disappointed! We follow librarian Izzy as she meets perfect-sounding bookshop owner Brodie online and wonders if he's too good to be true. Filled with the wonderfully warm cast of Izzy's family, and the swoon-worthy email exchanges with Brodie, I absolutely loved reading this book and felt like Izzy was a real friend rather than a book character! A book written by a book lover, about a book lover, for book lovers everywhere! I loved it! In fact, the only issue with this book is that my to-read list has grown exponentially from Izzy and Brodie's recommendations! It's a book lover's dream read!"

—Jaimie Admans, author of romantic comedies

Loyally, Luke

Other Books by Pepper Basham

Loyally, Luke

a novel

PEPPER BASHAM

THOMAS NELSON

Loyally, Luke

Published in Nashville, Tennessee, by Thomas Nelson. Thomas Nelson is a registered trademark of HarperCollins Christian Publishing, Inc.

Published in association with William K. Jensen Literary Agency, 119 Bampton Court, Eugene, Oregon 97404.

Maps by Lydia Basham.

Thomas Nelson titles may be purchased in bulk for educational, business, fundraising, or sales promotional use. For information, please email SpecialMarkets@ThomasNelson.com.

Publisher's Note: This novel is a work of fiction. Names, characters, places, and incidents are either products of the author's imagination or used fictitiously. All characters are fictional, and any similarity to people living or dead is purely coincidental.

Library of Congress Cataloging-in-Publication Data

Names: Basham, Pepper, author.
Title: Loyally, Luke: a novel / Pepper Basham.
Description: Nashville, Tennessee: Thomas Nelson, 2024. | Summary: "Sometimes love means embracing the good, the bad . . . and even the impossible"--Provided by publisher.
Identifiers: LCCN 2023055117 (print) | LCCN 2023055118 (ebook) | ISBN 9780840716583 (paperback) | ISBN 9780840716729 (e-pub) | ISBN 9780840716736
Subjects: LCGFT: Romance fiction. | Novels.
Classification: LCC PS3602.A8459 L69 2024 (print) | LCC PS3602.A8459 (ebook) | DDC 813/.6--dc23/eng/20231204
LC record available at https://lccn.loc.gov/2023055117
LC ebook record available at https://lccn.loc.gov/2023055118

Printed in the United States of America

24 25 26 27 28 LBC 5 4 3 2 1

To #rambodad
The first hero of my life and the man who
helped lead me to the Greatest Hero.
Many of Luke's best qualities I first saw in you.
I am so grateful I got to call you Daddy.
Until heaven.

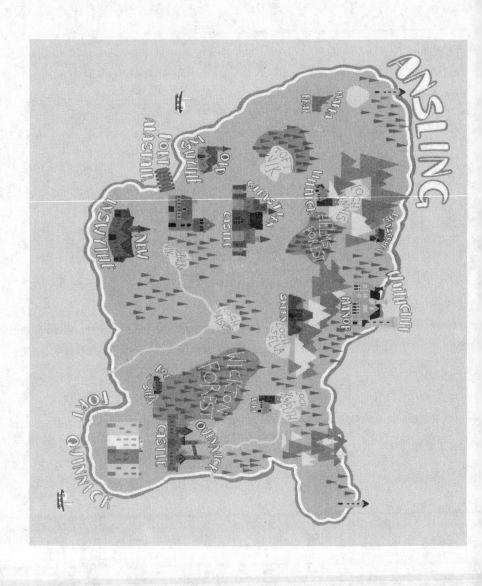

PROLOGUE

Don't read this book.

It's embarrassing.

And private.

I have a feeling my youngest sister has paid some sort of homage to the Hallmark pixies and they've turned my world into an ooey gooey, magical snow globe of romantic tropes.

Argh. Even my sentences are starting to sound like mush.

The whole situation is disgusting.

Well, not all of it.

The architecture was nice. And the work, which was mostly distraction-free.

Until it wasn't.

And there were some cute kids around.

And an actual ball. Not the March Madness kind!

I'm surrounded by pixie dust and romance and no amount of Rambo quotes will help.

And then there's this woman who is annoying . . . until she's not.

But she IS impossible.

I'm doomed.

Luke

PS: Send high levels of testosterone my way to combat the romance. Or send a gunship.

PPS: Help me, Obi-Wan—you're my only hope.

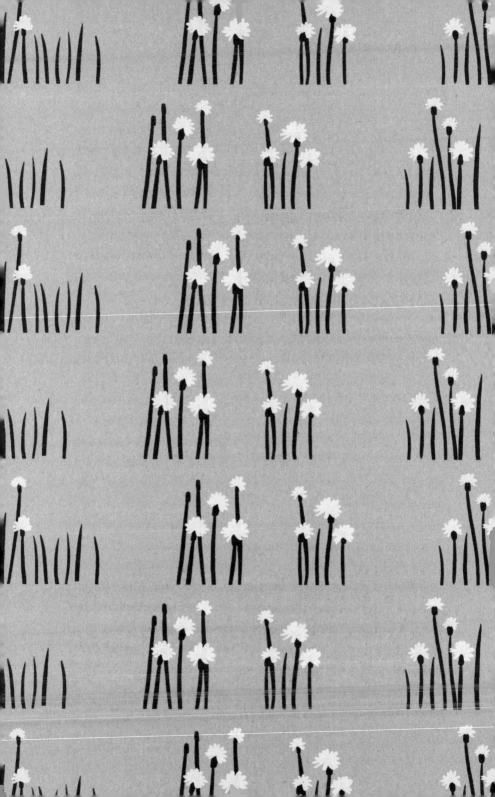

CHAPTER 1

*The Daily Edge: Social Tattle from
One Edge of Skymar to the Other*

It's been a while since we've heard much about Skymar's most notorious princess, but rumor has it she's stepping back into her position as a working royal. After a less-than-regal history, is Princess Elliana St. Clare, Duchess of Mara and the North Country, ready to take on the responsibilities she so shamelessly denounced three years ago? Only time will tell. And what may be on the radar for her future romances? Is there anyone in the aristocratic ranks willing to take on her past to plan a future? Share your tattle in the comments below!

• •

Text from Izzy to Penelope: You haven't happened to hear anything about Luke's arrival yet, have you? I'm waiting in the arrival line outside the airport (as he told me to do) but I've not heard anything from him.

Penelope: Are you surprised? He's probably going to leave us in suspense about whether he arrived safe just for spite. Or to cause us to develop worry lines. Besides, half the time he forgets he even has a phone.

Izzy: He's gotten better at keeping it nearby since I moved to Skymar. But his plane should have landed a half hour ago and I've not heard anything. He has to go through customs and get his bags, so maybe he still has his phone on airplane mode?

Penelope: I think he does things like this on purpose to annoy us. Like we're all waiting for his important words or something. He's such a BROTHER!

Izzy: Well, I AM kind of waiting on his words. And I'm so excited to introduce him to Brodie's family and show him Skern and have him see Brodie's house up close and personal! Oh, how I've missed you guys and it's only been three months since I left North Carolina.

Penelope: I'm glad he's getting to stay for a while too. And he's hired Charlie to run his business here while he's in Skymar, but I'm watching his dogs. Which, of course, makes me want to get one now. I've always loved Charlie. She's one of our few cousins who can actually carry on a conversation about important things. Like musicals and food. We tried talking about fashion once, but her style and mine are really different. The only hat she's ever worn is a baseball cap. Can you imagine?

Izzy: Not everyone has your shoe fetish or collection of hats, Penelope.

Penelope: I know. Sometimes it makes me sad to think about that. The right hat can really change a person's day. Or the right shoes. I think Luke wouldn't be so grumpy all the time if he had better shoe choices.

Izzy: Luke's fine. I mean, I hope he's fine. I'm going to text him again.

Text from Luke to Izzy and Penelope: I'm here and I'm not responding to any of your messages until I've had coffee. Thank me later.

Loyally, Luke

There were precious few things in life that Luke required.

Coffee was one of those things.

And with the headache pressing in on his skull with a viselike grip, stopping for coffee might be the difference between life and death . . . for other people. He walked through the airport, squinting as he scanned the shops on each side. Flying didn't usually bother him, until it did. And then it made up for lost time.

Thankfully, he'd been to Skymar once before, and since the airport wasn't large, he didn't have to think too hard about directions. Which was a mercy from God because he was having a hard enough time trying to think at all.

A mixture of English and the local language of Caedric blended around him as he waited in line, the noise and lights aggravating the ache. Pushing past pain wasn't new to him. He'd known the wrong end of too many accidents in his job as a carpenter and stonemason. Most left a scar or two. But headaches carried a different sort of internal, brain-distracting, teeth-grating kind of pain.

He rolled his suitcase behind him and adjusted his backpack on his shoulder as he stepped into the line at the nearest java joint. He'd appreciated his short visit to the island a few months ago to help his sister Penelope rescue a stage production of *The Sound of Music*. The folks had been friendly, the pace slow, the air fresh and clean. And the vastness of mountains and sea on the horizon promised plenty of space and quiet, which suited Luke just fine.

In fact, spending the last visit in the city of Mountcaster, though quaint, made Luke all the happier that most of his work in Skymar this time would take place in more isolated locations.

A cabin in the forest. An old stone barn by a lake. The small village of Skern.

Quiet, tranquil, with the added bonus of using his workman's hands to take something from broken to beautiful.

Safe and sound from following in the footsteps of his two sisters, who'd both experienced romantic adventures in this country. His headache sharpened at the very idea of romance. Nope.

The company of his dogs proved a lot less painful than his romantic past.

The scent of oranges mixed with some floral smell hit him in the gut and tightened his head all over again. With the added smell of coffee, he felt a fresh bout of nausea lodge in his throat.

Usually he liked the smell of oranges, but not today.

He swallowed and shifted a step back.

Ahead of him in line stood a woman who wore a light blue scarf over her head and massive sunglasses and kept her face bent over the phone in her hand. Something about her snagged his attention, which only added to his current annoyance.

With those heels and that tight skirt, it was hard to ignore biology. She had nice legs.

So he looked right back up at the coffee display, even though he already knew exactly what he wanted. Simple. Easy. One large black coffee. Hopefully, that order would be the same no matter which language or coffee franchise he used. Maybe desperation radiated off him in a language any coffee connoisseur understood.

His gaze dropped back to the lady, who'd turned just enough for him to make out her profile. A slightly familiar one? Maybe it was the fact that the scarf and sunglasses added a dash of mystery. Or fame?

Well, if she was famous, he wouldn't be able to pinpoint her. He and social media had as nonexistent a relationship as his current love life, which suited him just fine too.

His shoulders might be big from all the brick laying and stonemasonry, but they sure weren't big enough to hold all the problems dancing around in the cyberworld.

He grimaced at the very thought and glanced back at the woman.

Who did she remind him of? He pushed through his aching skull to land on a memory. Was it from a movie? A spy movie?

She didn't look like anyone from *Rambo*. He squinted. *Indiana Jones*? One of the blonde villainesses came to mind, but that wasn't exactly it. *Mission: Impossible*? No. Though that particular blonde was definitely easy on the eyes . . . and terrifying.

An older movie, maybe? And then the blurry recollection began to take shape . . . and his nausea took a turn toward disappointment—in himself.

Grace Kelly.

He closed his eyes and groaned, further frustrated that he'd actually remembered the actress's name.

Of course, he'd only watched the movie to appease a sick Penelope. And it hadn't been so bad because of Cary Grant. And fighting.

His lips curled into a snarl. But did he have to recall the actress's name? For some reason, that just seemed to hurt. Deep.

And . . . forced him to open his eyes and reexamine the woman's profile. Her posture was straighter than Uncle Herman's in a back brace, which somehow made him want to stand up a little straighter too.

Blonde hair slipped out from beneath the scarf, a few tendrils escaping some sort of bun. He grinned. The only part of her that didn't look under control.

Tense posture, tense bun—his gaze trailed down—tense skirt.

But those loose curls seemed to defy all the tension.

His attention came back to her face.

And she had a delicate chin.

Ouch. He shook his head. Delicate chin?

He'd blame that on the headache.

He immediately glanced away from the woman toward the cashier, who looked too young to even contemplate Luke's current inward struggle. Thirty really shouldn't feel so old.

Why was he even paying attention to the woman in the scarf anyway?

It wasn't like he hadn't seen pretty women before, in Skymar or otherwise.

She placed her order, or Luke supposed so, but she spoke in the local language. He'd only heard it a few times up close, and it held a lyrical quality. Like a folk song.

He rolled his eyes, but the motion hurt his head.

He'd forgotten how having a headache reduced his IQ.

Allowing his eyelids to drift closed again, he let the passing interest in the woman dissolve into the far back regions of his brain and drew in a steadying breath. The weakness of a moment, plain and simple. After all, he'd just been internally congratulating himself on his happy bachelorhood . . . or bachelor . . . ness?

Lord, help him! He was an idiot!

When the woman moved to the side, Luke stepped forward and placed his order, having to repeat himself three times. Evidently, ordering simple black coffee proved a puzzle in frou-frou coffee places around the world.

Or else his accent proved the real trouble.

He frowned. Was his accent really that bad?

Five minutes later, he raised the long-awaited cup to his lips, anticipating the healing powers of caffeine, and took a coveted taste of . . . flower java? He pinched his lips tight through a hard swallow. He'd been poisoned!

Was this even coffee?

And if so, it wasn't *his* coffee.

Making a quick pivot back toward the counter, he slammed directly into Grace Kelly. She greeted him with a look of pure disgust, probably just like his, and then stumbled from their impact. Luke reached out to steady her and the quick motion did two things at once: jostled the full coffees so that some of the liquid burst from the top, spraying in both their directions, and shook the sunglasses down to the end of her nose.

"Excuse me, ma'am."

Blue eyes—strikingly blue—stared back at him and then narrowed. "You were examining me quite thoroughly earlier, sir"—those pink lips dipped into a frown—"so I would have expected you, at the very least, to watch where *I* was going instead of playing some horrible game in order to speak with me."

The inviting tenor of her voice contrasted the belittling tone of her words, causing Luke's comprehension to take longer than usual. The headache didn't help.

Speak with her? Well, wasn't she just a bouquet of arrogance!

"And not only have you doused me in your vile liquid, but you've confiscated *my* coffee." One golden brow rose in challenge before she pushed the sunglasses back to cover those eyes, which seemed to help him find his thoughts more quickly. "Another one of your tricks to 'accidentally'"—she made air quotes—"meet me?"

He hated air quotes. It was sarcasm without the benefit of words.

"Wasn't *my* fault." He turned his cup toward her so that the name scrawled across the outside pointed in her direction. *Luke.* Crystal clear. "I don't have to resort to accidental meetings, thank you. In fact, I'm not a fan of meetings at all." He gestured toward her cup with his chin. "Besides, this ain't coffee." He swallowed to clear the taste from his tongue, pushing the cup toward her. "It's perfume in a cup."

She took the perfume from him as if touching a contaminant and shoved *his* coffee back at him. "Well, yours is petrol."

Luke frowned.

Nobody ought to talk about coffee that way, no matter what sort of pretty voice she used.

He plucked the lid off his cup and raised the coffee to his lips, all the while staring into those shaded eyes without flinching. The undiluted and, thankfully, unflavored liquid met his tainted tongue with glorious rightness. Even his head started feeling clearer.

Oh, his brain was clearing up just fine.

"Bitter, strong, and without a lot of fluff." He hummed his appreciation. "Just the way I like my petrol."

Her pink lips pressed as tight as her skirt and, with a glare he felt through those glasses, she raised her chin. "Of course—a drink to match your personality, I suppose?"

"Exactly." He'd play along. "Yours too, I'd guess?"

"Yes, as a matter of fact." Her lips tipped in a not-so-friendly smile. "Sweet, elegant, and refined."

"That what you call it?" He nodded, giving her back the same kind of smile. "Well, must be the language barrier for sure, 'cause those aren't the words I'd use to describe your coffee."

"There's no knowing what vocabulary you might use." He felt her gaze travel down him more than saw it. "And I wouldn't want to tax your faculties, so I bid you good day."

She swept past him and right out the door, taking her sickeningly sweet perfume coffee and tense personality with her.

And she'd just called him stupid.

He was a lot of things, all of which his vocabulary could identify, but stupid wasn't one of them.

Well, except when it came to women. And in that case, he didn't need a headache to reach the depths of his idiocy.

No wonder he'd called off dating.

He stared at her retreating form and took a long sip of his coffee just to spite her.

It was a good thing he'd met nicer Skymarians on his first visit to the islands, because if she'd been the personality of the general population, he wouldn't have come back. No matter how amazing the opportunity for a craftsman.

Loyally, Luke

Life was too short to voluntarily spend time with rude people.

Then the strange sense of someone staring drew his attention back to the counter.

Every one of the servers and two of the three people in line stared at him wide-eyed. One even stood slack-jawed.

Maybe they hadn't seen many Americans? He looked down over his body. Flannel shirt over a T-shirt, jeans, and tennis shoes.

Nothing out of the ordinary.

He looked back at them, smiled, and raised his cup in salute. "Good coffee."

And with that, he left the shop.

Text from Izzy to Penelope: I got him. But he has a headache, and it really must hurt because he kept asking me if people from Skymar drink black coffee. When I asked why, he said the folks in the shop seemed to have a strange response to his coffee. Or the fact he was an American. OR his argument with a Skymarian lady in the coffee shop.

Penelope: He had an argument with someone before he even left the airport?

Izzy: They got each other's coffee and then she acted rude and demeaning when they had to exchange. He said she looked like a high-class sort because she was in a suit and heels . . . and had some sort of arrogant vibe about her.

Penelope: Wait! They got each other's coffees, had an argument, and Luke actually noticed her shoes? Izzy, you must know what this means!!!

Izzy: I get a little nervous when you use extra exclamation marks while foretelling futures.

Penelope: Oh! Give me five minutes and I'm calling you!!!

Text from Penelope to Luke: Izzy just called me and told me
about your arrival and your . . . meet-cute! Oh, Luke! It's a
perfect movie moment!

Luke: Um . . . I don't recall ever using the word "cute" in my
conversation with Izzy about my arrival. In fact, I rarely
use the word "cute" at all.

Penelope: No, silly. A meet-cute! You know, in the coffee
shop! A meet-cute is a funny or charming first meeting
between two main characters in a movie. Meet . . . cute.
See? Cute meeting.

Luke: There was nothing cute about that meeting. Nothing.
She was arrogant and I had a headache. I ended up feeling
stupid and spilled half my coffee on my shirt. There is
nothing cute about losing one's coffee. Or feeling stupid.

Penelope: See? That's a perfect meet-cute! Ooh, like a Hallmark
movie or rom-com. Luke! I bet you'll see her again.

Luke: I don't want to see her again.

Penelope: That. Is. SO. PERFECT!

Luke: Exactly. It would be perfect to never see her again.

Penelope: Don't you know what this means?

Luke: That my headache is returning?

Penelope: It's the inevitable enemies-to-lovers trope! And you
were wearing flannel! AHH!! I can almost hear the Hallmark
Christmas chime going off in the background of your life.

Luke: It's not Christmas.

Penelope: Lucky for you, the magical Christmas chime
extends all year long.

Meet-cute? He growled down at his phone. Just the two words
paired with the definition turned his stomach. Ridiculous. Penelope
and her little powder-puff, sparkly shoes, glitter world.

What did *she* know?

Loyally, Luke

And the woman in the coffee shop wasn't cute at all. Her face flashed back into his mind, those large blue eyes of hers catching in his memory. Nope. Not cute. Pretty. Maybe even gorgeous, but not cute.

And looks lost their charm when distorted by sneers, glares, and disdain.

Ha! See there? Fantastic vocabulary.

Luke: I'm doomed. Oh, wait! I'm working about a hundred miles from where we met, so no, I won't see her again. And I refuse to respond to any comments you make about the "H" word. Or the Christmas chime. Ever.

Penelope: Twitterpated.

Luke: I'm turning off my phone now.

Penelope: Just you wait. I know about these things. You'll see. No one can truly escape the Christmas chime. Not even you, Luke.

Luke: Bah humbug, Santa isn't real, tiaras are for wimps.

Penelope: Only scared people resort to such senseless responses. Especially about Santa.

Penelope: *chime*

CHAPTER 2

Text from Ellie to Maeve: I am a horrible person.

Maeve: I try not to deny or confirm such statements until I've heard the whole story.

Ellie: There was an American in the airport coffee shop and our coffees were exchanged by mistake. Did I react nicely?

Maeve: I feel certain I can answer that one.

Ellie: It's no excuse, but I'd just read the recent tattle from The Edge and they'd pulled up an old photo from three years ago when I'd stumbled out of a bar wearing something atrocious. Will I never outlive those mistakes? I've made such an effort to distance myself from who I used to be. To change for the better.

Maeve: You have. You need to offer the media some positive photo ops, or they'll keep dredging up the past. And you have plenty for them to dredge up.

Ellie: Thank you for the encouragement, friend.

Maeve: I am surprised, though. Your brother has been a much worse royal than you, and he doesn't garner half the media coverage.

Ellie: Oh dear, I don't want to know what Arran's done recently. The last incident cost Father and Mother a small fortune.

Maeve: No, you don't want to know. But I will say it involves a French model and a bagpipe.

Ellie: I think I just became sick.

Maeve: So how nasty were you to the poor American?

Loyally, Luke

Ellie: Arrogant! A regular prig. After seeing The Edge's photo,
   I was in no mind to talk to anyone and then we bumped
   into each other, splashing coffee in all directions.
   Needless to say, Ms. Nasty raised her head.

Maeve: Well, at least it wasn't caught on camera.

Ellie: I'm groaning at the very idea.

Maeve: And the good thing about an airport meeting is that
   you'll never see him again.

Ellie: Right. Exactly. Though it doesn't stop me from feeling
   like a fiend anyway.

* *

From: Peter MacKerrow
To: Luke Edgewood
Date: March 3
Subject: Introductions and "roughing it"?

My grandfather, Lewis Gray, suggested I send you a quick
note to prepare you for your visit . . . and to introduce myself.
I'm Peter MacKerrow, Lewis Gray's grandson by his younger
daughter, Mirren. Mum married a Scot, so she lives across the
pond on the Isle of Mull, but I've spent summers in Skymar for
years and am taking a yearlong break from attending seminary
in Old Inswythe, so I count Skymar as home too. Since we'll
be renovating some of Grandfather's old properties, he's
planned to have us live at a cabin near the village of Crieff in the
northwestern part of Ansling, which is particularly nice for me
because it is one of the three Scots villages in Skymar (and is a
closer flight to Scotland when I travel home on the weekends).
I should also add that Grandfather has some secret project in

mind for us. He's not told me what the project is, but he has a twinkle in his eyes when he talks about it, which means . . . you should be forewarned. I don't know if you have a twinkle-eyed grandparent, but they're dubious, at best.

I should be in Skern to meet you by early afternoon for the drive to Crieff. Grandfather's arranged for a Mr. Holton to meet us to discuss the "secret job." He said Mr. Holton would explain everything. Sound a bit fishy to you too? If it hadn't come directly from Grandfather, I'd question the legality of the assignment, but Grandfather has an excellent reputation throughout Skymar, with some friends in very high places, so I have to trust it's all aboveboard.

I was relieved to hear that you're used to more simplistic accommodations since we will be living in the cabin while we renovate. However, Grandfather says the fireplace is in working order, so we "won't freeze." I do believe Grandfather is getting a bit of a laugh out of it all . . . and likely at my expense. Hopefully, I'll provide some friendship even if I'm not initially successful at striking a nail. (My father is a historian, and my mum owns a little family bookshop in the village of Glenkirk. Neither swings a hammer very well.) My eldest brother, however, is quite adept at handcrafting and building. I'm more of a bookish sort (another reason to be forewarned).

Grandfather thought you'd like to know that all of the materials and tools are stored at the cabin or on-site at our "secret assignment," which I believe may be ours whether we choose to accept it or not.

See you in a trice.

Peter

Loyally, Luke

Text from Izzy to Penelope and Josephine: Check out my new
ring.

Penelope: OH. MY. GOODNESS!! Is that an engagement
ring? Is it? AHHHHHH!!!!

Izzy: Yes, it is!! And I'm sending a few more photos of the
actual moment. Brodie had Luke on stand-by to take
them! It's been a little over a year since the email where
I thought Brodie was Josie and bared my soul to him. He
said his happily ever after started on that day.

Penelope: Isn't that the most darling thing ever! Oh, I love
him. Well, you know, I don't LOVE him, but I love him!

Josephine: Well, I knew it was inevitable. I'd resigned myself
to you living so far away, but this seems to make it more
permanent. It's a lovely ring. And you two look so happy.

Izzy: He is quite simply the most wonderful man for me. And
I'm living my little fairy tale, getting to work with books
and marry a bookish man.

Josephine: I am happy for you, dear Izzy. At least I know he's a
perfect match for you.

Penelope: And we can go visit, Josephine!! You'd love Skymar.
You've always liked oceans and knitted sweaters.

Izzy: We're not interested in a long engagement. How does
the first weekend in June sound to you guys? The twins
will be close to a year old by then.

Josephine: That's only three months away! What sort of
wedding do you plan to pull together by then?

Izzy: A simple one fit for us.

Penelope: Matt, Iris, and I were already planning to be in
Skymar in June for the annual Darling House theater
meeting, so it's PERFECT!! And I can help with last-
minute things! Oh, Izzy! You must let me cybershop with
you for the dress!

Izzy: And Luke doesn't leave until the second week of June
       so he'll already be here. We thought that would help with
       costs! YAY!! Guys! I'm getting MARRIED!!!!

G randfather suggested we stop in to see the place before we travel
all the way to the cabin."

Peter MacKerrow drove like he talked. Fast.

Luke took the mental lessons he'd learned from teaching Penelope
how to drive and relaxed his body. After surviving Penelope, Luke felt
certain God must have a bigger plan for his life, but Pete made him
question the notion.

"It's a good half-hour drive from the cabin to the village of Crieff,
so if we want to collect any messages . . . er . . . groceries, we ought
to do so now."

Of course, riding with Pete could be character development—
Pete took another turn like a Nascar driver—and if that were the
case, Luke's character was strengthening by the second. At Superman
speeds.

"Seeing both places should help us with planning."

Pete nodded, his dark, reddish-brown hair bouncing with
the movement. "That's what Grandfather said too. And, I think,
Mr. Holton is to meet us there." Pete skirted the edge of the road
where a rock wall lined the way.

Luke held in a wince, waiting for the side mirror to meet the wall.

There really must be something about red-haired people. Either
they lived with incredible security of their eternal destinies, or they
didn't care about destiny at all.

"I can't believe Grandfather talked the headmistress into getting
a second opinion from an outsider," Pete continued. "But Grandfather
seemed to think the other company was trying to undercut the place.

Loyally, Luke

He's had bad dealings with them in the past and didn't want the orphanage to feel the brunt of a scam."

Luke looked ahead as the tops of buildings came into view over a thick swath of pine. Scots pine, more sprawling than the Virginia pines back home. A good building lumber, should they need it. Of course, Luke noted some oak and cherry. Birch and willow too. But mostly, pine and oak feathered the way into the village of Crieff.

Like some of the other villages Luke had visited in Skymar, this one boasted a collection of stone buildings with slate roofs and a few with more modern shingles, but were some . . . thatch? Luke grinned. He'd only seen thatch on historical building shows, not in real life. Kind of gave the town a quaint look.

The village nestled in the crook of the mountains, as if protected by their intimidating heights, a lot like some of the towns back home in the Blue Ridge. Nice and isolated.

Luke relaxed back into the car seat with a smile. No worries about high-class rude airport women here.

"I've never been here before, so it's as new to me as you, but Grandfather shared a lot last night. It's the largest orphanage in Skymar." Pete's bright, pale eyes were alight . . . and not looking at the road. "Started during World War I because of the staggering number of orphans left behind, but really grew during the second war."

An unfortunate byproduct of the two wars, from what Luke remembered from school and information gathered from some of his favorite movies.

The road took them through Crieff and up a tree-lined entrance where a massive building of sandstone with a conglomeration of jagged towers rose into the gray-blue sky. Was that a . . . castle?

Luke readjusted his expectations to . . . well, he didn't have any experience working on castles. Somehow, the stone mixed with sky created a strange picture of the ocean, which suited a castle on an island better than Luke could have imagined.

"Cambric Hall is not as old as it looks," Pete said, as if reading Luke's mind. "This folly was built before World War I by a Scot who'd made his money in trade. Grandfather said something like 1905 or '07 . . . or '02?"

Okay, so not being very old took some of the intimidation out of the place, but not much. "A folly?"

"A fake castle, so to speak. The vastly rich at the time liked to show off, kind of the same as they do now." Pete chuckled. "When the war broke out, the Scot lost both his sons early on and in his grief returned home to Edinburgh, leaving the place furnished and untouched. News reached him of the large number of war orphans in Skymar, so he donated the folly for use as an orphanage and it's only grown since then. He kinna have chosen a better lot to guard his castle, though. The folks in the village take pride in hosting the largest orphanage in Skymar and being the homeplace for these kids." Pete shot him a wink. "Can't get better protection than a bunch of Scots. Or better stubbornness." He shrugged. "Or pride."

If the movies could be trusted, Luke would agree. Made him like the place even better.

Smatterings of children ran here and there across the lawns surrounding the folly, all ages, each in various states of winter dress. Their voices filtered over the crunch of gravel under wheels. Joyful sounds.

Something inside Luke's chest expanded a little. The idea of working on a castle didn't encourage a lot of peace of mind, but fixing up a place for kids sure did.

Pete brought the car to a stop beneath a portico at the front door.

Cool March wind bit into his face as he exited the car, inciting another smile. He loved this kind of weather. Crisp, cold, with the scent of pine on the breeze.

Then he looked behind him and realized, besides isolation, why someone would build a castle out here in the middle of nowhere.

The view.

Loyally, Luke

Over the forest, the world fell away to reveal dozens of mountain peaks with lakes cutting between them like rain puddles, before all the earthen colors ended in a horizon of dueling blues. Sky and . . . sea? He squinted, drawing in a deep breath of the fresh air. They could view the sea from here?

"Aye," Pete said, moving to his side. "A good and proper view."

Those words seemed much too weak to truly describe the scene in front of them, but since Luke couldn't quite think of worthy ones, he only replied with a nod.

"You're not much of a talker, are you?"

Luke looked over at the younger man. "No, not much of one."

"That must mean you're a good listener." Pete grinned and stepped toward the front door of the castle. "Which suits me."

His laughter reverberated off the stone of the portico, drawing Luke's attention toward the arched ceiling. Stone bricks patterned in diamonds stretched the length of the portico ceiling, displaying solid workmanship and craft.

Maybe fixing up a castle wouldn't be so bad after all.

And Luke liked working with stone.

"Luke, come meet Mrs. Kershaw?"

Luke looked over to find Pete standing next to an older woman before a set of large wooden double doors. Her soft gray-and-brown hair pulled back in a bun matched the softness of her eyes as he approached.

"Ma'am." Luke offered his hand and her smile brimmed.

"We're so glad to have you take a keek at our orphanage, Mr. Edgewood." She gestured for them to follow her inside. "Mr. Holton is in my office waiting for us, but he assures me you come highly recommended."

A flush of heat rose into Luke's neck. "I know buildings and stonework, but I've not worked on anything this grand before."

"Well, if you know a way to salvage our beloved building, you'll

21

be a hero in my book." She gave him another kind smile and continued leading them through a large entry hall.

Salvage the whole building? What was she talking about? He would have asked, if he hadn't been distracted by the grandness of it all. A double-story entry, half in stone, half in dark oak. Arched windows on each side, partly filled with stained glass. Stone columns, easily three feet around, lining the way. He'd never stepped foot in a church this big, let alone someone's house.

As they turned down a nearby hallway, a movement to Luke's right caught his attention. Two little girls, probably nine or ten years old, peered around one of the columns, contrasting in looks, but wearing similar smiles. The pale-faced redhead wore a sprinkling of freckles across her cheeks, her pale eyes wide. Her darker-skinned partner-in-peeking had even darker hair curled in tight braids around her head, the shade matching her large eyes.

His grin crooked.

Just before he disappeared into a room following Mrs. Kershaw, he shot the girls a wink.

A trill of giggles chased him into the room before the door closed.

He'd never get tired of that sound. Happy kids. A sound everyone should want to recreate in children.

Inside, a middle-aged man in a gray suit stood from one of the high-back chairs. He looked important and polished, with a well-practiced smile. Luke immediately thought "politician" but decided to give the guy the benefit of the doubt. No one needed that sort of first impression.

"Mr. MacKerrow, I presume." The man went directly to Pete and offered his hand. "You resemble your grandfather."

Pete's grin stretched. "I appreciate that, Mr. Holton."

"And Mr. Edgewood?" He took Luke's hand and sent an assessing eye down the length of Luke, a flicker of something lighting his expression. It made Luke stand up a little straighter. "I have been the vice president of Cambric Hall's board of directors for the past five years and work as a liaison between the board and organizations engaging with Cambric Hall."

Mr. Holton turned to Mrs. Kershaw. "Thank you, Mrs. Kershaw. I know you are very busy so I will apprise you of our discussion later, if you should wish to return to your duties."

"Yes, sir." She gave a small dip of her chin and left the room.

The room must have kept the same characteristics it held in the early 1900s. Floor-to-ceiling bookcases on one wall, dark wood crown molding, a large window with matching wood frame on one wall, and the scent of . . . books. Luke almost grinned. Izzy would love this place.

"Thank you for joining me," Mr. Holton began. "I'm certain you have questions about why we were seeking a lesser-known person to review our project here at the orphanage instead of using one of the larger businesses, so let me brief you with our reasoning." He folded his hands in front of him. "Three weeks ago, a construction company came to give an assessment of one portion of Cambric Hall. The floor was dipping, you see, which raised concern about structural soundness. However, Ms. St. Clare, the president of the board and supervisor of this Royal Trust project, felt concern over the findings, which led the two of us to question my father, who is retired from construction work. My family is one of the top supporters of this orphanage, as my mother was one of the children here."

"It's good to have a heart investment as well as a wallet investment in a place like this, I'd say."

"Indeed." Holton offered Luke an appreciative nod. "We know the value of Cambric Hall to the children it houses. When my father was in business, he was well-known throughout Skymar, and he still has a vast network of connections. I presented the case of the construction company's findings to him and he referred me to Mr. Lewis Gray, a lifelong friend of his. Once Mr. Gray knew the extent of the situation, he suggested we seek the counsel of someone less . . . influenced by the business demands in Skymar, but who also had an honest heart and keen eye." His gaze landed on Luke. "Mr. Gray recommended you, Mr. Edgewood."

Luke raised a brow. This entire situation seemed grander than the original cabin renovations that brought him to Skymar in the first place. Was Luke up to the task of a castle? "That was kind of Mr. Gray."

"Kindness has little to do with it," Mr. Holton responded with a shrug. "We need discretion and someone who isn't under the influence of those who could either mistreat the trust of the board or spread a great deal of harmful or misleading gossip."

Gossip? Over an orphanage? What kind of kids did they keep here? Celebrity kids?

Mr. Holton seemed to catch Luke's confusion because he continued, "There are, of course, delicate circumstances that bring children to our door, but there is another reason. The village of Crieff reserves the responsibility and honor of being a haven for the royals of Skymar."

The royals? Royals lived in Crieff? Or near it?

Now Luke knew he was in the wrong place.

"The most beloved country estate of the royals is only ten miles from here, hidden away in the mountains. They've had a longstanding relationship with the citizens of Crieff, which is a cherished agreement. The villagers ensure the royals' privacy when they are here, allowing the family freedom to mingle among the townspeople without concern for safety or being overrun."

"Scots," Pete whispered, his lips crooked.

"I hope and trust you will make a thorough and accurate assessment of the damaged area," Mr. Holton continued. "If your findings prove preferential to the previous assessment, and you feel the project is something you can complete within your stay here, you will be given sufficient workmen and compensation. There is only one rule for which we require your agreement."

Loyally, Luke

Luke raised a brow.

"Secrecy. Until the project is completed, we ask you to share nothing related to your work outside of those intimately connected to it. Do you feel you can agree to those terms?"

Pete rushed forward with his agreement, but Luke took in the request. Keeping secrets wasn't a problem for him, but why such secrecy about a repair job? Was it the fact that the Royal Trust had something to do with the orphanage? Luke had no idea how royals worked, but from his hit-and-miss views of England's royal family news, he imagined safety and privacy were at the top of the list of valued commodities.

And protecting vulnerable kids should be right up there too.

"So first things first, I make an assessment of the project and we go from there?"

"Yes." Mr. Holton's posture relaxed, which made Luke feel a little more comfortable too. "We will discuss your findings and then make a decision accordingly."

"All right." Sounded simple enough. One step at a time. No commitment just yet. "When would you like me and Pete to take a look?"

Mr. Holton released a genuine smile. "Tomorrow morning, if you are able?"

Luke looked over at Pete, who shrugged his answer.

"Tomorrow morning sounds fine."

"And Ms. St. Clare will be in attendance, so you can direct further questions about the project to her."

"And this Ms. St. Clare is to be our overseer for the project, should we take the job?" Pete took the question out of Luke's head.

"Indeed. The orphanage is her particular responsibility, and she takes it very seriously. Her opinion is held in high regard within the royal family, so first impressions with her are important, of course."

"Well, if we're both wanting the same thing—to help these kids have a safe structure to live in—then I suspect we'll see eye to eye without much trouble."

Luke thought he caught the briefest hint of a smile on Mr. Holton's face. "Indeed." The man stood and tipped his head. "Until tomorrow."

. . . .

From: Luke Edgewood
To: Izzy Edgewood, Penelope Edgewood, Josephine Martin
Date: March 11
Subject: The cabin

To keep from a zillion texts where I must repeat myself ad nauseum, I'm sending this bulk email to jointly answer some questions.

Peter is a nice guy. Probably close to Penelope's age. A real positive kind of guy. He likes to talk and I'm not sure he's ever been camping before. He drives like Penelope too. I'll let you figure that one out for yourselves.

The electricity is out in the cabin until the electrician can rewire some things in two days. That gives me some time to look over the place and figure out what sort of additional wiring we'll need for the expansion I'm planning. Pete's not too happy about the lack of electricity since he's a rather social sort, and I may be a disappointment as far as conversational partners go. However, I told him that I'd scare the bears and coons away if we saw any, but since I wasn't sure what other kinds of critters live in Skymar, I couldn't vouch for his safety from them.

I'm attaching pictures of the cabin. It's got great bones and is a good place to have as our base. Seems that we're only about three miles from the village of Crieff. Nice place. Small. Lots of stone buildings and a few thatched roofs. We can purchase supplies there or have them shipped in, so I feel content in not having to travel into any cities.

Loyally, Luke

The village is nestled in the mountains and a good half hour or more from anywhere else. The cabin is even more secluded.

I feel right at home.

The cabin's kitchen needs an update and we're turning a covered porch into a larger living area. The view is worth seeing (attaching a photo of the view too).

That's three photos. Be happy.

Otherwise, we're just winterizing the place and updating. The woodwork is great. And the wooden beams, but we're going to relocate them into the new living area.

The other project hasn't started yet but may end up being a big job. I don't know much else about it, except it's a secret.

That should be plenty for you all to chew on for a while.

Luke

PS: And yes, Izzy, I did tell Pete I was mostly joking about the critters.

PPS: BTW, Pete has never seen a coon. I'm trying to figure out if I'm saddened or envious.

Text from Penelope to Luke: Are you just saying it's a secret because you want to annoy me, or is it REALLY a secret?

Luke: **It's really a secret, but that doesn't mean I didn't want to annoy you too.**

Penelope: Ooh, Grandpa Gray knows lots of folks, so if he set it up for you, it must be very special. Famous people? Royals? Tell me if I'm hot or cold.

Luke: Nope. Didn't work with Christmas presents either.

Penelope: Ugh. I'll just keep teasing you about the meet-cute then. I looked for her in your picture of Crieff, but didn't see anyone resembling . . . who was it? Grace Kelly? *batting eyelashes*

Luke: Who is Grace Kelly?

Penelope: Nice try! Izzy wouldn't have made that up because it's way too unbelievable. So you must have REALLY said Grace Kelly and now I have a new thing to tease you about until the day you die.

Luke: I regret I ever mentioned the whole coffee scene to Izzy. It's a good thing I know how to keep secrets.

Penelope: I'm glad she told me. Now I can have such fun daydreaming FOR you!! Somehow, it makes you feel not so far away.

Luke: I know. I regret that too.

Penelope: BTW, I'm a great driver. I'm glad Pete is with you. SOMEONE needs to share some positive energy. Imagine being alone with all your sourness.

Luke: I smile every time I have that dream.

Evidently, Pete hadn't slept in a sleeping bag before either, because the guy tossed, turned, and groaned most of the night, occasionally attempting to start a conversation with Luke.

But Luke had learned long ago that only desperate times called for answering anybody's poke at a conversation in the middle of the night, so he kept his eyes closed and breathing steady. The cabin really wasn't so bad. No holes for critters to sneak in, and a fire that kept the main room nice and toasty through most of the night. Though Luke would be lying if he didn't admit to missing warm water for face washing and a fresh cup of hot coffee.

Loyally, Luke

No matter. Pete had secured them breakfast at a B&B in town, along with access to a shower too.

A few children had already made their way outside when Luke and Pete reached Cambric Hall, and as Luke exited the car, he caught sight of the two little girls from yesterday. They stopped their talking when they saw him and, with shy smiles, came a little nearer.

Kids were his kryptonite. He'd never admit it to anyone, especially his sisters, but he was drawn to spending time with and helping them. He coached baseball back home for that very reason. It was good for his heart.

Though baseball was made up of boys.

He had less practice talking to girls. He nearly groaned. Which proved true no matter what ages the girls were, in fact.

"Did I happen to see you two young ladies spying on me yesterday?"

The redhead giggled. "You sound funny."

"Do I?" Luke's grin spread. "Well, I'm from a different place."

The dark-haired girl's eyes grew wide. "You aren't from Nigeria."

Ah, from her accent, he wondered if that might be home for her. "No, I'm from America."

"Why don't you wear a coat?" the red-haired girl asked, scanning his flannel shirt and ball cap. "Aren't you cold?"

He lowered himself to a squat to be closer to their eye level. "Not at the moment. I like the cold."

"I do not." The dark-haired girl shook her braids. "I feel it in my bones."

"My name is Faye," offered the red-haired girl, pointing to herself. "And this is Amara."

"Nice to meet you, ladies. My name's Luke."

"Are you here to adopt a child?" This from Amara. "Because I cannot be adopted. My grandmother is coming for me."

"I'm afraid not. I've come to help fix some things around the place if I can."

Faye's expression deflated and hit him straight in the heart.

"Luke," Pete called from the doorway. "Ms. St. Clare is waiting inside."

"You ladies have a fine morning." Luke tipped his hat to the girls and resurrected their smiles. "If I stay on, I hope to talk to the two of you again."

Luke met Pete at the door, and the latter doffed a mischievous grin. "Charming the ladies, are we?"

"That age is about the only ones I can charm." Luke shook his head and followed Pete through the door. "I'm pretty useless the older they get."

They took the path they'd followed the day before, Mrs. Kershaw leading the way, and Luke took further inventory of the architecture and stateliness of the orphanage. He could spend a good month just investigating the bones and beauty of this place.

Mr. Holton greeted them at the office door, a practiced smile in place. "Good morning, gentlemen. I hope you enjoyed your first night in Crieff."

"I'm certain we'll like it better when the electricity works in our cabin," Pete said with an uncharacteristic frown. "And we have beds."

"No electricity?" Holton's brows rose. "Or beds?"

"The electrician is coming tomorrow and new furniture arrives this afternoon, so we'll be just fine, Mr. Holton."

The man nodded, humor lighting his eyes as he examined Luke for another second before gesturing them into the office. "Allow me to introduce Ms. St. Clare, the main overseer of this project."

Luke entered behind Pete and turned.

His welcome smile died a slow death on his face.

Before him, in a gray suit and with golden hair pulled back in a familiar bun, stood Grace Kelly.

CHAPTER 3

The Daily Edge: Social Tattle from
One Edge of Skymar to the Other

With spring around the corner, all our royal watchers keep their eyes out for news about the annual Wild Hyacinth Ball. Who will be invited? Who won't? And what special announcement will the royals make this year? No one comes to the Wild Hyacinth without a significant other, and this year the ball is dedicated to Princess Elliana as she steps back into life as a working royal. The rumor mill is spinning its tales on who Skymar's prodigal princess will bring as her possible future prince. Do you have any guesses?

Three thoughts rushed through Luke's mind at once:

1. He was never telling Penelope about this moment.
2. Grace Kelly's pale blue button-down really brought out the color of her eyes.
3. God had an unpredictable sense of humor.

What came out of his mouth was . . .

"You?"

. . . which proved even funnier, in hindsight, because Grace Kelly said the same thing at the same time.

Something in the back of Luke's mind made him think of Penelope's scenario, then the word *meet-cute*.

And everything within him suddenly screamed, *Retreat!*

"You've met?" This from Mr. Holton, whose brows rose so high they might have matched Luke's. Or Grace Kelly's . . . er . . . Ms. St. Clare's.

"In passing at the airport," Ms. St. Clare said quickly, her gaze meeting his. "Nothing of consequence, of course."

Of course.

Though his pulse beat a different response. However, that could be because the idea of working with this woman made him half annoyed and half . . . well, he wasn't even sure. But annoyed wasn't it.

"Do you still want me to take a look at the place?" Luke turned the conversation back to familiar territory. The job.

Mr. Holton looked to Grace Kelly . . . whom Luke needed to stop mentally referring to as Grace Kelly, because with his history, he'd inevitably make an idiot of himself and *call* her Grace Kelly. She shifted her attention with a little uncertainty and then brought her palms together, ushering up a smile as practiced as Mr. Holton's.

"I don't see why not? Unless Mr. Edgewood has any misgivings?"

She wasn't putting the blame back on him. "None at all." He pushed up his own practiced smile and glanced over at Pete. "You?"

Pete's gaze pinged from one person to the next, including the rather large man at Ms. St. Clare's right, who had yet to be introduced. "I don't think so."

A silence fell over the room as Luke locked eyes with Ms. St. Clare, waiting for her to take the next move. Pretty eyes or not, he was going to keep his word and do what he'd promised Lewis Gray.

"Well then, I'm glad we can move forward." She raised her chin and turned to the man beside her. "This is Mr. Brooks, a contractor for the Royal Trust. He's currently working on another project but came this morning to assist you in your estimate."

Assist? Hmm . . . or spy?

Luke shrugged off the inner growl. Extra caution made sense.

Ms. St. Clare and Mr. Holton didn't know Luke any better than he knew them, so for the kids' sake, and the reputation of the Royal Trust, bringing in a respected person sounded smart. "Morning."

Mr. Brooks dipped his head and returned the greeting.

"If you'll lead the way, Ms. St. Clare, I'll be happy to get started with the assessment."

Something flickered in those pale eyes as she stared back at him. What was it? A question? Concern?

He shook off the curiosity. He didn't know and didn't need to know. Instead, he'd just keep to his usual mantra. Do the job, enjoy the craftsmanship, play nice, and move on.

Besides, he had experience with not meeting high-class demands, and the reminder hit deep. His ex-girlfriend proved the sting of that choice all too well in her attempt to make him more "refined" just to impress her new friends. In the long run, he'd ended up miserable and with the clear understanding he'd never measure up to her world.

A hard pill to swallow when they'd both come from the same small town.

But she'd changed to suit her fancy.

A shift that only turned her into someone he didn't recognize anymore with expectations he would never, and didn't want to, meet.

Luke kept in step behind Mr. Holton, who followed Ms. St. Clare and Mr. Brooks.

"You're going to have to tell me the story of how you met her," Pete whispered, his grin almost impish. "I get the sense it wasn't ideal."

"Just a coffee mess-up. That's all."

Silence. But the kind of silence Luke could feel. Like a warning.

"Sounds like a movie meeting to me."

Yep. It was a redhead thing. Luke heaved a sigh. At least the man didn't use the term *meet-cute*. "Nope. Just a simple mix-up."

"But then to have her show up here? As our supervisor?" His voice was edged with humor. "It's a mad coincidence, is all I'm saying."

"Mad" matched the overall vibe of their first meeting, that was for sure.

The group's path took them through a classroom, which was currently empty of children; a massive room that must have been some ballroom in its former life, and which Mr. Holton thought was currently used as a gym; a large dining hall; and a few smaller rooms into a kitchen. A good-sized kitchen, if they were inside a house, but not the size suitable for a place serving dozens of children.

The room stretched into a few smaller adjoining rooms—ones Mr. Holton mentioned they'd like to bring into the renovations for additional space, a smaller dining area, a storage room, and a closet. From the looks of it, the kitchen had needed modernizing for a long time. Dated cabinetry. Nicked walls. Original fixtures.

And the floor dipped and dented from over a century of use.

Luke rested his hands on his hips, surveying the space. All cosmetic, from what he could tell. Straightforward fixes.

Assuming the foundation wasn't in trouble.

So, with an unwelcome audience of untrained viewers—apart from Brooks—Luke examined the concern areas in the kitchen and then followed Brooks into the crawl space for a look at the underbelly. The age and build of the space tempted Luke to linger a little longer within the dark corners, just to make note of building patterns and materials used over a century ago, but he kept to his goal: structure.

He'd restored old houses back home. Mt. Airy had a couple dozen Queen Anne–style houses and Victorians. The Smith and Merritt houses back home probably boasted the same age as this one, but weren't nearly as grand . . . nor made of stone.

He pressed on a board here and scraped at the stone of a wall there, carefully moving his trained eyes over every spot available to assess. After about an hour, he stood from his ducked position and plucked his flashlight from between his teeth before turning in Brooks's direction. "Do you know what the other company used to justify a weak foundation?"

Brooks gave his head a shake. "I wasn't available for their inspection, so I cannot tell you."

"Well, if you're seeing what I'm seeing, then it looks like that other company was trying to hoodwink this orphanage."

"That was my concern too, which is why I encouraged Ms. St. Clare and Mr. Holton to take a second opinion." Brooks raised his flashlight, larger than the one Luke carried in his pocket, and swept the shadowed space with another splash of light. "Once I heard the company's name mentioned—Westons is what they're called—I wondered if they were up to no good. Their investors are after property, and there aren't many places as pretty as this spot. Westons is polished, so they charm their way into business, from what I've heard."

"*Pretty is as pretty does,*" Luke's granny used to say. And the idea of somebody trying to trick money out of an orphanage? That just made him downright mad.

"You'd think kids like this would inspire a bit more compassion and a whole lot more virtue." Luke stepped toward the door, giving the space another look. "And from what I can tell, there's no need to tear down their home."

The two men reentered the kitchen where Mr. Holton, Ms. St. Clare, and Pete waited.

Luke took off his cap and ran a hand through his hair, certain he'd met with a few cobwebs, among other things. "The foundation looks sound and most of the underlying structures are in good shape." Luke turned to Brooks for confirmation and the man nodded his agreement.

Grace Kelly's posture drooped just a bit as if she were . . . relieved?

"But multiple floor joists are bad and need to be replaced," Luke continued. "So we'd need to tear out the floor, but since you were planning to remodel the kitchen anyway, it could all work together well."

"And save much more heartache and money in the process, I'd wager," Mr. Holton offered.

"Than tearing the castle down?" Luke chuckled. "You bet, but I ought to warn you, once we start peeling back parts of the house, we're bound to find other things to fix."

"Is that a common occurrence?" Ms. St. Clare directed her question to Brooks, as if double-checking Luke's words.

There was just no way to win with this woman!

"Yes, Your—" The man paused. "Ms. St. Clare. It's not only common but expected."

Her chin lowered just a smidge. Served her right.

"I can't vouch for what else we might find, but if you have the right team, most problems that arise should be fixable as long as the bones of the building are good." Luke shrugged a shoulder. "And they seem to be."

"This particular project is the most pressing and will lead to the greatest immediate help for the orphanage." Ms. St. Clare studied him with those blue eyes of hers. "But there are other improvements we hope to add as funds and time allow. And as we raise awareness, we hope for additional donors to support the orphanage in order to make those improvements more quickly."

"Which does bring us to the question of time." Mr. Holton steadied his attention on Luke. "The Donors' Banquet is scheduled for mid-May. Do you think these repairs and renovations can be completed by then?"

Luke looked over the kitchen area again, making another quick mental tally. "If you have a good team and not too many surprise complications, then I'd say yes."

"And you have experience leading such a team?" Ms. St. Clare's voice held a tinge of doubt.

"I've *led* a lot of teams, Ms. St. Clare," he answered, holding her gaze. "But we'd get the job done faster if it's a *good* team. At least a few workers who know about building. The others I can direct."

"Sounds like a hefty cost," she replied.

Luke had worked with women before, so the idea of having Ms. St. Clare as his supervisor wasn't the problem. The problem was her doubt and condescension. He almost grinned. Now there was a great vocabulary word too.

"Not as much as tearing down the place and rebuilding it," he shot back, and something in those eyes flickered with a hint of . . . fire? Humor? He couldn't tell and didn't want to find out. "Like you heard earlier, our cabin doesn't currently have electricity, but if you could point me in the direction of a place in town with public internet access, then I can do my research for material costs around here and get an estimate to you by tomorrow afternoon."

"Detailed?" Ms. St. Clare challenged.

"Line by line." He grinned. "I'll even use spell-check."

She narrowed her eyes a second and then looked away, one corner of her mouth twitching.

"You're welcome to use the internet here, Mr. Edgewood," Mr. Holton offered, speaking into the tense silence. "Mrs. Kershaw has made her office available for any of our needs."

"I appreciate that." Luke turned to Pete. "If Pete will drive me here in the morning, I'll try to have everything ready for your review by afternoon."

"Thank you, Mr. Edgewood." Ms. St. Clare's quick response paired with her softened smile caused him to do a double take. Was the woman. . . . nervous? He stifled an eye roll.

Nope. He'd gladly give the estimate and leave this job in someone else's hands. He didn't need to spend time working with a woman who sent his thoughts into some sort of ping-pong guessing game. Besides, she was clearly doubting his skills, and nobody needed to work under scrutiny like that.

As soon as he and Pete were in the car, Pete turned to him. "Ms. St. Clare reminds me of somebody, but I can't figure out who. Does she make you think of anyone?"

A villain. Luke shrugged. "A movie star?"

"Hmm, perhaps that's it, though I'm not up on my Skymarian actors." Pete put the car into gear. "But her bein' a movie star would suit the situation, wouldn't it? Since your life is kind of like a movie right now anyway."

Luke didn't respond. No way he was walking into that conversation.

"She does give off a sense of—"

"Arrogance?" Luke pressed back into the seat. "Entitlement?"

"Ah, you don't fancy her," Pete stated more than asked.

He shouldn't have opened his mouth. "I try to steer clear of folks who put on airs, that's all."

"Put on airs?" Pete repeated, appearing to mull over the notion. "If she's a movie star or high rank in the royals, she likely has reason to put on airs, as you call it."

"Being a certain social status or rank doesn't mean you stop being polite or kind. In fact, I'd expect folks who've been given more in life to be even kinder because they have so much already."

Pete paused, contemplating Luke's words. "I like that idea, but I don't believe it's as common in practice."

"No," Luke said, releasing a sad chuckle. "Usually the opposite."

"I wonder what her reasoning is. Why she seems so mad."

Luke stared out the window, those icy blue eyes of hers emerging in his mind against his will. "Most people who put on airs are either trying to prove something . . . or hide something."

He didn't know which one it was for Grace Kelly, but he had no interest in finding out.

Text from Ellie to Maeve: He is here! In Crieff.

Maeve: Maxim Thompson from that fabulous Italian holiday?

Loyally, Luke

Ellie: No! The American from the coffee shop. And why do you keep bringing up Maxim? He was a fiend.

Maeve: A delicious-looking fiend, who had a rather ravenous kiss, if I recall from your retelling.

Ellie: And the very man who made certain that the paparazzi caught us in a rather compromised position! I thought he was helping me with my sunscreen! Had I known he was posing for the paparazzi, I would have pushed him in the pool.

Maeve: Your royal life has been fraught with unfortunate moments.

Ellie: And poor choices.

Maeve: Remember, we are not wallowing in self-pity and regret. Though I do blame some of your ill behavior on your strange brunette phase.

Ellie: Why are we friends?

Maeve: Because I know all your secrets and don't treat you as if you're special. Now about this American? I happen to like most Americans, as I am one myself.

Ellie: You're only half American. Your mother is Skymarian. Besides, you've lived in Skymar for ten years. You can't claim your American status anymore. You've even lost part of your accent.

Maeve: Oh, I claim American status quite regularly when I want to. So did the American recognize you?

Ellie: He recognized me from the coffee shop, but not for any other reason. And no one from the orphanage has given any indication of who I am. The entire village of Crieff is remarkable at creating a space where I can just be a normal person.

Maeve: You will never be a normal person.

Ellie: Again . . . why are we friends? And I would love to be just a regular person for a little while to someone. I can only imagine how refreshing it would be.

Maeve: I'm a regular person. It's not super refreshing. But as someone who has only been a royal by living vicariously through you, I wouldn't want a constant fishbowl life either.

Ellie: Thus the reason Crieff is such a haven for us. Well, at least for me, especially during the last few years while I've been trying to reinvent myself.

Maeve: So what's he doing in Crieff? It's not a typical tourist spot for Americans. For anyone, really.

Ellie: He was recommended by one of Father's advisors as someone who could give an estimate for the orphanage project.

Maeve: Interesting . . .

Ellie: I can almost hear you plotting something that will make me nervous.

Maeve: Not plotting. There's not much to plot . . . yet. But your entire meeting in the coffee shop and then discovering you may be working with the man is interesting. Do you need an extra set of eyes? I could come help.

Ellie: I'm not certain anyone is ready for your sort of help, Maeve.

Maeve: Why do I get a sense that he's handsome? The less you talk about someone, it usually means the more handsome he is.

Ellie: That is not true.

Maeve: That he isn't handsome?

Ellie: No.

Ellie: I mean, yes. He is handsome, in a rugged sort of way. I meant, no, talking about someone less has nothing to do with how handsome he may be. Sometimes I want to forget the person.

Loyally, Luke

Maeve: So . . . I'm hearing that he's handsome.

Ellie: It doesn't matter if he's handsome, Maeve. I'm finished with short-term romances and he's not on the list. He'd NEVER be on the list. My parents have suggested some excellent options for my future, and I don't plan to disappoint them yet AGAIN. I've already done so much for which they've had to bear the brunt of the consequences. Considering their opinion is the very least I can do. Besides, I know they want what's best for me.

Maeve: Perfect. Then you ultimately get to choose, right?

Ellie: I'm not so certain I'm the best person to make the choice based on my past. No, I think it's time to trust their plans.

Maeve: You still should have some say, El. It's YOUR future.

Ellie: When you're a royal, it's never solely one person's future.

Maeve: I'm not going to have this argument with you again; however, I will say that I'd rather watch a handsome, well-built (see what I did there) carpenter work out, over one who doesn't improve the view. I think I may need to come and help you.

Ellie: I'm ignoring you. However, I must say he seems an honest, straightforward sort. And I was probably rude again. Or nonresponsive. Why can't I just be normal?

Maeve: Because you're not normal. We've covered this already.

Ellie: It is so difficult to be myself with new people. I'm always afraid they have some sort of ulterior motive and I must keep up my guard. I'm waiting for the cameras or the trickery. It's horrible.

Maeve: Maybe it's worth taking someone at face value every once in a while, El. It might restore some of your faith in humanity.

Ellie: Says the woman who would rather bury herself in her cottage and create music instead of talk to people.

Maeve: Dead composers and musical instruments are the best listeners. And we rarely argue.

. . . .

From: Josephine Martin
To: Izzy Edgewood, Penelope Edgewood, Luke Edgewood
Date: March 12
Subject: Re: The cabin

I'm glad to hear you're doing well, but I really think Mr. Gray could have taken better care of you and your assistant. A house with no electricity? Really, Luke! Though you've been on all sorts of adventures without electricity, so this should be manageable for you, at least.

And before you hear this from Penelope, I may have mentioned to Lori Creswell at church that you were single. I didn't make any plans, as you're not here, but I did plant the idea in her head. You'd be a great father to her children.

I look forward to hearing more about your trip. The photos are lovely, but I'm a little concerned about how remote you are. They do have hospitals nearby, don't they? You're notorious for putting nails through skin or getting hit with boards or . . . whatever else it is that happens to you and leaves scars. Or dents.

Love,
Josephine

PS: Charlie is doing a great job in your stead with the business. You'd be proud. I've tried to see if she's interested in dating right now, but she keeps avoiding me. Do you think those two things are connected?

Text from Penelope to Luke: You're having supper with Izzy? I'm so jealous right now. I bet you'll tell her your secret.

Luke: Well, since it's a secret, you'll never know.

Penelope: Izzy's not nearly as good as you are at keeping secrets. I bet I can get it out of her. In the meantime, I'm going with Matt to Iris's dance recital. She's having her first jazz concert. I braided ribbons into her hair. She's magnificent.

Luke: I should text Matt and tell him I'm sorry for him. Jazz recital AND braided hair talks? Poor man.

Penelope: You're not going to scare me. Matt's a dancer. He talks dance. As far as braided hair? He's just glad he has such enthusiastic help with girlie stuff now. Here's a pic. She says hi, BTW.

Luke: Now THIS is the definition of cute. Right here. Even the braids.

Penelope: The fact you even brought that up makes me wonder if you're not a little preoccupied with Grace Kelly. Or is that a secret too (insert wiggly eyebrows).

Luke: I'm currently preoccupied with ending this text conversation.

Penelope: And . . . since Izzy and I have found our romances in Skymar, I have high hopes you're next on the list.

Luke: I am not in one of your candy heart–flavored movies. Goodbye, Penelope.

Penelope: Denial is the first step to the Hallmark chime. Just so you know.

Pete dropped off Luke at Cambric Hall and left for the cabin, nearly giddy with the fact that the electrician had arrived. With a list of concerns and additions Luke made for him, Pete promised he'd ensure the electrician went through each one and text Luke should there be any questions. Already, Luke had created a blueprint for changes to enhance the place, as Lewis Gray had wanted, which was one of his favorite parts of the process. Visualizing. Seeing potential.

And then having the ability to make the potential a reality.

He spent the morning into early afternoon working on research and predictive costs, based on the manpower available. Mrs. Kershaw's office door stood open, allowing him glimpses of children of all ages as they passed in the hallway outside. He even caught sight of his two new friends, Faye and Amara, and he was pretty sure they made it a point to pass by the door more than needed.

Mrs. Kershaw had been kind enough to bring him lunch, which gave him freedom to keep working. The sooner he had this finished, the sooner he could get back to the cabin and start making renovation plans with Pete.

He'd just printed off the estimate to leave for Ms. St. Clare and her team when the sudden feeling of being watched brought his attention up from his laptop.

Two familiar little faces peered through the door, and they'd brought a friend. A little black furry one.

"How can I help you ladies?"

They skirted around the doorframe into the room, hands behind their backs. The little dog waddled forward, nose sniffing the air, tiny tail wagging like an energized flag.

"We brought you a wee bit to eat," Faye said, holding out her offering in a napkin. "Some of Mrs. Kershaw's biscuits."

"And a cup of coffee." Amara revealed a paper cup complete with lid.

Luke tucked the papers beneath his arm and rounded the desk

to approach the girls before lowering himself to a knee so that the dog could get better accustomed to him. "That was awfully nice of you." He gave the dog a scratch behind the ear before taking the offerings from the girls. "And who is your friend?"

"That's Clootie." Amara dropped into a sitting position, and the dog waddled over to land in her lap. "He's the house dog."

"Mrs. Kershaw has been the headmistress here for a hundred years." Faye nodded, her eyes wide. "And every time one dog dies, she gets another just like it, and they're all named Clootie."

"Well, that makes it easy to remember, I reckon." He took a sip of the coffee, welcoming the taste and warmth. If a cozy room like this office kept a slight chill to it, he couldn't imagine how the larger rooms felt. "Is there a special meaning to his name?"

"Aye," Faye offered, lowering herself beside him.

"It's a dumpling," Amara rushed to answer.

"No." Faye sent Amara a frown and then turned back to Luke. "Clootie is the cloth wrapped around the dumplin' for cooking. My gran used to make apple clootie dumplings for me before she passed on."

Luke studied the little girls. So much loss at such young ages. Made their smiles even sweeter.

"So the dog's named after a piece of cloth that wraps around a dumpling?"

Both girls nodded.

He could go along with it. He'd heard worse names for dogs.

"Do you have any dogs?" This from Amara.

"I have two, but they're both big dogs. Not nice and tidy like Clootie here."

"What are their names?" Faye ran a hand over the dog's head.

"Well, I have a shepherd named Chewy and a hound named Indie."

Both girls tilted their heads as if the names were new to them.

Luke didn't figure to explain since neither little girl had probably seen the corresponding movies.

A bell he'd heard throughout the day chimed, causing both girls to come to attention. "We've got to go, Mr. Luke." Amara took Faye's hand and they both started toward the door, Clootie tagging along behind.

"Thank you for my coffee and cook—biscuits." Luke raised the cookie-laden napkin in appreciation and followed the girls to the door.

He was rewarded with twin smiles and waves as they rushed down the hallway hand in hand. His grin stretched wide as he leaned against the doorframe, taking in the sweet view.

"A smile?"

Luke turned to find Ms. St. Clare standing a few feet away from the doorframe where he'd been leaning. "And a genuine one?" She followed his gaze to the girls disappearing around the corner of the hall, those eyes flicking back to him with a hint of curiosity in them. "I didn't realize you possessed one."

Her gaze was softer today. Not quite as . . . unwelcoming. The loose curls that had escaped her bun and framed her face probably helped. It was hard to look mean with a halo of curls around someone's face. He inwardly groaned. Halo of curls? Where on earth did *that* thought come from?

"I reserve smiles for *friendly* people." He finagled the cookies into his coffee cup hand and tugged the papers from beneath his arm. "I emailed a copy of this estimate to Mr. Holton per his request, but here's a paper copy I planned to leave for your review."

She hesitated, as if caught off guard, and then took the proffered paper. "Thank you."

He nodded, keeping to task. "I took some of the material costs from market prices, but I bet you could get a sizable discount if buying bulk. Do y'all have a contractor's discount at some of your building supply stores? I reckon the orphanage is tax exempt."

For the first time, Grace Kelly lost a bit of her posture. "I . . . I'm not certain about bulk purchases, but yes, the orphanage is under a special tax bracket."

"Well, both will save you some money. The more you can save, the more the orphanage can put back into these kids." He took a sip of his coffee and gestured with his chin in the direction Faye and Amara had disappeared. "I'm wondering if you ought to have someone inspect the heating system too. Make sure it's in good working order."

"I know these types of buildings aren't as insulated as newer structures."

He sent her a look, but her attention was focused down the hallway. She had a delicate nose too. He pinched his eyes closed. "I'd imagine so."

Quiet stirred greater temptation to look her way again, so he decided right then and there that he should probably leave. "The estimate has a detailed inventory of what's wrong, so whoever you get to do the work, you at least have knowledge about what needs to be fixed so another team won't try to take advantage of Cambric Hall."

Her attention flashed back to him. "Are you not interested?"

His brows flew skyward. "Interested?"

"In the job," she clarified, and he wanted to go hit his head against one of the stone walls, if for no other reason than to remove any definition of "interested" other than renovation.

"I figured you'd probably want to get someone else."

One of her golden brows rose. "Because of your ogling me in the coffee shop?"

"Ogling?" He turned to face her. "I can assure you I wasn't ogling, Ms. St. Clare. Ogling implies I had disrespectful thoughts or intentions, but that's not the case."

Her gaze searched his and some sort of itching feeling he couldn't reach buzzed in his chest.

"And exactly what sorts of thoughts were you having?"

"Human ones." Her stare held him, and his throat started to close up. Heat climbed his neck and scorched his face. Even his beard started tingling. Hitting his head against that stone wall sounded better and better all the time. "You're nice to look at. Like the view from these windows or the architecture of this building. That's as far as my imagination went. Nothing but simple admiration."

Silence followed again and he took such a large drink of coffee, it hurt to swallow.

"I think we may have gotten off to a poor start, Mr. Edgewood, and I'm afraid I'm to blame for that. I'm sorry." Her words drew his attention, those blue eyes examining his face, searching. "Would you allow me to start over?" She offered her hand, a hint of a smile on her lips. "I'm Ellie St. Clare."

Red lights started flashing in the back of his mind at her sudden gentling. Unkind and demeaning proved an easy person to dislike and avoid.

But a woman who took responsibility for her actions and attempted to rectify them? Nope. *Beam me up, Scotty!* He didn't need any reasons to like Grace Kelly, because then things like emotions started crowding in on solid good sense.

And Luke was a big fan of solid good sense and few emotional tangles.

In fact, he didn't like any sort of tangles.

Her golden brow rose higher, waiting.

Ridiculous. Silly. He'd just treat her like anybody else he worked with. No problem.

He pushed his palm down the side of his jeans, as if it were dirty or something, and then took her hand in his. Her fingers slid over his palm to take a firm hold, and a frisson of connection zoomed from the touch.

Her soft orange scent hit him in synchrony.

She didn't feel or smell like anyone he'd ever worked for or with.

He cleared his throat. "Luke Edgewood."

Those piercing eyes continued to study him. "It's nice to officially meet you, Luke Edgewood." She released his hand and stepped back, bringing the papers up. "I'll review these this evening. You should hear something from me by tomorrow."

He dipped his head in acknowledgment.

"But I hope you're prepared to take the job."

His turn to raise a brow. "You haven't even looked at the estimate."

"I know." Her chin rose, lips taking a slow curve into a broader smile that actually lit her eyes. "But I trust you." She paused, searching his face again. "And I don't trust a great many people. I believe you would have the children's best interest at heart, and that's what matters most to me."

And with that, she turned and walked down the hallway.

Luke barely smothered his groan.

Heaven help him! Why did she have to turn around and be nice? Even tell him she trusted him.

If she'd stayed mean, it would make things a whole lot easier for him. His gaze followed her retreat and then he looked away. Shoot fuzzy!

He didn't need to feel any sort of attraction to her. She was supervising the project. She lived in Skymar. And, most importantly, he wasn't looking for romance.

CHAPTER 4

Text from Luke to Penelope: How did you get Pete's phone number?

Penelope: He's my boyfriend's cousin. Plus, I'm resourceful.

Luke: I have a few other things I could call you. Busybody.

Penelope: You don't dangle a word like "secret" in front of me and expect me to do nothing. You really should know me better than that.

Luke: I had high hopes that being thousands of miles away from you would make you less annoying.

Penelope: Oh gracious! I'm sure it only makes me worse. Since I can't SEE how you're doing, I have to use my imagination, which can sometimes be much worse than reality.

Luke: I can't believe Matt betrayed me like this.

Penelope: Don't blame Matt! He just thought he was being helpful by giving Izzy and me Pete's information as an emergency contact. Then Matt and I had a video call with him while you were at the "secret" building preparing a "secret" proposal for a "secret" job.

Luke: The quotes and overuse of the word "secret" are pretty useless at this point.

Penelope: Don't worry, I'm not going to tell anybody. I just wanted to show you how clever I am at finding out your secret. Made me feel like a spy.

Luke: Meddler. Nosy. Troublemaker.

Penelope: If you hadn't challenged me, I wouldn't have had to resort to my sneaky self. Also, I wasn't going to

mention Grace Kelly, but now that you've called me
a troublemaker, I just wanted to add . . . I told you so!
chime

**Luke: I didn't believe you had Josephine's matchmaking
mayhem until now. Izzy is my only hope.**

Penelope: On the contrary, I don't try to match anybody, I
just make predictions. For example, Pete didn't tell me
the name of the lady or the place, so he kept the main
secret, but he DID say coffee girl was the same as the
lady supervising the project, so . . . my next prediction
is you'll get offered the job so then you two will have
forced proximity. That's usually what happens next in all
the rom-coms.

**Luke: This is NOT a rom-com. Gross. Now I'm turning off
my phone and going to bed. Which means good night,
Penelope.**

Penelope: Sweet dreams, Romeo.

Luke: I hate you.

Thank you for agreeing to meet with us, Mr. Edgewood."
Ms. St. Clare gestured toward the chair across the desk in
Mrs. Kershaw's office. Mr. Holton sat as Luke did. "I'm certain you
know why we asked to see you?"

Luke had been wrestling with the idea all the way over to the
orphanage. On the one hand, he liked the opportunity of working this
project for the experience and because of Mr. Gray's recommendation. On the other, he wanted to prove Penelope wrong.

He was *not* in some rom-com.

Or worse, a Hallmark movie.

"You reviewed my estimate."

"Your proposal was more in line with what we were hoping," Ms. St. Clare continued. She'd worn her hair partially down today and pulled back on the sides, displaying its length. He inwardly winced and focused back on her face. "And we would like you to head up the project, if you are willing."

"Timeline is mid-May or before?"

"That's right," Mr. Holton answered. "We would like everything completed so the donors can see how their generosity is being used."

"Apart from taking good care of these children," Ms. St. Clare added.

Luke hesitated, his pride at proving Penelope wrong fighting against doing the right thing. "What size team were you thinking?"

"We have three with experience whom you would oversee," Mr. Holton said. "Gordon Frasier is a longtime builder from Crieff, but he has recently cut back on his projects. He's agreed to join this renovation since it is so close to home and for a good cause. And, of course, you'll have Mr. MacKerrow."

"And me," Ms. St. Clare added, raising her chin as if expecting Luke to challenge her.

But he was of no mind for a challenge. She may not seem the sort to work in construction, but he'd learned a long time ago not to judge a book by its cover. His cousin Charlie proved to be one of the best carpenters he knew.

But Mr. Holton didn't seem so unmoved. Both his brows shot into orbit.

"I'm here to see the project through, John, and I mean to do so personally." Her expression brightened into a too cheery smile. "Besides, I like the idea of making something new again."

Mr. Holton paused, and some sort of awareness flashed across his features. Hmm . . . wonder what all that meant? Luke stopped his thoughts right there. Didn't want to know. Didn't need to know.

But the idea of some fancy woman slowing down the work, getting injured on the job, or distracting the whole team surely didn't bode well for efficiency.

Because she sure was distracting. He pulled his attention away from Ms. Distraction and back to Mr. Holton.

This project helped children. That alone was worth a yes from him.

Exactly. Focus on the children. And the experience.

"When do you want us to start?"

"Since you only arrived in Skymar two days ago and, according to Mr. Gray, you are completing another project for him, perhaps it would be beneficial to take the rest of the week to adjust to your new surroundings. Crieff is a charming village and one to explore." Mr. Holton looked to Ms. St. Clare. "That would give us time to make the necessary plans to move forward."

"Yes." Ms. St. Clare smiled, a reserved smile, but better than the high-and-mighty look he'd come to expect . . . until yesterday when she showed off her nice side.

He inwardly winced at his own mental observation. Nope. No need to think about any of her nice sides.

"Would Monday suit?"

Four days. A good bit of time to sort out his designs for the cabin and revisit his plans for the castle. "That'd be fine."

Of course it would be fine. Besides, a few days away from Cambric Hall and Ms. St. Clare would be just what he needed to clear his head.

In fact, distance sounded hunky-dory right now, but since Pete had the car and planned to come back for Luke in an hour or so, Luke was stuck.

"If you don't mind, I'd like to take another look around the work area."

"Of course." Ms. St. Clare stood along with Mr. Holton, those blue eyes meeting his in that same powerful hold. "Mr. Holton and I will finish up with our paperwork here. Can you find the kitchen on your own?"

"Yes, ma'am." He backed toward the door. Even if he couldn't remember, spending less time around her seemed a good idea for his peace of mind.

A long row of cabinets and a commercial sink lined one wall of the kitchen with a window of the view just offset from the sink.

Shame. A kitchen sink should have a window if at all possible.

Since the plumbing wouldn't have to be extended too far, sliding the sink over a few feet wouldn't cost much and would add a valuable view for anyone having to wash dishes. A weight-bearing wall into the next room proved they'd best make an archway from one room to the next instead of removing the wall altogether, and one large closet and one small one would be perfect to open into each other to increase the size of the pantry.

He pulled his hammer from his ever-present backpack and nudged some of the baseboard loose. Time, some paint, and decades of dirt caused the board to stick, but he worked at it until he could carefully slide the baseboard from the wall opposite the cabinets. The wall seemed in good shape. Age-worn, but nothing significant. So he kept working, taking his time removing a few more pieces.

"It seems you're doing much more than taking a look."

Luke glanced up to find Ms. St. Clare inside the kitchen. She nudged a piece of discarded baseboard with her foot. "Do you always carry a hammer with you?"

He stood from his crouched position, measuring her statement. Was she attempting to joke with him? "Actually, I have two."

Her smile flashed for the faintest second, as if she hadn't meant for it to, and then her expression returned to neutral. "You're not meant to work until Monday."

"Just checking a few things. So far the walls are in good shape, except for a few spots where I'd already noticed some slight water damage." He gestured toward the two closets with his hammer. "If we opened those two closets into each other, they'd make a good-sized pantry, which is one of the items on the list of improvements."

He directed the conversation into safe territory. Work.

"It's amazing how much you've already removed in such a small span of time."

"It's always easier and faster to break things." He shrugged a shoulder. "Much harder and longer to rebuild them."

Her gaze caught in his, her entire expression falling. Even her eyes seemed to go darker. A frown puckered her brow. "Painfully true words, Mr. Edgewood."

His chest tightened as she stared at him, and he had the sudden urge to hug her. Though she didn't seem the huggy sort. He cleared his throat and searched for words. "If you don't mind, since we'll be working together, I'd rather you call me Luke."

Evidently the words worked, because her lips shifted a hair upward and out of that sad, "help me" sort of look. "Then you should call me Ellie."

She didn't look like an Ellie. For some reason the name seemed too short or simple for her. Luke mentally slapped himself at the ridiculous notion. And what did it matter anyway? Ellie was a fine name. Rolled off the tongue easily enough.

She pulled her gaze from his.

Was she trying to figure out if his name fit him? It did. Concise. To the point. His mama told him once that the name meant "light-giving," which he never shared with anyone because the meaning sounded like it fit Penelope more than him. But there was something . . . nice about the sentiment. Bringing light to folks.

"I see Mrs. Kershaw has already emptied out everything from the cupboards."

"The closets too." He gestured against the door with the hammer.

Had he always talked with his hammer? And why was he suddenly noticing it now? Being in a different country brought out all sorts of weird things.

"She's keen to have a new kitchen. It's been a dream for a long time, but the last few years other projects took priority, like updating the plumbing and wiring." Her focus zeroed in on the two closets and she proceeded to walk over to them, examining their positions. "Yes, this would add a great deal of space for storage."

"And you already know what cabinets and updated appliances you want?"

She nodded, peering into the smallest closet. "Mrs. Kershaw and I have those ordered and I'll email you the specifics to help with your planning. There are no lights in these closets either." She cast a look over her shoulder as she stepped inside. "I don't think I added that to our list."

Luke took a few steps closer. She'd worn simple navy slacks and a white dress shirt today. A little more approachable than the suits, but still clearly a physical reminder of their differences. High-class. Country grown?

Keep your head down, boy!

"It's on the estimate. Any sizable pantry needs good lighting."

She sent him a brief smile and then turned on her phone flashlight, stepping farther into the closet.

What on earth was she doing?

"Are you looking for something in particular?" He waited at the threshold of the door. The closet was easily five feet by five feet, but it was still too small for him to enter with her.

Well, not literally, but . . . in all other ways.

"Mrs. Kershaw told me that this particular closet has some preserved signatures of children from the World War II era." Her words came muffled from inside the shadowed closet. "They're not visible when the closets are full, but with them empty, I thought I'd try to find them."

The lilt in her voice, the childlike curiosity, pulled him another step.

"Oh yes! They're here."

He barely recognized her voice at this point. Gone was the distant, controlled woman. She still seemed pretty prim and proper, but something had shifted in her personality, and it was more than just going from Ms. St. Clare to Ellie. He'd even noticed it when they met an hour earlier. Could it have something to do with trusting him?

Curiosity drew him, like a loon, around the doorframe. The sweet scent of oranges and flowers almost had him hightailing it right back out of the space.

Oranges never smelled so distracting before.

He gave his head a strong shake. As soon as he got back to the cabin, he was watching *Rambo*. These "sweet" references in his mind had to go.

She looked back at him as he entered, a broad smile his unexpected greeting. "Look there. These are the reasons preserving this place is so important."

Dozens of names marked the old wooden, paneled wall at the back of the closet. Different handwriting. Some sharp, others curved. Dates like April 1940, September 1941. The earliest he could see from his cursory view was November 1939. Almost a century ago.

"Malcolm Ferguson was an orphan himself before he worked his way in trade to become one of the wealthiest men in Scotland." Her finger slid across one of the names and she dropped to her knees, the light from her phone following her movements. "He met and married a woman from Crieff and built here. When he lost two of his three sons in the Great War, he and his wife left Skymar, taking their remaining son with them back to Scotland, but as he left, he donated Cambric Hall to the royal family in hopes of it being used to care for the many orphans of Skymar." She looked up at him from her crouched position, her eyes glowing from the flashlight . . . or the story. "It's one of the reasons I requested this appointment." She turned back to the names, her voice lowering. "It seemed a good place to find hope."

He ignored the sudden softening around his heart and stepped back. Within twenty-four hours, she'd gone from being Cruella de Snarl to an . . . interesting anomaly. Snarky with tenderness underneath. Reminded him a little of Princess Leia and Han Solo's first few meetings. That was definitely an enemies-to—

He halted his thoughts right there. How on earth was Penelope sneaking into his brain, even ruining one of his favorite classic movies with her crazy, heart-eyed romance talk?

And the last thing he needed to do was focus on any "broken" parts of Ellie St. Clare. The fixer inside him was already having a Rambo-style war with his rational don't-get-involved side.

So he just stayed quiet and took another step back.

"I wonder why they would cover the bottom part of some of the names by placing this board here?"

Her words brought his focus back to the nice, predictable wall. Near the bottom, a wood piece, several inches thicker than regular baseboard, cut off a few of the names.

Had someone tried to cover a damaged part of the wall? Could it have been from a previous renovation?

He frowned. That wouldn't make sense, since the wall was clearly still original to the house. But Luke hadn't noticed any other such renovations. And it wasn't a particularly professional job.

"Is it loose at all?"

Ellie gave the wood piece a tug. "It moves a little and I think, well, it's covering something." Then she turned, looked up at him, and plucked his hammer right out of his fingers. "Thank you," she added, with a crooked grin, before pressing her phone into his empty hand. "Would you mind directing the light for me?"

And there he stood, hand in the air like the Tin Man from *The Wizard of Oz*, or maybe he was more like the Scarecrow, because his brain went completely blank. She'd just taken his hammer right out of his hand. No hesitation. *His* hammer. He looked down at his palm where the pale blue mobile phone sat in its place.

Then . . . she worked the hammer like she knew how.

Ms. Perfume-Coffee held the tool in her hand with familiarity and hooked the claw to the edge of the wooden slab without a hitch. With a push to leverage the claw deeper between the wood and wall, the board separated a little from its hold.

"Something is definitely down here." Her volume rose with excitement and his mind still didn't know what to do with the change.

If his brain hadn't been muddled, he'd have responded more quickly, but before Luke could warn her about the possible somethings hiding in dark, cold places in old houses, she gave the hammer another twist. The wood popped loose and, immediately, two things happened at once.

Ellie screamed.

And then her arms flew up as she jumped back and the hammer hit Luke square in the eye.

Well, thankfully, his cheekbone and forehead caught most of the impact.

And the claw wasn't pointed in his direction. Just one of the flat sides.

He grunted and stumbled back, reaching for his head, but only succeeded in hitting it with the phone he still held. Ellie half-turned and fell into him, slamming into his chest as his back hit the opposite wall. His free arm came around her to keep her from toppling over, which meant they both slid together, her head in his neck, all the way down into a seated position . . . with her on his lap.

Everything stopped for a second, and then his formerly muddled brain shot into overactive mode. *She* distracted any pain in his face. Her scent surrounding him. The softness of her body against his. The tickle of her hair brushing his neck.

And then she buried a little deeper against him, her fingers clutching his flannel shirt, and Luke wondered, for a second, if maybe he *had* stepped into one of Penelope's movies . . . complete with orange petals invading his senses.

Then Ellie's grip tightened on his shirt and she sat upright, her face mere inches away. He'd heard some sappy statement at one time or other about a man falling into a woman's eyes, and had dismissed the idea as something a person like his sister would write . . . but at that moment, he understood. Maybe it was the head wound or the way the light from her phone shone at just the right angle to reveal a glimmer within the blue, but for a split second, he forgot how to move his eyeballs.

She didn't release him from his fall immediately. Only stared. Wide eyes so mesmerizing, he didn't just fall but practically jumped right back into their depths.

Maybe she'd fallen in too, but that didn't sound right. Women didn't fall into men's eyes, did they? Seemed men proved the clumsy ones in that case.

And . . . he gave himself another mental slap.

"There . . . there's something brown and furry down there," she whispered, a shiver moving through her into him.

His palm instinctively tightened on her back.

And then she seemed to realize their intimate position, because she pushed off him but didn't go far. Twisting into a seated position beside him, she pressed her back into the corner of the wall farthest from the hole. With an audible swallow, she gestured with his hammer toward the partially revealed space on the other side. "The . . . the brown something . . . was *not* small."

Deep in the recesses of his foggy brain, his sense of humor emerged, and he bit the insides of his cheeks to keep from grinning. Life had afforded him a lot of construction experiences, but this was new.

"It's not funny." She raised the hammer like a pointy finger.

"Not one bit."

The tension in her lips loosed ever so slightly from what he could see in the dimness. "I'm serious."

"Very," he said, nodding.

Those eyes narrowed as if in warning, so before she could fire back some retort, Luke braced his palm against the wall and struggled to a stand, the pulsing in his face confirming swelling.

Well, that was likely the reason he'd fallen into her eyes. A head wound. Plain and simple.

He slid his fingers gently against his head, then cheek, as he stepped across the small space. At least he didn't feel the sticky warmth of blood. One bonus. Of course, part of his cheekbone was numb, so he may not have felt it anyway.

"There's a good chance that if it didn't run away from the noise you made moving the board, it's not alive."

She whimpered in response.

His guess was that it wasn't a sad whimper.

But instead of a dead animal smell, all that filled his lungs were oranges and flowers. He pinched his eyes closed, then winced at the slight sting in the wounded side, and turned her phone so the light shone toward the hole. The board still partially covered the spot, so Luke gave the board a poke with his foot.

"What do you see?" Ellie peeked around his shoulder, keeping him as a shield from the dangerous something.

His lips twitched again, but he wrangled them into submission. "Not sure." He began to lower to his knees to peer down into the hole, but she caught his arm.

"What are you doing?"

He turned just enough to see her in his periphery. "Believe me, Ellie, I've seen a whole lot worse than what's down there, so just stay behind me and we'll figure this out."

And she did as she was told. Which almost brought a smile to his face, if the motion hadn't hurt his cheek so much. He kneeled. She followed along with him.

The pain might have been worth that grin.

As he shone the light down into the space, Ellie gasped, her hands tightening their hold around his arm. And for some reason, he felt like he could take on an entire alligator if it jumped out of that hole just to show her how strong those arms were.

He coughed to hide his laugh. He was crazy. And might have a teensy bit of a concussion.

Or at least he could blame all these ridiculous thoughts on the hammer. Which made him feel a whole lot better than blaming them on any alternative reason.

The light hit something brown and misshapen. But it didn't look like an animal.

He reached his hand down into the hole.

Ellie's fingers dug into his arm as he touched something soft and clothlike with a firm center. The grin started to emerge again, along with a rascally thought. He fisted the cloth in his hand and, despite the voice in his head sending off warning shouts, released a pained cry.

Ellie screamed in response. "Oh no! Did it bite you? Give me my phone. I'll call emergency. Luke!"

He lost control of his grin, despite the pain, and started laughing, holding whatever he brought up with him at his side.

In the faint light, Ellie's features transformed from terror to confusion and then . . . hardened into pure fury.

"How . . . how dare you!" She slapped his shoulder.

"Just getting even."

"Getting even?" Those eyes now narrowed to blue slits. "What on earth do you mean?"

He gestured with her phone to his face. "You nearly took out my eye with that hammer."

Her expression slowly unraveled. "I . . . what?" And with only a slight hesitation, she grabbed his arm and pulled him into the light of the kitchen.

He blinked and his left eye didn't open quite as quickly as it should.

Yep. Swollen.

"Oh my word." She studied his face, her bottom lip dropping into a pout. "I'm so sorry, Luke. I had no idea."

"It's not the first time I've been hurt on the job." He tried to grin again.

She winced. "But a first by me." She raised a palm. "Ice. Let me get ice."

Ellie rushed to one of the two remaining appliances—the refrigerator—and dug through a bottom freezer, slowly pulling out a handful of ice. "Here. Put this on it."

He would have complied, but one hand gripped her phone and the other held whatever he'd pulled from the hole. As if suddenly aware, he raised the item into the light.

"It's a leather bag?"

Luke squeezed the bag, feeling the firm contents. Box-shaped?

He offered the phone to Ellie, who placed the hammer on the counter and slid her phone into her pocket, ice still in one hand.

With the bag between them, he carefully tugged at the drawstring and drew out . . . a book?

Ellie stepped closer and slid a slender finger over the leather cover. "A book?"

She gently opened the cover, a gasp puffing from her lips. She looked up at him. "It's a journal." She pointed down at the writing on the inside cover for him to see. Or at least, see with his good eye. "Blair MacKee, 1918." Ellie gave her head a shake, bringing more of the scent of oranges toward him. "Could it really have been under there all this time? Decades?"

Luke tried to peer down at the pages, but it was becoming increasingly difficult to see out of his left eye as the swelling continued. "Over a century."

"Remarkable." Her attention flitted to his swollen eye. "I'm so sorry. Your poor eye." She raised a cube to his cheek and he flinched at the shock of cold and sting. She grimaced. "I imagine this makes you even more excited to have me work with you."

A soft laugh slipped through his grin. "At least you've given me fair warning."

Her smile dawned slowly, like it had to work out the kinks. And despite how ridiculous the thought was, he liked that he'd somehow made that smile bloom. Even if only for a moment.

Daggone it.

"Oh, pardon me."

Luke and Ellie turned to find Mrs. Kershaw standing in the doorway of the kitchen, her gaze shifting from him to Ellie to Ellie's hand on his cheek and back again.

Heat traveled into Luke's face and likely started melting the ice at record speed.

"Mrs. Kershaw, you've arrived at the perfect time." Ellie looked away from him, her expression moving back into the well-controlled category. "We're in need of more ice."

"What happened?" The woman rushed forward, examining Luke's face.

"A building accident," Luke offered. "Nothing that a few pieces of ice and a pain reliever or two won't fix."

Almost imperceptibly, Ellie slid the journal from Luke's hand behind her back. "He's being too generous, Mrs. Kershaw. I'm the one who accidentally hit him with the hammer when I thought we discovered a dead animal under the floor in the closet."

The older woman's eyes grew wide, and she pressed a palm to her chest.

Loyally, Luke

"It was just this leather bag, Mrs. Kershaw," Luke explained to keep the woman's eyes from growing any wider.

"But we did see the old signatures on the wall."

Mrs. Kershaw's face relaxed into a smile. "Aren't they lovely? Such a part of the history here." She turned her pale eyes on Luke. "You won't destroy them in the renovations, will you?"

"No, ma'am. We'll find some way to keep what we can of them."

"Very good." Mrs. Kershaw waved for him to come closer. "Now, let's see to your eye before it swells to a close."

Luke looked back at Ellie, who offered a tight smile, one hand still keeping the journal behind her back. Those eyes implored his silence, his mutual camaraderie.

And Luke realized something.

When Penelope mentioned forced proximity, he had no idea it included a small closet, a secret one-hundred-year-old journal, and the tactile memory of an off-limits Skymarian in his arms.

CHAPTER 5

***The Daily Edge: Social Tattle from
One Edge of Skymar to the Other***

Could a duke become the awaited prince charming? *The Edge* has it on good authority that Princess Elliana was seen Friday night in New Inswythe with Christopher Montgomery, the Duke of Styles. Unfortunately, the princess didn't give our tattlers as much entertainment as she's shown in the past, but this photo reveals the two enjoying a private dinner. Could our princess shake up Spotless Styles's reputation? Perhaps bringing some "style" could boost his reputation with readers of *The Edge*, since the duke hasn't given us anything to talk about . . . ever. What are your thoughts about the possible match? Leave a comment online to join in the latest tattle!

• •

Text from Penelope to Luke and Izzy: Luke! Izzy! Do you
    have time for a video call? I'm babysitting the twins and
    they've just gotten big enough to fit into their hobbit
    outfits!!

Izzy: Aww, I want to see!

Luke: Just send me a photo.

Penelope: A photo is not the same thing. They're making
    some of the cutest noises. Ember is so bald, I almost
    slipped and called her Smeagol in front of Josephine, but
    I'm afraid Josephine may never let me babysit them again

if I do that. Besides, Ember laughs every time I say "my precious" and you can't hear that through a photo.

Luke: **We can do a video chat next week.**

Penelope: Is there a reason you can't right now? You met Izzy for lunch today, so you're not sick. It's too late in the evening for you to be working. Are you on a DATE????

Luke: **I would not be texting you back if I were on a date.**

Izzy: He's not going to video chat with you tonight, Penelope. He had a work accident and his left eye is swollen shut and purple.

Penelope: He went out to lunch with a swollen eye?

Luke: **No, Izzy brought pizza over to the cabin. I didn't want to scare the small children of Crieff.**

Penelope: It couldn't be worse than the permanent paint of the Spider-Man mask you had last year.

Izzy: Um . . . there is a distinct possibility it might.

Penelope: Oh my goodness, what happened to you, Luke??

Luke: **I'd rather not talk about it.**

Penelope: It has something to do with Grace Kelly, doesn't it? Did she hit you? That's not what I meant by forced proximity.

Luke: **And I repeat, I'd rather not talk about it.**

Penelope: So . . . is it a secret? *batting eyelashes*

Luke: **Penny-girl, leave it alone.**

Text from Ellie to Maeve: Will I never outrun my reputation?

Maeve: What is it now?

Ellie: Clarice Kershaw, the longtime headmistress of the orphanage, walked in on me and Luke at a less than ideal moment and proceeded to speak with me in private afterward about my conduct.

Maeve: What do you mean?

Ellie: She not so subtly reminded me of how my actions influence the impressionable children at the orphanage and she'd prefer any romantic liaisons remain clearly outside the orphanage. She also alluded to my past as being a less than stellar recommendation of my ability to maintain decorum.

Maeve: First off, Mrs. Cranky Kershaw doesn't know the princess you are NOW, so it's going to take some time to show her how you've changed and grown.

Maeve: But more importantly . . . what on earth do you mean by "less than ideal"? Is Luke the American? And if he's already kissing you, then he moves pretty fast.

Ellie: Kissing is not the point. And there was no kissing. He had a wound on his eye and I was applying ice to it. That's when she walked in.

Maeve: I feel as though kissing should always be some kind of point in a story.

Ellie: Maeve!

Maeve: El, you're going to have to keep choosing to do the right thing over and over again. It's much harder to climb out of a bad reputation than to sully a good one. So just keep choosing right and let all those right choices speak for themselves.

Maeve: And getting the right kind of kiss now and again is definitely a good choice in my book.

Ellie: You are no help at all!

Text from Rose to Ellie: Are our parents forcing the Duke of Styles upon you?

Ellie: Mother recommended him from their list of eligible suitors for me.

Rose: Ah, the list.

Loyally, Luke

Ellie: He has an excellent reputation, which Mother feels will
   help clean up some of my messy past.

Rose: Marriage is not mercenary, Elliana.

Ellie: Depends on who you ask. Besides, I'm not attached to
   anyone, so they made a recommendation or two. It was
   only dinner. And their list worked wonderfully for Stellan.
   He's the perfect Crown Prince with the perfect wife.
   Even his sons are perfect.

Rose: You wouldn't say that if you've ever attempted to watch
   them.

Rose: As far as Christopher, it would be fine if you really liked
   him, but as your elder sister, I know you can't. He's very
   nice, but his personality is . . . well, does he even have one
   of his own?

Ellie: He's reserved.

Rose: Ah, perfect royal marriage material. The media is not
   your measuring stick. Take care, Elliana, that you do
   not continue to pay for a debt that has been forgiven.
   Despite all their expectations, our parents would never
   wish for that.

Ellie stared down at her phone, her sister, Rosalyn's, last text niggling
deep into her heart. Simply accepting their forgiveness seemed too
simple for all the trouble her mistakes had caused.

All the horrible press.

All the heartache.

The very least she could do was try to make things right. To take
their suggestions into consideration.

She wasn't too certain she trusted her own ability to make the best
choices anymore.

Especially about relationships.

When men discovered she was a royal, everything changed. And in her experience, not in a good way. She'd been such a fool to think any of them really cared for her.

They'd only wanted popularity or spotlight or whatever they could get by being associated with her. None of them had been genuine or honest. None truly *saw* her.

How could she have been so stupid?

She pressed a palm into her stomach, forcing the memories into submission. Years of therapy and thousands of prayers had brought her to the other side, and she would not go back.

No, it was time to turn her hopes and expectations to serving others. To embrace her royal life and duties. Love could grow in time as it had for some of her ancestors.

Her parents cared for her. They loved her through all the messiness and ramifications of her choices, so surely their recommendations held weight enough for her to push back any dreamy romantic notions and embrace solid good sense.

Luke Edgewood came to mind, unbidden. Perhaps it had been the word "solid," or maybe the phrase "good sense," for surely it had nothing to do with romantic notions. Something about his genuineness was so refreshing. He had no idea of her past or her pedigree. No kid gloves. No deference. Her lips tipped ever so slightly at the memory of the kitchen closet scene. He'd teased her. And brought out her laugh. She couldn't remember the last time she'd laughed with a man.

Her fist pressed against her chest.

And she'd instantly felt safe near him. Safe enough to lower her guard, even for a few moments.

She rarely experienced such a feeling outside of her family.

Why?

She shook her head.

It didn't matter why. Even if she admitted to a modicum of

attraction, he most certainly didn't fit on any royal list and didn't even live in Skymar. However, becoming the patron to the orphanage had been the right choice. And taking up her primary residence at Perth Hall had been the right choice. And choosing Luke to take the lead on the construction had been right as well. Those things she *knew*. And perhaps they would prove the beginning to a great many future choices in the right direction.

Because she desperately needed to trust herself again if she was ever going to take control of her own life, let alone prove a capable royal patron to the North Country.

She tugged her coat more closely around her and walked up the cobbled main street of Crieff. Staying in the country estate of Perth Hall gave a sense of separation from the demands of royal life and fewer opportunities for her flaws to be on display, but this secluded village offered a glimpse into an almost regular life. Though the storybook world of thatched roofs and quaint cottages likely proved as unique to "regular" life as castles and ballrooms.

Maybe finding the journal had resurrected all these thoughts of a simple life. From what Ellie could tell, Blair MacKee had been an orphan-turned-kitchen maid and she'd fallen in love with a nearby farmer named Gabriel. The journal told the tale of a simple and sweet love, from their initial meeting to the day she left service to marry him.

Love.

Like the fairy tales.

She shook her head and continued her walk toward a large building near the center of town. One of her favorites. Rudan Air Chall Antique Shop. The owners, an older couple, had owned the antique shop for decades and, like most family-owned businesses in Crieff, they passed it to the next generation.

A few newer shops had come into the village, like an ice cream shop, a fine clothing store, and several restaurants, but most other small businesses—especially if they didn't fit with the overall . . . atmosphere of Crieff—ended up relocating elsewhere.

Crieff was safe.

At the thought, she glanced behind her to find Cameron keeping an unhurried pace. She frowned. Well, at least he kept his distance, at her request. She'd had to compromise with her parents by agreeing to one person on security detail in public to be free to live and work in Crieff at her leisure. He was a good sort. Early forties, extremely serious, but reliable and strong.

And had been royal security for over a decade.

Which meant he knew this world.

And her history.

Rudan Air Chall welcomed her out of the cold afternoon air into a world of visual activity. Vintage chairs, hand-hewn tables, old-fashioned lanterns, picture frames, and myriad other unclaimed treasures cluttered up as much space as was possible . . . and still, by some miraculous feat, looked inviting.

The Frasiers at work. Or likely Nessa Frasier, the matriarch of the establishment. As if called from Ellie's thoughts, the woman emerged from the back of the shop behind a massive dresser, her white hair drawn back into a ponytail that defied her age.

But of course, Nessa seemed to have the energy of a younger woman too.

"Well, it's always a pleasure to have you visiting us, Your— Ellie," she corrected, as she always did when first meeting after a short sabbatical. "Gordon told me he'd heard you were back from New Inswythe. I hope your family is all well."

The twinkle in her eyes revealed her pleasure in their shared secret. How much of a secret it truly was, though, was debatable, since the entire town knew about it. "They are. Quite well. And your family?"

"Besides Gordon being a wee crabbit this morning, we're all right as rain. The grandweans are with us for the day and have cheered his heart." She winked. "Though you wouldn't know it to see him all dour-faced as usual, but he's quite keen on 'em."

"As any good grandda ought to be."

"Aye, and he preened like a parrot when Mr. Holton rang him yesterday about joining the renovation team at Cambric. He nearly laughed his delight."

"Gordon Frasier nearly laughed?" Ellie offered a mock look of shock. "And you didn't get a snap of it?"

Nessa's laughter filled the space. "It's a rarity for certain, but he's been without a large project for a few months, and this will set him to rights for a while." Nessa examined Ellie, her gray eyes soft. "Now, what will you be wanting this afternoon?"

The dips and curls of her thicker accent soothed Ellie's nerves and gently reminded her that in Crieff she wasn't under the microscope of the public. At least, not as much as usual.

"Only looking." She lowered her voice and drew closer to the woman. "Though my parents have given me leave to decorate Perth Hall to my own liking with the design of moving in by autumn."

"Well, I was hoping you'd make Crieff your permanent residence."

Nessa's welcome spread healing warmth through Ellie's chest. "It's proof they have more confidence in the future direction of my life and choices. And since one of my titles is Duchess of Mara and the North Country, it has been my hope to settle here so that I might be a part of the people whose lives I mean to serve."

"You're speaking very much like someone with the right perspective." Nessa brought her palms together and drew in a breath. "Well now, we have some new paintings in the back that Olivia found a few months ago at a charity sale, and as you know, my daughter has a keen eye for art. Come along and I'll give you a keek." She tossed a glance toward the front. "And tell Cam if he's going to stand at the window, he might as well come inside and have a spot of tea."

But when Ellie turned, Cam had already moved out of sight.

"I'll send Gordon to tease him inside once he's finished with a customer." Nessa waved a hand and then led the way, weaving among the lovely and . . . not-so-lovely conglomeration of antiques.

Just as they turned the corner into the next room, Ellie nearly ran headlong into a wall of flannel, big shoulders, and . . . logs?

She blinked the man into view only to find she'd come face-to-face with Luke Edgewood. She glanced down at his wood-laden arms and then back to his face.

"Luke?"

His eyes widened—well, partly. The wounded eye, with a bluish hue around it still, drooped just a bit. But it looked much better than it had three days before. "Ellie?"

"My, my," Nessa cooed. "I had no idea you two were acquainted."

"We're both working at the orphanage," Luke started.

"The project of which Gordon is a part," Ellie continued.

Nessa's gaze flickered from Ellie to Luke and back. "Well, how delightful. We've only just gotten acquainted with Luke but already feel he's going to be rather regular here, since he's keen on antiques too."

"Not so much the antique part as the well-made and less expensive part," he corrected. The way his deep brown eyes lit as he grinned over at Nessa held a mesmerizing sort of quality.

How strange.

Brown eyes weren't all that common in Skymar, so no wonder they'd prove a bit of a novelty.

"He's collecting items for the cabin he's renovating on Yarrow Fell."

"Yarrow Fell?" Ellie looked over at him. "That's a rather secluded spot in the mountains, isn't it?"

"Seems to be." Luke shrugged one shoulder, drawing her attention to the sturdy span from one arm to the other. A warm, strong shoulder she'd burrowed into when they shared a moment in the closet.

Heat shot into her face.

Shared a moment? No. When she overreacted—yes. That was all.

Loyally, Luke

And thank heavens there were no paparazzi around to snap a photo of her sitting on his lap in the dark closet of an orphanage! Her throat tightened. And praise God for small favors that Mrs. Kershaw didn't show up *then*!

"Pete's a bit skittish about the distance to Crieff, but I like the quiet." Luke nodded, turning his attention back to Nessa. "And you can't beat a view like that every morning."

"Oh, I wouldn't wonder that it's one of the best in the North Country," Nessa said, shifting her focus between them again, one of her brows raised.

Ellie noted Nessa's humor-filled eyes and quickly gestured toward the wood in Luke's arms. "What have you found?"

He raised one of the pieces, its dark wood bearing intricate carvings of . . . children and animals? "I came in trying to scope out what I could purchase locally, things like furniture and light fixtures, but when Gordon figured out what I was doing at the cabin, he showed me his back room where he keeps unique wood and scrap pieces." He gestured to the wood. "Thought these would make nice frames for the signatures in the kitchen closet."

"What an excellent idea." Ellie stepped closer, slowly sliding her fingers across one of the pieces. "Mrs. Kershaw will love it, and it's perfect for celebrating Cambric's history."

"There's not enough of the carved pieces for the full wall, so I'll use these two for the top and bottom and put something simple on either side to complete the frame." He had such a pleasant smile. Kind. Gentle. "Seemed a good way to honor the past."

Her gaze caught in his, the mutual understanding palpable. "Indeed."

"I kinna wait to see the finished product, Luke." Nessa tapped one of the wood pieces. "And you've made Gordon's day. To have another craftsman to blether on with. He's keen to work with you at Cambric too. Does his heart good to find a like-minded sort."

"I feel the same, ma'am."

Every time he said the word *ma'am*, Ellie wanted to smile. There was something about the quaintness of the word paired with the way he spoke it that made her think of chivalrous knights. How preposterous! Ma'am?

"This whole village seems filled with talent."

Nessa's smile bloomed. And, to be honest, Ellie's did too. After spending such an extended time in Crieff and the North Country, she'd fallen in love with these people, their welcome, and their many skills passed down through generations. Whether from their clannish history or more old-fashioned ways, they'd embraced her without ceremony.

And she'd truly grown into their patron in both heart and position.

"There's such a heritage of handcrafts in these mountains, Luke. From overhearing you and Gordon, it sounds as if the people where you live aren't too different from those of us in Crieff. Using the earth to create beautiful things. Keeping to our heritage, if we can." Nessa raised a finger as if coming up with an idea. "You've not toured Crieff, have you?"

"Only seen a few shops yet," Luke answered. "But I think I found—"

"Ellie, you should give him a proper tour of the village, especially since he'll be staying here for some time."

Ellie looked from Luke to Nessa, attempting to send a mental message of how bad an idea that was. "I don't think he needs—"

"He'll find the people friendlier and most apt to help him if he comes along with you." The twinkle in her eyes deepened. "Everyone's a wee bit suspicious of strangers here, you ken."

"Sounds like home to me," Luke said, laughing. "We've got a whole lot of Scottish heritage in my part of the world. Folks will be friendly enough to point you in the right direction, but they're not quick to trust."

"Then it's all settled." Nessa nudged Ellie's arm back toward the way she'd come. "You take Luke here on a wee tour of the village, and by the time you get back I'll have some bacon batties, scones, and tea ready for you."

Luke narrowed his eyes for only a second as he looked at Ellie, likely for an interpretation.

With another not-so-subtle nudge or two, along with a farewell of "Now you two enjoy yourselves," Ellie found herself outside the shop with Luke at her side.

"You don't have to take me on a tour. I'm sure I can find my own way."

"Are you truly suggesting I defy one of the most powerful matriarchs of Crieff?"

His grin split wide and somehow inspired her own. "Yep, this sounds a whole lot like home."

"You have terrifying small-town matriarchs there too, do you?"

He leaned in, one brow raised in a playful way, causing her breath to stumble the slightest bit. "And there's no crossing them, so you just do as you're told."

She cleared her throat and drew back. "Exactly."

He shoved his hands back down into his jeans and blinked a few times, as if a little uncomfortable too. Clearly, he'd not meant any sort of flirtation. He'd just responded as if . . . as if they were friends.

Her intentions congealed around that thought.

And why not be friendly? She had no design to date him. The relationship couldn't go anywhere because she was determined to keep to the plan—earn back her parents' trust, and if she married, he would be Skymarian. Simple.

But friendships didn't have the same expectations.

She gestured with her head toward the steps and he followed, moving in step with her up the cobbled lane.

"Bacon batties are basically strips of bacon on a roll. Nessa will likely add eggs or cheese with some brown sauce, but it's a fairly basic sandwich."

"With Scottish flair," he said.

"Yes." She smiled. "That's the part you may need to watch out for. The Scottish flair."

He had an easy grin. "If it's got bacon in it, I'm all set."

"Well then, the North Country should suit you well. Bacon and sausage are found in over half the meals."

"This place is sounding more and more like home every minute."

"Really? I suppose I always equated America to massive cities like New York or Los Angeles. Not something like"—she waved her hand toward the cobblestone street lined with quaint little shops—"this."

A glimmer lit his dark eyes as he arched a brow. "Do I look like I fit into a place like New York or Los Angeles?"

"No." She chuckled. "Not at all."

His gaze took in the village. "My town, Mt. Airy, North Carolina—it's small like this and hugs the Blue Ridge Mountains, but . . ." He shook his head and sighed. "I have to drive a good distance to get views like you have here, if I can even find anything close. There's a wildness to it here."

"Which often frightens people." She raised her brow in challenge and watched his grin tip in such a way her heart fluttered a bit. "The wildness and . . . solitude."

"I'm a fan of both." His brow and words challenged her right back.

She smiled and he sighed, looking back ahead of them. "Especially the solitude right now. Pete's a talker. And a singer." Luke sighed again. "He even talks in his sleep."

It had been much too long since she'd laughed so readily. It felt good and . . . strange at the same time. Luke offered a comfort in conversation she hadn't often experienced. Perhaps it had to do with the fact that he had no idea who she really was, so there was an ease to the conversation. But the longer she spent in his company, she was beginning to think it was just him.

He was incredibly genuine and sincere.

Qualities with which she'd had little experience in previous . . . friendships. Besides Maeve, of course. And Maeve's brand of genuineness came off as terrifying sometimes.

"I got the sense he was the more outgoing of the two of you."

He chuckled, soft and low. "I'm glad you're so good at reading people."

"In this case, the process wasn't difficult." A sudden chill shivered the smile away. "Actually, it's a learned skill after reading poorly so many times in the past."

He looked her way, taking in her words with a nod.

His silence held a simple and welcome acceptance. No quick praise, censure, or ridicule. No unwanted curiosity. And she realized that perhaps acceptance wasn't so simple after all.

What was it about this man that felt so . . . familiar? Well, perhaps not familiar, but so . . . good.

With a blue-and-black flannel shirt covering a black T-shirt, his hands in the pockets of his jeans, and worn brown boots, he looked almost as much a part of this village as any native. Could he truly be as authentic as he appeared?

"You like this village, don't you?"

She sighed and glanced up the building-lined street, a few lampposts dotting the way. "Love it. I'd stay here all the time if I could."

His brows rose in surprise, but he stayed his response.

"Ah, I'm too proper and poised for simple village life, you assume?"

He shrugged a shoulder. "I wouldn't say our first few meetings gave off country girl vibes."

"Maybe you've gotten me wrong?"

"I think that ran both ways." He gave her a pointed look.

Her attention never wavered from his. "Yes, but I've admitted my fault."

"You're right." He chuckled and looked down at her, his gaze as warm as the sound of his laugh. "Sometimes I don't mind being wrong."

She glanced away first, the moment teetering on an awareness she *couldn't* appreciate. Not with him. She desperately needed to move the conversation onto safer ground.

"Your eye is looking better."

He raised a brow. "You're gonna have to try that again if you want me to believe you."

And there went her smile again. "I'm serious. It does." She groaned. "I am so sorry."

"Really, Ellie. It's just fine." He gestured toward his face. "This is small in comparison to some of my other work wounds. Construction isn't the most accident-free occupation."

"I would imagine those accidents aren't usually caused by someone else."

"It's fifty-fifty."

They moved on a little farther and she filled in some of the amiable silence by pointing out various places here and there. Bratha's Treasures, one of the most special places in Skymar for its hand-crafted ornaments; Seelie Wight's Bookshop; St. Peter's of Crieff, one of the oldest churches in the North Country; and Bree's Bakery, a newer addition.

He commented and asked questions in an unimposing sort of way, drawing out her conversation rather effortlessly.

"There is a shop you might enjoy." She waved toward his chest. "Since you seem so fond of flannel."

He followed her gaze to his shirt. "I never thought of the Scots as flannel lovers."

"The Scots have worn flannel shirts for centuries. Not quite as long as the kilt, but some as long as your country has been . . . a country." She gestured toward the nearest close, which wound between two narrow stone buildings. "There's a fantastic shop for them just down this close."

"Close?"

"Alleyway, I believe is the word with which you are more familiar. Some lead to pleasant little discoveries and others to rubbish bins."

"Sounds like life." His grin broadened and she almost laughed.

"I'd prefer the pleasant discoveries."

He nodded. "Me too."

And her gaze caught in his, or was it the way his lips tilted just the slightest bit to hint at his teasing?

She turned away, frustrated with herself, but her foot landed on one of the loose pavement stones. Her ankle made a little twist and she started to fall. In a second, Luke was by her side, taking her by the arm, but they both stumbled, the slightest cry rising from her throat as her ankle bent again.

Then, out of the corner of her eye, something dark blue rushed into view. Before she could prepare herself, Cameron was there, taking Luke by the arm and jerking him back toward the opposite wall of the close.

The motion sent Ellie off-balance again. "Cameron!" But her protest sounded strained as she attempted to right herself on the weakened ankle, stumbling as she did so. Concern flickered on Cameron's face and he hurried forward as if to steady her.

Her gaze found his. "It's not what you're—"

Before Ellie could finish the statement, Luke dashed back to where she stood and, with Cameron distracted by her, succeeded in slamming a fist into the man's jaw.

CHAPTER 6

Text from Luke to Izzy: So . . . I punched a royal guard,
or something, today. I'm not sharing the news with
Penelope because I don't care to go into the story, but
I thought you'd appreciate my dual sense of power and
humiliation.

Izzy: What on earth happened????

Luke: Evidently, he was in Crieff checking up on security for
the people who are working for the royals, like . . . let me
refer to one of my supervisors as Holt and the other . . .
as much as I hate it . . . Grace Kelly. So since this project
is important to the royals, and these people are working
for the royals, he was sent in to check security. Or that's
how Grace Kelly (ugh, I hate writing that) explained it.

Izzy: So you decked him?

Luke: Only after he pushed me out of the way and then
went for Grace, at which time I tried to protect HER
from HIM, thus the punching. Evidently, he thought I
was putting her in danger, when really I was just trying
to catch her after she twisted her ankle. Her cry of
pain was taken as a cry for help and he bounded to the
rescue. It was a big misunderstanding.

Izzy: Which ended up with a royal security guard having a
black eye and you . . . ??

Luke: Busted lip, but my teeth are okay, so I take that as a
win. I'm glad Grace stopped him because he is trained
to protect, so I'm pretty sure he could have killed me
quick.

Loyally, Luke

Izzy: This is clearly what happens when you forget your
Rambo knife.

**Luke: Actually, the guard and I talked weapons after Grace
smoothed things over and explained to him that she was
giving me a tour of Crieff.**

Izzy: Oh my word. I hate to sound like Penelope . . .

Luke: Don't.

Izzy: But this sounds like a movie moment.

Luke: You can't join her side, Izzy. You're the reasonable one.

Izzy: Did the whole town see what happened?

**Luke: Thankfully, no. It all happened in a little alleyway. So
we didn't have an audience to witness me almost getting
arrested.**

Izzy: Do they have dungeons here? I should ask Brodie.

**Luke: All the more reason not to tell Penelope. She'll make
it into some weird romantic movie reference about
happily-ever-after mush. Especially if there is a royal
connection or dungeon reference.**

Izzy: So now you have a swollen eye and a busted lip? My
introduction to Skymar was better than yours. *Brodie*

**Luke: I am 100% certain I don't want Brodie to introduce me
to Skymar like he introduced you. Gross. The cabin has
a great view, the typical menu consists of mostly meat,
and I get to do what I love without one hint of ooey
gooey kissing stuff. Semantics really does change who
has the "better" introduction.**

**Luke: On a different note, you and Blighty should come
visit Crieff. I imagine Brodie's already been here since
he's a native of Skymar, but he should bring you. You'd
love it. All sorts of quaint shops. Unique ones. Lots of
trade work and craftsmanship. There's a whole shop
of handmade Christmas ornaments, a luthier, a quilt**

store, handmade jewelry. It's like visiting places in
Appalachia back home, except with this culture's own
distinctiveness.

Izzy: That was a super-long text from you. Wow! You must
really like the place.

Luke: Rural. Quaint. Grumpy Scottish men who talk sense
and friendly Scottish ladies who will feed you? Perfect.

Luke: Gotta run. We just pulled into work for our first day on
the job.

Izzy: Try not to damage anything on yourself that won't heal.

Luke: I never make those kinds of promises.

It only took a little while to mentally sort the building team into two groups, the experienced and the wannabe experienced. Since both teams were interested in working, though, Luke had no trouble making all their dreams come true for a solid eight hours.

Two of the men, Gordon Frasier included, had good heads and experience for building, so he put them on the demo team along with him. The other group he placed under Pete's care as the gofer boys, though Luke didn't share that particular label with the men. However, a good building team always needed folks to go for more wood or tools or to take the scrap to the scrap pile.

And with a new floor to lay and floor joists to fix, plus an entire kitchen to remodel, he needed folks in their lane.

He'd just finished instructing the men on the initial floor demo plan when the energy in the room changed. He'd heard Penelope talk about that moment before, but he'd ignored it as another of her magical romance-y thoughts.

But he felt it. Even noticed it on the men's faces as their posture straightened and their eyes shifted behind Luke toward the kitchen doorway. For some reason, he had a strange idea he knew exactly what or, more precisely, who had caused the change.

He drew in a breath, raised his gaze heavenward in a quick prayer for strength, and turned to see Ellie entering the room. She offered him a smile as she took off her coat, and his thoughts froze. She'd pulled her hair back in a long ponytail, but what really captured him were her clothes.

Gone was the formal attire. In its place was a pair of dark jeans, a long-sleeved green T-shirt, and a pair of calf-high work boots. Even her makeup, if she wore any, looked more simplistic.

And the same feeling he got when he'd visited a three-story Bass Pro Shop for the first time tightened his chest with a terrifying realization.

This moment would change his life.

His mind shoved the movie moment idea back so fast, he nearly got dizzy. Because his sudden mental fog could *not* have anything to do with Grace Kelly.

She tilted her head in question at his stare, and he looked away.

Pantsuits and skirts were one thing. Nice. Fancy. Somewhat ignorable for the *most* part.

But a woman who rocked simplicity?

His brain revolted against the interest.

Well, that could undo a man.

Or at least the kind of man he was.

He was pretty sure he needed to keep her out of his sight for the rest of the day. Or at least the morning, so he could adjust to the annoying attraction nearly knocking him over.

Luke shot another gaze heavenward and pinched back a complaint.

He always appreciated God's sense of humor in *other* people's lives, but he couldn't say the same for it in his own. At least not about—he frowned—the heart.

With a few short commands, he sent the men off in various

directions and braced himself as the orange, floral scent slipped around him at her approach.

Time to shove any ooey gooey romance thoughts into the far recesses of his mind, deep into the nothing box.

"I thought we weren't starting until nine." He turned to her voice, her head tipped back and eyes narrowed. "Did you tell me the wrong time on purpose?"

And he pushed his attraction to this woman into the nothing box too. "Nope, it's just that the men all showed up early, so there was no use waiting around to start the job."

"Well, next time I'll make sure to arrive early too." She folded her arms across her chest. "Now, where do I start?"

He gestured with his head toward the group of men to the right. "I'm placing you with Pete and the gofers."

"The what?"

Don't grin. It's a sign of weakness.

"In a building crew, there are usually two groups. The ones who have more experience and know how to be most effective and efficient with our time, and the ones with less experience but plenty of good sense." He raised a brow. "Well, I'm *hoping* there's plenty of good sense in our gofer crew, but I haven't seen what sort of workers they are quite yet."

Shucks. Why did he feel compelled to tease all the high-class right out of her? It was like his mouth didn't listen to one word his brain was telling it.

"You're not implying anything, are you, Mr. Edgewood?" Her brows rose, the slight tilt of her lips revealing her playfulness in the conversation.

Daggone it. A sense of humor was about as attractive as those eyes. He pushed that thought into the nothing box too . . . and then his shoulders deflated.

There were a whole lot of somethings piling up in that nothing box.

"No implication whatsoever," he shot back, watching the glint deepen in her eyes. "Time will tell."

Her bottom lip dropped the slightest bit before slipping into a smile. "Good sense learned through trial may be more my speed."

He studied her for a second.

Hmm . . . there was no mistake she was trying to overcome something in her past from the smattering of remarks she'd made so far.

Nope. Stop, Luke. Don't think beyond, "Hi, nice to see ya. Would you help carry that piece of shoe mold to the scrap pile?"

"That's probably the best kind of good sense."

She paused her gaze in his before dipping her chin. "Good." She started toward Pete and then tossed a look over her shoulder. "But for proper reference, I know my way around a hammer. I may not be able to do much else as far as construction, but interior design taught me that much."

Interior design? Hmm . . . then her comfort with a hammer made sense.

He pulled his gaze away from her retreating form and put his mind to task.

The process moved rather smoothly from there. Luke only had trouble understanding Ross and Gordon a few times, and they weren't big talkers either. Sometimes he'd overhear them making comments to each other in Gaelic or Caedric—he wasn't sure which one—but otherwise, they kept to work talk. Good craftsmen related to good craftsmen for the most part. And mostly used work talk, which suited Luke just fine. The understanding of the work and the desire to do a good job transcended different cultures and backgrounds in many ways.

It was another reason he liked working in building over accounting. He'd always been drawn to creating with his hands. Sure, it started with some mean LEGO skills, but his uncle had seen the carpentry gift and taken Luke under his wing. His father's handcrafts through furniture making only enhanced Luke's skills and interest.

His mom had said it was because Luke liked fixing things.

His gaze traveled up from his place by the window and fell on Ellie, who was carrying scrap wood from the kitchen floor out to a safe place away from the children. Pete came along and offered to help, but she shook her head, continuing on without complaint. She'd been working as hard as the rest of them all morning.

Well, Pete seemed a little distracted by one of the lower-grade teachers. The teacher seemed pretty distracted by Pete too, from the way she kept making eyes at him.

Luke frowned and returned to his work. He wasn't making eyes at Ellie like that, was he? Oh man, that would just be embarrassing.

His brain scanned through all of his favorite movies. *Indiana Jones*? *Rambo*? Ethan Hunt in *Mission: Impossible*?

Nah. Indiana wasn't the best example with his track record.

Rambo either.

His brain paused on Aragorn.

Okay, so maybe there were some not-so-embarrassing examples of "making eyes."

Luke gave his head a strong shake. Nope. Wasn't going there.

He turned all of his mental energy back to wood and nails and dust.

And away from Ellie St. Clare.

Text from Izzy to Penelope: Luke starts the job with Grace Kelly today.

Penelope: Of course he does. Ooh, I wonder what sorts of connection moments they'll have. Will he brush her hair from her face? Will she help tend his wound? Will their eyes catch across the room of tools and sawdust? Um . . . not sure that last scene in my head is as romantic as the others.

Izzy: Penelope, Grace Kelly doesn't seem his type at all. Reserved. High-class. Working for the royal family?!? I mean, Luke hates anything princess-y, let alone girls who act like they ARE princesses (I mean that in the bad princess way, not the way you act like a princess). It's definitely not a match for him.

Penelope: I'm shocked at you, Izzy. Where is your love for tropes? Enemies to lovers? Opposites attract? Fish-out-of-water romances? AND he's even wearing flannel. He's living his best Hallmark movie dream right now.

Izzy: Penn, I think we can safely say Luke would never put the words "best," "Hallmark," and "dream" in the same sentence in reference to himself. Ever.

Penelope: Well, that's all right. We can dream it for him. Isn't it fun??? And I can give him pointers from my vast movie-lover experience so he won't be blindsided by what happens next. I've already predicted the forced proximity. Hmm . . . what do you think would be next?

Izzy: Predictions with Luke might be too dangerous for me.

Penelope: Coward. It brings my fierce daydreaming skills to the forefront. Plus, I feel some sort of justification for all the ways he's teased me my whole life.

Izzy: For some reason, I can actually hear you cackling right now.

Penelope: I wasn't THAT loud.

Izzy: Working with the coffee shop girl is just a coincidence.

Penelope: Izzy, there are no coincidences. Only wonderfully designed divine appointments. Or . . . well-scripted scenes. Or those moments when we're just clumsy.

Penelope: So they'll have to engage in a few awkward
moments. You know what I mean? Catch her when she
falls. Or reach for the same cup.

Izzy: Or hammer, in Luke's case.

Penelope: Right. Or show up at the same place unexpectedly.

Izzy: And find out they have some similar interests.

Penelope: Right! Be surprised that their first opinions aren't
true. EEEE!!!! It's like writing Luke's love story while it's
happening. This makes me so happy. We should share our
ideas with him.

Izzy: He would hate us. Mostly you.

Penelope: Pssht! I'm not worried. He's hated me before.

Mrs. Kershaw provided a nice lunch of vegetable soup and rolls—hearty enough to get the workers through the rest of the day without much trouble. She'd even had a few of the older kids bring in cookies, or what they called biscuits over here, as well as offer tea and coffee.

Luke took his cup of coffee and walked out onto a large veranda connected to the back of the castle. He still shook his head every time he thought of working in a castle. If this had happened to Penelope, he wouldn't have blinked an eye. But he wasn't the castle sort.

Though he had to appreciate the architecture.

And the perfect situation of where the owner had chosen to build the place.

Even as a chilly bite clung to the March breeze, Luke had to take any opportunity to appreciate the view. Miles of views. Rich green hills rolling up to jagged mountains. A lake off to one side.

He squinted.

And what was that in the far distance? Some sort of estate house?

He'd never admit it out loud, but this whole island was like stepping into a storybook. He preferred thinking of it more like something out of an epic movie like *The Lord of the Rings*, but he couldn't help the occasional turn of thought, despite his attempts, toward the fairy-tale story direction.

"It's a pretty spectacular view, isn't it?"

He turned to find Ellie joining him at the veranda railing, her gaze focused on the view ahead. He'd spent most of the morning reordering his thoughts and tugging his emotions to comply, so when she turned up, looking all comfortable and cozy with that cup of coffee between her palms, it only took five seconds to pull his attention from her profile.

Five.

That was much better than the last time.

"Like nothing I've seen before."

She turned toward him. "Didn't you say there were some lovely mountains near where you live? Something bluish?"

He tilted his head, studying her. "You were listening that carefully, Ellie?"

"Maybe. And I might have googled images." Her lips twitched. "Trying to see this world from a novel point of view is difficult. It's all I've known."

"I get that." He nodded, taking another sip of coffee. "Besides going on a few mission trips to South America, I've not traveled much from home either."

"Do you . . . like home?"

Her hesitation drew his gaze to her face. "I do. I like the place, the people. I like knowing who to call when I need something and where to go to find it. And I like the scenery and the quiet. And that my family is just down the road."

"I always thought people like you were from fairy-tale stories."

He nearly spit out his coffee. "What?"

Her grin resurfaced. "You're, what do they call you, one of the good guys?"

"Not sure good guys are just reserved for fairy tales, or at least I hope not. I'd like to think they're a lot more . . . real than that."

She rolled her eyes with a sigh. "You know what I mean. Honest, reliable, authentic." She waved toward him. "But instead of a knight's armor, you wear flannel." A chuckle wrapped around her words.

"And instead of a sword, I carry a hammer?" He narrowed his eyes at her. "I'm not sure whether you're trying to compliment or insult me."

"I'll let you sort it out then." She took a sip of her coffee and wiggled her brows, and the nothing box exploded from all the extra things he started stuffing in it at that moment.

"I'd like to think I'm those things," he said, rushing ahead before stopping himself. "Not the fairy-tale things but the other parts." He drew in a breath. "But I've got feet of clay like anybody else, and sometimes it's stubborn old red clay that refuses to budge."

She stared at him, a soft smile on her face. "Hmm . . ."

"Don't get me wrong." He called on some humor for cover from any romance-y ideas. "It's all the flannel. It sets off good guy vibes."

"So lose the shirt and you're a scoundrel?"

He gave his head a firm shake. "Now why would anyone want to get rid of a perfectly good flannel shirt?"

She chuckled again but let the conversation dim into silence. Good. He had plenty of things God was working on in him, so any idea toward a fairy tale would definitely lead to the wrong conclusions.

He nodded to himself. Exactly. Bah, fairy tales! No good. They set unreasonable expectations and led to Penelope singing too much for anyone's peace of mind.

With a turn back toward the horizon, Ellie took a sip of her coffee and sighed. "Coffee is perfect for days like today, isn't it?"

"I can smell the sugar in it from here." Now, why did he keep teasing her if he didn't want to keep talking to her? Stupid brain!

She tipped her cup toward him. "Sweet rewards for sweet personalities, I suppose."

"Or"—he raised his mug—"you're already so sweet, no added sweetness is necessary."

Her laugh burst out and somehow made him feel taller. Better.

He really was losing his mind.

Ellie squeezed her coffee cup so hard she thought she might puncture it. Just the idea of Luke losing his shirt had her mind going much too close to the ogling direction! She'd been the one to accuse him and now found herself having a hard time pulling her attention from the way his T-shirt hugged his arms.

It wasn't like she hadn't seen attractive men before, even after she'd turned her life around, but his subtle humor and focused attention, paired with those arms and shoulders, proved the real attraction.

She squeezed her lips closed to stifle a grimace.

What was wrong with her?

And why had she even come out to talk to him? Any relationship with him couldn't go where her interest wanted it to go! She knew this! He'd just stated how he loved where he lived because his family was "just down the road."

But then he'd said her name—*Ellie*—in that deep, rumbling voice of his, and she'd nearly buckled at the knees. Heaven and earth! Why?

She'd been with plenty of men.

Too many.

And all the wrong ones, so a simple thing like someone saying her name shouldn't have her wanting to curl up inside that flannel shirt of his, but here she was. Daydreaming and ogling like one of the best oglers in the world.

But she couldn't seem to stay away, drawn to something in him she craved.

What was it? His goodness?

"You know . . ." She turned and rested her hip against the railing, looking up at him, the sunlight brightening those coffee-colored eyes. "You haven't brought up the journal we found. Aren't you curious at all?"

He stared down at her, his height and the size of those shoulders intimidating but for the glint in his eyes. She'd seen him with two of the orphan girls, overheard his conversation. He held a gentleness within his strong frame. A kindness.

And she . . . trusted him. More than she should at such a short acquaintance.

Her lips gave way to a grin. Perhaps he was more knight than he realized.

At heart.

"I'm curious, but I figured you'd tell me if you wanted to."

Her emotions glitched in response. No games. No manipulation. "You are a very low-pressure sort of person, aren't you?"

His smile widened and she forced her gaze not to drop to examine the tiniest indention at one corner. Was that a dimple? No! Not a dimple! On such a man? That just seemed like the cruelest sort of combination!

"I have my high-pressure moments. Mostly related to movies or building techniques." His expression sobered. "I hate cutting corners and not giving people my best."

He was definitely proving one of the good guys. "Well, that's certainly worthy of high pressure."

"And my sisters would say I can be high pressure on the teasing side or in competitions. I can get pretty hot during those moments." Then he gestured toward her with his cup. "So what about this journal?"

"Ah, did we spend too long talking about you, Mr. Edgewood?" She watched a tinge of red creep into his cheeks as she took a drink of her coffee . . . and, simply put, it was one of the most attractive things she'd ever seen.

He narrowed his eyes at her. "If you don't want to share, we can just head right back inside."

"Very well." She released an exaggerated sigh. "It's simply that. A journal. From what I can tell, it belonged to one of the former maids of the house and tells of a romance she developed with a local farmer."

"Of course it'd be about a romance." Despite his growly response, she almost felt him smile, so she continued.

"I read it all in one night."

"That gripping of a romance, or were you just bored?"

Her grin spread. "Actually, it was simply beautiful and I mean both of those words. It held a simple beauty. Nothing grand or glorious. No fencing, fighting, torture, or revenge."

"Monsters?" He raised a brow. "Chases or escapes?"

A laugh burst out of her at his continuing the quote from *The Princess Bride*. "No, but there was true love, it seems, and that was the miracle."

He scrunched up his nose as if he'd caught a sour scent. "We leave gross talk like that away from the jobsite, Ellie."

And she lost her laugh again. "Well then, I'll save the talk for another day and place so as not to sully the jobsite. But there was something incredibly sweet about such a simple sort of love. Straightforward and tender."

"I reckon the best kind of love is simple in one way." He looked back out over the horizon. "Choosing each other over and over and over again."

She stared up at him, the declaration taking her by surprise. And yet it fit him. Direct and tender without any frills. She liked that.

He looked down at her then and shook his head, a new wash of pink coloring his cheeks. Ah, he hadn't meant to say that.

The sound of hammers and falling wood broke into the quiet, and Luke glanced behind him back into the hall. "Looks like the break is over." He took a few steps back, his words rushing out as if someone had given him an escape.

And it just made him more endearing.

No, Ellie. No. You promised yourself that the next time you gave your heart, it would be to the right man or not at all.

And American carpenter Luke Edgewood wasn't an option.

She pushed away from the railing, raising her cup to him in salute. "Well then, I suppose it's back to being a gofer."

"I have to say you're one of the best-lookin' gofers I've ever worked with." His eyes shot wide and he looked away, clearing his throat as he took a few more steps back.

Oh, she couldn't let him get away with a sweet comment like that now, could she? "Ogling again, are we?"

His jaw twitched but he leveled her with a look, almost like taking a challenge. "Just stating facts." And then the resident twinkle reentered his eyes. "And I don't know how much of a compliment you should make of it. I work with mostly grumpy, seasoned men who smell like sawdust and sweat. Your presence would be an improvement on all fronts."

With a lift of his own cup, he turned back toward the hall, and to her own dismay—and delight, if she was being honest—she ogled him all the way back inside.

The smile fell from her face as the door closed behind him. What was she doing? She'd worked so hard to move in the direction her family wanted her to go. Spent three years trying to renew her thinking toward solid, wholesome plans any princess should have for her family and country.

Loyally, Luke

And she'd worked hard to earn her parents' trust and confidence again.

They were finally reinstating her, officially, as a working royal at the Wild Hyacinth Ball, and she wanted that. She wanted to prove to them she was ready.

Her gaze went back to the hall and her heart constricted from a sudden pang.

Which meant another hard lesson of royal life.

Making choices for the greater good.

Not for her heart.

CHAPTER 7

The Daily Edge: Social Tattle from
One Edge of Skymar to the Other

Another tattler spotted our reformed Princess Elliana out with Stoic Styles on what appeared to be a walk in Hyacinth Park on Wednesday evening. Did we even see the Duke of Styles smile? With a little PDA (note his hand on her back), could these two become a royal possibility for the future? She brings the crown and he brings the reputation. It's a match fit for a princess trying to leave her past in the past.

• •

Text from Maeve to Ellie: I only read The Edge so you don't have to, but what the what? I met Stoic Styles once and it was like talking to a door.

Ellie: He's actually very nice. Soft-spoken. Quiet. Very quiet. But nice.

Maeve: Reading between the lines, I'd say he's nice and boring.

Ellie: He's not boring. Not really. He's merely quiet . . . and nice.

Maeve: You've typed "nice" three times in two messages. Just thought you ought to know. When I think of nice, I think of certain shirtless movie stars who will remain nameless.

Ellie: Sometimes I wonder if you're a good influence on my reformation.

Loyally, Luke

Maeve: Of course I am! I say all the things you won't say, so you can stay demure and . . . nice.

Ellie: Oh hush! Christopher is a good man, I think. And once I get to know him better, perhaps I'll find a sense of humor and bantering abilities beneath the decorum.

Maeve: There is nothing like great banter! It can tell you so much about a person.

Ellie: Yes, it's delightful. And fun. And makes you laugh when you haven't laughed in so long.

Maeve: Whoa . . . whoa . . . THIS is not Spotless Styles talk. Who is he, El? He's the coffee guy, isn't he?

Maeve: You're not commenting, so I'm right. Oh! Didn't you mention at lunch this weekend that he was a rather tall, dark, and handsome builder?

Ellie: I do not recall using any of those words besides tall and builder.

Maeve: Was there something about his shoulders . . . ??

Ellie: I am certain I didn't say anything about his broad shoulders.

Maeve: Broad? Ahh! I knew it. You've always had a thing for shoulders. Why aren't you going after this guy?

Ellie: You are ridiculous! 1. He is an American who will return home in three months. 2. He is not interested in a life on display, I am certain. 3. He is not on the list and never will be. 4. See #1.

Maeve: 1 and 2—People do a lot of amazing, crazy, and unthinkable things for love. 3. Lists can change.

Ellie: Not this list, especially since the expectation is to marry a Skymarian. And there is NO talk of love. There's not even talk of like.

Maeve: You don't have to say the "like" part. I can tell there's already like.

Maeve: Don't you think your parents want the best man for
you? Sometimes, the very best things don't come on a
list. They come out of nowhere.

She'd been keeping her distance the past few days. Which was good.
Especially for the way his thoughts responded to being near her. So
why did he find his attention slipping in her direction or himself
aching for another conversation?

Because he was stupid. That was why.

And because emotions led to their own private torture chamber. If
he'd learned anything from the movies, let alone his past experiences,
the poor guy usually had his heart beaten to smithereens before he ever
made it to the end of the story.

And Luke wasn't interested in smithereens, unless it was after
Rambo took out his revenge.

Right. Exactly.

And he'd keep telling himself that until he believed it . . . or
returned home.

Why was it that just at the time he'd gotten settled with the idea
of being single for a while, he was struck upside the head with an
impossible attraction? Well, the attraction wasn't impossible. His roving
attention could confirm that without any trouble, but any possible
relationship sure was.

Emotions, in the romantic sense, had rarely served him well. He
wasn't a half-hearted sort of person. Once he dove—or stumbled—
into a relationship, he was all in. And any sort of anything with a
Skymarian Grace Kelly didn't bode well for hearts and futures.

He continued his internal monologue as he moved from the back
of the castle up the stairs to the kitchen, his arms laden with lumber.

Loyally, Luke

Pete followed, whistling some song that sounded nauseatingly chipper for only one cup of coffee. They'd arrived a little early to make sure the worksite was set before the others arrived. It made things move faster and better.

"Have you noticed that lovely primary grades teacher I've been chatting with?" Pete's voice lilted. The man had more enthusiasm than most women Luke knew. "The brunette, dark skin, fantastic eyes."

"I think so." Luke rounded the top of the stairs and entered the kitchen, subfloor showing from one end to the other. In truth, his focus had been split between the job and the perfume-drinking distraction.

"I'm thinking of asking her to dinner this weekend." He placed the tools in his hands down on the floor and then sighed. "But I'm not certain she's interested in me or just being friendly."

Luke pulled his tool belt around his waist, sending Pete a nod. "That's a pretty regular dilemma."

"You're older than me." Pete waved a hand in Luke's direction. "And likely much more experienced."

Don't count on it.

"How do you know if a woman is interested in you?"

Luke drew in a breath and clicked his belt in place. "I just assume she's not."

Like with Ellie. She had a lot riding on this remodel, he could tell. And her friendliness stemmed from creating a positive work environment, he guessed, and likely making up for a bit of their bad start. But interest? Nope. Not a high-class woman like her and a regular guy like him.

A movie scene popped to his mind, unbidden. A movie star and a bookshop owner? Hugh Grant, was it? He nearly got sick at the idea. Had he watched that movie with Izzy for a birthday?

Clearly, the nothing box was not working.

"A bad history with women then?"

Luke paused, thinking of how he could end this conversation as soon as possible, when a set of little faces peered around the kitchen doorframe. Yep, he was okay with the girls rescuing the guys sometimes. Especially in this case.

"Looks like we've got some company."

He walked over to the door and kneeled down to match their eye levels. "You ladies are out and about early this morning."

Amara offered him a wrinkle-nosed grin. "We're not outside. We are inside."

"That is true." His grin spread and he looked up at the ceiling as if in thought. "So what has you coming to visit me this morning?"

"Jamie said you've broken the floor." This from Faye.

"We did." Luke gestured behind him to the room. "We have to break it to make it better." Then Luke caught sight of a boy standing in the shadows nearby. Thin fellow. Maybe fourteen or fifteen?

Luke leaned close and in a stage whisper said, "Is that Jamie spying on us?"

The girls giggled and nodded, so Luke continued, "Well, if Jamie is interested in learning more about what we're doing"—Luke raised his gaze to the boy—"then just tell him to check with his teachers and I'll put him to work."

The boy stared at Luke with wide eyes before he disappeared around the corner of the wall.

"My grandmother is coming to get me in two days," Amara said, hugging a stuffed animal—was it an elephant?—against her chest. "She is going to take me back to Nigeria. I have lots of family there."

"Well, I am happy for you, Amara. I think family is a good thing." Luke caught sight of Faye's wobbly lip. "And you've had a whole bunch of family right here in Cambric Hall, haven't you?" He nodded to Faye. "The two of you stick together like you're close as sisters."

Amara's eyes brightened and she wrapped an arm around Faye's waist. "We've been friends for a whole year."

"Whew. That's a long time." Luke gave the announcement enough obvious respect to see both girls smile in return. "I heard a secret once about friendships like that." He leaned in closer. "Wanna hear?"

The girls' eyes grew wide and they edged in. He lowered his voice. "I've heard that the best friends stay friends no matter how far apart they are."

They stared at him, waiting for him to continue, so those words needed more . . . something. "Because we carry memories around with us that help us think of good times, and if we close our eyes real tight—" He closed his eyes and then opened them just enough to notice that both girls had closed their eyes too. He wrestled against a burgeoning grin, the itch to hug both girls nearly knocking him over. "We can see those folks we love as if they were near enough to touch."

When he opened his eyes, both girls stared back at him, nodding.

"And we can write letters," Faye said.

"Or emails," Amara added.

Luke nodded, his grin twisting for release. One reason he liked kids so much. They liked practical more than sentimental too. "That's exactly right."

"Do you have people you email from where you live?" Faye asked.

"I do. I have three sisters." Because he always counted Izzy as a sister instead of a cousin.

Both girls' eyes grew wide. "And no brothers?"

"Nope." He shook his head, sighing. "Not a one." He tapped Faye's nose. "But both my dogs are boys, so I could try to even out the score a bit."

Both girls giggled, but another chuckle behind him sounded much too mature for a little girl. He closed his eyes with a sigh, almost certain of who it would be. He turned to find his fear confirmed. Ellie leaned against the doorframe, arms crossed, staring down at him with a crooked grin on her face.

He rolled his gaze heavenward as heat traveled up into his face, almost enough to make his beard sweat. He wasn't ashamed of talking to kids at all, but for some reason, her seeing and hearing it just niggled at him the wrong way. With all her high-class, she probably thought he was ridiculous.

Luke stood and the girls smiled and waved at Ellie.

"Hello, Ms. Ellie," they said in unison.

"Hello, Amara, Faye."

She knew the girls' names?

"Are you making a new friend?" Ellie looked from the girls over to Luke. He kept his gaze away from hers and gave a tug to the collar of his T-shirt, just to have something to do.

"He's breaking the kitchen floor to make it better," Faye recited.

"He is."

"Are you helping him?" This from Amara.

"I'm trying, but I have a lot to learn in regard to building."

"What do you usually do?" Faye asked. "When you're not here?"

Which meant she was probably at Cambric more often than Luke expected.

"She visits castles and rides horses." Amara nodded, looking expectantly up to Ellie. "And wears beautiful dresses."

Luke slid a glance over to Ellie to catch her response.

Ellie wrestled with her grin, her cheeks pinking a bit. And the look didn't hurt her at all.

"There are a lot of castles in Skymar and they need lots of work." She stepped closer to them. "And I do like riding horses, but I much prefer comfortable clothes than lots of dresses. However . . ." She drew out the word and dropped to one knee. "If I were going to wear a special dress, I would certainly want it to be a beautiful one."

"Do you have lots of crowns too?" Faye asked.

Ellie's smile faded. "Crowns?" She looked over at Luke like she'd lost what to say.

"It's all right if you still wear crowns, Ms. Ellie." He shrugged a shoulder. "I've got a sister who does too. Often. And without one apology."

Ellie's wrestling match with her smile took on a whole new force.

"Your sister wears crowns?" Faye's eyes grew wide.

"And fancy dresses and she sings *all* the time," Luke added, lowering back to the girls' level next to Ellie. "But you know what she loves even more than her crowns?"

Both girls shook their heads.

"Her shoes. She's got more shoes than windows in Cambric Hall."

A collective gasp from all three of the ladies came in response.

"Faye, Amara," a teacher called from down the hall. "It's time for classes, girls."

Both girls stood, their body language screaming that the last thing they wanted to do was follow the teacher, but with half-hearted smiles and a wave or two, they made their way down the hallway.

Luke stood, offering a hand beneath Ellie's elbow as they both rose. Her orange scent invaded every breath.

And she'd worn her hair down in the back today instead of the ponytail she'd worn the rest of the week. Long, thick, golden.

Like Rapunzel.

He flinched. Where on earth had that thought come from?

"Three sisters?" She raised her brow, those blue eyes dancing.

He nodded and shoved his hands in his pockets.

"Are you the eldest?"

He shook his head. "Second or third, depending on how you count it."

She tilted her head, studying him. "I . . . don't understand."

"My folks have three kids, but we adopted my cousin when her parents died, so I'm second born as far as biological siblings are concerned, but third in line if we count Izzy."

"A middle child no matter how you put it." The teeniest twist to her smile hinted at her tease. "That explains so much."

How could he miss having conversations with Ellie, someone he barely knew, after only a few days? But he did. Or maybe it was the company he'd kept lately. Quiet builders and . . . Pete.

"Best kind, in my opinion." He held her gaze. "What about you? Any siblings for you to boss around?"

"Boss around?" Her smile flashed wide. "I'm fifth of five. I'm told what to do by everyone else."

"So you just take out all that pent-up frustration on me then?"

The way her grin responded to him shouldn't matter so much, but it did. It mattered a whole bunch. And he liked it more than he should. Like a coffee addiction.

Her gaze trailed from his face to his chest and back. "You looked like you could handle it."

He nearly stepped a little closer, drawn in by those eyes. What was it about her that had him thinking romance wasn't such a bad idea after all? If she'd even consider him.

Which was unlikely.

But with her dressed in those jeans and that baggy sweater, the distance between them didn't feel so insurmountable.

"So you're the baby of the family, are you?" he said, returning her challenge. "That sure explains a lot." He tossed her words back at her, complete with raised brow.

"That I'm well prepared to manage big personalities?" She held his stare, the glimmer on full display, and for one quick second, the desire to kiss her jumped right into his head.

As if she'd read his mind and didn't like the direction of his thoughts, she looked away and stepped back.

"We ought to get to work." She moved toward the kitchen door, her smile barely hanging on. "As you said yesterday, this kitchen won't fix itself."

Luke released his breath, his shoulders dropping. Whatever

broke the spell of that moment probably saved him from making even more of an idiot of himself. Women like her didn't fall for men like him, and a woman seven hours away by plane, at that. So despite this crazy magnetism toward her, he needed to keep clear of her.

Do his job. Enjoy this new experience.

And go back home.

Text from Penelope to Luke: Pete says you're working on an orphanage. How perfect for you, Luke! You love kids.

Penelope: And it fits right in with the usual romance trope of "save a business," "save a homestead." You really should watch more Hallmark movies to best prepare for your life right now.

Luke: I can think of five million better things to do with my time, Penny-girl.

Penelope: That's all right. I'll just keep narrating your life for you because I know you love it so much.

Luke: That threat ALMOST works, but not quite.

Penelope: Well, at least one of us is trying to be prepared for the possibilities of your romantic future.

Penelope: Your orphanage is in a CASTLE???? Luke! It's . . . perfect.

Luke: How on earth . . . ?

Penelope: I asked Matt about orphanages in Skymar and told him that you were in the northern part of Ansling. He said there was one rather well-known orphanage in the North Country, so of course I put on my best detective hat and went to work . . . virtually. I'm even more certain you are in your own romance movie. A castle???

Luke: Penn, even if I were working with someone like Grace Kelly, romance is not in the future. Don't throw your romance confetti on me. It won't work. I'm immune.

Penelope: *chime*

Text from Matt to Luke: I had no idea she was researching where you are. But I will add that the North Country has some excellent lakes for fishing, should you get the opportunity. Text Grandfather and he'll give you more details.

Luke: Thanks for speaking sense. I needed it after the Penelope love-tornado just blew up my phone.

Text from Penelope to Matt and Luke: Just so you know, I'm only being extremely hopeful because I want you to be as happy as I am. I am NOT matchmaking. I don't possess that skill. I'm only giving you little hints as to what might happen in your life. Just think about how wonderful it all could be!

Matt: I didn't know I was dating a fortune teller.

Luke: Busybody.

Penelope: It's not fortune-telling. It's just excellent social prediction skills. For example, I'm predicting that you'd really like me to make you some strawberry tarts tonight, Matt.

Matt: If fortune-telling is related to your baking, then the answer is always yes. As far as the prophecies into Luke's love life? You didn't see our romance coming.

Penelope: That's true. I should have. All the perfect Maria von Trapp signs were there, but that's why my predictions are so helpful. We often can't see clearly when we're in the thick of it, so we might need outside observers.

Loyally, Luke

<u>Luke:</u> I'd prefer silent outside observers.

<u>Luke:</u> PS: Could you guys continue your cute little lovefest in a private convo?

<u>Matt:</u> Sorry, mate. Don't worry. I know how to distract her.

<u>Luke:</u> I'm not sure your last text helped with the lovefest ideas, Matt, but thanks for trying.

Nessa Frasier promised a magnificent find.

Early-nineteenth-century sconces, similar to what Ellie had been in search of for the cottage. And the dear woman had seemed almost giddy with the discovery. She truly was one of the kindest people. She and her husband had taken Ellie into their lives when she'd first hidden away at Perth Hall and helped her with her healing and reentry into the world.

Crieff had been the best place to hide. And heal.

And orient herself to what she really wanted.

This village offered only a small sampling of the good people filling Skymar, people she could find a way to help and support as they'd done for her. She fit here.

She sighed. But at times, she fit in the real royal world too, more in the service part of things, especially for the past three years. Still . . . she knew now that her position came with power to change things for the better. She'd worked so hard garnering funds for the orphanage. It had been in dire need of improvements, but after almost a year of meeting with prospective donors and businesses, her work had finally paid off in a solid positive trajectory to expand the orphanage and associated school.

She'd also worked on improving the roadways in the usually forgotten North Country. And with its unique collection of ruins, particularly castles and old houses, she'd slowly been making progress in finding particular properties to convert into useful buildings—whether holiday homes, office space, or residences.

All in the hopes of building up not just the North Country but all of Skymar. Bringing in more people. Tourists-turned-residents.

It was one tangible way of bringing something good out of her own brokenness.

And the people of Crieff, Mara, and the North Country recognized her efforts . . . and heart.

Ellie's mind trailed back through the most recent day of hard work at Cambric. Despite several of the men attempting to deter her, she insisted on helping unload lumber for the new kitchen floors while Luke and Gordon made additional repairs to the floor joists.

Luke only tried once. But then, as she'd come to expect, he took her at her word and left her to work alongside Peter, who'd become a bit of a curious confidant of hers. Well, *she* wasn't sharing anything, but *he* shared a great deal about Luke Edgewood.

The carpenter kept proving more and more of an anomaly. Peter told how Luke rose early most mornings to drink one cup of coffee while reading his devotions and then, after a quick breakfast, he took a short walk before getting ready for the day.

Something about that knowledge of this strong and capable man choosing to spend each morning reading a devotion and enjoying nature only deepened her curiosity about him and made him all the more intriguing.

She slowed her pace down the path. Why would God send someone so . . . interesting into her life when she couldn't allow herself to even consider a future with him? To strengthen her self-control? To help her prove she'd changed?

She shook the thought away.

Not that Luke would choose her, especially when he learned the truth about her.

Loyally, Luke

What quiet, behind-the-scenes man would want a royal life?

And he'd almost found out. If Luke's princess-loving sister hadn't already dulled his curiosity about women who wore crowns, Ellie would have had some explaining to do.

She frowned. Perhaps she should tell him anyway, but the anonymity was too addicting. The fact that he treated her as he did, simply as Ellie, made their interactions all the sweeter.

And the way he bantered with those girls? And then he'd brought Jamie MacGregor into work, slowly teaching him how to help lay flooring? Something about a strong, gruff, quiet man like him lowering to a knee to comfort little girls and taking an insecure, broken boy under his wing should prick at any person's heart.

She shook her head as she entered the Frasiers' shop.

Perhaps she should return to New Inswythe for a few days to distance herself from this distracting interest in the impossible Luke Edgewood. Even if he didn't have any interest in her, nursing her own fascination didn't help with her need to discover whether Christopher Montgomery was her future or not.

And the more time she spent with and learned about Luke, the more she found herself comparing the two. One offered "everything" her role as princess needed: rank, reputation, stability, history. The other offered some things that called to her heart: tenderness, humor, gentleness, strength.

Her pulse certainly responded much more quickly to one than the other.

She pressed her fingers into her forehead as she navigated one of the back ways to Rudan Air Chall, taking a few quick turns to bypass Cameron's hawk eyes. She'd learned special ways to get around the good-natured man, but he usually guessed her movements. Though in Crieff, his alertness remained more relaxed than in the city.

The bell over the door announced Ellie's entrance into the shop. A few visitors hovered on the far right, talking quietly about some piece of furniture. Ellie veered in the opposite direction. Most tourists didn't recognize her, which was a mercy. When she'd been at her worst, she'd colored her hair dark and worn clothing she winced even now to remember. It was almost like she'd tried every way to defy her royal life.

On the back side of the kitchen items section, she found Nessa and Gordon deep in conversation with . . . Luke Edgewood. She raised her gaze heavenward. How had this happened again? She was trying to distance herself from the man, not appear as if she was stalking him!

"Oh, Ellie, how good of you to come." Nessa stepped forward, her light blonde hair spun back into a bun. "Just in time for dinner." She waved behind her, her eyes alight. "And Luke has just agreed to join us as well."

Ellie's gaze zeroed in on Nessa, who did nothing to hide the pixie glint in her eyes.

The woman knew Ellie's situation. Had basically lived through it with her for the past five years. As a longtime friend of Ellie's mother, Nessa should be well aware how any sort of relationship with a non-native was out of the question, but here the woman was, smile in perfect form, wearing an apron that read "Make Love Not War."

And playing matchmaker for an impossible match!

With a tight smile at the two men, Ellie took Nessa by the arm and steered her out of earshot into the book section.

"What are you doing?" Ellie whispered, peering over Nessa's shoulder into the next room to make sure Gordon and Luke weren't following.

"Making dinner for friends, as I always do on Friday evenings."

Ellie narrowed her eyes at the woman. "Nessa, just because you are one of Mother's oldest and dearest friends doesn't mean you should meddle."

"Meddle?" Her brows shot high. "I dinna know what you mean, dearie. I was simply being hospitable for a lad who's new to our wee village. If that's what—"

"You know very well what I mean." She sighed. "Why would you even contemplate such a thing when it will only lead to someone getting hurt?"

"Hurt?" She tsked and shook her head. "Havin' nice friends who will treat you well is never a bad thing, Ellie. I dinna know if there's any romance brewin', but I will tell you this: the lad in the next room is a one-of-a-kind sort and is worthy of your friendship, if nothing else."

Nessa returned to the room, casting a knowing look over her shoulder. Ellie followed, attempting not to grumble like a disappointed six-year-old. As soon as she turned the corner, her attention fell on Luke. He'd changed from his work clothes and was wearing a simple green T-shirt and dark jeans, his jean jacket hanging open. He had a wonderful wave to his dark hair, as if it was brushed back by the wind.

He didn't seem the sort to spend a lot of time fussing over his hairstyle, so the wave must be natural, softening his face probably more than he'd ever want to know. She pinched her lips tight to keep her grin intact. The fact she knew him well enough to guess such a thing made the wave even more tempting.

Her gaze traveled down him with a thrill of appreciation.

Friendship? *Have mercy.* Mere friendship wasn't exactly what her heart wanted to investigate with Luke Edgewood.

At all.

And her response proved two things: the Ellie of the past was still alive and well, and this time she may very well be in real danger of losing her heart.

CHAPTER 8

When Luke had gotten a call from Nessa Frasier about some special period-appropriate tile Gordon had located for Cambric Hall's kitchen, the question of Nessa calling him instead of Gordon only flickered through his mind.

He'd just check out the pieces and have them sent up to the castle if they fit with the new backsplash. It wasn't but a mile or two walk from the village to the hall, and the clouds didn't seem threatening. Pete promised to meet him there after his date.

Little did Luke know that the threat inside the shop was much more dangerous than any possible one outside.

Nessa had invited him to stay for dinner along with Ellie St. Clare.

And from the twinkle in the older woman's eyes, her intention was clear.

Matchmaking. His lips fought a snarl. It was like he couldn't escape it.

Nessa's subtle hints about Ellie's history of betrayers and her need to have trustworthy people in her life didn't help Luke's struggle against attraction at all. The protector in him rushed to the defense.

Luke raised his gaze to hers across the table.

She had her hair pinned on the sides again today and she'd worn blue. Two things that, for some reason, brought out her beauty all the more. He'd noted the vulnerability in her words a few times during their past conversations. Something about brokenness.

Whoa there, pal. It is not your sole purpose to prove chivalry still lives! Nope.

Loyally, Luke

"Is this your first visit to Skymar, Luke?" Nessa asked, cutting him a piece of some sort of cake.

"No, ma'am." He nodded his thanks as he took the cake. "Last fall, my youngest sister worked at a theater in Mountcaster and I came over in December to help with some of the set work for their year-end performance."

"The Darling House theater?" Ellie asked.

His attention shot to her. "You've heard of it?"

"*The Sound of Music*. Wasn't it?" Ellie said, her eyes glittering in the soft light cast over the table.

Luke turned his attention back to the cake and away from those eyes. "That's right."

"You traveled all the way to Skymar to assist your sister with a project?"

"I had the time." He wished he could shrug off the conversational turn with as much ease as shrugging his shoulders. "And they needed the help."

"And now you're swooping in to rescue our orphanage," Nessa added. "Like a regular hero."

The cake soured in his mouth.

"He's doing his job, wife," Gordon grumbled around the food in his mouth. "There's nothing heroic about just doing your job like the man you ought to be."

Thank you, Gordon. Sense . . . and distraction.

"I heard the performance was a huge success for the theater. As I understand it, the queen even made an appearance."

"The queen?" Nessa's comment held a lilt. "Well, did you have a chance to meet her, Luke?"

"Sure did." He offered a grin. "She was nice. Kind. Not nearly as high and mighty as I thought she'd be."

Ellie coughed.

"Well, of course she's not. She's from Crieff originally," Nessa

115

added. "Her father was the pastor of Christ Church in the center of town."

Luke pushed his food through a hard swallow. "The queen is a PK?"

"PK?"

"Preacher's kid," he clarified and chuckled. "Well, that does change the sheen, doesn't it? A queen as a preacher's kid?" He shook his head. "I figured most royal folks had to marry other high-class sorts. Or at least that's the way it seems in the movies my sisters watch."

"It's usually the case that royals marry someone of rank or position, but not always." Nessa looked over at Ellie. "Sometimes love wins over position. In fact, it is so for our own king and queen."

Ellie's expression didn't quite match the theme of the conversation. She looked mad. Maybe she wasn't interested in royals all that much either.

"In fact, the queen is a lifelong friend of mine." Nessa tapped the table. "We went to school together and have remained very close throughout our lives."

A sound like a horse snorting came from the head of the table. Gordon, who'd been busy eating his cake, gestured with his fork toward his wife. "The lad didn't come here to talk nonsense about queens. He's come to talk about the work." He turned toward Luke. "Do you hope to modernize the look of the kitchen or keep to the original?"

Luke offered Nessa a grin in hopes of softening the turn in conversation before looking back at Gordon. "I have a few ideas I'd like to talk to Ellie and Mrs. Kershaw about before I make definite plans, but my goal is to keep the look historic while giving the kitchen more modern conveniences."

"Oh, well, you and Ellie should have a good discussion," Nessa interjected. "She has a degree in interior design, and she's a keen eye for it too."

"Nessa—" Ellie interjected, a slight edge in her voice.

"And she appreciates the history of the place," Nessa continued. "I'd make wise use of her skills and time, Luke, if I were you."

Ellie rolled her eyes and shook her head at him as if she were about done with Nessa for the night. Luke wasn't sure why, but her response nudged his grin a little wider.

Could a relationship, friendship or otherwise, be possible with her? Izzy and Penelope had made the seemingly impossible work, but could something that crazy work for him too?

Crazier things had happened, right?

Ellie checked things off a list he didn't even realize he had until that moment.

Smart. Talented. Sarcastic. Easy on the eyes.

Heat traveled up his neck, so he rubbed at the spot. He didn't even know classy was attractive to him, but she wore it well.

And was fun to talk to.

He pulled his attention back to safer ground. Work and Gordon. "We should be finished laying the new floor by midweek." He glanced back at Ellie. "I have your original plans. Do you still want to stick with those?"

Her brows rose. "Do you think we should change them?"

"Sometimes when folks see the space with the new floor, they get a different vision for the room. Now's the time to make any additional changes and consider colors for the walls."

"I do have some ideas about colors and fixtures." She leaned toward him, resting her chin on her hand and staring up at him in a distracting sort of way. Maybe it was the tilt to her smile or the glint in her eyes or the way her hair fell over her shoulder.

Daggone it. He was losing his ever-lovin' mind.

"And the new cabinets, well, I'd love your opinion on hardware for them—what you think would work best."

Work talk and a smart, pretty woman.

He was done for.

Fact.

And needed to get away ASAP before he did something really crazy like ask her on a date.

"Don't you both have to walk back to Cambric Hall?" Nessa offered. "It would be a good time to talk about it, I'd wager." Her smile spread wide. "How's that, Luke? Unless you're afraid Cameron will have another go at bustin' your other eye?"

Luke pulled his attention back to Nessa and chuckled. "I had a talk with him before coming into the shop. Thought an apology was due on my part, so I think now we're in good standing again. I'm not much of a royal sort, so his being part of the guards didn't even occur to me."

"The guards?" Gordon repeated. "Cameron? Well, he's not one of those—"

"That was very good of you," Nessa interrupted. "Cameron's from this village too. It's why he was chosen for the job." She stood, glancing out the window. "The clouds are coming in and the gloaming is close. Should the two of you start back toward the hall?"

Gordon's brows rose and he smothered what sounded like a laugh with another bite of cake. Yeah, Gordon saw the matchmaking madness too.

Luke and Ellie had barely made it out the door when Ellie looked up at him and sighed. "I'm so sorry about Nessa. She likes to engage in well-intentioned meddling too much for her own good."

"Well-intentioned meddling, eh?" He took the steps down from the shop door behind her, a slight wind bringing the nearby scent of pastries with it.

"After my rather difficult history, I'm afraid she thinks I'm in need of some good friends."

"Aren't we all in need of good friends?"

Her gaze flashed to him and then caught for a second before she returned her focus to the cobblestone lane ahead of them. "Yes." A soft sound like a chuckle slipped from her lips. "Yes, I suppose we are."

The silence took a tense turn, so Luke pushed himself into conversation. "My oldest sister has her beat by a long shot. It's a relief to be so far away from home for a little while just to get some peace from her good-intentioned meddling." He sighed. "Though my youngest sister is trying to do her fair share too. Evidently, her vast knowledge of movies helps her predict other people's futures."

"Movies?" Ellie laughed as they started down a path away from the main street. "Well, I suppose if you were fighting Batman or attempting to save the world from aliens, having a thorough inventory of certain movies could help. But from the sound of it, I suppose she relies more heavily on the romantic variety?"

The fact that her first two movie references were not romances piqued his interest more than it should. "Are *you* the sort that relies on the 'romantic variety'?"

"Don't." She chuckled at his attempt to mimic her. "I prefer your natural accent."

"It's not quite as nice to the ears as yours," he murmured, and then replayed his sentence and wished the ground would grow teeth and swallow him whole.

What in the world was wrong with him? Why couldn't he speak like a normal person around her, rather than an idiot?

"I suppose it's listener's preference then. I think your accent carries a certain calming quality."

Well, at least if he spoke like an idiot, his voice had a calming quality.

The path led along the forest's edge away from town but in the direction of Cambric Hall. More private, he supposed.

"But I like all different sorts of movies. Adventure, action, historical, some biographies. The occasional rom-com, if it's done well."

For the real test, though . . .

"If you had to choose between watching *Mission: Impossible* or *You've Got Mail*, which would you choose?"

"*Mission: Impossible*, hands down." She tossed him a grin. "You get so many more movies, and Tom Cruise to boot."

"Tom Cruise." He pushed the name out through a good-natured growl. "But at least you chose wisely."

She looked up at him, her eyes lit with her smile. "Nice reference." His gaze shot to hers and she continued, "*Indiana Jones? The Last Crusade?*"

He may have just fallen in love with her on the spot. He frowned. She couldn't be this perfect. "All right, what about *Star Wars* versus a Hallmark movie?"

She slowed her pace, turning toward him. "What's a Hallmark movie?"

She *was* perfect. "You don't need to know. Ever."

Her eyes narrowed. "Well, now I have to find out."

"Don't waste your time and ruin the solid brain you've got for movies right now. Hallmarks are these predictable, sappy, romantic finger-food movies that basically use the same eight actors in three different settings with two basic storylines. If you're interested in action, there is none. And if you're interested in thoughtful romance, well, it's few and far between."

"And they're popular?" Her laugh choked out. "Why?"

"Beats me." He shrugged and thought of Penelope. Even Izzy fell for them sometimes. "You know how there are people in the world who prefer the sugar icing instead of the substance of the cake?"

"Oh dear, that sweet?"

"Worse." He nodded, their path bringing them to the outside edge of downtown Crieff, where a small park diverted the road in two directions. "They all have the same sorts of things that happen to the folks to fabricate romantic tension. The guy wiping a smudge of food off the girl's cheek, catching her from a fall off a ladder, offering his coat to her, their first kiss getting interrupted by a cell phone, reaching for the same drink at the same time, an undercover royal—"

"What?" She came to a complete stop.

"Yeah, that one is really far-fetched." He rolled his eyes. "You'd think folks would know if a person was royal or not from the get-go. Well, folks like me wouldn't because I don't follow that sort of news, but the regular folks would."

She started walking again, at a bit faster pace. Man, she really must not care for royals.

"I think since the royals are from make-believe countries that no one has heard of, the fact that they're undercover works better."

She cleared her throat and tossed him a narrow-eyed glance. "For not liking Hallmark movies, you seem to know a lot about them."

"Three sisters." He held up the appropriate number of fingers. "And even the most sensible one will binge-watch them at Christmas. It's like some sort of magical hold on their psyche."

Her laugh returned. "You're not really keeping my curiosity down, you realize."

They walked a little farther, the scent of baked goods and the sound of distant voices from the main street carrying to them over the cool breeze. Snow was in the air. Even in Skymar, Luke could smell it.

He glanced ahead as they started the climb up the hill. A large oak, like so many he'd noticed around here, branched out so wide the path had to detour a good ten feet to get around it.

"That's quite a tree."

She raised a brow and looked over at him. "It is."

And he continued to display his utter brilliance. "We just don't have oaks that big where I'm from. Maybe in the deep south, but not in my neck of the woods."

"My brother used to say those are the best ones to climb."

Luke nodded. "The branches basically create a stairway."

She paused, staring up at the tree. "I . . . I've always wanted to climb a tree."

He turned toward her slowly, trying to decipher her sentence. "You've never climbed a tree?"

He didn't mean to say it as bluntly as he did, but the idea of never having climbed a tree sort of stumped him. It was as common in his world as eating PB&Js. He blinked. Did she eat PB&Js?

Did they even have those in Skymar?

A rush of pink flew into her cheeks.

"Sorry, I . . . I'm sure there are lots of different things about Skymarian childhoods than Appalachian ones."

"I'm certain there are, but tree climbing isn't one of them." She studied him a moment and then resumed their walk. "There are many things I seemed to miss that I'm only now truly realizing. In fact, I have an entire list of things I missed as a child that I'd like to do someday."

"What happened?"

Quiet lingered, the only sounds their feet crunching the leaves scattered across the path and the voices from the village growing fainter. A bird chirped here or there. A squirrel rustled out of the way.

It was life as he liked it.

"When I was young, I had cancer for a little while."

The declaration struck him in the gut. Cancer hit hard enough, but as a kid? The idea nearly crippled him. How helpless and scared her parents must have felt.

"There were a lot of hospital visits and medications. I had to be home-educated for a few years. And then, after all the abnormal, I had to learn how to enter back into a normal world again as a ten-year-old." A burst of air came from her. A laugh? A sigh? "My mother became extremely protective of me because I wasn't very strong then."

"Fear."

"*Now* I understand it, but then all I felt was that everyone else's lives had moved on in ways mine hadn't. And since it took some time to gain back my strength and build my immune system, she continued to be overly protective to the point I felt trapped."

"Trapped?" He watched the late afternoon sunlight bathe her face and hair in gold.

"Suffocatingly so." She kept her gaze ahead, her expression sad. "There are . . . high expectations in my family, for everyone, but I felt I was coming into the fray not only at a disadvantage but attempting to free myself too, so I fought hard. As hard as I could to prove myself. In fact, it seemed I tried to do everything in complete defiance of how my parents raised me and what they wanted for my future." She paused then and looked up at him. "I'm fighting a very different battle now. Trapped, perhaps, in a different way by a collection of horrible choices. And now I'm fighting to prove I am not who I was. That they can trust and rely on me. That I have my priorities in the right place." Her gaze faltered. "But like you said in the building process, it truly *is* much more difficult to restore something that is broken than it is to break it."

He took everything in. The words and the ramifications of those words. The pain lacing her voice. The desire to make things right, but most of all the hope. Hope that after all the work and good choices, she'd be able to be seen in a new way, maybe the way he was beginning to see her.

"What were some things on your list?" He followed beside her as she resumed their walk. "The things you didn't get to try?"

Checking off a list, he could do. Fixing a broken past, well, that wasn't his job as much as hers and God's.

Her lips quirked, as if she recognized his detour too. "Much like the journal we found, my list is comprised of simple things. Climbing a tree." She waved behind them to the oak they'd passed. "Having a snowball fight."

"You've never had a snowball fight?"

"No." She shook her head, orange scenting the air as she did. "My mother was afraid to send me out in the cold and to have any of my siblings accost me with snowballs."

"I bet you'd have a mean throw. I've seen you swing a hammer."

She laughed. "You should see my painting skills. I'm rather excellent at painting."

He tipped a brow, his gaze roaming over her face. "I can put you to work with that too. Once you stop dawdlin' around with scrap pieces and get to *real* work."

"Real work?" Her eyes lit. "Then teach me how to lay the flooring next week?"

He narrowed his eyes as if considering. Maybe someone like her could consider someone like him. With her interior design degree, they'd make a great team, but—heat began a slow rise up his neck—he imagined they'd make an even better team off the job. "Were those the only things on your list?"

She narrowed her eyes right back at him and then chuckled. "Oh, I had other silly things like roast food over an open fire at night, swim in a lake."

"There are plenty of lakes around here." In fact, except for the ones that required snow, this list seemed pretty doable.

"Go sledding." She looked over at him. "The kind with an actual sled, not the horse and sleigh type."

The horse and sleigh type? He never would have thought of that one. Must be common in Skymar. Horse and sleigh?

"Build a fire. I've never learned how to do that and think it would be a rather important thing to know." If his body temperature counted, she already had a winning skill. "Sleep under the stars." Another picture that didn't help his man-brain. "Go fishing."

"Fishing is a great pastime." He cleared his throat, their steps seeming to grow slower the closer they came to the castle. "It's one of those quiet things in life that calms your mind and somehow makes life a little sweeter."

Loyally, Luke

The lights of the castle blazed into the growing dusk in the distance, but she stopped just within the tree line and turned toward him. For a moment, she didn't say anything, just looked up at him, a crinkle on her brow.

"I've never met anyone like you." She breathed out the words. They didn't sound as if she thought he was crazy. No, her voice was tinged with a teensy bit of . . . wonder? Naw, that couldn't be right. He never inspired wonder, except when it was with people below the age of ten and he pretended to take off his thumb. "You pretend to be gruff, but anyone who is looking can tell there's a big heart beneath"—she waved a palm toward his chest, her smile brimming wider—"all the flannel."

He chuckled. He could fall for her so easily. Without one bit of trouble. He was already on the edge, ready to trip over the cliff, barely hanging on by his boot strings.

"Didn't you know? Flannel is heroic." Which made him think of Penelope for some reason, and nearly had him backing up to break whatever magnetic pull and stupid-inducing connection Ellie inspired, but Ellie's expression clouded, so he stayed close.

"After all the ways I've messed up and been hurt, I never imagined someone like you still existed. So . . . good."

"Flannel or not, we all mess up, Ellie. We make stupid decisions that impact us in immediate and long-term ways. But we also have the choice to grow from our mistakes." She stared up at him, her eyes softening with something that drew him even closer. "Sounds to me like your past and your mistakes have only made you a stronger and better person." He tilted his head, holding her gaze. "Certainly from what I can see."

He wasn't sure who moved first. He felt her grip his jacket at the same time his palms framed her cheeks, but at the moment, it didn't matter. Oh no—all that mattered was the way her lips felt against his. The scent of oranges wrapping around him with the same possession as the tightening of her grasp on his jacket. The taste of cake on her lips. The sense of coming home to a place he'd never even imagined, right here, in front of a castle, kissing Grace Kelly.

He pulled Ellie into his arms, accepting this strange and wonderful sense of belonging. She made a soft purr of a sound, encouraging him to continue investigating the contours of her lips, to drown in the scent of her hair. Have mercy, he'd never wanted to kiss someone as much as he wanted to kiss her . . . and didn't even know it until it happened.

Whatever her mistakes, he didn't care.

And whoever those hurtful men had been? A sense of protectiveness swelled through him with the force of a storm. They'd have to get through him first.

Somewhere in the back of his mind, he thought he heard a . . . chime?

He almost stepped back, but she had such a nice hold on his lips, he decided to stay a bit longer.

And then the chime sounded again?

"What?" Ellie pulled back, her eyes wide, her breath fast, and her lips deliciously swollen. "What was that?"

Luke decided not to even mention his initial thought because there was no way he was proving Penelope—or Hallmark—right. And was she talking about the chimes or the kiss, because the kiss seemed pretty self-explanatory.

The chime happened again, coming from down below in the village.

"It's . . . it's the church bells?" She stumbled back from him, her palms to her cheeks. "Is it seven o'clock already?"

Bells! Not chimes. At least it wasn't chimes! Though, after that kiss, he might not mind a few Hallmark chimes here and there. Or explosions. Explosions sounded much more like what was happening inside his chest.

"We . . . we need to go." She stared back at him for a moment longer, as if trying to decide whether she wanted to vault back into kissing mode or take off like a terrified squirrel.

The squirrel idea won. Off she skittered up the hill.

He wasn't sure whether she was running away from his kiss or toward shelter, but one thing was for certain: he was already ready to kiss Ellie St. Clare one more time.

⌐

Text from Ellie to Maeve: I can't return to the orphanage for the next two months.

Maeve: Are the renovations that bad? I thought what's his name—Luke?—was a good carpenter.

Ellie: He's a great carpenter. And a good man.

Ellie: And . . . an excellent kisser.

Maeve: Um . . . what?

Ellie: I'm not sure what happened. One minute I was telling him about my childhood, and then he looked at me so tenderly with those big brown eyes of his and we were kissing.

Ellie: Excellent kissing. I need to stop thinking about it.

Maeve: As I've said on numerous occasions, I never mind a good kiss. A great one is even better.

Ellie: But I'm not supposed to be kissing a man with whom I cannot continue a long-term relationship, Maeve. I'm supposed to be showing my maturity and growth. My readiness for life as a royal.

Maeve: Royals don't kiss? I'm sure your parents would beg to differ. Stellan and Ariana shared an impressive one on their wedding day too. I think they probably breached ten royal protocols with that kiss.

Ellie: It was just a kiss, right? A harmless kiss. Simple.

Maeve: Was it?

Ellie: No. It wasn't. My mind went completely blank for a solid ten seconds and all I wanted to do was linger there. He . . . I don't know, he made me feel safe and treasured and completely overwhelmed.

Maeve: Yep, that's not a normal kiss. You'd better run from this guy since you're determined not to have a happily ever after.

Ellie: Maeve! He's not on the list.

Maeve: Then it's a stupid list.

Maeve: What are you going to do?

Ellie: Apologize.

Maeve: For the kiss?

Ellie: It doesn't feel right apologizing for such a kiss . . . or a few kisses, truth be told, but I am going to apologize for allowing the kiss to happen and carefully explain that I can't pursue a future relationship.

Maeve: Sounds horrible. Not the kiss-ES but your reasoning.

Ellie: It sounds responsible.

Maeve: Responsible for who?

Maeve: Aha, you've stopped responding. Another point for me.

Ellie: I'll admit to it being an amazing kiss and one I may remember for the rest of my life. But it can NEVER happen again.

CHAPTER 9

The Daily Edge: Social Tattle from
One Edge of Skymar to the Other

Our tattlers have been busy drumming up your royal news for this week. Never one to stay out of the limelight too long, Prince Arran made his appearance at the debut premiere of *Verona Rising* with his newest conquest on his arm, actress Maria Lansing. We can depend on Arran to keep all our tattlers on their feet with news from his latest exploits, to his cars, to his many adventures and ladies. As the third royal son, he's truly taken his freedom and popularity liberally. However, his sister, Princess Elliana, returned to the cyberstage with her first post from her previously defunct social media page, sharing a photo of the North Country mountains. Word has it that she's been held away in Perth Hall these past three years while working behind the scenes to improve various parts of Mara and the North Country. Could this be a sign that she's also ready to return to the stage of the online world?

• •

Luke was already plotting how he could get another kiss from Ellie St. Clare. First of all, it was one of the best moments of recent memory, and second, they'd had no time to talk about the "after kiss" situation.

A guy didn't recover too quickly from something like that with a woman like her. And as little as he liked emotional talk, some situations required a healthy dose of it. Preferably with a kiss at the end.

Maybe in the middle too.

Well, shucks, they should probably just start off with one for good measure.

He thought about her all Saturday morning while working on the cabin, with Pete sharing the news of an upcoming date. He thought about Ellie through lunch, wondering if she'd be interested in a date. (Since they'd already engaged in a very datelike kiss, an actual date seemed a natural progression.)

In fact, the date and kissing idea took up so much space in his head, he visited Cambric Hall Saturday afternoon. When he discovered Ellie wasn't there, Luke spent some time with a few of the kids who were outside playing some kind of game that looked like a weird combination of baseball and bowling. If he recalled, it was named after a bug.

Text from Izzy to Luke: How are things going?

He took a seat on a bench in the park and paused. How was he doing? *Better focus on the job or she'll know something is up.*

Luke: Good. I haven't killed anybody yet, and the team follows direction just like I like it.

Izzy: Ah, stroking the ego, are they? How are things with the cabin?

Luke: Making good progress on that too. I sent some photos to Grandpa Gray and he likes what we've done so far.

Izzy: And . . . Grace Kelly? Are things getting a little better with her?

His grin twitched.

Loyally, Luke

Luke: I think so. She's not as high-and-mighty as she used to be.

Izzy: I suppose she just couldn't resist your southern charm. Wait. Do you have southern charm?

Luke: I save it for special occasions.

Izzy: You must have pulled out your best.

Luke: I tried.

Izzy: Well, I'm glad she's come around. It would be horrible to have to work so closely with someone who added tension to the work environment.

Luke: Unless it was the good kind of tension.

Um . . . how do you delete a text?

Izzy: Sure?

Luke: I think we just got off on the wrong foot. She seems to be one of those cautious folks who take a little extra care to get to know, but once you do, they're worth it.

Izzy: You like her, don't you?

Izzy: Luke! When you get quiet, I know I've hit on something true. Oh my goodness! Penelope was right!

Luke: Don't ever say that, even in a message.

Izzy: What happened?

Luke: Are you and Brodie headed this way anytime soon?

Izzy: Deflection. A definite yes!

Luke: Not deflection, just that if I'm going to talk about anything important, I'd rather do it the old-fashioned way. In person.

Izzy: Actually, I was texting to see if we could go to dinner with you somewhere in Crieff on Wednesday. Now there's no way I'm missing it.

Luke: It's nothing to get all excited about. And likely won't amount to anything because I'm not crazy like some

people who pick up their roots and move across the world.

Izzy: Love is a pretty powerful thing. What was the quote you told me? "Being deeply loved by someone gives you strength, while loving someone deeply gives you courage."

Luke: There is NO talk of love on this end of the phone. We just moved from being annoyed by each other to tolerating.

Izzy: Well, that's half the battle right there. See you Wednesday!

Luke: Don't expect much. Seriously. Very little.

Luke: And don't jump to conclusions.

Luke: And don't tell Penelope.

⚒

"I spoke with Sir Reginald last night and he gave a rather stellar report of your work on the North Country housing project."

Ellie looked up from her breakfast to meet her father's gaze, his gentle smile belying the depths of pride in his eyes. Her heart pinched. Oh, how they wanted her to succeed.

"I'm glad his report was favorable." She relaxed back in the chair. "Sir Reginald has been an undeniable asset in the process of making the best improvements. He seems to know *everyone* in the North Country."

"He mentioned two school visits you made last week," her mother added, glancing over the top of her teacup. "You know that leads to visibility."

"I know." Ellie nodded. She'd only just begun to forge her way back into the world of social media. A strategic and thoughtful plan.

Loyally, Luke

And all had been going according to her life strategy until a certain woodworking American and an unexpected kiss. She'd made no plan for him. And definitely not that kiss. Her face grew warm at the memory. She couldn't afford another similar slipup.

"If you are to formally reinstate me as a working royal, I think a gradual reintroduction to the media will be better for me than a sudden emergence. It will allow me time to adjust to their persistent presence again, so I've begun a thoughtful reentry."

Her mother dipped her chin, a subtle show of approval. "The fact you've mostly remained out of the public eye for so long is a testament to your mindful caution, but I agree with you." A glow lit her mother's pale eyes. "You are ready."

"I've heard good reports from Holton about your progress at the orphanage as well. Are you enjoying being on-site for the work?"

"I've loved it." Ellie looked over at her father, confidence growing at their choice of conversational topics. "You know how I adore those children, and the renovations are coming along at an excellent pace to be completed before the Donors' Banquet. Our team leader has truly made the process efficient and positive."

"This was the man Lewis Gray recommended, was it not?" This from Mother. "The American?"

"Yes, Luke Edgewood." Ellie smiled as she said his name, but quickly stilled her response. "I believe you met him at the Darling House last December in Mountcaster."

"Oh yes!" Mother's eyes lit with her grin. "He'd flown in to help his sister and the theater rescue their production. Yes."

"He flew from America to help his sister on her project?" Father asked.

"He's the sort you'd appreciate, Father," Ellie answered, her smile returning. "Thoughtful, hardworking, a good craftsman, and he cares about doing his best work for the children, but also for the craft."

"It sounds as if you've gotten to know him?" Mother tipped her brow.

"As one of the people overseeing the project, I have continual contact with him, plus I've been assisting with the work."

A sound burst from her father. "As in, the construction?"

"Of course. I enjoy getting my hands in the middle of the projects. It's one of the reasons I thrived in interior design. We were given ample hands-on learning experiences."

"Excellent, Ellie." Her father's compliment paired with the use of her nickname warmed her heart. "That heart of service is the whole reason I have every faith in you to become a long-lasting working royal." Her father tapped the newspaper on the table to his left. "And those photos you sent of the plans? I can see how the remodel will be beneficial to everyone at Cambric Hall."

"Luke's even offered to install a few wheelchair ramps and widen several doorways to make them more accessible for anyone requiring such modifications. And at my and Mrs. Kershaw's request, he's drawn up a plan for the placement of an elevator as well."

"It would do well for your visibility to share a few photos of your work there, Elliana," Mother added. "Send it through Taugen House and they can release it to the media, especially before the ball. *We* know the hard work you've put into recreating yourself, but the world could benefit from a few more glimpses."

Ellie held her composure despite the erratic hammering of her heart at the thought. Engaging the media felt too much like Russian roulette on most days, especially with the way they'd taken the smallest of her mistakes and turned them into character-demolishing rumors.

"They're going to find you no matter what," her mother continued. "It was a hard and long lesson to learn in my entry into royal life."

"What is our media protocol, dear girl?" Father raised a brow.

"Control what you can and ignore what you can't." Ellie repeated the mantra, which was much more difficult to enact than recite.

"Exactly. And with Cambric and your work in the North Country, you have excellent control." He reopened his newspaper. "Could you send a few snaps of the progress on the renovations as well? I should like to see what this Luke Edgewood has been doing to garner your praise."

Heat flew into Ellie's face, but she maintained her composure. "Once I return to my room, I can send a few I have on my phone."

"Excellent."

"I hear you have a third dinner with Christopher Montgomery this evening." Mother's attempt at disinterest failed miserably. "He's always seemed like such a nice man."

"He is. Nice." And without much of a personality. Ellie held her smile.

"Well, if he doesn't turn out to be the one for you"—her mother raised her serviette to her lips—"there are three others I would recommend without hesitation. All from long-standing Skymarian families with good reputations."

"But there's no hurry, of course." Had Father caught her look of desperation? "And you could stumble upon some excellent North Countryman none of us have ever heard of who will embrace the royal life as beautifully as your mother has." His attention fell upon his wife with the open tenderness he often kept reserved from the public eye.

Mother paused, her gaze lingering in Father's, before she turned to Ellie. "Of course there is no hurry." Her golden brow rose. "But so long as he's a good Skymarian man, I'll be happy to support your choice. And I'm quite fond of good, honest North Countrymen." She rattled off a statement in Scottish Gaelic without a hitch. "We can live too long in the royal life that we forget the everyday Skymarian, and I hope I brought such a perspective into the family."

"Without a doubt." Father raised his teacup to Mother, his smile disappearing within his well-trimmed beard. "And I still consider her brother someone who keeps me grounded."

Ellie laughed. "Because the two of you stay in a cabin on Kernvick for three weeks out of the year?"

"It's refreshing to disappear for a little while and just live in the quiet."

"A truth I've appreciated more than I can say over the past three years." Ellie pinched off a piece of her scone and tossed it in her mouth. "But I am also ready to formally return to my duties."

"A fact we look forward to celebrating at the Wild Hyacinth Ball." Mother sighed, a smile playing across her lips. "All you need to do is sort out who your special escort will be. There is a lovely history of partners who come to the ball together and end up married very soon after. Your eldest brother is a prime example."

"I don't know that my perfect match will happen this year, Mother." Ellie tossed another bite of scone into her mouth. "But I am more than content with the announcement of officially returning as a working royal during this ball."

"Don't underestimate the power of the ball, Elliana." Her father chuckled. "Or your mother's excellent skills at matching. She made such a good choice with Stellan, she's rather determined to do the same with the rest of you."

"Aleksander!" Mother tossed her serviette down. "I plan no such thing. It's merely that I knew our children well enough to see a good option when one presented itself. But there was no matchmaking. Only suggestions. As with the Duke of Styles."

"Of course, darling." Father's eyes lit as he took a sip of his tea. "Merely suggestions." He shot Ellie a wink and then sobered. "As a small country and one that is losing its population, we have to attempt to bring out the best of Skymar, not only to make us stronger but to bring people back. The Foreign Spouse Initiative has helped some, but we've seen the most growth in promoting our tourism. There are not significant numbers yet, but the preliminary view suggests that tourists are coming . . . and then choosing to stay."

"Sander, you're bringing work talk to the breakfast table." Mother's teasing reprimand held Father's grin intact.

Ellie almost smiled. Her parents' affection for each other came in subtle hints but was true and beautiful in its way. Even amid the trials and expectations, their united front paired with a healthy relationship with the Houses of Parliament had brought Skymar from the brink of bankruptcy.

And keeping a united front and sending a positive message of the privileges of their heritage were a part of that continued growth.

The people here needed to see the stability and hope provided by the Skymarian leadership.

A choice Ellie would make, no matter the consequences to her heart.

Christopher Montgomery sat across the table from her in an open-collared white shirt and gray sport coat, his well-made mouth hanging open.

"What did you say?"

"At the next snow, would you like to go sledding with me up in the North Country? There are excellent hills and I've overseen some of the building programs for holiday houses. It would provide privacy." Perhaps he would relax some in a less populated setting? If deepening the relationship was their plan, then why should it be a surprise to try something more real-life than simply dinner at a high-end restaurant? "And perhaps a more relaxed environment to become better acquainted."

He closed his mouth and took a deep breath, extending the silence by patting his lips with his serviette. "Elliana, as much as I'd like our relationship to go to the next level, I feel spending the night together wouldn't be the best choice for your reputation."

It was her turn to sit agape. Her reputation? "I wasn't expecting us to spend the night together. Only spend time together in less formal situations."

"What else can you learn in a different setting that you cannot learn over dinner?"

She blinked a few times. "Conversations can happen over dinner, of course, but other settings provide new information."

"Like what sort of information?"

She racked her brain for an answer. "Well, for example, if we were going to see a movie, what sort would you choose?"

"Whatever you like," came his quick response.

"But what do *you* like?"

He appeared genuinely confused. "I have no opinion on the matter." His perfect smile spread. "It's the reason why we're well suited. I can follow your lead."

"But a relationship is built on two people making decisions, not just one."

"Yes, but this isn't a typical relationship, you must admit." One of his blond brows rose. "You're a princess and I'm a duke. There are expectations well beyond typical."

"Behind closed doors it will be typical." She studied him. Would he be like this behind closed doors as well? Complying with her wishes? Agreeing without opinion?

Her sister, Rosalyn, would say, *"Isn't that every woman's dream?"*

"If you would like for me to come to the North Country and see your work, I'll be happy to take a day trip and explore with you." His smile returned. "Perhaps that will allay some of your concerns about our compatibility 'behind closed doors,' so to speak."

But something told her Christopher Montgomery wouldn't prove any more interesting behind closed doors than across the table.

Loyally, Luke

She swallowed her doubt. "Let's make plans for that to happen within the next month. What do you say?"

"Your wish is my command."

⚓

Text from Ellie to Maeve: I'm in a tree!

Maeve: You're in a tree? (I feel like this is significant for some reason. Either that or I should be concerned.)

Ellie: I climbed it! I've climbed my first tree! It's one of the things on my list.

Maeve: Wait. THE list?

Ellie: Yes! My secret "simple things" wish list.

Maeve: So you just woke up this morning and said to yourself, "Today is the day I climb a tree"?

Ellie: No. Luke arranged it all for me.

Maeve: Luke knows about the list?

Ellie: Yes. We had a rather intense heart-to-heart on the night we kissed and I mentioned the list and a few things about it.

Maeve: And he helped you climb a tree?

Ellie: Actually, about midmorning, two of the girls in the orphanage came up to me, gave me a pair of gloves, and asked me to come with them. They took my hands and led me to this tree. It is secluded and can't be seen from the hall. I know he had to have chosen it to ensure I'd have privacy and not feel embarrassed. And he put a little box at the bottom to use as a step so I could reach the first limb.

Maeve: Um . . . I think you should stick with Stoic Styles.

Ellie: What?

Maeve: Then I can have Legendary Luke.

Maeve: Are you getting a photo of this moment?

Ellie: I hope so. I've sent the girls back to ask Luke to bring my camera from my purse.

Maeve: Smart. Don't want any easy access to the photos on your phone like that one time before.

Ellie: Exactly. And it's nearly lunch break so I think Luke will have a moment, if he doesn't mind.

Maeve: If he doesn't mind? He put a little box on the ground, gave you gloves, and helped you fulfill one of the things from your simple list? Plus he kissed you. I think he'll MAKE time.

Ellie: Maeve, why am I crying right now? I'm not sad. I'm actually . . . happy? It feels like more than happy. I don't know.

Ellie's phone rang in her palm and she brought it to her ear as she nestled deeper into the crook of the tree, staring out at a horizon of wavy mountains.

"I am going to forgo my usual devil-may-care attitude and answer your question." Maeve's voice came through the phone. "Understand that you are not allowed to make fun of me after said sentimental moment, nor are you to expect a return to this type of talk, except in dire circumstances. Are we clear?"

"Crystal," Ellie said, chuckling through her response. "This conversation only happened in my mind."

"Exactly." Maeve drew in an audible breath as if bracing herself for the next sentence. "From the beginning, there's been something different about this guy and the way you responded to him. He got under your skin in all the right ways, even the aggravating ones. This latest move only brings that point home all the more. Luke heard your heart and responded to it in a simple and beautiful way that shows he sees you . . . for you. No strings, as far as I can tell. From what you've said through messages and phone calls, he seems a pretty honest kind of guy."

"He does." Ellie smiled at the memory of walking into work that morning and finding him mentoring not only one teenage boy but two. Jamie had brought a friend.

"So maybe you've convinced yourself that it was impossible that someone like him existed. That someone like him wouldn't want someone like you for two reasons: either he was too good to overlook your past and still care about you, or the crown defined how people showed their care about you. Here's a pretty clear example that the impossible can happen."

"It's still impossible, Maeve." She leaned her head back against the tree. "I need to tell him who I really am before anything serious begins. He needs to know it's impossible."

"I know this is premature, but if Luke does turn out to be the man for you, what would have to happen for it to be a possibility?"

She'd tiptoed around the question in her mind, no answer resulting in a happily ever after. "I'd have to renounce my title as a working royal."

"Which is not something you should have to do, especially after working so hard to get where you are now."

Ellie sighed. "Find a way for my parents to accept him as my option."

"Which they've done before. Your mother is a prime example."

"Mother was a very special case of close friends to the royal family." She looked up at the blue sky. "And if my past had been less tainted at this point, perhaps it would be a more viable option, but when they helped me through all this, my parents strongly encouraged me to find a husband with a widely known good reputation and strong Skymarian ties. I agreed to that."

"You can change your mind, El."

"Maeve, after all the ways they've supported me, this is all they ask. And it's a good request for my future as a princess. The people need to see that sort of support for our country. Besides, I already know he wouldn't choose a royal life, even if we could be together. It's not him."

"Sometimes the best people to come into our lives are the ones we least expect. The ones who we can't see fitting, but they change everything. Even the things they don't plan to change."

A noise from the distance drew Ellie away from the conversation to see Luke coming across the field, hair tousling in the breeze, gaze focused on the horizon. Her heart squeezed. He was certainly unexpected. Wonderfully unexpected.

"I've got to go, Maeve." Ellie kept her attention on Luke.

"Is he walking toward you through a field or something?"

Ellie sighed. "Kind of." And with his flannel shirt casually open, blue T-shirt beneath, and his hands in his pockets, he reminded her of a few of the characters she'd seen in her recent binge-watching of various Hallmark movies.

He was the quintessential small-town hero.

The one she was supposed to end up with if her life really were a movie.

Maeve seemed to read her thoughts.

"It sounds like you need to have an important conversation with Likable Luke."

But this wasn't a movie. Ellie's smile fell and she pinched her eyes closed. "Yes, I do."

CHAPTER 10

Going through a woman's purse was not something with which Luke had a great deal of experience. Actually, he didn't really want that sort of experience. A mixture of awe and terror had accompanied his perusal of Ellie's massive bag, and he took the camera out as soon as he found it, pulling his hand back as if the mouth of the purse would close like a booby trap.

Maybe the intimidation was from being a southern boy whose mama had either used her purse as a possible weapon or protected it like a holy grail.

But he was certainly glad to find the camera and place the bag safely back beneath the desk in Mrs. Kershaw's office.

He alerted Gordon that he was taking his lunch outside and made the trek down the hill behind the hall, his grin growing with each step. If she'd sent for the camera, it meant she was happy with the surprise. And if she'd sent the girls for the camera, it meant she'd actually climbed the tree.

He wasn't sure why the idea of her taking him up on his little surprise made his steps a bit lighter, but he liked the feeling that the image of her smiling face left behind. He'd pondered and prayed about their conversation, when he hadn't been distracted by kissing thoughts, and had come to an unexpected conclusion.

Since he couldn't predict the future and how plans shifted and changed, then he'd just embrace the now and deal with those consequences as they came. He'd never have predicted Izzy would meet her perfect match on an island across the sea, nor that she'd have the courage to pack up her life and move here. He was sure Matt hadn't expected to find his match in the disgustingly optimistic personality of Luke's sister Penelope and then pack up his whole life and move to America.

That was the thing.

In the beginning of the story, there are a whole lot of impossibilities, like a Death Star or three challenges or the defeat of a revenge-hungry sheriff. None of the characters could have guessed how things would turn out. He paused. In fact, that sounded like a Samwise quote from *The Lord of the Rings*. Another great example of impossibilities being overcome in unexpected ways.

Why not something as crazy as a woman from Skymar and a man from America?

Ellie had climbed up higher than he thought she'd try, which made him like her even more. Not only was she a little sassy, she was smart, brave, and a little funny. He had a feeling there was more humor beneath all that high-classiness and, of course, the type of person who wanted to do the right thing.

And she was beautiful, which was an added bonus he didn't mind at all.

She had her hair in a long braid over one shoulder of her navy jacket, and her grin welcomed him forward. Once she'd decided to like him a little, he'd lost all sense, but at the moment, he didn't mind.

If nonsensical led to kissing her senseless and having fun conversations, he'd adopt nonsensical as his new MO. And that was saying a lot. He'd steered clear of pursuing any romantic relationships for two years because his last girlfriend kept trying to change him to fit her ideals.

She'd been the high-class, big-money sort.

And there was nothing wrong with that, if they were more like Ellie. Genuine underneath all the high-class.

But Clara hadn't been that way.

Which meant he never would have been good enough for her.

"Well, look who found her way up a tree."

Her smile spread as she looked down at him, golden braid swinging like Rapunzel.

He would have frowned at his thought if her smile hadn't been so pretty.

"I can't believe you did this for me."

He tucked his hands into his pockets, settling into the pleasant feeling of pleasing her. "It's not too hard to find a tree around here."

The way she looked at him had him standing a bit taller. "You know what I mean, Luke."

He liked the sound of his name on her lips. Well, he liked those lips, too, and needed to explore them some more. "Smells like snow's on the way too." He shifted another step closer to get a better view of her through the limbs. "Which means there may be a few other things we can check off your list."

A burst of air escaped from her and she shook her head. "You don't have to help me with my list, you know." Her words were weighted with emotion.

"Well, I'm not a fan of making them, but I'm pretty good at helping out friends with theirs."

Her gaze held his, so filled with warmth and invitation, and he started to have the slightest inkling why someone would leave their entire world for love. He flinched. But this wasn't love. Maybe it could turn into love, because his heart veered really close to falling, but right now it was like. A lot.

A kissing lot.

"We're friends now, are we?" Her question came breathlessly, and the look in those eyes confirmed what was going on in his head. Friends . . . plus. "By the way, I spent the last few nights watching those Hallmark movies you talked about."

"Whoa." His palm came up as if to fend off the very idea. "Why would you go and ruin your brain like that?"

"You do remind me of one of the heroes, Luke." Her lips seemed to wrestle with her grin.

"We can't be friends anymore."

"Only you're much better," she finished, holding his gaze long enough to bring a little heat to his chest. "The only thing you're missing is a dog and a Christmas tree farm."

"I hope I have a bit more sense too," he murmured and then squinted back up at her. "I don't have a farm, but I *do* have two dogs."

She shifted down a little closer to the trunk, lowering one booted foot to the next branch. "Do you? What are their names?"

"Chewy and Indie." Would she get the references?

She paused and looked back down at him, her braid swishing and her smile growing. "Nice choices. I have a cat named Loki."

"Loki? That's 'bout right." He bent his head and shook it slowly, wondering how in the world she could get any better. Well, being willing to move across the world would probably be a good start. He drew in a breath. "So, *friend*"—he placed his hands on his hips—"you gonna come down from there, or should I build you a tree house?"

Her mouth dropped wide. "Have you built one before?"

"A couple. My favorite was for my cousin's children."

She began a slow descent. "I asked my father for one once, but he had a small cottage built instead. Not exactly the same thing."

"Gotta give him props for going big, though." He held his palms out as she wavered a bit on one of the branches, ready for a slip. Hadn't he seen a movie where something like this happened? He winced. *Oh Lord, help me.*

He almost pulled his arms back.

Ellie chuckled. "You could say that, I suppose, but there's something magical about the idea of a tree house, don't you think?" Then she froze. "Oh wait, Luke, a photo! Did you bring the camera?"

He raised the device up for her to see. "But I'm not great at using one."

"That's all right. I just want it for my memory." She posed, looking at him expectantly, so with careful movements, he took a few shots.

And she looked great in all of them.

She thanked him and finished her descent, but just as she neared the lowest limb, she slipped and, like the flannel-wearing Hallmark hero he didn't want to be, he caught her.

Her orange scent slipped around him as her body crashed into his chest.

"Well, it's a good thing you were here . . . isn't it?" Her words hitched and their gazes locked as he lowered her to the ground, her body pressed against his.

Maybe this hero gig wasn't so bad after all.

There was only a slight pause as he stared down at her and she stared right back, and then . . . their lips found each other. She seemed to anticipate the kiss as much as he did because her fingers slipped right up his neck to bury in his hair as if she knew exactly what he wanted. *Heaven and earth!* He pulled her closer, stumbling in the process, but neither broke the kiss. Of course, with the grip she had on him, she was about as interested in stopping as he was. Her back pressed against the tree, their position likely hidden from view with the tree trunk behind them and the limbs hanging low.

One of his palms came up to frame her cheek before it trailed slowly down her neck to hook onto that braid. The silken softness of her hair slipped beneath his rough palm like one of the best feelings in the world.

She made a whimper of a sound and pulled back—or tried—but there was a tree in the way. He'd always liked trees.

"We . . . we can't keep doing this." Her fingers entwined into his jacket, almost like her brain and her hands wanted two different things. "It doesn't make sense."

"It makes about the best sense of anything I've ever done."

"That is not your brain talking." Her lips tilted into a very kissable smile.

"Even if a man finds a woman kissable and she sees the man in a similar way and they both commence to act accordingly with a great deal of enjoyment?" He raised a brow. "From your nonverbal communication, I'm assuming it was mutual."

She sighed in answer and his grin spread wide. "Makes pretty good sense to me."

Something flickered in her eyes and her smile fell. "Luke, it would be ridiculous to deny that there is a real attraction between the two of us."

"Very ridiculous."

She nodded, her gaze searching his. "And I think you could turn out to be one of the very best men I've ever known."

He tilted his head, studying her, a sudden wariness rising in his chest. "What do you want to say, but aren't?"

Her shoulders drooped. "We can't keep acting on these feelings."

He shrugged. "Seems a shame to waste 'em, Ellie."

Her smile flickered afresh but she shook her head. "But how will this work out between us? Do you plan to move here?"

No, he didn't. Not at all. The scenery was beautiful and the village was growing on him too, but he knew where home was, and Skymar wasn't it. His parents needed him within driving distance, not so far away it would take two days to get home.

He kept silent.

"And I don't plan to leave." She sighed. "So the best thing would be to accept what we cannot have and, perhaps, embrace the friendship we can for the remainder of your time here."

Her eyes were the most startling shade of blue.

"That would probably be best."

She nodded, some of the fight in her expression dimming as she stared up at him. "And much easier," she whispered.

"That too."

She tugged him right into another kiss, which didn't seem to settle her mind because she pushed away almost immediately. "This isn't working."

"Feels like it's working pretty well to me."

She rolled her eyes. "You're not helping at all." And then a pucker creased her brow as she looked back up at him, almost pleading. "I do care about you, Luke, and if our lives were different, I'd risk about anything to explore what a future between us could hold, but I can't do that. We don't have that sort of choice."

He understood the dilemma. He'd thought about it too, and he wasn't the sort of guy who made plans with a woman half-heartedly, so the fact that he wanted to continue learning more about her, bantering with her, and most definitely kissing her, meant he knew good and well he was putting his heart in danger.

And people always have a choice.

"Ellie, I'm trying to decide what would be worse—being near you and not acting on my feelings for the next two months, or enjoying what we can while we can, then figuring out the rest as we can."

Her golden brow rose. "Almost poetic?"

He growled and pulled her into another kiss.

"No, no." She pushed away again and this time succeeded in creating distance. "We can't do this. I mean it. And you'll understand once I tell you the truth."

His whole body stilled. Truth?

He waited, crossing his arms to have something to do with them now that she'd left them.

She closed her eyes, as if bracing herself, and then looked back at him. "I don't usually have to tell people this, because they usually already know, so . . . this is new for me." Her voice shook a little and he edged a step closer. "And at first I didn't tell you because I didn't think it mattered since I didn't expect to start really caring for you." She paused and rubbed her palms together in front of her. "But now . . . it does matter. And I should have told you sooner, as soon as I realized I was beginning to care for you, but I was selfish and didn't want things to change between us. It was wonderful being known as just me for a change."

"I don't follow." He shook his head, a chill slicing through him. "Are you married?"

Her eyes shot wide. "No, though my parents wish I were, particularly from their extensive lists of choices."

"They have a list?" He blinked, trying to piece her reaction and words together. "That sounds like my sister Josephine."

"I think my parents' list may look a bit different than your sister's."

He tilted his head, studying her. "So . . . I'm not on this list, I'd guess."

"How could you be? They don't even know you." She placed her hand on his arm.

"We can change that." He'd met parents before. Some could be intimidating or downright crazy, but not enough to turn him away from the right woman. "In fact, I'd like to meet your parents."

Her smile took on a desperate sort of look. "I'm bungling this beautifully." She drew in a breath and steadied her shoulders. "Luke, I . . . I'm . . ."

He narrowed his eyes, waiting for the blow of whatever left her so flustered, and then . . . a chime sounded.

A chime?

He stared at her as if she'd explain, and the chime sounded again.

This was not the time when the Hallmark chime sounded.

As if he even knew.

She groaned and offered him an apologetic look. "Perfect timing."

At least they weren't about to kiss when the phone went off.

"That's my father." She reached into her pocket and pulled out her phone. "I need to check this."

She turned away from him, sending another grimace of apology his way.

"Hey, Dad."

And then she turned slowly toward Luke, her eyes growing wide as she listened.

"What?"

She held Luke's gaze, her face growing paler and eyes wider.

"In five minutes?"

After saying goodbye, she pulled the phone away from her ear, staring at Luke before sliding it into her pocket.

"The king is coming here to see your progress." She swallowed. "And he'll be here in five minutes."

Ellie barely got the words out, still trying to wrap her mind around the fact that her father was on his way to Cambric Hall.

Her father never just showed up places.

Any official call he made, he informed people well in advance.

She tried to catch her breath. Unless he planned for this visit to be unofficial?

Her gaze met Luke's. He stood staring back at her, waiting for an explanation.

And she had to tell him now.

"Let's get back to the hall to alert the workers so they'll know." She bypassed Luke, gesturing with her chin for him to follow.

"We don't have to do anything special because the king is coming, do we?" He fell into step with her. "I mean, I reckon we won't start back to work until he leaves?"

She kept her face forward, working up her courage. "Probably not. He'll likely want to ask questions about your plans and progress."

Luke nodded. "I worked on a vacation cabin for a governor once and he was a down-to-earth sort. Didn't have any trouble speaking with him at all."

Ellie held back a whimper. They topped the hill and the hall came into sight. A few of the workers stood on the veranda finishing up their lunch.

"Luke, the king is a good sort. The best, in my opinion." Her throat tightened. "And he appreciates honest and creative people, so I'm certain he will appreciate you." She refused to look his way. "And I know he's going to like you."

"Why do I feel a 'but' coming?"

They made it to the path to the back door of the hall and Ellie sent him a look from her periphery. "There's no 'but.'" She breathed out the fight. "Only the fact that I'm his daughter."

She reached for the back door, but he placed his palm over the handle so she couldn't grip it. "Wait a minute."

She looked up at him then.

He shook his head as if to clear it. "Did you just say the king of Skymar is your father?"

She bit her bottom lip and stood to her full height. "He is."

Luke stared at her a long time, eyes narrowing by slow degrees. "Wouldn't that make you a princess?"

She attempted a smile. "Yes, in fact, it would."

The only thing that moved on his face were his eyelids as he blinked a few times. However, he did loosen his hold on the door handle, so Ellie, being the complete coward she was, took the opportunity to move forward.

He stumbled behind her. "You're a princess?"

"I'm so sorry I didn't tell you sooner."

"A real princess?"

"I didn't want you to see me differently." She raced down the hallway, keeping her voice low. "You were so genuine and I felt like I could just be me."

"I . . . I kissed a princess?"

Her feet slid to a stop and she turned around to face him. He stood with his hand on his head and a grimace on his face, staring at her as if she'd grown a horn from her forehead.

Or maybe he was envisioning a crown.

"I tried to end things back there under the tree, don't you see? For your own good, because my life is not my own and you didn't step into my world knowingly." She breathed out a sigh. "And I didn't want to hurt you."

He looked away, exhaling audibly, before turning back to look at her again. "When were you planning on telling me? Or were you just gonna keep dancing around the topic until I was contemplating marriage?"

"I was planning to tell you back there. Under the tree." She waved toward the way they'd come. "If you'll recall, I was trying to end things and you kept kissing me."

He moved close, those dark eyes on fire. "If I recall, the kissing was mutual. I never pretended to be anything other than what I am, and I certainly never pretended to care more than I did."

"I wasn't pretending to care for you either," she shot back. "I *do* care for you, which is the whole reason I was trying to end—"

"Ellie!" came Mrs. Kershaw's frantic cry from the top of the stairs. "The royal entourage just drove up to Cambric Hall. Would you mind shedding some light on this, please?"

She held his gaze. "I'm so sorry, Luke." And to keep from seeing more of the disappointment in his eyes, she dashed up the stairs.

Mrs. Kershaw stood wringing her hands, the only visible sign of her mental state.

"It's not an official visit, Mrs. Kershaw. I believe he's only popping in to support me and Cambric Hall."

"Support you?"

"Since this is one of the first larger solo projects he's entrusted to me in a very long time, he's heard a great many good things and wishes to see for himself."

The woman raised her chin, a hint of pride in her eyes. "Well, I prefer a bit more notice when presenting Cambric Hall and its children to His Majesty, but we will make the best of it. Yes, we will."

A collective gasp from down the hall pulled Ellie toward the crowd of children who were crowded around a few of the front windows, peering out. Ellie turned to find Luke hovering near the hallway, his hands in his pockets and his attention focused on her.

She couldn't read his thoughts.

And maybe she didn't want to, because the look in those eyes shone with something like disappointment and . . . hurt.

Mrs. Kershaw opened the door to reveal Ellie's father with several of his advisors behind him. Brandon, Marks, Tristan? Why had they come? Even Cameron hovered in the background.

And to confirm her thoughts that this was an unofficial visit, her father had worn slacks and an open-collared shirt beneath his sport jacket. The appearance always gave him a more youthful look, though her father was barely in his midfifties.

"Thank you, Mrs. Kershaw, for your generosity in welcoming us with such short notice. I've brought some books for the school's library that I think the children will enjoy." Her father's gracious entrance and specific gift clearly curbed any of Mrs. Kershaw's previous ire. "But I hope you'll see this more as a friendly visit to check in on the progress of my daughter's hard work, rather than anything else."

"Of course, Your Majesty." Mrs. Kershaw gave a slight curtsy. "You are most welcome."

In her father's usual fashion, he took his time getting to the point of the trip by greeting others. The nearest children, some of the teachers—he even leaned down to pet Clootie. Ellie never grew tired of watching his tenderness defuse a room, a gift she'd not appreciated when she was younger, but she now hoped she carried at least a little of it within her.

Father enlisted Tristan to take a few photos, and then when her father finally finished his extensive greetings, his small entourage following along behind, he turned to Ellie, his eyes alight with expectation.

"Wish to take me on a little tour of the progress, Elliana?" He leaned close and lowered his voice. "I should like to meet this American of yours."

Ack! That certain phraseology did nothing to help her frayed emotions at present for two reasons: one, he wasn't hers, though she wouldn't mind figuring out if he could be, and two, he couldn't be.

"If he's here, he'd likely be with the team. They've just finished lunch."

Had he eaten lunch at all? Pain stung anew at the thought of his little surprise and her perfect way of ruining everything. Even when she'd done so much to turn her life around, she still had a way of messing things up. Perhaps she should continue to stay very well hidden in the background, like the Quasimodo of the royal family.

The large room, now even larger from opening up one wall, stood in disarray with the old cabinets and appliances removed, leaving the walls bare but highlighting the new glossy wooden floors. Well, what parts of the floor could be seen.

Luke had placed cardboard down for the workers to walk on so that as they put in the new cabinets and details, they'd keep the floors safe.

Luke kneeled near Gordon on the far side of the room as they installed a new set of doors from the new wall into the small staff dining area. Ellie had chosen beautiful oak doors to go with the sage-green paint color waiting to add soft vibrancy to the plain white walls.

At the noise from their entrance, all the workmen came to a stop and stood to attention. The Skymarian men dipped their heads in reverence to their sovereign. Luke removed his cap.

And now there were three boys from the orphanage helping. Justin had joined. And was Kimberly keeping to the shadows of the room? Had she started helping too?

Ellie almost smiled. Did Luke have a tendency to enlist followers? With his easy personality and subtle wit, she imagined so.

"You must be Luke Edgewood, the project leader." Father stepped forward, his smile wide in greeting. "Elliana sings your praises."

Luke's attention flicked to hers, wary. The hurt stung afresh through her.

"I haven't heard much about you, sir." He grimaced and then squinted as if in pain. "Your . . . Majesty."

Father glanced to Ellie, a question in his expression before he continued, "Ah, well, I believe we should become better acquainted, especially from the high report I've received. Not from Ellie alone, but Holton and even Marshall, who has worked on other projects for the Crown."

Luke looked over at the burly Scottish man, who dipped his head in acknowledgment. "I appreciate that, sir . . . um . . . Your Majesty."

Ellie tried not to cringe at Luke's clear discomfort. Another failure for her. If she'd prepared him a little better, he wouldn't have had to face this embarrassing moment. When Luke looked her way again, she attempted to infuse as much of an apology into her expression as she could.

"Ellie and Holton mentioned that you've saved the orphanage a great deal of money with your plans."

"The more we can keep to use for the children, the better." He pushed his hands in his pockets. "Most of the time, it's pretty simple to just do the right thing."

Ellie wasn't certain if that barb was meant for her, but she felt it. To her heart.

"Would you mind explaining to me some of the things you've done?"

And with that one question, some of the tension dissipated. Luke took the lead then, taking his time explaining about repairing the floor joists and replacing the floor, sharing how this type of flooring was a good fit for the kitchen. He freely gave credit to the workers, including Pete, who'd made his job easier by their ready willingness to work hard.

"And . . . are these some of your added helpers?" Father greeted the boys, who all stood with faces down as if embarrassed. Kimberly made no move to leave her hiding spot.

"They were keen to learn, and as some of them don't seem interested in university, I thought helping them learn a few practical skills would do them good."

Father turned a sharp eye to Luke. "Yes, of course it would."

Luke drew in a breath like he might say something else but stopped.

"What is it?" Ellie interjected, maybe only to have him look her way again. He'd clearly been avoiding doing that as much as possible. "I'm sure your ideas would be worth hearing."

His jaw tightened and he returned his attention to her father. "Crieff is a great village with lots of different shops. Mostly skilled labor shops, like seamstresses and butchers, welders, woodworkers. There's even a blacksmith." He shook his head. "And I met a real shepherd. Never done that before." His lips twitched just a little, then he sobered. "From what I can tell, they're good people and I wonder if the townsfolk would be willing to apprentice some of these kids."

"Apprentice them?"

"It would take matching the kids to the people and skill, but I've seen it work before and it's a great way to give back to the community and build a stronger connection. Even if the kids later decide to go to college, they'll have learned some solid skills along the way."

Ellie stared at him, her smile growing. He may not be much of a talker, but what he did have to say was worth hearing.

"So you've had experience with this sort of project?" This from Father, who'd drawn closer to Luke. One of his advisors stood nearby, scribbling away on his iPad, likely taking notes.

"As a matter of fact, I volunteered at a children's home back in Virginia where we set up an apprentice program with local businesses." He gestured toward the boys with a nod. "Saw a huge turnaround in how the kids made better choices for the future and found some real support within the community there."

"A volunteer?" Father had that look about him, the one that meant he was already plotting something. "How did you volunteer?"

Luke's lips quirked a little, as if he may have seen the spark in Father's eyes too. "I was one of what they called Buddies. I'd take a few of the boys under my wing and spend time with them and teach them some of my skills. Still in contact with most of them."

"That is an excellent idea with great impact, I should think."

"I agree." His expression sobered. "Most of those kids have had hurts like I can't imagine, Your Majesty. So we created a careful selection process of trustworthy people, and not only did it end up helping the kids with job skills, but the connections they made with the families and the community helped heal some of the pain they carried with them."

"Would you be interested in talking this idea over with me in further detail?"

"Yes, sir." He grimaced. "Your Majesty."

"Excellent." Father waved toward Tristan. "Please collect Mr. Edgewood's contact information." Father turned his attention back to Luke. "I look forward to more dialogue with you, Mr. Edgewood."

He turned to her. "Ellie, I have some things I need to discuss with you."

Ellie pulled her attention from Luke and back to her father. "Yes?"

Loyally, Luke

"Let's go into Crieff and visit some of these businesses Mr. Edgewood celebrated, and then we can talk over dinner."

She looked back at Luke as she followed her father from the room and found him watching her. Sadness hovered in those eyes. Disappointment. She'd praised him for his honesty, but she hadn't reciprocated with the same authenticity.

And he valued authenticity.

Something in her heart shuddered.

Why did it feel as if she'd lost something she wasn't even supposed to want?

CHAPTER 11

Text from Luke to Izzy: Can you and Brodie come up tonight for dinner? I need to talk.

Luke: Or wake up from a nightmare.

Luke: Or be hit by a 2x4.

Luke: Probably the latter.

Izzy: You need to talk?!!!!!

Luke: Might as well spill the beans. It's going to be all over the news soon.

Izzy: The news? Are you in trouble? What did you do?

Luke: Why is it something I might have done?

Izzy: Do you remember Uncle Lee's motorcycle when you were fifteen?

Luke: Fair, but that was over a decade ago and it was a really fast motorcycle.

Izzy: Brodie says we can be there in an hour and a half.

Luke: Great. Thanks.

Luke: And maybe you shouldn't watch the news. Just . . . in case.

Text from Penelope to Luke: You're working with a princess??? And you had your photo taken with the KING???!!!

Penelope: I know you saw my last text. It shows "read" at the bottom.

Penelope: You realize I watch Skymarian news religiously. Even more than Matt and that's *his* home.

Loyally, Luke

Luke: Gossip columns aren't the same thing as news.

Penelope: Well, that actually depends on which news shows you're watching. (See, I can be funny.) Anyway, it doesn't matter when your brother's photo pops up in the same shot as the KING. LUKE!!! Your life has just become more exciting than mine and I never thought I'd type that!

Luke: Is that supposed to make me feel better?

Penelope: Wait! Oh my goodness, Princess Elliana? Is she . . . GRACE KELLY?????? She looks like Grace Kelly and I didn't see any other Grace Kelly look-alikes in the photo. LUKE!!!

Luke: How did you . . . ? Oh, I forget, you're some sort of movie guru/sleuth wannabe.

Penelope: I'm sure I don't need to tell you how much this is like a movie. I'm sure you already feel it in your bones.

Luke: More than you know.

Penelope: Oh, that wasn't a good response! Have you started caring about her? Have the two of you had one of those heart-to-heart moments that switches the enemies into . . . more? Did you know she was a princess?

Penelope: I saw that you read my last comment and didn't respond . . . so you DIDN'T know? Oh my goodness, LUKE!

Luke: Why is it that I can almost hear you screaming and we're thousands of miles apart?

Penelope: But I want to hug you. I'm so sorry. A royal! I mean, every time you even say the word "royal" you grimace, so this can't be a happy discovery.

Luke: Would you please keep it private, Penelope? I'd rather not make a big deal out of this, okay?

Penelope: Of course! I've only talked to Matt and Grandpa Gray. I may be exuberant, but I'm not a betrayer. My heart just hurts for you right now. Because despite all your grumpiness, when you care about someone, it's the most magnificent thing in the world. Addicting because it's like finding the chocolate in the center of a Tootsie Pop.

Luke: **You've compared me to a Tootsie Pop? I have no response.**

Penelope: And if she's anyone worthy at all, she would have figured that out pretty fast. Matt says she's had a tough history. Grandpa Gray said she's really been trying to make amends for a lot of the past, so it makes perfect sense that when she meets someone as great and authentic as you, then she would want what you have to give. And she would even be able to overlook the beard, constant flannel, and possible fish smell.

Penelope: And you give great hugs.

Luke: **Princesses don't give up their worlds for guys like me, even with my amazing beard and great hugs. And I wouldn't ask her to. She's got responsibilities I don't understand. And once I get some time to sort it all out, I'll be okay with it. I just need to go cut down a few trees or walk a few hard miles uphill in the cold to get to that point.**

Penelope: I'm not going to give you a list of all the times princesses and regular guys have gotten together.

Luke: **Fiction, Penny-girl.**

Penelope: And nonfiction. There are some, so it's possible.

Luke: **This time, Penn, I need you to leave the fairy dust out of the conversation. Okay?**

Penelope: Okay. I'll just be sad for you, then pray for you, and then daydream about your next romance until I feel better.

Luke: **Fine. As long as those daydreams stay in your mind and out of my texts.**

Loyally, Luke

Penelope: I love you. And I'm sorry you're hurting. And just so you know, you're better than any prince wannabe could ever be.

Luke: Thanks, Penn.

🔨

Text from Ellie to Maeve: I messed things up again, Maeve. Because I was too afraid and too ashamed to do the right thing, I did the wrong thing, and I hurt Luke.

Maeve: You told him about being a princess?

Ellie: Yes, but not at the most opportune time.

Maeve: I'm guessing he's the hottie in the blue flannel in the photo online?

Ellie: The photos are already out?

Maeve: Within the last hour. Quite the stir too, since most folks are wondering about you. BTW, so you don't have to read the comments, everyone is in agreement that they prefer your natural hair color.

Ellie: Maeve! This is serious. I'm not sure what to do.

Maeve: Did you apologize?

Ellie: Of course, profusely, but there's nothing else I can do.

Maeve: Exactly. Then you'll know.

Ellie: Know what?

Maeve: If he's all you think he is.

Ellie: And if he is?

Maeve: I think only you can answer that, El. And I don't envy you. But I rarely envy you, no offense, because that princess gig is not all the movies make it out to be. As your friend of . . . lots of years, I've seen all sides.

Ellie: And I've made my choice about things, Maeve. I won't go back on it now because I know it's the right thing.

Ellie: But what happens when you have two possible right
answers which oppose one another?
Maeve: We pray for a door #3?

"Wow!" came Izzy's response as she sat across from Luke in the small Crieff pub called The Wee Dram, Brodie by her side.

He looked less shocked and more . . . sad?

Well, Luke could relate to all the emotions—the bad ones anyway. The shock was definitely wearing off to leave a big hole of hurt and disappointment behind. Some anger too.

"No one revealed her true identity to you?" Brodie shook his head, his grin almost emerging. "I'd heard the royals had a special place they found refuge, but to such an extent? It's remarkable."

"I thought Pete should have picked up on something." Luke raked a hand down his face, his entire body weighted from some internal struggle he didn't even know how to define. "But he just said the last time he'd seen photos of her, she'd had dark hair. I asked how her last name—St. Clare—didn't give it away, and he gave me the strangest look and said, "How many people who aren't royal stalkers know the royals by anything other than Prince Stellan or Princess Rosalyn?"

"Our neighbors, Prince William and Princess Catherine, are cases in point," Brodie gently offered. "And St. Clare, or some variation thereof, is not an uncommon surname in Skymar."

The realization took the edge off Luke's discomfort a little . . . but a very little.

"And you haven't talked to her since?"

Luke looked over at Izzy and shrugged. "I'm still trying to wake up from some weird dream caused by listening to too many of

Penelope's conversations. The last thing I need is to talk to anybody besides you guys."

"The whole village and the orphanage just speak to her as if she's a regular person?" This from Brodie.

"It seems there's some kind of agreement between the folks in Crieff and the royal family so they can have a sense of . . . normalcy?" Luke shrugged, a wave of hurt tightening his jaw. "Like I was, I guess. A little experiment to feel normal."

"I'm so sorry, Luke," Izzy whispered, covering his hand on the table. "I guess she's just an entitled sort of person."

Luke met Brodie's gaze and something in him flinched at Izzy's words. No, Ellie . . . or Elliana . . . seemed more of a guarded, lost person than an entitled one.

"She apologized." His shoulders drooped as he remembered the way her eyes pleaded with him. "Several times."

"Before her father came to the orphanage?" Brodie asked.

Luke nodded. "She was trying to tell me about it, I think, before her father showed up, but his arrival certainly moved the confession along."

"You know her behavior isn't a measure of who you are." Izzy sighed. "I mean, I can't even believe we're having this conversation, but she's a princess! She should have known better than to go around dating a commoner, right? Of course, you could view it as a compliment that she was so drawn to you, she forsook common sense."

Forsook? He tempered his eye roll at Izzy's love of old-fashioned words. "I doubt my special brand of charm held that kind of mind-numbing power." He raked a hand through his hair. "And we never dated, per se."

He must have hesitated because Izzy's gaze zeroed in on him. "What? What did you do?"

"What do you mean?"

"If you didn't date but you did do something to show that you two were romantically interested . . ."

His face heated. "We may have kissed a couple of times." A country couple, and then some. His beard started tingling from the warmth in his face from those memories.

"You kissed her?"

His palms came up. "In my defense, she kissed me back."

"She kissed you back?" Izzy's mouth dropped open. "The princess kissed you back?"

He looked over at Brodie. "I hate it when they rephrase what I just said into a question. It's usually not a good sign."

Brodie's grin crooked a little and he smoothed his palm down Izzy's back. "I'd put a little thought into what Isabelle said, though, Luke. You probably don't know that Princess Elliana has a rather difficult past relationship with the paparazzi and certain men, if the news is any indicator. But it's common knowledge she drew back from the spotlight and her royal duties to seek treatment for her difficulties with alcohol, as well as counseling for whatever happened in the shadows of that past." His hand came up. "I'm not justifying her behavior by any means, but I am curious if the interest was genuine, all the more so because you weren't judging her based on her position or past."

Izzy looked over at her fiancé. "It still didn't give her the right to play a game with his emotions, Brodie."

"No, not at all, but it does make one wonder if you were as much a surprise to her as she was to you." He gestured toward Izzy. "I know it's not of the same caliber, but that's how I felt when Izzy came into my life. Unexpected and rather perfect for the awkwardly bookish man I am."

Izzy wove her arm through Brodie's and leaned over to kiss his cheek.

"It's no excuse for her not telling you the truth, Luke," Brodie continued. "But perhaps it would help to understand her perspective a little. I'm not certain what she's had to overcome to venture back into active royal life, but I would hazard a guess there is more to it than the media reports. There usually is."

"I imagine there is." Luke rested his head back on the booth. "But that still doesn't change the fact that she's Princess Elliana of Skymar and I'm carpenter Luke Edgewood from America. And whatever was happening between us before today was as real as Penelope's fairy tales when seen in the light of real life." He braced his shoulders. "I'm just glad it didn't continue on any longer, or I might . . . well, I could have—" He didn't finish. Didn't want to. The idea of hurting from feeling anything more than he already did nearly caused him to be sick.

"Will you still have to work with her?" Izzy asked.

Luke took his time with a sip of Coke before answering. "I'd expect so."

The table grew quiet and an unwanted scene filtered into Luke's head. One of Ellie playing hide-and-seek with the kids, laughing. Then another, of her conversation about the journal . . . and then their walk back from Crieff to the castle. She may have been a princess all that time, but she was also just Ellie all that time.

What was he supposed to do about that?

The conversation shifted from Luke's dilemma to cover all kinds of other things like Brodie and Izzy's wedding plans and the work Luke was doing on the cabin, but as they walked out of the pub together, Brodie stopped and turned.

"I don't know why I feel the need to tell you this, Luke, but I was reminded of something my father once told me about a situation in which he found himself wronged."

Luke pushed his hands in his pockets and waited, hoping for guidance, comfort.

"The best stories are like a diamond. They have many sides, and the true reader is the one who attempts to understand more than one."

He offered a small smile. "I know you're not used to living with royals as a regular part of your world, but I can tell you from a lifetime of watching and listening to the stories, there is always more than one side. I don't know if you want to see any of the other sides of this one, since you're only here for a short while, but it might provide more clarity on how to manage the next steps."

⊤

The comments were brutal. Tearing Ellie apart. A few loyal royalists defended her, but most people ripped into her like rabid dogs.

Luke barely recognized her in the online photos when he first started the search because her beautiful hair was short and dyed a very dark brown. She looked pale and sickly. Too thin. And the clothes she wore in the photos were nothing like the style he'd grown accustomed to seeing on her. Gone were the pantsuits and simple button-downs. Gone were the jeans—his throat tightened at the mental appreciation of those on her—and the tasteful T-shirts. And in their place, she wore ill-fitting, gaudy, and rather revealing dresses. Some super short. Others leaving little for the imagination.

One photo showed her stumbling out of a pub with a man attempting, and failing, to catch her. Another showed her attempting to cover her bare upper body with a towel while sitting on a yacht, the man to her right grinning a little too broadly for Luke's liking.

Another showed her being escorted from a car into a rehab facility. The photographer must have caught her at just the moment she looked back over her shoulder. Her face was gaunt and those large eyes of hers stared back as if at Luke, haunted and sad.

Everything about that picture screamed "broken" and "afraid."

He'd caught small glimpses of that woman in the one he'd met.

Looks. Snippets of conversations. The ghost of the shamed Princess Elliana hovered beneath the surface of Ellie St. Clare.

And ghosts could be powerful if they were left to haunt without being reminded that they were nothing more than memory.

His gaze skimmed back over the comments.

"Look what happens when people have everything but want more."

"Or have too much and can't control themselves."

"She doesn't deserve the crown."

"How can she help us at all when she can't even keep herself in check?"

"Move to America if you're going to behave like this."

"I can't imagine how ashamed her parents must be."

"I hope she got what she deserved."

The photo of her being led into a facility was posted two and a half years ago.

Two and a half years.

And he'd not been able to find anything else about her in any more recent online searches, except for a sentence here or there. She'd kept away from it all.

Trying to heal? Trying to become strong?

Trying to figure out how to return to life in her fishbowl world?

Luke breathed out a sigh and relaxed back in his chair at the little table in the cabin. He glanced out of the window toward the mountains in the distance, grateful that Pete had gone out on a date so Luke wouldn't have to talk . . . or listen.

No, Ellie hadn't handled the situation well, but if he thought about it, he wasn't even sure how else things could have happened for them to begin a friendship without the shadow of some crown falling over it all.

He'd have steered clear of her as much as possible because he knew he'd never fit. And wouldn't even have been sure how to talk to her, which would have made him even quieter than usual.

But he had gotten to know her a little more. Enough to start to really care.

Enough to kiss her.

He pinched his eyes closed and ran a hand over his beard.

Enough for him to rethink all the assumptions he'd had about royals. Though, to be honest, except for Penelope thrusting any news or movies about them toward him, he didn't think about them at all.

Until now.

Luke's phone flashed a message and he picked it up.

Text from Izzy to Luke: Are you looking at some of these same past stories about her?

Luke: Probably.

Izzy: Some of these commenters are harsh, especially about her going into rehab.

Luke: I know.

Izzy: I can't even imagine what life must have been like for her. When you mentioned her childhood cancer and feeling trapped, and then to have every wrong thing you do blown up over the internet?

Luke: I can only imagine.

Izzy: Don't any of these folks understand the need we all have for a second chance? I remember all the horrible rumors when Chip left me at the altar. Don't you? Crazy things that made no sense. And none of them were true, but they hurt so much. My smallest insecurities became the topic of the whole town's conversations. Or that's the way it felt. I can't even imagine how much worse it would feel on such a bigger scale.

Luke: With the added responsibility of a high-profile family.

Loyally, Luke

Izzy: I know all I wanted to do was disappear.

Luke: Yeah, get away from it all.

Izzy: So I wouldn't have to keep rehashing the same stories over and over again.

Luke: And to find a safe place to heal.

Izzy: Yeah. And I just pressed into the love of my family and the people closest to me because they knew me and the truth. And I could just live my life without having to relive my mistakes.

Luke: Right.

Izzy: I don't know how much of these things are true, Luke, and I don't know if you care to find out, but like Brodie said, I bet there's a whole lot more happening than what Mr. Google shares. And it sounds to me like Ellie's scared. I can't even imagine what the pressure would be like as a royal, but how much more as a broken royal trying to prove herself again? If she saw anything in you like I see, then no wonder she wanted to keep the situation secret as long as possible.

Luke: But lying is never okay.

Izzy: No, but it makes her actions more understandable. She was looking for that safe place just to be herself, and here you came.

Luke: What do you mean?

Izzy: Don't you know? Why is it that Penelope and I always come to you with the hardest things? Call you when we really need someone to talk to, even if we know we'll probably get some teasing thrown in for good measure? When you care about somebody, you're the type of person who evokes this massive awareness that you'll do whatever is necessary to protect them and love them. You somehow create a sense of safety and acceptance.

Both of those things are kryptonite to a frightened heart.
We know we can trust you with our most broken, hurting
selves and you'll be there for us.

Izzy: Isn't that what everyone is really looking for? Even
princesses?

**Luke: Izzy, I'm not the type of person, even if it were
possible, to want a royal life. Ever.**

Izzy: I'm not saying I expect you to marry her, Luke. But
maybe she could use your friendship. That's a pretty
amazing thing all on its own.

His gaze flashed back to the photo on his computer screen.

She needed people to believe in the person she was now. He saw
that. Felt it.

But he wasn't sure he was strong enough to offer friendship without
losing his heart.

CHAPTER 12

Ellie didn't show up to work the next day, but left a message through Mrs. Kershaw that she was on business in the North Country and would be back the following day.

Maybe it was a good thing to allow Luke the time to focus on work instead of the woolly mammoth in the room when he'd see Ellie again. But the atmosphere sizzled with a new type of tension.

Guards had been posted at the gates of Cambric Hall, requiring Pete and Luke to show identification before entering. Mrs. Kershaw shared that the king had sent them in preparation for any news crew that would likely follow the story of the orphanage and anything associated with the "princess-in-hiding."

Luke had noticed some extra traffic in Crieff as they'd passed through. Could that really be from the media yesterday? He had no idea how people responded to royals in general. His only real experience was his younger sister, and he really hoped she was the exception to the rule. Penelope created an entire "experience" for watching any of the royal weddings and hoped to name one of her children Catherine.

Luke sighed as he helped Gordon, the man he'd become closest to among the workmen, install another cabinet. Having Penelope as his sister even meant that Luke knew exactly who people were talking about when they mentioned Will and Kate by their first names.

"She's been good for this orphanage," Gordon murmured, almost too quiet for Luke to hear, the older man casting a look over his shoulder as if some of the other workers may have overheard him.

Luke didn't have to ask who "she" was.

He knew.

The air simmered with her absence.

"And the North Country," Gordon added, his voice even quieter. His pale gaze rose to Luke's. "I ken she's had her ways in the past, but she's ours and she's proud to be."

Luke may not have understood everything behind Gordon's words, but the meaning was clear. The people who saw Ellie's reform embraced it deeply.

"Dinna believe all you read." He paused, holding Luke's gaze in his steely one before giving a curt nod. "You ken who she is."

It wasn't a question.

And down deep, Luke wondered if Ellie from the last few weeks was much more "real" than Princess Elliana, whatever, of the North Country.

The situation from a few days before gnawed at the back of his mind. He hated unresolved conflict. Even if the situation wasn't going to turn out the way he'd hoped, the idea that it lingered without an answer kept distracting him throughout the morning.

When lunch break came, he retreated to the front lawn of the castle, just to breathe in more space or the quiet or the simple peace of being alone. He took a bite of the sandwich Mrs. Kershaw had offered and looked up at the sky.

He'd always prayed that God would help him make a difference in the small part of the world where God had placed him. Simple things, like helping a neighbor with some house repairs, or giving a stranger a lift to the bus station, or even working with the children's home—a temporary choice that turned into a long-term arrangement.

Even agreeing to travel here for Lewis Gray had been a choice to help, as well as see a little more of the world. But surely God hadn't chosen Luke, of all people, to help a princess heal? And if God had chosen Luke, why hadn't God also taken away the attraction from day one? Because there was no mistaking the two of them shared a mutual attraction.

Loyally, Luke

Could he even offer friendship without wanting to kiss her silly every day?

Seemed like too big a feat for a simple man like him.

And a princess? He raised a brow to the blue sky. Really?

A sudden sniffling sound nearby pulled his thoughts from contemplating God's sense of humor and toward the corner of the front portico. There, sitting on a step, coatless and crying, sat Faye. Her little body shivered with her quiet sobs, and there was nothing else to be done but to take his jacket off and lay it over those little shoulders as he lowered himself to her side.

"Now, what's got you all upset?"

Faye rubbed her fingers into her eyes as if to plug up the tears. "Amara left today."

Luke's chest deflated and he slipped an arm around the little girl's tiny shoulders. "That's hard for sure."

Faye nodded, another tremor quivering through her. "I don't want her to forget me."

"You think she will?"

"She didn't cry very much."

"Well, she had to show she was happy to see her granny too, right?" Luke gave her little shoulders a squeeze. "But I bet she was torn up too. Half happy, half sad."

"I don't want her to be all sad."

"Of course you don't. What friend would?"

Faye looked up at him. "She gave me a little journal with notes from her for thirty days."

"Wow." Luke released a low whistle. "That's a really nice gift. Helps her still feel close for a while, like she's talking to you every day."

"That's true." Faye blinked, tears dangling on her long eyelashes. "For thirty whole days."

"And she seemed to like to talk, so I bet those notes will be nice and long."

"They are long. Some are a whole page." Faye wiped another hand over her eyes. "She didn't talk when she first came. I had to do all the talking. She was too afraid."

Luke's grin stretched. "And I bet you did a fine job talking to and for her, didn't you?"

Faye's lips trembled into a little smile. "I did."

"So fine, in fact, that she couldn't help but start talking too."

Faye's smile grew into dimples, and paired with those freckles, it about did him in altogether. "Ms. Faukes said I loved her so well, she couldna help but grow right into talking so we could all get to know who she was on the inside."

Luke nodded, allowing the little girl's simple sentiment to sink in. "Well, I've always heard that love has a way of doing things like that."

Her eyes sparkled, half with tears, half with joy. "Like magic. That's what my gran used to say. Love is like magic. When you pour it out on someone, it makes wonderful things happen."

His smile faltered just a little because that sounded too much like something Penelope would say, but the heart behind it was true. He'd seen it happen over and over again, especially with the boys he'd worked with at the children's home.

Love held power, a truth he knew soul-deep. The earthly sort didn't always prove magical—he had a track record to support a failure here and there—but the heavenly, pure, all-in kind sure did. Luke's experience with real romantic love could be counted on one finger and hadn't proven magical enough to have Clara love him back the same, but he'd begun to realize the problem had more to do with the receiver than the love.

"It's a pretty special thing to know your love is so big that it makes magical things happen." Luke smiled down at her.

She nodded, the tears not as intense as they'd been before, thank the good Lord!

Loyally, Luke

"And I'd imagine it's even big enough to stretch all the way from Skymar to Nigeria. What do you think?"

Her smile dimpled again. "I know it is."

"And hers to you, because she seemed like she loved you a whole lot too. Notes and all."

Luke escorted Faye back into the castle and left her in the capable hands of her teacher, Ms. Faukes, before returning to the kitchen, his head and heart nearly aching with . . . emotions. He pressed a palm to his forehead and sighed. Nasty things. No wonder he didn't enjoy talking about them.

For some reason he always felt a little nervous when emotion-talk or feelings started pressing in, but how could anyone blame him? He was raised with three sisters. His testosterone levels constantly felt threatened.

Even here, working with mostly men, the little girls found him with their tears and their freckles and . . . he was sitting on a front porch sipping his coffee and talking about love and magic.

He grimaced.

He needed another large cup of black coffee and a massive hammer.

Nah. The nail gun. Powerful and loud enough to drown out his thoughts for a while.

It was plum disappointing that demo day only came around once a job.

Ellie slipped into one of the side doors of Cambric Hall, attempting to time her entry with dinner for the children and the end of a workday for the workmen. Luke and Pete would stay behind, as they did every evening, to make certain everything was "prepped," as Luke called it, for the next day.

In truth, she'd had a meeting with one of the larger timber

companies in the North Country to discuss distribution of the natural resource (since the northern part of Skymar provided over 60 percent of timber for the island), reforesting, and a few new ideas she'd gleaned from conversations with Luke on how to salvage some of the unused buildings scattered throughout the North Country for tourism and business.

He had so many ideas, and she'd wanted to pelt him with questions, but she'd kept her curiosity curated to fit the interior designer he'd thought she was before today. Of course, she did have a degree in interior design, so at least she hadn't lied in that respect.

But his compassion and intelligence burst out of him when he spoke of building, farming, protecting nature, and so many other things. It was very possible he didn't realize how much he had to offer to those around him.

The sound of men's voices drew her down the narrow storage hall that opened into the kitchen. Pete and Luke, as she'd suspected. She smoothed her palms down her stomach and drew in a breath.

She had to talk to him.

Seek his forgiveness.

Pray for his understanding.

And release this absurd connection she had with him.

"We should be able to finish up those cabinets tomorrow and install appliances," Luke was saying, gesturing in the various directions as he spoke. "We need to finish up some trim work, too, and work on the pantry and the adjoining room, but it looks like we're ahead of schedule."

"Sounds like a good day to stop in at the Kilted Duck for supper." Pete's voice lilted, almost drawing out Ellie's smile. "Besides, we ate the last of what you cooked yesterday."

She could almost see Luke's sigh as she stood in the shadow of the door. His back was to her, his broad shoulders slightly bent. Oh dear, she'd been surrounded by those arms before. A glorious feeling.

She closed her eyes to calm the sudden rush of butterflies in her stomach. *Silly woman. You are not a girl.*

Her gaze flashed to him, her body in full revolt.

Losh!

"Sounds like a plan." He waved Pete toward the door. "I'll check the back to make sure it's locked."

Ellie steadied her shoulders and stepped from the hall. "Excuse me."

Luke flinched. Pete cried out.

"I apologize for startling you." She shifted her attention from Pete back to Luke, searching his unreadable expression. "Would you mind if we talked before you left?"

Luke stared at her a second and then turned his focus to Pete, whose gaze shot between the two before his grin tightened. "Right. How 'bout I pop on down to the pub and you join me when you're all finished here?"

"I'll meet you there in a bit." Luke nodded toward Pete before walking past her to the back door of the kitchen.

Pete offered a dip of his head and half a wave before he fled backward through the double doors of the main entrance to the kitchen.

Nothing but the sound of Luke's movements as he walked to the door filled the silence. The lock clicked into place. When he turned, he took a few steps forward, his attention fixed on her, and with a gentle motion, he leaned a hip against the nearest newly installed cupboard. "I don't—"

She raised a palm. "Please, let me go first."

He paused, nodded, and then folded his arms across his chest, his expression not as foreboding as she'd expected. Serious and intense, but not . . . lost to her?

Why did that fact bring a sudden tightness to her throat? He should be furious. Maybe even hate her, but she didn't sense any such response from him.

Her eyes stung and she looked away to gather her thoughts before meeting his eyes again. "I'm sorry, Luke. I'm sorry that I wasn't forth-right with you from the beginning. At first, I didn't think it was important because it was merely work, but then . . ." She swallowed and gathered another breath of courage. "But then it wasn't merely work anymore. It was real and fun and I could live in this little fantasy where I was just me and you were just you." Her vision blurred and she looked toward the window. "I don't ever have that opportunity. There are always expectations of my . . . position. And caution for what another person's motives might be." Her gaze found his again. "But you are so . . . likable and you made me believe I could be just Ellie, the woman, instead of Elliana, the princess. And we fit like people do in those silly movies. Simple and sweet and . . . real." She shook her head. "I didn't want to give it up, you see? I liked who I was when I was with you. Because I didn't have to be anyone else. And that seemed to be all right with you."

He tilted his head ever so slightly, studying her, his attention un-moving, focused, warming her skin. She moved a step closer. "Please forgive me. When you've made such poor decisions in the past, it's easy to doubt that when all the glitz and glamour and prestige are stripped away, you will still be worthy of someone's affections just as you are. And you've shown me such tenderness and understanding. I never wanted to hurt you. And I never expected to care for you as I am beginning to do. You've been so authentic and genuine with me, and I didn't reciprocate with similar honesty. I'm sorry."

He studied her a moment longer, his gaze gentling, his lips almost smiling. And then he cleared his throat and drew in a breath, standing to his full height. "I just want to know if you're gonna use this princess thing as an excuse to stop working. Because if you want to keep this job, I don't plan on pampering you."

Air burst from her lungs. "What?"

"You may have used the princess gig to get out of real work before, but don't expect it with me, all right, Ellie?" He grimaced. "Or do I have to start calling you Princess now?"

Her mouth dropped open as she stared at him, replaying his words and attempting to sort him out. "You . . . you're not angry?"

"It took me a bit to work through it." His expression sobered. "I googled you."

She winced.

He shrugged a shoulder. "I still don't like it, but it made sense, why you didn't tell me." His brow rose. "No more mysteries, though, all right?"

"How can you be so . . . fine about it all?"

"Well, I'm not exactly fine." He ran a hand over his chin, his gaze slipping down and then back to her face. "I can't see our relationship moving in the direction I'd hoped, so that part of acceptance is tough to swallow." He gave his head a firm shake. "Downright disappointing, to be completely honest, but your past? The reason you didn't tell me who you were? That made sense."

"Did it?"

"Izzy, my cousin, told me a quote once—I think it was by Oscar Wilde—that says, 'Every saint has a past and every sinner has a future.' You sift through anybody's backstory long enough and you'll find messes we're all trying to heal from, cover up, or forget." He sighed, his dark gaze roaming her face as if he cared. And he did. She felt it like the hug she craved from him. "Yours just happened to be strewn across the internet. If someone did that to all *my* sins, I'd want to duck and hide forever too." His grin widened. "But you're not staying there. Which means you're strong . . . and brave. And on the right side of your brokenness and heart struggles."

She wasn't too certain about that, since her heart felt a little too fragile to be steady at the moment. His words reached out to her in some magical way, soothing her insecurities like a balm.

"And if anyone looks at you like you're still living in that past life, then they're the ones with the heart problem. Not you."

Warmth infused her inner being. She'd heard similar comfort from her parents, siblings, and closest friends, but to hear it put so gently and directly from this man, for whom she was beginning to care, touched her soul like nothing else—as if his large, rough craftsman's hands had reached into all the vulnerable places of her heart and strengthened the weak spots.

She stepped closer, wanting those powerful arms to capture her in a hug. "I wish I could offer you . . . something more."

"I suspect you're planning on remaining a princess?"

She nodded. "And you have no interest or desire for a royal life or to leave your family."

"No." His gaze held hers, his smile sad. "I'm not meant for a life like yours."

The declaration hit like a barb, even though she knew the truth before he spoke it. "Then what are we to do? Act as if nothing has happened between us? We're still working together every day." She shook her head with a little fierceness. "And . . . and I don't want to go back to being strangers."

"I've thought about that too." He leaned back against the counter again. "I mean, I did promise my friend Ellie that I'd help her mark off some things from her list, and I like to stay true to my word."

"I'd never hold you to that." She couldn't help but smile. "But I adore you for still wanting to help me. And be my friend." She nibbled at her bottom lip and then addressed the massive elephant family in the room. "Do you think being friends is a possibility? Please say it is."

His eyes creased at the corners with his smile and she wanted to hear his laugh again. "Well, if I can work really hard to keep thoughts of kissing you out of my head, I think it's a real possibility."

She shouldn't agree to this. She should distance herself from him as much as she could until he returned to the U.S., but the very idea of him being in the same country and her not spending time with him hurt nearly as much as the thought of hurting him. "You're not the only one who'll have to fight those thoughts, I assure you. I was just having an internal monologue about how wonderful it would feel to be in your arms."

His jaw tightened and his stare intensified. "Yep. Sounds like we both need to turn our thoughts in a more friendly direction." He gave his head a shake. "Or less friendly direction?"

"I'll take friendship, if it's a choice between that and nothing at all." She stared up at him, now a step closer. "I know it's horrible. If things were different, it wouldn't be a problem. I just can't change my life."

"And I'm not asking you to."

"I know." Which endeared him to her even more. "But if all I have is two more months with you in my life on a regular basis, then I'd rather have you as my friend than nothing at all."

"All right then." He drew in a breath as if preparing himself for his answer. "If we're going to be friends after kissing like we have, then I think we need to set some ground rules."

"Ah, yes. Very good idea." Ellie clasped her hands together, hating the idea but pushing up a smile because the right thing and the preferable thing didn't always go hand in hand. "No more dates?"

"I don't know if we've officially dated anyway." Amusement lit his eyes. "Though that would have been my next question if—"

"I wasn't a princess." She sighed.

"It does put a damper on our relationship."

"Touché." She rolled her eyes with a chuckle. "Another *Princess Bride* quote?"

"It fit too well not to use it."

She stared at him too long. Too heartachingly long. And then she looked away with a shrug. "I suppose it would be best if we weren't left alone for long periods of time."

"It would certainly help keep temptation at bay."

"Two months, Luke." Her gaze moved back to his, her breath shallow as she stretched her hand out toward him. "Can we be friends for two months and then go on with our lives?"

Dangerous. Impossible. She held his attention. But she didn't want to let go.

He took her hand into his, the rough edges smoothed with fresh familiarity against her skin. "But just so you know, Princess"—his smile brimmed in his eyes—"I still expect you to work as hard as you did before."

"Deal." She raised a brow, though a voice in the back of her mind told her that the hardest work—to not fall in love with Luke Edgewood—had only begun.

CHAPTER 13

Text from Luke to Izzy and Penelope: I feel certain that Penelope knows even more than I do about my current situation, likely from some ability to place spies among the orphans at Cambric Hall, so I figured I'd just get it all out of the way in one text thread. We've agreed to be friends until I leave in two months.

Penelope: Friends? With a princess? I wonder what could possibly go wrong. (Or right, if you ask me.)

Luke: I didn't ask for feedback, as I recall.

Izzy: Are you sure you can DO that, Luke? The friendship thing?

Penelope: Izzy, Luke has lots of friends who are girls. Why wouldn't he be able to be friends with a woman who also happens to be a princess? *chime*

Luke: No chimes, Penny-girl, or I'll stop texting you anything at all.

Izzy: Wouldn't it be difficult to move to friendship after kissing her?

Penelope: YOU KISSED A PRINCESS???!!!!

Luke: Izzy, I will no longer message you for the rest of time.

Izzy: Ack! Sorry, Luke! I thought with all her movie-induced foresight, she'd have known already.

Penelope: But, Luke! It's too early to have kissed her. That always leads to trouble. You're not supposed to kiss a princess until near the end of the story, or right after you two agree on happily ever after. Early kissing is sure to lead to turmoil.

Luke: You have no idea.

Penelope: I feel as though I need to rewatch a few royal movies so I'm better prepared for your life, Luke. How exciting!

Luke: Not exactly what I'd call it, but I will say, as strange as it sounds, if we're going to be working together, I'd rather have us on friendly terms than acting like we don't know or care about each other.

Izzy: That's going to be tough.

Luke: Sure is.

Penelope: What if she wants you to be her prince, Luke? Oh my goodness, I can't even believe I typed that IRL! Prince Luke . . . hmm, maybe you should go by your middle name. Stephen is more princely.

Penelope: Oh, sorry, Luke. Matt just reminded me that Ellie is expected to marry someone from Skymar as part of their effort to build back the population and support for the country. I wonder how long getting citizenship takes?

Luke: I'm not the prince sort, Penny-girl. I've already been down the road of trying to measure up to the impossible. I'm not interested in doing that again. Besides, I'm a happy citizen of the Blue Ridge Mountains in the U.S. of A. So keep the royal romance talk out of the conversation. I just shared so you'd realize we're moving forward as friends and that's that.

Izzy: Well, I'm glad you guys can be friends now. And hopefully it won't negatively impact your work.

Luke: Shouldn't. And her dad asked if I'd meet him and Ellie for dinner tomorrow evening to talk about some of my ideas.

Penelope: You're having a private dinner with the KING OF SKYMAR???!!!!

Penelope: Sorry. Matt just told me that the royal family are incredibly approachable and that King Aleksander is highly involved in learning new ways to help his people. Doesn't he sound like a lovely man? You'll have to tell me all about him after your dinner. Wow! With the king!

Penelope: Matt also said that no matter how loud I talk while I text, you still won't be able to hear my exclamations from North Carolina to Skymar. So that's his subtle, sweet way of letting me know I'm getting too loud. He's such a doll!

Izzy: Is there anything we can do to help you?

Luke: I wouldn't mind some prayers for wisdom and . . . patience. Lots of patience.

Penelope: And self-control? I mean, how can you un-kiss somebody in your mind? A princess too?

Luke: Living with you and all your ridiculousness has fostered a whole lot of self-control in me, Penny-girl. If I said everything I thought, you'd realize just how much self-control I use on a minute-by-minute basis.

Luke: And, Izzy (since Izzy is actually taking this situation seriously), if you think of it, send up some prayers for Ellie. I think somewhere along the way she lost sight of who she is and that she was created for a purpose.

Izzy: Then I'm glad you're her friend, Luke. You may not always say those things with your words, but you're great at showing people how important they are through the way you care about them.

Penelope: I'm taking it seriously! I always take royal romances seriously.

Penelope: But on a really serious note, I'll pray too, Luke. To step back out into the world after feeling as if she'd ruined so much—that already shows how brave and strong she is. She just needs to see it. It's such a good thing God sent you into her life to be her . . . friend.

Izzy: I think another dinner date should be on the planner. Next week? And I can show you some of the simple LotR-inspired wedding ideas I have. You'd appreciate the Bag End cake.

Having the whole evening to process his conversation with Ellie may have helped him go into work the next day with a clear head. Or at least with great intentions of keeping his end of the bargain.

Of course, it wasn't like they'd been dating.

And they'd only kissed a few times. His inner rogue replayed just how fantastic it was, so he shoved those thoughts into the broken nothing box.

He could do this. He *had* to do this.

And then she walked in with her hair in a ponytail, wearing a baggy sweater and jeans.

Luke groaned and shot a glance heavenward. The pantsuit would have been a better choice to keep his mind from temptation. She looked more like a princess that way.

This way . . .

Well, she just looked . . . cuddly.

He grimaced and turned back to Gordon before his thoughts derailed into an even more embarrassing direction. Gordon's attention flicked to Ellie and back to Luke, his pale eyes taking on added humor.

Luke raised a brow in warning to the man. His only response was a momentary wider grin and a sound like a muffled chuckle.

Perfect.

Luke had left directions with Pete to have the gofer crew move the final cabinets into the kitchen for installation and to start clearing out the adjoining room to the kitchen so that repairs could begin in there while he finished up the pantry over the next few days.

Once he sat down with Mrs. Kershaw and Ellie to go over the trim work and additional details along with their plans, he'd have an even better idea of how much longer it would take them, but they were well ahead of schedule already.

Always a good feeling.

So with Pete in charge of the gofers and Luke keeping somewhat solid focus on the cabinetry, he went all morning with nothing more than a few pleasantries with Ellie St. Clare.

And there may have been some occasional looks.

She was in his line of sight sometimes, so he *had* to look.

He probably shouldn't have winked at one point, but she'd come by with broom in hand and made some comment about "sweeping him off his feet." What was a guy supposed to do about that? And from a princess?

Gordon's not-so-subtle grunt-chuckles didn't help.

And neither did Pete's not-so-subtle grins.

Even young Jamie had started to raise his brows at Luke when Ellie entered the room.

He was in a losing battle, which meant only one thing.

He needed to watch *Rambo* tonight.

After dinner with the king.

He gave his head a hard shake. He should probably watch more than one of them.

Well, one good thing about having Ellie on the gofer team was that most of the time, they kept a healthy distance from each other. Which was good for him, because he'd started craving oranges with a passion and they weren't easy to find in Crieff . . . in April.

During his lunch break, he slipped into the small office outside the kitchen that Mrs. Kershaw had set up for his use. A few days ago, he'd gone over the plans and reordered certain supplies, but with the progress going so well, he pulled up his 3D designs for the cabin to review.

Of course, the cabin work was coming along much more slowly than the orphanage. Pete was his only coworker on that job, and Pete only helped when he wasn't eating, playing video games, traveling home "for a quick trip," or going on dates.

Which basically meant Luke was on his own, and for the most part, it suited him fine. He'd save the work that required an extra hand for when Pete was around.

But he'd been attempting to restructure the living area of the cabin to give it a more open feel while also keeping it cozy, heat efficient, and practical. The kitchen needed more storage space since he had plans to turn a tiny closet into a washer-and-dryer spot.

"Hey."

Luke didn't have to look up to know the owner of that voice. He turned to find Ellie standing in the doorway, shoulder braced against the frame as if she'd been standing there a little while. His neck grew hot.

"Hey to you."

Her teeth skimmed over her bottom lip in a smile and she stepped into the room. "I just wanted to confirm dinner tonight with Father?"

"I brought a change of clothes so I'd be more presentable."

Her gaze swept over him, not more than a few seconds, but enough for his body to know it was more than a cursory glance. Lord, help him. They were a mess.

He shouldn't keep craving time with her. Shouldn't. They couldn't be together, and he had no desire to even attempt to live up to expectations he could never meet. Royalty? Nope. The very idea doused some of the attraction.

Only a little.

Definitely not enough.

"He wouldn't mind what you're wearing, just so you know." She looked away. "As I understand it, he was always a bit of a rebel when it came to protocol, which has proven a boon for his reign. The people love him for how willing he is to be a part of their lives."

Luke nodded. "I like that."

She folded her arms across her chest, studying him. "You remind me of him in that way. Good-hearted. Keen to hear a person's perspective."

"How's he look in flannel?"

Her smile shot wide. "Actually, in more private life, he wears it well."

"Sounds like the right sort of king." Even saying that out loud sounded weird, but he also never imagined he'd have kissed a princess, so there was that.

She took another step forward. "I have to leave early today to attend a meeting with the transportation board of the North Country, but I should be back in time for supper. He wanted me to let you know he'd send a car to Cambric Hall for you. Around seven?"

"Would it be easier to have Pete just drop me off somewhere?"

"Well," she said, her nose wrinkling with a little frown, "to avoid considerable publicity, he's secured a private dining room for us at the Ivy Hotel on the edge of Crieff, and sending his car for you will keep you from having to go through security and the like."

"Okay . . ." He drew out the word as he processed the situation. Private car. Private dining room. Meal with a king and his daughter.

Weirder and weirder.

"Is that a 3D design model?" She gestured toward his computer, moving way too close for him to keep his thoughts friendly. "The cabin?"

"Yeah, I'm trying to figure out how to create some more storage space for the kitchen." He gestured toward the screen. "See how I'm taking this closet and turning it into a laundry room? Well, it eats into kitchen storage."

"And this is the new room?" She pulled up a chair, her shoulder brushing his.

She didn't seem aware of how close she was. Perfume-smelling close. Definitely deal-breaking close.

He tried to hold his breath. "Yeah. I have some good storage in mind for that room. Bench seats beneath the windows there and I've designed a banquette for this corner, since there wasn't space for a table and chairs before the renovation."

"I love it." Her smile and praise had him sitting a bit taller. Not quite as straight as her posture, but better than usual. "The view must be on that side?" She pointed to the additional windows.

He nodded. "Spectacular view, so I wanted to take advantage of it."

"Of course." She studied the model with familiarity. "Are you bringing the cupboards around here to create some extra counter space?"

He followed the direction in which she pointed. No, he hadn't thought of that, but bringing out the cabinet just a bit there would add another whole cabinet. "That'd be an easy addition. Worthwhile too."

"And some open shelves would be nice. On this wall. Beside that window."

He watched her out of his periphery, her attention shifting over the screen, intelligence dancing in those eyes.

"What's beneath the stairs there?"

It took him half a second to pull his mind from examining her profile to the fact she'd asked him a question. "Um . . ." *Brilliant, Luke! Top-notch smarts right there.* "I haven't checked if there's anything."

"If it's merely empty space, you could make it into a closet, couldn't you?" She turned toward him, her face beautifully close.

He drew his attention, much too slowly, back to the computer screen and cleared his throat. "I'll check it out tonight and see, but if you're right, it could be a good use of available space." He turned toward her, leaning back a bit to give himself some more distance.

A deal was a deal. And he'd attempt to keep it for both of them despite her . . . her-ness.

"Interior design, eh?"

"I love it." Her grin spread. "But I rarely have the opportunity to use my skills. When Mrs. Kershaw requested someone to review the needs here at the orphanage, I thought it would be a wonderful combination of my duties as well as my education." She gestured toward his computer. "She allowed me to create the designs." She wiggled her brows. "And I get to be a part of watching them become a reality."

He nodded slowly, watching her come to life. "And if Mr. Gray were going to have someone come in and paint the walls, what would you suggest?"

"Oh, colors! I love them." Her gaze brightened anew. "What is the fireplace made of? And the kitchen cabinets, since the two rooms open into each other."

"Rock fireplace, mostly sand-colored rock." He kept staring. Why did she have to be a princess, of all things? He might have preferred a lawyer over a princess. Or a politician. He grimaced. No, that was pushing it too far. "The cabinets are light oak."

"Then you must use something darker on the walls. Like a soft red or green. If I could see it in person, I'd know for certain." Her gaze met his and one brow rose. "What?"

"Just nice to see you enjoying this."

Her cheeks blushed, but she didn't look away. "More than I should, I believe," she whispered, drawing him a little closer.

A chime sounded in the distance just in time to stop Luke's forward motion toward her lips.

He heaved a sigh and sat back. "That chime!"

"What chime?" And then the sound came again. "Oh, you mean the church bells?"

"Right. Bells." He shook his head. "Not chimes."

Her laugh burst out, the sound a whole lot better than any chimes. "What are you talking about?"

"My little sister, Penelope, the romance-y, royal-loving one I've told you about?"

"Yes?" Her shoulders shook with her chuckle.

"Well, she's been sending me little reminders of the Hallmark Christmas chime in hopes of inspiring my faith in magical romance." He gave his head another shake, though the idea of magic and romance did go together when he thought of Ellie. And holding her. And feeling her hair through his fingers. "It's annoying."

"It's a good thing we're not close to Christmas or we'd have no chance at keeping our bargain at all, would we?"

"Oh no, you've been watching more of them, haven't you?" He narrowed his eyes, watching her wrestle with her smile. "You're just going to cause more trouble than is necessary thinking romance can happen like that."

"It's true. Hallmark Christmas involves magic at a whole new level. I doubt we'd stand a chance against Kriss Kringle and all his little elves."

"The last thing either one of us needs is anything nudging us in the romantic direction any more than we've already gone." He looked back at the screen to avoid making eye contact. Those eyes were magical too. "You should stop watching those, if for no other reason than to save *my* sanity."

Sounds of work resuming in the kitchen traveled down the hallway, and Ellie pushed up from the chair and moved back to the doorway. "I don't need a chime to know my feelings, Luke, and *there* is the difficulty." Her smile took a dive into a frown. "If only real-life troubles could find such charming resolutions as in the Hallmark world."

Exactly. Fictional. Impossible. Pixie dust fluff and nonsense.

Chimes or not, Luke refused to think about any future with Ellie,

other than finishing the remodel for Cambric Hall. With a deal between them and an impossible romance to boot, dwelling any longer
than his errant brain already did would only lead to a greater disappointment when he broke down the facts.

Distance. Families. And the biggest of them all, he could never
be royal material.

So he closed off that side of his thinking.

Which was much easier to do when Ellie wasn't within seeing or
smelling distance.

However, he *could* do his best work and maybe even offer ideas
for helping these kids have better futures, which would at least provide
two good outcomes from this Skymarian adventure.

Besides, just because Izzy and Penelope found perfect romances
halfway around the world didn't mean he would too. He usually ended
up being the odd one out anyway. Being the only boy in a houseful of
girls certainly proved that point more than once growing up.

The day ended with the team finishing up the cabinet install
and completing most of the trim work around the cabinets, with a
good plan for finishing it up the next day. Pete and Gordon helped
straighten up the workspace for the next day so Luke could change
into the only "nice" outfit he'd brought with him: khaki pants, a light
blue button-down, and a navy sport jacket.

It was a miracle he'd even packed that outfit, and he wouldn't have
if Penelope hadn't presented him with at least a dozen scenarios for
which he might need it—a dinner with the king of Skymar, however,
was not on that list.

As Luke loaded his tool belt into the back of Pete's car, a large
black SUV pulled up alongside them. A man stepped from the driver's
side of the car in a black suit with matching shades, something about
his walk seeming familiar. Was that Cameron, the royal guard? The
one he'd punched?

Luke held in a wince.

"Luke Edgewood?"

Luke stepped forward. "Yes?"

Cameron nodded, his expression unreadable. "I will take you to your appointment with the king." And the man proceeded to open the back door of the SUV.

Now, Luke had seen this scenario play out enough times in movies to get the slightest tension in his stomach. Usually, once the folks got into the vehicle, they didn't come back without a fight . . . and possibly Bruce Willis.

But that was just in the movies, right?

Luke looked from Cameron and then back at Pete, whose brows rose.

"Mr. Edgewood?" Cameron asked, hand still on the open door.

With a deep breath and a nod to Cameron, Luke slid into the vehicle. Cameron took his place in the driver's seat and started the SUV forward.

"I thought you were Ellie's bodyguard."

Cameron looked up in the rearview mirror. "I am."

"Well, shouldn't you be with her instead of coming to get me?"

The man's lips twitched. "I already delivered her to her father at the hotel, at which time they sent me to collect you."

Luke studied the passing scenery outside. All familiar. They weren't headed anywhere he didn't recognize just yet.

Cameron still held a small smile on his face, so Luke leaned forward. "You volunteered to collect me, didn't you?"

"I dinna what you mean."

"Right." Luke shook his head slowly from side to side. "You didn't enjoy picking me up in this vehicle like I was some James Bond villain getting ready to die."

Cameron's grin took a wider tilt. "Concern you a wee bit, did it?"

"Let's just say I checked if the doors were locked when you started driving."

Loyally, Luke

"You're a guest of the royal family. You're safe." Then Cameron chuckled. "But I dinna mind getting you back a little for hitting me in the mouth."

Luke relaxed back into the seat, fighting a smile. "We can call it even then?"

"Aye, we can."

Text from Penelope to Luke: How did dinner go?

Luke: Do you remember everything?

Penelope: Only when it involves royals and you having dinner with them. (And movie/musical things. And all things Matt and Iris.) If you didn't want me to remember, you shouldn't have told me on the phone yesterday.

Luke: You're right. A moment of weakness.

Penelope: I think it was more like bragging rights. You're always weaker when you know you can hold something over my head. I've learned to take advantage of it instead of getting frustrated.

Luke: I didn't realize how annoying superpowers could be until this moment. Yours are.

Penelope: Thanks. So . . . did you share all your vast knowledge about rescuing lost boys like a veritable Peter Pan? Hmm, you're mischievous and sometimes act like a twelve-year-old boy, but I'm not sure you'd really strike me as the Peter Pan type. Maybe more like Captain Hook sometimes.

Luke: I was actually going for Smee.

Penelope: Ha ha. You're too cute to be a Smee.

Luke: Calling a man cute is like stabbing him in the stomach so that he bleeds out slowly.

Penelope: Gross. Now you're trying to distract me from the point of the texts. How did things go with THE KING??!!!

Luke: Fine. He was nice. Not very kingly, if you ask me. Too down-to-earth. Maybe he was a doppelganger.

Penelope: Grace Kelly would have known if he was.

Luke: He seemed to like what I had to say. Asked me to present it to some board of directors he and Ellie work with, who are over all the orphanages of Skymar. I think I'll just type something up and give it to Ellie to present. I'm not much of a presenter.

Penelope: You can do it! It would mean more coming from you, Luke. You've done the work firsthand.

Penelope: I know you read what I typed! You're not a middle schooler anymore who is being teased about the way you talk! You're wayyyyy beyond that. You even taught Sunday school! That can be the hardest crowd of all!!

Luke: It was high school boys.

Penelope: My point still holds.

Penelope: Just remember, you are braver than you think. I've seen your closet.

Text from Josephine to Luke: I love the reports I'm getting from Penelope and Izzy about you. It seems that your work in Skymar is going so well! Penelope even showed me a photo of the orphanage where you are working. How lovely, Luke! What an amazing experience for you.

Luke: Thanks, Josephine. But I feel as though there's a question in the wings.

Josephine: Well, actually, would you mind sending any advice about traveling there? Izzy and Penelope have told me that the temperatures may be a bit cooler than here, but not much. Would you please confirm whether this is

true or not? I know Penelope and Izzy both tend toward
exaggeration, especially about this island.

Luke: Weather? Josephine, why are you really texting me?

Josephine: Why does there have to be an alternate reason?

**Luke: Because you live life by the weather app, so . . . I'm
pretty sure you've already mapped out outfits for you and
the kids each day of the two weeks you'll be here in June.**

Josephine: You're the only male child of this family, Luke. Our
parents depend on you being close by.

Luke: Yeah, I know.

Josephine: I just wanted to make sure you knew that.

**Luke: I'm here through Izzy's wedding and then it's back to
the Blue Ridge. That's home for me, Josephine. I don't
have any delusions of moving across the world.**

Josephine: Good, because though your cousin Charlie is
doing a fabulous job with your business, I can tell she
would prefer you were here. I can see it in her eyes. I
know these things.

Josephine: And Charlie isn't an up-front person. She's quiet
and gentle. Some people need a more forceful delivery,
or at least the appearance of intimidation.

Josephine: And Amber Lawson has moved back to Mt. Airy
and has been attending church quite regularly the past
three weeks. Did you two date in high school?

**Luke: Charlie is doing a fine job. We keep in regular contact
and I don't think she's missed a beat since I left.**

**Luke: I refuse to comment about any matchmaking,
Josephine. You already know how I feel about that. If you
feel the urge to start it up again, spend more time with
your husband and the twins . . . or get a dog.**

CHAPTER 14

The Daily Edge: Social Tattle from
One Edge of Skymar to the Other

Our rebel princess has finally crawled out of her hiding place and returned to the cyberworld. Not only has she been seen out on another date with Stoic Styles, but she's been posting on social media. Nothing to give us any real idea of her romantic future, but it looks like Princess Elliana is on her way to proving she's ready to be reinstated as a working royal. Her recent posts have been related to some of the North Country organizations and groups of which she is patron, as well as her work at the orphanage at Cambric Hall. Has our favorite bad girl truly turned the corner? We're only slightly disappointed, but would love your help in securing the truth. We need your assistance in locating the tattle. Do you have any incognito snaps you've taken of Skymar's defiant darling as she's returning to the spotlight? Share them in our comments below.

• •

Text from Maeve to Ellie: How come I had to read on The
   Daily Edge that you had another date with Styles?
Ellie: I thought you'd stopped reading The Edge.
Maeve: It's the best rubbish in town. I'm embarrassingly
   addicted. So . . . Styles?
Ellie: It was not a date. We were both invited to the same
   dinner party, so not technically a date. Mum gently

encouraged me to think about Christopher as my date for the Wild Hyacinth Ball since his reputation is so stellar, but I don't know if I want to spend a whole evening with him. I'd prefer Mum's other choice, the Earl of Tallon. At least I can feel more comfortable with him than Styles.

Maeve: You could just go alone.

Ellie: There is no way I'm stepping out in front of all the media and aristocratic world as the only person without a date to the Wild Hyacinth. Especially on a night when there's so much at stake for me. If I can make it through the Board Luncheon next week, then the Donors' Banquet after that, and then the ball, I'll feel as if I'm on the right track forward. But showing up alone? No, I can't do that.

Maeve: Hmm . . . I love your mother, but sometimes she can be rather fixated on appearances. And you're much braver than you think you are.

Ellie: It's from her upbringing, I think. As a veritable nobody, she had a lot to overcome in the public eye when Father started his romance with her. I think it really impacted her view of her children and public perception.

Maeve: Which is entirely lost on your dear brother, Arran the Unruly. (Nice refusal to respond to the latter part of my text. Very brave of you.)

Ellie: Is that what The Edge is calling Arran now? (Purposefully ignoring.)

Maeve: It has a better ring than Errant Arran. And it's easier to say (feartie).

Ellie: Mother has been so focused on helping me reinvent my public appearance, I think she's left Arran to his own devices a bit too liberally. (Are you name calling like a child?)

Maeve: And I'd advise you to keep your nose out of the news if you don't want to see how very unruly your brother has been lately. He really is putting your reputation to shame. (No, I'm name calling like an adult who prefers fun Scottish insults.)

Ellie: Thus the reason Mother is hoping for such a stellar presentation at the Wild Hyacinth Ball, to overshadow some of his behavior too, I'd imagine.

Ellie: Good heavens, what is he wearing?

Maeve: I told you not to look at the headlines. And the real question should be about what he's NOT wearing. Though, I must admit, he's certainly working out. Very fit!

Ellie: Ugh. Well, once they make everything official with me, they can turn all of their attention to remediating him. I'm sure he'll love that.

Maeve: No doubt. And where does Lovable Luke come into all this?

Ellie: Lovable Luke?

Maeve: I can practically see you grinning as you contemplate the moniker.

Ellie: He doesn't. He can't. I have convinced myself that I will treat my meeting with Luke as a sweet dream to cherish, but nothing more.

Ellie: Or a lovely acquaintance, but nothing more.

Ellie: Well, maybe a friend.

Maeve: But nothing more?

Ellie: I refuse to acknowledge that remark.

Maeve: I need to meet him. How can we make that happen?

Ellie: I'm not certain that's a good idea, though Father did invite him to the Board Luncheon at Cambric next week. He's going to meet with the board members after lunch to talk about his excellent ideas for supporting the future training of some of the children.

Loyally, Luke

Maeve: Wait, Dad's on the board. And he probably needs a plus-one. Hmm . . .

Ellie: Oh dear.

Maeve: And since you can't have him and I'm available, this could be kismet! Plus, I have no qualms about romancing an American.

Ellie: Perhaps I should encourage your father to bring your sister instead of you.

Maeve: Nice try.

⊤

Two full days of working with Ellie and, apart from glances and superficial conversation, Luke had stuck to the plan. Now, if anyone had been able to see into his head for the first five seconds of looking at Ellie every morning, they would have known that internally, Luke was teetering very close to the *t* word from *Bambi*—he shuddered, almost hearing Penelope say "twitterpated" in his mind, complete with a chime—but otherwise, he was quite proud of his appearance of self-control.

But that hair.

And those jeans.

And her eyes.

Well, it was a miracle of God alone that Luke hadn't crossed the kitchen and tossed Ellie over his shoulder like some caveman, just to take her right back out to the tree and finish what they'd started over a week ago.

Self-control indeed.

And a healthy dose of *Rambo, Mission: Impossible*, and World War II movies.

He'd even tossed in *Braveheart* for good measure.

He tried *Star Wars*, but every time Han Solo and Leia came on the screen, he got distracted by the idea of a regular guy and a princess.

Bad idea.

Not even *The Lord of the Rings* helped, because Arwen was close enough to a princess.

His shoulders drooped for a second. Princesses were everywhere!

"Edge?"

Luke looked up at the nickname Jamie, Cade, and . . . the new kid staring back at him had given him over the past week. The boys had connected among the fellow builders in the same way Luke had seen back in the States. He wasn't too sure about girls, but he knew most guys craved purposeful work. And the ones he mentored usually wanted a way to work with their hands.

Besides, since Jamie, Cade, and—what was the new kid's name?— had started helping out with the renovations, the boys had also gotten a little more attention from some of the girls in the house. Not a bad byproduct of hard work.

"What do you boys need?"

Jamie gestured to the chair rail molding in his hands, a piece Luke had freshly cut to spruce up the long, empty wall on the opposite side of the kitchen cabinets. And the perfect spot for Mrs. Kershaw's framed names from the closet. He'd run it by Ellie and she'd agreed. Putting the framed names back into the room where they found them held meaning.

"Do you want us to try to place these like you taught us yesterday?"

Luke kept his grin subtle despite the warmth of pride in his chest. "How far up the wall for these nine-foot ceilings?"

"Thirty-two inches," came Cade's quick reply.

Luke's smile gave way then, and he nodded. "Go on then."

The boys cast each other a bright-eyed look and scurried off to the far side of the room.

Gordon came up beside Luke. "I'll keep watch over them, ya kin?"

"Sounds good, but I think they're going to do just fine."

"Aye," the man responded low and deep, like a soft growl. Reminded him of his grandpa. "They got minds for the task, if they can keep their focus."

Luke moved back toward the additional room to finish up some trim work, and as soon as he stepped through the newly widened doorway, the scent of oranges hit him. Ellie turned at his entrance, her hair pulled back in a long ponytail, a pale pink sweater falling around a pair of black leggings.

She looked like she needed somebody to hug her.

And that somebody needed to be him.

"You mentioned I could help you with the trim this afternoon."

He studied the room to give himself time to place his mind in the direction of their deal, the fresh-cut pieces of baseboard lying against their designated spots catching his eye. His attention flipped to hers, a smile pulling at his lips. "I know you're handy with a hammer, but have you ever used a nail gun?"

Her brows rose. "No, but I'm sure you can teach me."

He rested his hands on his hips, giving her the once-over. "I reckon I can."

And daggone it if she didn't imitate his stance and give him the once-over right back. "Then we'd better get to work."

Lord have mercy! He'd never imagined falling in love with a princess, let alone one who wanted to learn how to use a nail gun. Without a hitch, his thoughts veered quickly in the direction of kissing her.

After pressing the baseboard in place, he demonstrated a few times with the gun and then handed it to her. "Now, the first few times you nail it, you might be a little surprised at how intense it feels. It's fast. So be careful of where your hands and feet are."

He lowered himself to his knees beside her and she positioned the nail gun against the wood, but at an odd angle.

"Just turn your hand a bit like this." He covered her hand with his, his body almost cocooning her. Her ponytail brushed against his chin and he drew in a long, deep breath of her oranges. His throat nearly squeezed closed.

She shifted her fingers beneath his. "Like this?"

Yep, her voice sounded about as tight as his.

"That's right."

She pressed the trigger and the nail drove into the wood.

"Perfect," he murmured, reluctant to move from his spot, but the longer he stayed in position, the greater the temptation to lower his nose to nuzzle her neck, so he shifted away and cleared his throat. "Try the next one."

The second time worked as well as the first, and she grinned at him. "I believe this scene is a replay of some rom-com or another. The telltale moment when the hero touches hands with the heroine to guide her along on some task?"

"What?" He shook his head, trying to keep his smile in check. "Don't bring up such things and ruin a perfectly fine day."

Her smile dimmed a little, but she kept the glint in her eyes. "Would you prefer I recount all the ways a nail gun could protect us from a possible assault by a sociopathic hit man?"

He stared hard at her. "Are you referencing the movie I think you're referencing?"

"I've always had a small crush on Denzel Washington."

She had just referenced *The Equalizer* and Luke wanted to kiss her silly for it. "So have I."

Her laugh burst out. "It's nice to know you have good taste."

And she went back to working the nail gun, leaving him to reconsider what he thought about royals and futures and happily ever afters. He gave his head a shake. It was a good thing the orphanage would be finished in less than two weeks, because he needed distance from her to get on with his life.

Because every time he tried to think about the future, her face kept popping into his head.

"Oh, I like this tool," she said as she came to the end of that particular stretch of baseboard and stood. "Efficient and powerful."

He raised a brow. "Just wait until I let you use my chainsaw."

Her grin tipped and she handed him the tool. "I don't know if I'm quite ready for that amount of power."

"I'd say, Princess, the fact you're in line for a real throne means you're definitely ready for some chainsaw-like power."

"Princess, is it?" She folded her arms across her chest.

"Never had a nickname fit quite so well."

A sudden commotion resounded from the next room and caught his attention. The teen boys stood by one of the windows with Pete leaning over to see as well. Luke sent Ellie a shrug and stepped around the loose baseboard on the floor to take his own peek out the nearest window.

With a tilt of his head, he studied Ellie's face as he said, "Looks like we can mark another thing off your list."

Ellie's forehead wrinkled as she moved to stand beside him at the window, comprehension dawning.

The window framed a world of white.

Large flakes of snow fell like feathers covering an already dusted ground. The blurry horizon promised that this was only the beginning of the snow. Gentle. Soft. And if Luke judged correctly by the looks of things, the perfect weather for sledding.

Snow wasn't uncommon in the North Country, even all the way through May during colder winters, but the boyish grin on Luke's face proved an entirely unfamiliar attraction.

One Ellie wanted to get used to.

Without breaking eye contact with her, Luke called to the other room, "Pete, I think we are more than prepared for this occasion."

Pete stepped up to the threshold of the room and sighed against the doorframe. "Aye, we are."

Luke sent her a wink, which inspired her own grin, and then walked into the kitchen. "Team, we're well ahead of schedule on this project and it looks like the weather's taking a turn. If you need to leave for the day, you're welcome to do so. Otherwise"—he grinned over at the teen boys who basically followed Luke around like disciples— "do you know what a sledding party is?"

All three boys' smiles swelled to Grinch-like proportions. "Aye," they said, almost in unison, already moving toward the hallway for, most likely, their winter wear.

Luke turned back to her. "You'd better get bundled up, Princess, 'cause we've got some sledding to do."

He might as well have asked her out for a romantic dinner from the way the look in his eyes sent a thrilling shock to her pulse. With a crooked grin, he dashed off toward the hallway with as much enthusiasm as those teen boys.

Ellie stared at his retreating form and then looked over at Pete for clarification.

"He's been carrying around sleds in the back of the car for weeks now." Pete shrugged a shoulder and started in pursuit. "He must *really* like sledding."

For weeks?

Ellie's palm pressed to her chest as awareness dawned. He'd not only purchased some sleds but had kept them nearby just in case it snowed . . . for *her*. He had nothing to gain from this act. In fact, they'd both already agreed to part ways once the work on the orphanage was completed, yet still he cared enough to turn this item from her little wish list into a reality?

Warmth spilled through her like a hug.

And he seemed so excited to give her this gift, for which she could offer him nothing in return but her gratitude. Her fingers balled into a fist against her chest and she squeezed her eyes closed for a moment, embracing a feeling she'd never experienced.

Not like this. So vast and amazing and filled with all sorts of hopes and wonders meant for fairy tales and happily ever afters.

She refused to name it. If she did, the pain at having to give it up would be excruciating, but she'd appreciate it while she could.

Here and now.

"Don't dally, Ellie," came Gordon's gruff reprimand, his eyes agleam. "Bundle yerself up and get out in the snow."

Ellie's body ached all over.

She'd pulled the sled up the hill behind Cambric Hall at least twenty times, each time ready to glide back down it again, usually with a child or two in tow. She couldn't remember ever having so much fun.

After carefully showing her how to settle the sled, steer, and then push off, Luke left her to her own fun, sharing his own sleds, as well as pulling from the ones Cambric Hall kept on hand "somewhere in the basement," as Mrs. Kershaw announced.

Lights from the hall glowed into the fading afternoon, glinting off a wintry world. The snow had stopped at least an hour ago, but multitudes of children and adults still clamored across the hillsides, taking in the wonder and fun.

Up ahead, some of the boys engaged in sled races down one of the steeper edges of the hillside, teasing each other, tumbling (or being pushed) off sleds midride, Luke and Pete in the midst of them, playing just as hard.

Ellie tugged her sled closer to where the most aggressive races were happening, with Luke directly in the middle of them. "So who's winning the races so far?"

Luke shot her a grin. "Well, if we don't count cheating, I am."

"Now, now, Edge." Jamie tsked, shaking his head in mock consolation. "You can't help bein' older and slower."

"Slower? I think you boys have a tendency to sled in the way of the little children, and then I have to hop off and rescue them."

"Och." Cade shook his head. "Excuses is what I hear. What about you, Jamie?"

"It's five for five, Miss Ellie." Jamie looked over at Cade, and something unspoken passed between the boys. "I don't think Edge has got it in him to win one more."

"Don't I?" Luke shot back, tossing his sled on the snowy ground and narrowing his eyes at the boys. "I've got as much as either of you."

"Well, now, sounds pretty serious to me," came Cade's thick Scottish accent as he stepped closer to Luke. "But you can't win if you don't have a sled."

And with that, Cade hopped on Luke's sled before he could move.

"Sorry, boss." Jamie laughed as he took the next sled and called behind him, "Smart and fast."

Luke released a burst of foggy air and then looked from the boys back to Ellie. His gaze settled on her sled.

"Get on the sled," he called, stepping over to her.

"What?"

Without repeating himself, he took the sled from her hand and threw it to the ground. "Get on. We'll go faster with more weight." Before she fully comprehended what was happening, she'd slid to a sitting position. The sled jerked into motion and Luke took a running jump and joined her, slowly situating himself behind her, and they took off faster than any of her previous runs.

His arms caged her in on both sides, his strength surrounding her as the cool air stung her cheeks.

"Steer to the right." His voice came near her ear. "Let's show Jamie how it's done."

Ellie wasn't certain how they were going to show Jamie "how it was done," but she relaxed back into Luke's hold and pulled the rope to the right. The sled followed her guidance and, within a few seconds, they slid past a wide-mouthed Jamie.

"What's the matter, Jamie? Too much snow in your boots slowing you down?"

"Watch out, Cade!" Jamie called.

Cade turned at the sound of his name as Ellie and Luke neared him, but in his turning, he redirected his sled into their path. Luke placed his hands over Ellie's on the ropes and jerked the sled in a different direction, barely missing Cade as they passed, but in doing so, their sled edged over the steepest part of the hill.

"Luke!" Ellie called, pressing harder back into his chest, her gaze focused on the fast-approaching forest at the bottom of the hill.

He attempted to turn the sled away from the trees, but the incline and speed proved against him.

"Let go of the ropes, Ellie." His low comment lingered in her ear.

She obeyed. The trees edged closer, and in one smooth motion, Luke released the rope, tightened his arms around her, and rolled with her off the sled, his body buffering hers against the impact.

For a second, all went quiet and still. One of his arms pillowed her head against the snow and the other kept a tight hold around her waist. He'd burrowed his head against hers as they rolled, and now he pushed up on his palms. His gaze roamed over her face, those brown eyes taking in every detail.

Her breaths puffed shallow.

His look of concern slowly melded into something much more . . . tempting, warming the air between them.

His attention dropped to her lips and then returned to her eyes, one dark brow jutting high.

She stared back, her chest rising with her breaths, every prolonged second increasing her hope that he would breach the short distance between them.

With a little growl, he shook his head. "You sure don't make this deal easy, Princess." He sighed and rolled off her, placing his hands on hers to help her to a sitting position, his gaze sending off signals her pulse understood. "Because all I want to do is kiss you until you forget we're in the middle of the snow with a bunch of wild kids all around."

From the few previous experiences she had with his kiss, she didn't doubt his abilities. "You're wonderful, Luke Edgewood."

He tilted his head and studied her a moment, the slightest beginning of a frown flickering into place before he drew in a breath and stood, offering her his hands to draw her to a stand. "I think that was ten times better than any movie-worthy sled ride I've seen. What do you think?"

He changed the topic for her sake. For both their sakes.

Despite what they both wanted—this perfect dream of a romance—it couldn't be theirs, could it?

But was it really possible to embrace the now? Enjoy what time they had for the next two weeks in order to carry these wonderful memories with them into the future?

Before she could broach the subject, a group of children and adults broke the intimacy of the moment to see if they were safe and well.

Ellie caught Luke watching her, those dark eyes offering such tenderness, such focus.

Yes, she was well.

But her heart was anything but safe.

Not from heartbreak.

Because she knew for a fact she was falling in love with Luke Edgewood.

CHAPTER 15

"Do you think the sledding was too much for her?"

Pete's question pulled Luke's attention away from caulking the new crown molding in the kitchen's additional room. He looked down from his lofty height on the ladder, catching a raised brow from Gordon as he did so.

"I'm sure she has a lot of responsibilities that don't include Cambric Hall, Pete."

Pete's brow crinkled as he stood holding an extra caulking gun and some paper towels. "I just thought, well, it seemed the two of you were gettin' on so well—"

"Pete." Luke shook his head and went back to caulking, attempting to ignore the nauseous weight in his stomach.

"So you're gonna end up like that movie, are ya?"

Luke refused to look the man's way. "Movie?"

"Yeah, it was one of my sister's favorites. Princess and a commoner who had to make the choice to separate at the end. I think it takes place in Rome or someplace like that."

Luke grimaced, as much because he knew exactly which movie Pete referenced as because of the actual truth of his statement. *Roman Holiday*. One of Penelope's many favorites.

"I don't know that I'd call my relationship with Ellie a romance." Luke cleared his throat and kept his focus on his work. "A friendship, maybe, but I never expected a future with a princess, Pete."

Which was true. Not once in all his plans did he contemplate anything close to a romance with anyone remotely famous or rich, let alone a princess. He'd daydreamed a little about something with Ellie, the interior designer, but not Princess Elliana, the royal.

Luke gestured toward the kitchen. "Would you go check on Jamie and Cade's progress with puttying the nail holes in the baseboard in the kitchen? They're good kids, but probably need a little extra nudge to keep on track."

Luke finished up his work and then climbed down the ladder, meeting Gordon as he rose from the floor. The older man narrowed his eyes as he examined Luke.

"She's stayin' away because she's afraid."

"Afraid?"

"She cares for you. Anyone with two eyes and half a brain can sort that one out." Gordon raised a brow and gave a slow shake of his head. "She's trying to make it easier, I suppose, though I doubt it helps much."

Luke studied the man. "And I suppose you have a better idea?"

Gordon chuckled. "There's no way around getting your hearts broken at this point, lad. You're bound for it, one way or the other." He shrugged a shoulder. "So if I knew I was going to hurt anyway, I think I'd be tempted to make it worth the pain."

Gordon left Luke standing in the empty room staring, unseeing, at the doorway. As completely ridiculous as Gordon's advice was, it made the most sense of anything related to him and Ellie thus far.

Luke couldn't change the fact he wasn't meant for royalty.

And Ellie couldn't change the fact that she was.

So if they couldn't change the future, could they leave with enough sweet memories to make the heartache more bearable? Was that even possible?

"Come home with me for supper, yeah?" Gordon gave a curt nod to brook no refusal. "Young Pete is off on another date, and you're in need of company." His grin quirked. "I'll drive you home after. Nessa'll be glad to see ya."

Loyally, Luke

"This isn't another accidental meeting between me and Ellie, is it?"

Gordon's bushy brows took an upswing. "I leave those accidents to Nessa. But if you come over, you can rest assured the conversation will be worthwhile."

†

Text from Luke to Izzy: Any idea what I should wear to a board luncheon?

Izzy: Your Hulk Underoos. That should liven up a "bored" meeting.

Luke: Did I just text Penelope by mistake? Because that was horrible.

Izzy: Sorry, I've been texting her most of the afternoon about wedding ideas, so I think she's probably rubbed off on me.

Luke: It's for the donors of Cambric Hall. The king asked if I'd come and talk to the group about what I did at the kids' home.

Izzy: Oh wow, Luke, that's amazing. I'm so glad you're stepping out in this. You've always had an amazing ability to influence people for good. Okay, some bad. Especially when pranks are involved.

Luke: I'm hoping I can convince Ellie to do the talking or read off my ideas. I hate speaking in front of people. You know that. You were in middle and high school with me. You've seen it.

Izzy: I hate that those guys made fun of you because of your accent. Just because we were a few of the only country kids at the city school gave them no right to be so mean, but that was so long ago. You're not that kid anymore. And you only fainted once.

Luke: In front of the entire student body.

Izzy: Hyperventilating will do that to any eighth grader.

Luke: I just don't see the point in having to stand up in front of a bunch of people I don't know and won't need to know when Ellie already knows them and has a lot more influence than me.

Izzy: The king wouldn't have asked you unless he thought it would matter, Luke.

Izzy: Wow, that's so weird to type IRL. I mean . . . wow!

Luke: Back to clothes. Ball cap or no ball cap?

Izzy: You can't see me, but I'm rolling my eyes. What if Brodie and I come up tomorrow, join you for lunch, and then help you figure out what to wear? He's wanted to come back and visit that little bookstore in Crieff anyway.

Luke: Sounds good.

Izzy: We could check out that kilt shop too. That would really make an impression on the donors.

Luke: A kilt and my ball cap. Got it.

Izzy: Ugh! See you tomorrow.

Luke: Thanks! See you then.

Luke: PS: They were Captain America Underoos. If you're going to attempt to tease me, get your story straight.

Mrs. Kershaw and her staff at Cambric Hall knew how to throw parties. And since Luke had introduced the idea of looking for ways to turn these moments into teachable, and possibly occupational, opportunities, Ellie had been inspired to think in the same way. She'd even encouraged Mrs. Kershaw to use a few of the teen girls, who were particularly interested in the field of hospitality, to join in the last parts of the planning.

And everything looked lovely.

People moved from the buffet to the tables. Some chose to stand and have their conversations. Each had their own place setting so that when Ellie stood to speak to them, everyone would be able to see the small platform where she would stand.

Her gaze skimmed over the tables of fresh-cut hyacinths, their lavender hues an excellent complement to the pale gold tablecloths. If the Board Luncheon proved this well executed, she could only imagine how much better the Donors' Banquet would be. Ellie preferred the Caedric word for it—*Ceilirach*, or beautiful gathering.

It fit the current setting so well.

Cambric and another orphanage, Mara Caladh, on the Isle of Mara, housed the highest percentage of orphans on Skymar between the two of them, and their donor presence had always been significant. Another reason to love her people.

A gathering to ensure some of the most vulnerable children of Skymar were provided for and educated well. And now, with her heart and head in the right place, she felt all the more her calling to these children, these people.

Ellie smiled.

Her people.

Additional attendees dotted the space. This year, the board had invited some of the media to attend in order to increase visibility.

The idea of their presence sent a tremor through Ellie's stomach, but she stilled the nerves as best she could. It was time to accept this part of her life again . . . and try to use it for good. Besides, she wouldn't be alone. Luke would be with her.

But where was he?

Quietly, she moved back through the hallways, nodding to several workers and newly arriving guests as she passed. She should have contacted him to remind him, but having his phone number tempted her toward another level of intimacy—texting.

And she loved good texts.

Their banter confirmed they'd have equally enjoyable texts.

She gave her head a shake to push back temptation and rounded the hallway to the kitchen. A familiar silhouette caught her attention and she skidded to a stop at the threshold of the room.

Luke stood on the far side of the kitchen, staring out the window and brushing his hair to the side with his fingers. Was he using the window as a mirror?

She slipped back a step into the shadows for subtler observation.

She liked his hair. Dark and thick with a bit of wave. Her fingers twitched from the memory of brushing through it during one of their kisses. She hadn't seen him in a few days, partly by choice and partly because of the demands of other commitments, but she hadn't expected to see him in green.

A green button-down, open at the collar, to be specific. He'd paired the quality dress shirt with black dress slacks that fit him . . . well— her neck heated—very well.

All the interest and emotions she'd experienced while cocooned in his arms during the sledding rushed back at full force. Absence had indeed made the heart grow fonder.

Or it only confirmed all the more why she needed to keep her distance.

Because she wanted him too badly.

His conversations, his smile, his look of admiration, his strength, and especially his kiss.

All of it.

Badly.

He cleared his throat and pulled a folded piece of paper from his slacks pocket, unfolding it and staring back at his reflection.

Mumbling something to his reflection, he gave his head a hard shake and then seemed to try again . . . except this time, he must have caught sight of her because he turned, offering her that crooked smile.

Right, she'd forgotten how much she wanted to see that crooked smile. Every day.

"Think I look civilized enough?"

"Very nice." She stepped forward, trying very hard to keep her ogling to a respectable minimum. "Dark green is a good color on you."

He refolded the paper and placed it back in his pocket, his body tense. "Blue is a great one on you. The suit is nice, even if I prefer you in sweaters and jeans."

Her laugh burst out. "Do you?"

"Without a doubt." He tilted his head, studying her as he met her halfway across the room. "Few things are quite as sexy as a beautiful woman looking cozy and huggable."

Any response fled her brain as the magnetism his words inspired drew her body and heart another step closer. "You really shouldn't say things like that."

"Probably not." He sighed. "But I think things like that a whole lot more than I ought to."

"So do I." She nearly whimpered and then shook her head. "I mean, I don't think those things about me. I think them about you."

His grin took a steady and dangerous slide from one corner to the other. Be still her heart! "Haven't seen you in a few days."

"Miss me?"

"It's probably the worst thing to do, but I'd prefer to see you while I can." His eyes glinted. "You're much better on the eyes than most of the people I work with."

"I think Gordon might take offense to that."

"He pretends to take offense to a lot of things."

Silence followed his statement and Ellie stared back at him, taking in those eyes . . . but more so the way those eyes looked at her. She wanted to bask in it.

"You stay pretty busy, don't you?"

"At this time of year, I do." She nodded, pulling her gaze from his. "It seems that most of the meetings and parties and all the other royal business for the North Country get smashed into the first half of the year. By July, I get a bit of a respite until Christmas planning starts, though."

"Well, at least there's a break in the crazy." He glanced toward the hallway and sighed. "I guess we'd better get to the luncheon?"

A sudden thought flickered across her mind. "You're . . . you're not concerned about speaking, are you?"

He grimaced. "I'm just not that great at speaking in front of people. I'm more of a behind-the-scenes kind of guy."

"But you spoke to Father so well. Clear and focused. With passion."

"That was to you and your dad, not a roomful of people." He raised a brow. "And definitely not to any media."

"I know you're going to be excellent." She gestured toward the hallway. "But we do need to make an appearance at least. However, if you find you're becoming overwhelmed, you could just imagine you're saying it to me."

His grin partially resurfaced. "That might help a little."

They turned toward the door and Ellie's gaze caught on the far wall: the old boards of children's names framed in aged oak poised on the pale wall.

"Luke, it looks marvelous." She stepped closer, staring at the evidence of lives lived within these walls and now brought out into the light. "Mrs. Kershaw must adore it."

"She seemed pretty pleased." His shoulder brushed hers as they stared at this special piece of history for Cambric. "I think she plans to give the donors a tour of the renovations once all the speaking is over, so I wanted to have it up and ready for her."

"I know you've mentioned how your youngest sister has some magical quality of helping other people believe in themselves, but I think it must be a family trait."

"I'm not magical." He wrinkled his nose with his grimace. "I'm practical."

"Perhaps your type of magic begins with wearing overalls and carrying a hammer but ends with making other people shine or find where they belong. You may be behind the scenes, but you are no less important than those who take the stage. In fact, without you, they may not even make it to the stage."

He held her gaze for a moment, his expression uncharacteristically sober before it dissolved into a mock frown. "Now I know you've been watching too many Hallmark movies. You're starting to sound all sentimental, like them."

She laughed and took his proffered arm as they made their way to the luncheon room.

They had paused at the threshold when a sudden sight sent a chill from Ellie's neck all the way down to her feet.

On the far side of the room, near a set of tables set aside for the media, stood an unwelcome familiar pair. Drake Stephens, the reporter who'd taken the photos that led to her royal exile, and Maxim Tatem, Ellie's ex-boyfriend who'd led the paparazzi to her.

After all the media coverage, interviews, and even a book from which Maxim had benefited, his popularity landed him a daily television spot. A placement that wasn't as popular as it had once been.

"What's wrong?" Luke asked, his voice low.

Ellie knew how to remain calm externally. Her family trained her for the careful control of a person in the spotlight, but Maxim and Drake's presence brought her past and insecurities to the surface, rattling her new confidence.

"That man, in the navy suit and pale blue shirt."

"Next to the guy in the crazy orange?"

Ellie almost grinned at Luke's description of Drake. "Yes, him. The one in the orange is the man who took the photos of me on the yacht over three years ago."

She didn't need to clarify the type of photos those had been. Or what little she'd been wearing. At the time, in her wrong thinking and blind trust, she'd believed Maxim meant to protect her, to provide her privacy.

She'd been horribly wrong.

"And the man in the navy suit . . ."

"The scoundrel who set you up." Luke's tone rumbled low, threatening. Without a word, he placed a palm to her back, both calming and safe. "What's he doing here?"

Luke's presence, his touch, took a little of the sting out of Maxim's presence. She wasn't alone. The one time she'd seen Maxim after the photos and stories ruined her life, he'd looked at her with such arrogance and self-conceit.

She'd wilted beneath his stare, a victim of his deceit all over again.

Because not only had he betrayed her, but when she'd tried to break up with him, he'd spread horrible lies to anyone who would listen. And even continued to share private photos of them for the whole world to see.

Shame scorched her cheeks with such heat, her eyes began to water.

For months, she'd taken all the blame for his response, embracing what the media called her. Receiving her just deserts. After all, she'd chosen to be with him. She'd ignored the warnings of those closest to her, rebelled against the good and right.

She'd "earned" the soured reputation. The mishandling.

But with the love of her family and months of counseling, she'd begun to see how very wrong her thinking had become.

"His show's ratings are down, so I imagine by somehow reconnecting our stories, he hopes to gain some views." She looked over at

Luke as a shiver climbed up her arms. "And likely intimidate me. He was always good at that."

"Well, he'll have to get through me to get to you." Luke gestured with his chin to a man poised nearby. "And Cameron."

Who seemed to recognize his name surfacing in the conversation, because he and Luke shared an understanding nod.

"Are the two of you friends now?"

Luke smirked. "I'm not saying we're going to take up Xbox together, but I think we have a healthy respect for each other, especially when it comes to a certain princess we know."

She readied her response when a movement to her right caught her attention. Maxim saw her . . . and was walking in her direction. All confidence fled her body as she kept a threadbare hold on her expression.

"Maybe you should pretend to be my date?"

Luke's brows rose so high they hit the strands of hair that fell over his forehead. "I'm sorry? Did you just say pretend to be your date?"

Maxim was stopped by someone during his approach.

Ellie attempted to control the sudden quiver in her voice. "Maxim is on his way over here and I . . . I can't let him think I'm alone, Luke. Not him."

"You're not alone. I'm right here with you." He waved toward the crowd. "And there are a few dozen other people."

"Luke." She hated the pleading in her voice. "He's the sort who won't let it alone."

"So . . . fake dating?" He pushed the trope out of his mouth like it hurt.

"Might as well stick to as many tropes as we can while we're at it, right?" She pushed up a tense smile. "And it would only be for today. With him."

He squinted down at her for a second and then grinned. "What if I want it to be real for one day?"

"We've already been over this." She huffed. "How can it be real between the two of us when it's so temporary?"

"Being temporary doesn't make it less real."

She squeezed her eyes closed, trying to ignore the pull of his gaze.

"How about it's real for me but fake for you?"

She nearly laughed. "How can that even work?"

"I'll just mean it and you won't."

She rolled her gaze heavenward, wrestling with her smile.

"If I do this"—he lowered his attention to her lips, his lashes sweeping low—"will the kisses be fake too?"

Heat exploded in her face. "Luke!"

"Ellie!" he countered with the same voiced emotion, only his was rather teasing.

She narrowed her eyes at him in powerless reprimand.

He leaned closer. "I don't like being fake." The soft curl in his low voice nearly melted her to the floor. "So, Ellie, would you go on a date with me today?" He wiggled his brows. "If you say yes, then we won't have to lie."

She couldn't actually think well enough to speak.

"And then my reward kisses won't have to be fake either."

She stared up at him, wishing there was a way to make him her future because she . . . she wanted every date, every feeling, every kiss to be very real. She rallied from the wonderful aura of his nearness and stepped back a little from his distracting touch. "But we can't present ourselves as a *serious* relationship, Luke."

"Great, I prefer humor anyway."

"Luke," she said through her laugh, "I mean it. The media won't leave you alone and they'll distort whatever they see." Her gaze pleaded with him. "I don't want you to have to manage any of that. It's horrible."

His expression turned thoughtful. "We can weather a lot of things for the people we care about." The gleam returned to his eyes along with an added wiggle to his brows. "But I'll try to play nice."

"Oh dear." She couldn't control her grin resurfacing.

"You promised the aforementioned reward, so this whole room could do about anything to me and I'll be *just* fine."

"I did not promise—"

"Princess Elliana?"

The voice brought unwelcome and shameful memories with it, even souring her own name to her ears. She turned to find Maxim in a suit he'd somehow managed to make look too relaxed, with Drake by his side, the latter staring with wide, ravenous eyes in search of the next story.

"Mr. Tatem." She turned to Drake. "Mr. Stephens. How good of you to come to support our children here."

"Mr. Tatem?" Maxim raised a golden brow. "Such formality. Should I bow?"

Her left hand shook from the effort to contain her emotions, so she fisted it at her side. "I don't know that you suffer from following the 'shoulds,' Mr. Tatem, so I'll leave your response to your own discretion."

"Still nursing old wounds, are we, Elliana?"

Luke's palm warmed her lower back, reminding her of his presence. Somehow, strength passed from him to her. She stood a bit straighter. "Oh no, Mr. Tatem. I have no need nor desire to highlight or waste time on insignificant scars. I prefer to learn from my past and move forward with a much better perspective, instead of renewing grudges or dwelling on past mistakes." She turned toward Luke. "May I introduce you to my guest, Mr. Luke Edgewood."

"Guest?" Maxim's gaze roamed over Luke with unveiled humor before he turned back to Ellie. "I hope you and the Duke of Styles haven't fallen out."

Ellie stilled her expression. Oh no! She hadn't told Luke about Christopher.

Luke held out his hand in greeting. "The duke was unavailable, so she had to settle for the peasant."

She looked over at him and he shot her a wink.

And at that very moment, she knew she loved him.

Maxim scoffed and stared down at Luke's hand for a moment before taking it. "How do I know your face? I rarely converse with peasants."

"I'm only here to help with some renovations for the orphanage." Luke gestured toward Ellie. "Princess Elliana was kind enough to include me in the festivities surrounding some of the work I'm doing."

"What a boon for your confidence, to be the guest of royalty!" Drake interjected, like the approval-seeking pup he was.

Ellie stifled a cringe.

"I suppose that speaks to the type of person the princess is, doesn't it?" Luke didn't miss a beat. "Aware enough to make the changes necessary to help others, but humble enough to realize we're all the same at heart. Royal or not."

Oh, he really wanted his reward, didn't he? And deserved every bit of it.

"Which is why we're all here, isn't it?" Ellie added, matching his lighter tone. "Through service and love to these children, we encourage a better future for them and for Skymar. They are the future, aren't they?"

Maxim's smile failed to resurface, which only teased Ellie's wider.

"Or they'll only end up moving away as many others have," Maxim challenged.

"If you knew your current news, Mr. Tatem, you'd realize that trend is subsiding due to many of the programs my parents have initiated, as well as growing interest in Skymar across the globe." She gestured toward Luke. "And Mr. Edgewood has suggestions to advance those ideals further."

The light left Luke's eyes, and he merely nodded in agreement.

Maxim's doubt splayed across his features without any subtlety.

"It should be interesting to hear what you bring from your experience, Mr. Edgewood." He bent his head toward Ellie. "Princess."

Ellie turned to him as soon as they were out of earshot. "Luke, I'm sorry I didn't tell you about Christopher." At Luke's confused look she clarified, "The Duke of Styles. We are friends, but presently I've made it clear that I have no other feelings toward him."

"This guy on the list?"

"One of several." Her shoulders drooped a little. "I didn't mention him because I didn't want you to think—"

"I knew about the duke."

Her bottom lip dropped. "You did?"

His knowing look took a sympathetic turn. "Ellie, I googled you, remember? Your life is pretty available to see. I think the duke may have taken you out for Italian on the last date?"

"That particular instance was not a date; it was a coincidence." She winced, searching his face. "I hope you know I'm not as I was, and even now, what they publish, it isn't the real me."

"Except when it has to do with what you love." He looked around the room. "I think the real you is mixed up in things like this a whole lot."

All her worries deflated with his one sentence. Maybe he did see her still. The real her. And perhaps he saw her even better than she fully understood. Was that one of the reasons she felt so drawn to him so quickly? He saw and still wished to keep seeing?

"You are marvelous, Luke Edgewood."

"I don't know about that." He shook his hands at his sides. "Right now I'm sweating like a ten-year-old sitting outside the principal's office."

She covered her mouth to cloak her laugh. "Spoken like someone who is well acquainted with that feeling."

He grinned. "More than I plan to admit." Then he looked around the room and released a sigh so large his broad shoulders sank a little.

"How on earth do you do this all the time? I can't even imagine meeting after meeting, people always watching you." He shook his head. "No wonder you just wanted to be Ellie for a while."

"I wouldn't mind it so much if there were more opportunities for respite. And, I suppose, if there were people like you to allow me the freedom to just be me." Her sigh matched his. "But one does get used to wearing a public face, I'm afraid."

"To reference our earlier conversation, I'm not great at pretending. Never been good at it, really."

"I'm glad you're so genuine." She scanned him from top to bottom. "But no one would think you're uncomfortable at all. You were the very model of charming to Maxim the Monster."

Luke's attention shot back to the *monster*, who had made no secret of his continued observation of Luke and Ellie. She could only imagine what scenario he conjured up in that maniacal head of his, plotting some next headline or talk-show selling point.

"Hmm . . . ," came Luke's response, which sounded more like a growl, then he turned back to her. "I'm glad I'm faking it so well, but my heart's beating like a ping-pong ball inside my chest right now." His grin inched up. "And it only has a little to do with your presence."

"At least I'm in there somewhere."

"If we were alone, then you'd be the full reason."

And yet again she fought her grin and the rising warmth in her cheeks. "Luke, you can't keep saying such things, you know? It only makes things harder for both of us."

"But it's date talk." He raised a brow. "And as I recall, we are on a date."

He rushed on before she could interrupt. "So, since we're on a date, and you kind of owe me a favor, I was hoping you would be willing to present my ideas today." He reached for his pocket. "I wrote everything down."

"What?"

"I've never been good at speaking in front of people." He shrugged a shoulder. "And who's to say they'll even understand me with my accent, so it might be better coming from you."

What was he talking about? "Luke, you speak fine." She made to reach for his hand, but stopped. As Ellie, she found it so easy to respond naturally with him, but as Princess Elliana, with eyes possibly critiquing her every move, she hesitated. "And it will mean more coming from you because it's *your* story. When the board asks you questions, you can answer from your own experiences. I can't do that. You were meant for this moment, Luke, just as much as you believe I am."

He still didn't look convinced, so the woman who cared for him nudged the poised princess to the side. She leaned closer to him, lowering her voice. "And I promise to reward you privately for your wonderful work."

His lips edged up on one side as he narrowed his eyes. "I'll hold you to that, Princess."

⚒

"Mr. Edgewood?"

Luke looked from his conversation with a few straggling donors to find Cameron standing at the entrance of the room, his towering presence difficult to ignore.

Luke approached, giving the room a quick look before turning back to Cameron. "Are you as disappointed as I am that we didn't have to teach Maxim what's-his-face a lesson in humility?"

Cameron's stoic expression broke into a slight grin for only a second before melding back to neutral. "The fact that the princess chose a peasant over a talk-show celebrity may have been a start."

"Maybe, but I would have felt better with a little more hands-on teaching opportunity."

"Aye." The slight grin reemerged for a moment. "I would have been keen to see it too."

Only a few donors remained speaking with Mrs. Kershaw as the luncheon came to a close. From what Luke could tell, the event proved a success with more support than Ellie or the board anticipated.

Good.

Maybe installing an elevator and updating the heating system weren't too far in the future after all.

Luke shrugged off his sport jacket, searching for the princess of the hour. "It is my understanding that Mr. MacKerrow is waiting for you at the Frasiers', sir."

Luke looked back at Cameron, always a little unnerved at the man's knowledge of things. As Ellie's protection officer, Luke supposed he kept tabs on a lot of people. "He is. And likely getting his fill of good Scottish food too."

"I'm here to drive you to the Frasiers'." Cameron's gaze held Luke's as if he were trying to communicate something.

"I appreciate that, Cam, but I don't mind the walk. I'm sure you need to tend to Princess Elliana." Luke sent the room another look. "Wherever she is."

"I do, sir," Cam continued. "And I insist on driving you."

Luke tilted his head and studied the man. Cameron's expression gave nothing away, but the insistence hinted at something else . . . a possibility? "All right. I'll take you up on that offer."

Without another word, Cam led the way to a side entrance of the hall where his solitary SUV waited, carefully framed in by a rock wall surrounding this side of the hall and drive. Luke looked over at the man, attempting to sort out the unspoken message, but Cameron merely walked forward and, with a shift in his position, turned his body so it created a barrier between the SUV door and the castle.

With a nod and almost a smile, he opened the door. "Her Highness suggested the two of you were unable to finish your conversation from before, Mr. Edgewood."

What?

And then Luke looked into the dark interior of the vehicle, his gaze landing on a blue suit that led directly up to a pair of familiar and lovely matching eyes. "Um . . . thanks, Cam," Luke murmured, climbing into the seat. The door closed behind him and Cameron took his place in the driver's seat before raising a partition, blocking his access to where Luke now sat next to Ellie.

"I didn't trust us to find any privacy in the hall after such a successful and full event," Ellie rushed to say, the shadows of the moving car failing to hide the heightened pink in her cheeks.

She looked pretty kissable right now.

"Probably a smart call."

"And meeting you like this is probably idiotic, but at least better than being caught in a closet by Mrs. Kershaw." Her brow rose the tiniest bit as she turned toward him.

A closet sounded good to him, but he wouldn't complain. With her orange scent invading each breath and Ellie staring up at him with those eyes, he'd probably be content about anywhere. "I see you have Cameron in on your plans, so at least you're guarded."

"Undoubtedly." Her lips slid into a full smile. "And though he might not show it, he likes you."

"No better way to start a friendship among men than a solid hit to the face."

Her soft laugh and a scoot or two brought her closer. "I feel you're owed a substantial reward for your amazing work as a champion for children across Skymar."

His pulse took an upswing at her reference. Yep. She kept getting better and better.

"And for contemplating the very idea of fake dating." He frowned, even though the closer she came, the happier he felt.

"I was trying to stick with some of the tropes that keep popping up in our lives." Her palm settled on the collar of his shirt, giving the slightest tug. "But I agree—I only want the real dates." She edged closer. "And the very real rewards."

There were times in life when a man needed to take charge. This wasn't one of them.

Being a princess and all, Ellie seemed to have the situation well in hand . . . or, in this case, her lips had his. And boy, did they. Certain. Soft. Taking their ever-loving time to show him a great deal of appreciation.

How on earth was he supposed to go back to anything else after her?

Sure, he didn't belong in any sort of royal life. And he could never measure up to the expectations her family likely had, but his heart teetered on the edge of throwing every one of his own fears aside to jump headlong into a future with her.

If she would have him.

As the SUV drove away from the Frasiers' a half hour later, his lips still happily tingling, a bruise of pain ached in his chest.

She was a princess.

He wasn't on the list.

And there was a good chance those kisses weren't so much a reward as a goodbye.

Text from Izzy to Luke and Penelope: So . . . how did the luncheon go?

Luke: I think it went pretty well. The board seemed really supportive of my ideas.

Loyally, Luke

Penelope: Well, the gossip columns are all aflutter about you, Luke. One even hinted that you were trying to steal Princess Elliana from her duke, or earl, as the case may be.

Penelope: But I'm not too impressed with the duke anyway. You're much more handsome and actually change your facial expression.

Luke: I don't really care what the tabloids say, Penny-girl. They're not where I go for news. Or truth. Or even reading material.

Izzy: The two of you do make a nice pair, though, Luke. And you looked great in that green! Brodie really has an eye for that sort of thing. *sigh* He's wonderful.

Penelope: Do you think it's a Skymarian thing? Matthias is great at fashion too. He even bought a hat for me last week and it was PERFECT.

Penelope: See what a little fashion can do for you, Luke? You're practically dating a princess!! Just imagine where your life could be if you shaved that beard!

Penelope: Stop sending me photos of Aragorn with and without the beard!

Izzy: Did Ellie seem pleased with how things turned out at the luncheon?

Luke: Yeah, she did. I think it was a good step for her too. The more she can show the public how much she cares and how she's grown from a few years ago, the better for her. And she's getting a little more confident, I think.

Izzy: Well, when you're not teasing us into delirium, you're really good at encouragement.

Penelope: AHH!!! I can't believe we're talking about Ellie as if she's a regular person!!!!

Luke: She is a regular person, Penn!

Penelope: A princess kind of regular person! Which is not regular at all. But you would know better than me. *blinking eyelashes and thinking twitterpated thoughts for you*

Luke: She's a pretty good encourager too.

Izzy: Did you have any trouble speaking?

Luke: At first I did, but then I took Ellie's advice and finished off just fine.

Izzy: Well, I'm so glad she showed her appreciation for your ideas and efforts.

Luke: She was very thorough in her appreciation.

Penelope: I don't know why that makes me think you mean something more than what you're saying, but I feel as though you do. However, I'm just going to bask in the secondary glow of watching you live out a movie. This is the time in the movie when someone declares their feelings and the couple kiss, but since you've already done the kissing, I suppose that's a little anticlimactic. Maybe you'll rescue her from something or other next. That could work.

Luke: When Penelope starts predicting my future, it's time to end the conversation. Good night, ladies.

Izzy: Good night, Luke.

Penelope: Good night, big bro. *chime*

CHAPTER 16

***The Daily Edge: Social Tattle from
One Edge of Skymar to the Other***

It looks like our reformed rebel is at it again, except this time she's juggling an earl and a . . . carpenter? We all know she has a past of enjoying the romantic journey, but all her previous exploits have been more in line with aristocracy or "Hollywood" royalty, not some unknown carpenter from an unknown place in the U.S. And has she left Stoic Styles behind? Because Princess Elliana was spotted having lunch with the introverted and camera-shy Earl of Tallon yesterday. Perhaps the earl is more open to sharing? It certainly looks as if our princess hasn't shaken off as much of her former life as she's claimed. Or is she only taking after her father in searching for love in the most unlikely places? It seems as if there's something magical in the North Country air that woos royalty to color outside the lines. What are your thoughts? Team Styles, Tallon, or Edgewood?

- -

Text from Maeve to Ellie: Now I really hate that Dad got
    sick and we missed the luncheon. Luscious Luke looks
    fantastic in green.

Ellie: Oh no! Have photos already found their way into print?
    How bad is it?

Maeve: If we're talking about Luke in green, so bad I think you ought to give him to me. If we're talking about the "news," then . . . you'd better not read it.

Maeve: Those shoulders, El. Those shoulders. Can you imagine how well he'd fill out a tux?

Ellie: I do not need help with my imagination on that score, Maeve.

Maeve: And what's this about Timid Tallon? You didn't tell me you were meeting him. Did he talk at all?

Ellie: He was on the list, so Mother suggested I ask him to be my escort to the Hyacinth. I feel as though he'll prove less dull than Christopher, which suits me better too, and he's been a good friend for most of my life.

Maeve: Why don't you shake things up and ask a certain builder?

Ellie: Maeve! He is not interested in royal life, and I can't imagine anything would induce him to attend a royal ball. He's already had to deal with paparazzi finding him in Crieff. I don't want to make things worse for him. Besides, why would I encourage something that cannot continue? I've already gotten my heart too entangled as it is.

Maeve: Because seeing him in a tux would be worth it?

Maeve: Ignoring me, are you? Or daydreaming about Legendary Luke in a tux?

Ellie: Oh heavens! The Edge is already suggesting I've fallen back to my old ways after three years because of ONE meeting where I touch a man's arm???!! This is ridiculous.

Maeve: It's what tabloids are all about, friend. Besides, the real problem probably has more to do with the way you're looking at him, rather than a touch to the arm. Maverick Maxim must have gotten a glimpse of something.

Ellie: He'll do anything for a story.

Loyally, Luke

Ellie: And I probably need to contact Luke to warn him.

Maeve: You've got to learn to ignore the tabloids like your family usually does. (Well, everyone except Arran, who seems to enjoy them a little too much.) I mean, you've always said that one-time stories like this aren't really the problem—it's when the same ones keep happening over and over that it becomes an issue.

Ellie: True. I need to take a deep breath and not look for a catastrophe behind every headline. It's just so difficult to retrain my brain.

Maeve: Here's the thing, people are going to look for a story, and they have the freedom to spin it any way they want. So do you. Have you ever considered that you can use the media as a tool? They may not bite on everything you put out there, but it will give you a semblance of control to have your own version for people to consider.

Ellie: You're right. In fact, I was just contemplating the idea before you texted. If I want more visibility for what I care about, I need to make it more visible so the media will focus on the good.

Ellie: And I need to distance myself from Luke. He will finish with the renovations next week and then the following week is the banquet. Then he'll be gone from Crieff to finish up another project near Skern, and I'll have no reason to see him ever again.

Maeve: That is one way to look at the problem.

Ellie: Why do I feel as if you have something else you want to say?

Maeve: If someone I cared about was going to leave—and I knew I would probably never see them again—I'd try to find ways to spend as much time with them as I could.

Ellie: You're thinking about your mother, aren't you?

Maeve: I would do just about anything to have her back, El. She's been gone a year and I still think she'll show up at my flat to ask if I'd like to join her on some ridiculous shopping excursion.

Ellie: You were with her, Maeve. All the way to the end.

Maeve: And I have those memories, along with all the others I've collected through my life. I would rather have those memories and the love wrapped within them than have "spared" myself the hurt by creating more distance than necessary.

Ellie: It's so risky.

Maeve: Do you want to know what I'd tell you as my friend? Or as a princess?

Ellie: Why do they have to be so different?

Maeve: They just do. It's your life and, now, your choice.

Ellie: Then, as my friend.

Maeve: Is he worth the risk, El? Even for just this little while? He's not going to be a prince. You're not going to leave your country. But which will you regret more? Making memories and then having to say goodbye or never trying at all?

Luke had expected Ellie to be AWOL at Cambric the next few days. She'd told him after taking full advantage of their one-day date with a lip-on-lip reward that she had responsibilities to attend to in Mara.

But the thing he hadn't expected was his sudden popularity.

As he exited Gordon and Nessa's shop Saturday evening after dinner with them, a half dozen reporters stopped him on the main street of Crieff, bombarding him with questions.

Loyally, Luke

He'd never been a fan of attention, unless it involved the very thorough private attention of a princess (evidently), or the attention to detail needed to build something the right way. But this type of attention fit neither of those criteria.

Though, from the look on Pete's face, you would have thought he'd won the popularity lottery.

From what Luke could make out from the multiple reporters talking at the same time, mixed with their accent, the questions all revolved around one thing: him and Princess Elliana.

"Are you dating the princess?"

"Sources say you two are on intimate terms. Is that true?"

"What do her parents have to say about her dating a foreigner?"

"Are you considering relocating to maintain your relationship?"

Half the questions he didn't even know how to answer. The last one, he did, but he refused to give them the satisfaction. Blocking people's way to their car was just rude and he didn't care much to appease rude people.

Luke tried to push through the crowd and was making slow progress when Gordon burst from the front door of his shop, yelling threats in Caedric, Gaelic, and English. Evidently, he wasn't too keen on rude people either.

With some help from a few of the other Crieff residents, the crowd dispersed and Luke and Pete made their way back to the cabin.

And as weird as it sounded, Luke kept a look over his shoulder to ensure no one was following them to their secluded location. Of course, why on earth would someone follow *him*? It wasn't like he'd get captured and the royal family would receive a ransom note or something. That was just ridiculous.

But at the current moment, his life looked a little too much like a movie to discard caution, even the ridiculous kind.

"You're all over the news, mate." Pete sat up from his reclined position on the couch, where he'd been looking at his phone. "This one photo from the luncheon does make it look like the two of you are close."

Luke moved from the finished banquette to peer at the photo on Pete's phone. Someone, likely Monster Maxim, had taken a picture of the moment when Ellie placed her hand on his arm and leaned close. From their position, one could almost guess she was leaning in for a kiss.

Luke rolled his eyes and took a giant bite of his sandwich to keep his words from offending his own ears. No wonder Ellie wanted to seclude herself back in Crieff. Dealing with this all the time would drive anyone batty.

He took another large bite of sandwich.

Another item to add to his list of reasons for avoiding social media.

"What are you going to do?" Pete looked up from his phone.

"What is there to do? Isn't it some sort of usual royal protocol to keep a stiff upper lip and go on? Keep quiet?" He raised the rest of his sandwich as if toasting a glass. "That I can do."

"And what if . . ." Pete's smile took a mischievous turn. "What if she wants you to be her prince?"

Every bone in Luke's body revolted against the idea of him and the word *prince* in the same sentence. "She's not going to ask."

At Pete's skeptical expression, Luke sighed and rested his hip against the back of the couch. "Ever watch the *Mission: Impossible* movies? Or *Indiana Jones*?"

Pete only blinked.

"*Rambo*?"

Nothing.

Pain pinched in Luke's chest at what Pete had been missing in his life. "Well, they're not romance movies. They're adventure movies. And in those, the guy doesn't usually get to keep the girl. Or maybe the girl doesn't get to keep the guy. It's not that they stop caring about each other, but life happens and hard choices have to be made." Luke shrugged. "Well, in Indie's case, he's just really bad at choosing the right woman, but anyway, the point is, just because two people care about each other—and I'm not saying Ellie cares about me in the way you're implying—doesn't mean they get to choose to be together."

"And you're going to be okay with that?"

"Life's full of hard choices, Pete." Luke looked down at his half-eaten sandwich, his appetite gone. "Sometimes, between two good choices, you have to pray, consider, and hope you choose the best one for all the right reasons."

"And if you don't?"

"You make the best of your choice and do the next right thing." The weight of the declaration pressed him to sit on the back of the couch. "I'm not going to say it doesn't feel awful. I feel like someone's repeatedly punched me in the stomach, but I'm also not so short-sighted or hopeless to think that God can't turn choices—the best or not—into something good and right."

"Even if you missed your soul mate?" Pete looked utterly horrified.

Luke gave his beard a scratch as he pondered how to answer. Not the most popular opinion either. "My granny once said that love is much stronger than any feeling. It's a *choice* you make over and over again. Choosing her and what's best for her every day." He shrugged, sifting through his own words for consolation and strength. "It's real nice to think of all the magic of finding that one person in the whole universe who will make *you* happy, but I feel that's going about it inside out."

"Really?"

"Focusing on what I can get out of it? Doesn't sound like real love to me. Does it to you? If I'm spending so much time stewing over my own happiness, I'm bound to cook up a whole lot of discontent, self-focus, hurt feelings, and pride—and to be honest, I don't know if any of us need to spend too much time inside our own heads." Luke shuddered. "Scary place in there."

Pete's grin quirked.

"But real love isn't so much looking out for myself as it is the other person's best. Helping them shine."

"Like what you want for the princess?"

Love? Yes. He did love her. Luke looked away. But there was no way he was going to say it out loud. Especially to Pete, the chatterbox.

Luke's phone buzzed in his pocket, so he pulled it up to view.

An email? From HRHStClare?

HRH?

What business did he know that used those initials? St. Clare? Wasn't that Ellie's last name?

Did princesses have *last* names?

He groaned. He was in way over his head.

But the email wasn't from Ellie.

It was from her dad.

Was it okay to call a king "Dad," or did he immediately warrant the name "Father"? His head started to ache.

And then the realization hit him. The king of Skymar had sent him an email? Why would . . . The press! And the implications for Ellie!

His face went cold. This was much worse than the principal's office.

"What is it?" Pete's voice broke through Luke's mental chaos. "You look like you just got hit in the stomach."

"Not sure." He opened the email and skimmed across the few short lines.

Thanks for the meeting . . . grateful for your thoughts . . .

Luke froze.

There is a current situation I'd like to discuss with you. If you are open to meeting with me, I can have my secretary contact you to

242

set a time within the next few days. I feel in-person would be best. I shall be residing at Carlstern Castle leading up to the Donors' Banquet at Cambric Hall. It is an hour drive from Crieff. Would you have available transportation to meet or should I send a car?

Gratefully,
HRH Aleksander

"What is it?" Pete had moved from his place on the couch and attempted to peer over Luke's shoulder, but since the man stood several inches below Luke, he wasn't succeeding.

Luke swallowed through the lump in his throat and released a sigh. "Do you think Carlstern Castle has a dungeon?"

Text from Ellie to Luke: Hi, Luke. It's Ellie. Nessa contacted me and told me about the reporters in Crieff. I'm sorry for involving you in this way.

Luke: How did you get my number?

Luke: Not that I mind. It's just, I think I would have remembered if we exchanged numbers because . . . well, I had to fight the urge to ask you for yours about twenty times before I found out about the whole princess thing.

Ellie: I'm one of the royals of Skymar. I have my ways of getting the information I need.

Ellie: However, all I really had to do was ask Holton.

Luke: Clever. And I'm not sure how to react to such power. It might be a little intimidating.

Ellie: I adore the idea of being intimidating. You ought to see me when I shoot pistols with Father.

Luke: Ellie, if you're trying to create emotional distance between us, you shouldn't mention shooting pistols to me. It only makes you more attractive.

Ellie: What would you do if I told you I'm currently taking your advice and watching Hacksaw Ridge?

Luke: You're not playing fair right now, Princess.

Ellie stared down at the phone, almost able to hear him say what he'd just written. The ache that began the moment he responded to her first text branched throughout her chest. Her breath shook from her effort to control her emotions.

She knew what she had to do, but everything within her rebelled against it. Was Maeve right? Could she spend time with him as friends just to make the best of what they had left?

Luke: I have a feeling you won't be visiting Crieff anytime soon, will you?

Her eyes burned. He knew.

Ellie: It will be better if I keep my distance until the banquet.

She slid her fingers beneath one damp eye. She'd never imagined anyone like him in her life. Wouldn't have even known how to imagine him, but here he was, caring for her with such genuineness and goodness.

Helping her realize how good life could be, how fun.

Luke: I imagine it would.

His simple admission redirected every plan she'd made for the conversation.

Loyally, Luke

Ellie: But I don't quit so easily on a job when I start one, so I
   suppose I'll be a gofer for a little longer.

Luke: A lady who shoots a pistol, watches good movies, and
   finishes what she starts? Woman, you're not helping my
   mind stay on the friendly path at all.

Her grin stretched wide, and the sweet warmth of attraction
bloomed through her chest.

Ellie: It's only a few more days. Hopefully I won't tempt you
   over the edge in that time.

Though, judging by her pulse, her heart had already galloped over
the edge and right into his arms without one look back.

Ellie: And I'll really only be there for one of those days since I
   have other business to attend to.

Luke: Well, at least I can get some distraction-free work done
   sometime this week. That's awful friendly of you.

Oh, how she wanted to hold on to this as long as possible. Even
if only as friends.

Ellie: I'd rather have your friendship than nothing at all.

Luke: Oh, you got my friendship, Ellie. And anytime you want
   to tiptoe over into the gray area of kissing friends, I'll
   gladly be your friend then too.

CHAPTER 17

Luke walked through Cambric's kitchen and the adjoining spaces, giving a last check to all the team's work. Mrs. Kershaw had gone through things with him an hour before, oohing and aahing at all the changes and additions.

The new kitchen would certainly serve Cambric much better than the old. Two new industrial ovens, a massive griddle, an additional sink, a much larger pantry as well as additional storage, and some better insulation would only prove to keep the cooling and heating more efficient than before.

And the soft green wall color paired with the oak cabinets made the space not only functional but pretty too. All Ellie's suggestions.

He grinned, his gaze moving to a painting here and a light fixture there that they'd added at her recommendation. She really had a gift for adding beauty.

He gave the room a final nod before meeting Gordon and Pete in the hallway.

"Nessa's expecting you two for supper, you ken?"

"Aye." Luke imitated Gordon's usual response, bringing a wry smile to the man's face.

"Now you're embracin' our world, lad." Gordon placed a palm on Luke's shoulder. "You ken you are always welcome in Crieff? With us?"

"I know."

"I'd welcome the opportunity to work with you anytime."

"And I you."

"Not me, Gordon?" Pete offered with a wink. "Though, I have to say, I've learned enough on this job to whet my appetite for more."

Loyally, Luke

"May the Almighty help us all!" Gordon sighed, incurring a laugh from Pete and a smile from Luke.

"I'll meet the two of you in town." Luke nodded, drawing a deep breath and stepping back. "But I need to speak to a few people before I leave Cambric."

"A few small people?" Pete's grin broadened.

"One small and two who are nearly as tall as me," Luke corrected and turned to Gordon. "I'll meet you in an hour. Will that work for Nessa's supper plans?"

"Aye," he said, drawing out the word for emphasis. "And if the bairns can come, bring 'em on. Jamie and Cade have proved good workers and fine boys, and Faye would be good for Nessa's heart since she's not seen the grandweans in a month."

"I still can't believe the two of you are old enough to have grand-children." This from Pete. "My parents are older than you and only have one."

Reminded Luke of his parents. They'd been high school sweet-hearts and had Josephine in their early twenties. Probably similar to Gordon and Nessa. Neither of them could be more than fifty.

"Ah, but when you love young, you parent young." Gordon gave his hefty brows a shake. "And then you still have movin' bones when you have grandweans. You may be sore after they leave ya, but you can still move the next morn." He groaned. "Mostly."

Luke smiled as the two men left, Pete regaling, or attempting to regale, Gordon with a story about his nephew's antics in usual Pete fashion. Lots of words and animation.

Gordon offering a gruff response or teasing look here and there.

This side of the world kept growing on him, especially when a certain drop-dead-gorgeous blonde came to mind.

He raised a gaze heavenward, wondering what God was trying to teach him. As he'd told Pete, life brought choices of all sorts. Some were easy. Others difficult.

And some left you asking yourself what you really wanted and treasured.

But in all truth, he didn't have much of a choice about this one. Whatever "list" royals had for their children's spouses, he didn't make the cut. And even if he did, could he really see himself giving up his home and life for somewhere he didn't belong at all? Sure, he could help out here and there with remodels or coming up with ideas to help kids, but banquets and balls and meetings with lots of fancy people all the time?

He groaned at the very idea.

And he wasn't a big fan of the media, but he could ignore their nonsense for the most part. His grimace deepened. Until he couldn't and ended up punching somebody important. He shrugged. But at least then that would overshadow Ellie's past.

After receiving permission from Mrs. Kershaw—who basically offered Luke permanent residency at Cambric Hall for how well he'd worked with the kids—Luke found Jamie and Cade more than willing to take a trip to the Frasiers'. In fact, the boys had developed almost as close a relationship with the grumbly carpenter as they had with Luke. He paused on the thought. Did he come off as a grumbly carpenter? By the time he was Gordon's age, would he then?

He nodded to himself. He could certainly see that in his future.

He found Faye sitting on the side steps of the hall, doll in hand and a very impressive pouty lip on display. Luke slid down to a seat beside the little girl and allowed the silence to encourage her response.

She rubbed a hand against her sniffling nose, looked up at him, and then sighed so loudly, he was pretty sure she'd only done it for his benefit.

He wrestled with his grin and attempted to portray the seriousness her exaggerated emotions warranted. "Is something wrong, Faye?"

She tucked her doll close and buried her chin into the worn strands of the doll's hair, releasing another sniffle.

Loyally, Luke

He waited.

"Are you leaving today?"

"I finished my job."

She sniffled again. "I don't like it when nice people leave."

Luke leaned forward, his elbows on his knees, staring out at the view. "I don't like leaving nice people."

"Could you stay?"

He looked over at her, at those big eyes searching his, and his heart pinched. "It's a really nice place to consider staying, that's a fact. But I have folks back home who want to see me too."

She nodded and nestled her face back into the doll. Luke couldn't imagine the dozens or more of "goodbyes" Faye had experienced. And he was another one. A person who came into her life, showed her he cared, and then left.

He'd thought and prayed about some small way he could make this transition a little easier. Probably not the best idea, but he'd seen the necklace in a shop in Crieff and it just fit.

He reached into his shirt pocket and brought out a little box. The shopkeeper even placed a tiny pink bow on top when he'd told her the reason for the purchase.

"But I got you something."

She looked down at the box and then pushed her doll to the side. "What is it?"

He grinned and pushed it into her waiting hand. "Open it and find out."

The box lid slipped away to reveal a small gold necklace. Faye looked up at him with wide eyes.

"I got a gold necklace for you because gold is pretty and special, like you are. But you know what is the most like you?"

"What?"

"Gold is strong. And you are strong."

She looked down at the necklace, studying it.

His throat tightened. "And it's a heart because I want you to remember something."

Her gaze fastened back on his. "What?"

"That you are loved by lots of people." He nodded toward the hall. "Mrs. Kershaw."

Faye wrinkled her nose in disagreement. Luke held in his smile.

"Mrs. Rue."

Faye liked that name a little better.

"Amara from all the way in Nigeria."

Her smile brimmed at that one.

"Lots of your friends at the orphanage." He tilted his gaze upward. "God."

She looked up at the sky.

He swallowed through the tightness and worked the words through his lips. "And me."

She smiled up at him and his heart nearly broke into a zillion pieces. "You too?"

"Me too. You were one of the very first friends I made when I came here."

Her cheeks dimpled with her widened grin and his throat squeezed tight.

"I spied on you."

"You did." He cleared his throat. "And that heart necklace"—he tapped the box to give him something else to look at besides her face—"well, when you wear it, I want you to remember all those things."

She touched the heart with her little finger, her smile fully intact. "I'm pretty and special." She looked up at him. "And lots of people love me."

"And you're strong." He nodded. "Strong enough to keep hold of that kindness and sweetness inside of you, even when things are hard."

Her eyes rounded. "I'm not always sweet."

"Who is?" He shrugged a shoulder, glad for the levity in the subject change. "But I hope you can hold on to your sweetness long enough to join me for supper with Mr. and Mrs. Frasier tonight."

Her little mouth dropped open. "Mr. Frasier from the old treasure shop in Crieff?"

"That's right. He's specifically invited you, Jamie, and Cade to join me and his wife for a supper to celebrate finishing up the kitchen work." He refused to say a goodbye supper because somehow the word kept getting stuck in his throat.

Text from Izzy to Luke and Penelope: Thanks so much for the photos. Faye is the cutest thing. Those eyes just sparkle.

Luke: They sure do. With a whole lot of sass and mischief.

Izzy: Anyone with sass and mischief is your kind of someone.

Penelope: Oh my goodness, Luke! She looks like a little fairy. In that one picture, is she getting ready to throw a cup of something on one of those boys?

Luke: Yeah, Nessa caught her in time so it didn't happen, but Jamie was teasing her about redheads.

Penelope: Some of the best people are redheads. *batting eyelashes proudly*

Luke: Is it possible to bat eyelashes humbly?

Penelope: You're not funny.

Izzy: So . . . will you see Ellie again before you leave Crieff?

Luke: She'll be at the Donors' Banquet, so I'll see her there.

Izzy: Are you still being followed by the paparazzi?

Luke: Yeah, a little. I just move through them or go around them. If Ellie isn't here, I don't think they'll stay long. And they'll likely lose interest once the banquet's over and I get out of town.

Penelope: I know you think I'm crazy and too stuck in

movie-brain, but I just feel like it can't be the end of your story with her.

Luke: Penny-girl . . . real life. It happens.

Penelope: I know you're not as laissez-faire as you're pretending to be. And she CAN'T be. A girl just doesn't forget a guy like you.

Izzy: Actually, Penelope is right. Despite all your faux grumpiness . . .

Penelope: And faux arrogance.

Izzy: And short sentences.

Penelope: And facial hair.

Luke: You can end the list now, thanks.

Izzy: You really are the type of person who leaves a lasting impression.

Penelope: And not just the kind like permanent markers . . . or that time with cousin Thomas and the iron. You may not want people to know, but you listen. That's an amazingly attractive character trait (despite the beard).

Izzy: And you find ways to show people you care about them so they FEEL it.

Luke: Okay, y'all. Stop or you're gonna make me cry. Oh wait, I don't cry.

Penelope: Well, there was the time you ate the ghost pepper.

Luke: Not the same thing.

Penelope: Are you going to be okay? Really? I'm so far away I can't tell whether you're just being your regular grumpy self or you're really sad.

Luke: It sucks to fall for a princess you can't have, but I suppose this may be as close as I'll ever get to feeling like you did most of your young life, Penny-girl. Oh wait, all the princes you fell for weren't real.

Loyally, Luke

Penelope: Never underestimate the heartbreak of fictional romances.

Izzy: She does have a point, Luke. Fictional characters can be very powerful. But we just want you to know (even if you don't want to know) that we think you're pretty amazing.

Penelope: Totally worthy of any princess. EEEE!!! That sounds so magical.

Luke: Okay, I'm getting off here before you start singing some movie song performed by animated creatures. Besides, I'm getting ready to rewatch The Expendables, grill some hamburgers, and try to clear my head of all your emotional talk.

Penelope: Love you BIG, bro!

Text from Izzy to Luke: Just so you know, if you need me, I can be there in an hour.

Luke: I'm okay, Iz. I wish things could be different, but they can't.

Text from Maeve to Ellie: I still think you ought to ask Luscious Luke to the Hyacinth, Ellie. Timorous Timothy of Tallon is nice-looking and all, but really can't compare. In looks or conversation.

Ellie: Timothy is very sweet and only sees me as a friend. It's a good pairing for the Hyacinth. I can have a date and he can appease his own mother by attending a social engagement now and again. Besides, after the Hyacinth, I plan to turn my attention to my duties.

Maeve: Because your heart needs time to heal.

Ellie: I haven't known him so long as that, Maeve.

Maeve: It doesn't have to take a long time to care for
someone, El. And when it's the right person, it doesn't
have to take long at all.

Driving a car in Crieff proved a lot different than driving one to a castle.

A real castle.

To meet a king.

And possibly end up in a dungeon for dating his daughter?

In all honesty, it was only one real date.

Heat crept up his neck.

And about a half dozen unofficial ones. Or more. Sort of.

Gordon and Nessa had assured Luke his fears were unfounded. That the king was a reasonable and kind man, which was what Luke believed after having dinner with him. But that was before Luke went around . . . what was the Scottish word? *Snogging* his daughter?

He gave his head a shake. Nope. He still preferred the word *kissing*. *Snogging* sounded like something you'd spit up rather than the fantastic activity kissing really was. Or at least, how it was with Ellie.

After doing a little research online, he'd worn his best jeans, a white button-down, and his sport jacket for the occasion, hopefully balancing casual with a "fit for a king" meeting. If Prince William could make the look work, surely Luke could get by with it.

Even with a beard.

And, maybe, a scared rabbit expression.

He parked in the allotted spot indicated by a detailed email on protocol and then proceeded to pass through a series of security checkpoints, including one set of guards who opened the gift he'd brought for Ellie that he planned to leave with her dad. Thankfully, he'd purchased a box with an easy slip-off lid and separate bow. He didn't even realize they made boxes like that. Game changer.

The castle itself looked like something off some show Penelope loved to watch about royals. Like the Biltmore Estate back home . . . only on steroids. Gold-trimmed mirrors, crimson and dark green wall colors. Woodwork with the most intricate designs carved to frame doors or accent crown molding. Massive stone, marble, and ceramic fireplaces. The furniture didn't look like you were supposed to sit on it, and if you were supposed to, it wouldn't be comfortable.

Even the ceilings glistened like works of art, from their designs to their colors. One even had a painting covering the entire ceiling, very much like the Biltmore's library.

Though everything glowed with more grandeur than the estate back home, something about having a frame of reference eased a little of his discomfort in walking through the space. The craftsmanship shone through, only highlighting things he'd already come to appreciate from Skymar. They valued woodwork and stonemasonry.

And quality.

Luke followed his black-suited escort up a narrower stairway and less ornate hallway, still well maintained, but the atmosphere changed from grand to . . . something else? Luke glanced behind him the way they'd come, trying to remember the direction in case he needed to run for it.

The servant leading the way stopped in front of a large oak door with wood carvings of flowers twining up each side in distracting detail. The leaves looked fragile enough to be real.

Luke didn't have time to study the designs further because the manservant—did he call him a manservant? Butler?—knocked and a voice within beckoned entry. Unlike the previous and larger rooms, Luke stepped into a space of cozy, pale blue couches and white walls. The chairs looked more comfortable, though it seemed pretty clear that no one had been eating Doritos while watching movies here.

As weird as it sounded to his brain, this place felt more like the middle ground between how he imagined Ellie's life and what he knew of his own. This was comfy-class. He cringed. Where had that thought come from? He'd only watched HGTV a few times, and those were only during emergency moments involving Izzy and *Wuthering Heights*, Penelope and boy drama, or Josephine and some of her strange diet crashes.

King Aleksander stood from behind a desk by one of the large windows in the room and walked forward, hand extended. "Happy to see you again, Luke."

"Your Majesty." Luke gave a small bow before taking the man's hand. He got a little help from research for that protocol too. "I'm grateful to have a chance to talk with you again."

"Good. Come sit." The king waved toward one of the matching chairs and then turned to the two men in the room. "You can leave us, thank you."

No witnesses. Luke watched them leave. But that also meant no ganging up on Luke. He studied the king. The man looked in good shape, but Luke thought he could take him, if he had to.

The king sat and Luke followed (another tip from the cyberworld).

"You didn't have to bring a gift." The king gestured toward the box in Luke's hand.

Luke looked down at the offering and heat rushed to his face. "I'm sorry, sir, but I actually brought this in hopes you could give it to Ellie—Princess Elliana for me, since I've finished my work at Cambric Hall and we don't plan to see each other in casual circumstances again."

The king scanned the long, rectangular box with a raised brow.

"It's a fishing rod." Luke leaned forward as if someone else might overhear. "PENN Spinfisher."

The king's eyes widened. "You bought my daughter a fishing rod?"

"Yes, sir."

"And you think this is a good choice?" The king's lips crooked just a little beneath his golden beard.

"I do, in fact, sir. It's something on her list."

"Her list?" The king tilted his head, studying Luke with curiosity more than skepticism.

Did her dad not know about her list? Maybe he shouldn't have mentioned it.

"I beg your pardon, sir, but it's a private list your daughter has. I imagine she'll be glad to tell you about it if you ask her, but if you don't mind, I'd rather not betray her trust about it."

The king dipped his chin in acceptance and his smile returned. "Well, first I'd like to thank you for your presentation to the Board of the Children's Trust. We have already begun making contacts in the community to review possible individuals who would be willing to mentor and train any of the children in our children's homes who are seeking trade work."

"That was fast."

The king's grin widened. "With great power comes expediency." He raised a brow. "Sometimes."

"I'm sure a great deal of children will benefit from that choice, sir."

"I believe you're right." The king relaxed back in his chair with a sigh. "But I'm certain you are curious as to why I asked to meet with you. I have a long acquaintance with Gordon and Nessa Frasier. They speak very highly of you, and Gordon praised your work ethic and quality."

"It's been a real pleasure working with Gordon." Luke had attempted to keep his posture straight, but now he noticed that the king had relaxed into his own chair just like a regular guy. So Luke followed suit. "He knows a lot about building, but even more than that, he loves his town and the North Country."

"Yes, he's advised Ellie and me on several conservation projects we've started within the last year." He folded his hands on his lap, appearing much more like a regular guy than what Luke knew he actually was, which added a whole different level of weirdness.

Sure, he'd welcomed Luke during dinner a few weeks ago and they'd engaged well, but now they sat in a study in the man's castle. Was he supposed to be more kingly here? Or could he really be this . . . semi-normal?

"He took me on a few drives into the forests you all have up there. Fantastic areas. Beautiful too."

"Yes, which is why I hope to create more wildlife reserves, but also capitalize on what we offer as a country to bring in more tourists and hopefully transplants." His smile flashed a little, the movement reminding him of Ellie. "Which is one of the reasons I invited you here. Gordon recommended you take a look at a few additional properties I am contemplating for renovation into holiday homes—one may even prove an excellent option for a hotel. But Gordon mentioned you'd worked in . . . what is it called in your country? Wildlife management?"

Air burst from Luke's lips like a cough. "Um, I worked in that a bit during college."

"Received a double major, I believe."

Luke blinked. "Yes, sir, wildlife management and accounting."

"Neither of which you use at the present time?"

Had the king run a background check on Luke or something? "I got out of accounting because it really wasn't what I wanted to do. I prefer being outdoors or working with my hands. The wildlife management degree was a way for me to study something in school that I liked while studying something my parents liked." He shrugged a shoulder. "The accounting smarts come in handy for running my own business and during tax season." He chuckled at his own joke, one that the king seemed to understand because he responded in kind. "But I saw that I could make more money in building than I could in wildlife management, so when I decided to start up my own business, building made the most sense."

"And how did you learn carpentry and stonemasonry?"

Was this the real reason the king had invited him? Work talk? Luke's whole body relaxed. "I had an uncle who mentored me from the time I was twelve. I even worked with him in college during the summer to earn some extra money."

"You're quite the jack-of-all-trades, aren't you?"

"Maybe if those trades are manual labor or more outdoorsy." Luke gestured toward the room. "But I'm not into diplomacy or political meetings or anything fancy enough to fit this place."

The king's grin spread wide. "My mother used to say that God gifts different people for different jobs so they can use their gifts to their fullest potential."

"I like that." He nodded.

"But He's not afraid to stretch us."

"No, sir. He's not." Luke's grin twitched. "I've learned a great deal by being here and seeing how things are done in building on this side of the pond versus my side. And I look forward to working on another renovation for Mr. Gray before I return home."

"Did you like Crieff?"

"Yes, sir. Small-town folks are small-town folks no matter where you go in the world."

"Indeed." The king's expression turned thoughtful. "I've learned to appreciate small-town virtues by marrying into the family I did. It was not my family's first choice, but it taught me the value of those who have lived lives very different than my upbringing."

"Which is why I think your people appreciate you so much, Your Majesty. Most folks value good-hearted genuineness and understanding."

"Yes." The king studied Luke again with an intensity that Luke wasn't quite sure how to handle, but he managed to keep from fidgeting or moving beneath the stare. "Would you ever have any interest in relocating? I could use someone with your experience, integrity, and knowledge to assist in a great many ways."

Luke's jaw slacked a little. Was King Aleksander offering Luke a job? His brain stopped working completely. A job from a king?

He could just see Penelope's head explode with confetti.

But a job? For him?

His brain started working again, piecing together what that meant. He could be with Ellie. And he'd live near Izzy.

He could learn new skills and enjoy the countryside here.

But it would also mean leaving his parents, selling his new and thriving business, embracing a life of paparazzi, ballrooms, suits, and—he groaned inwardly—dress shoes. He cared for Ellie, so much more than he imagined in such a short time, but his parents relied on him for help. Josephine did too. Living so far away meant they'd suffer from his absence.

And he'd even miss Penelope, which he'd never admit out loud, but it was enough to admit it in his head.

He drew in a breath and steadied his attention on the sovereign. "I can't tell you how honored I am that you would consider me worthy of a job in service of you and Skymar. Truly, I'm humbled by your faith in me and my skills."

"But?" The king held his gaze.

"I can't leave my parents to move here, sir. Or my business." He leaned forward. "Coming here for a few months to work is one thing. I'll be back home in a month or so to help with all the things they've been storing up for me, but relocating here, especially as my parents get older?" He sighed. "A good family is a precious thing in life and something I value a great deal. I don't know that I'm ready to make a move like that."

"I can understand that, Luke, and it only makes me respect you more." The king's expression softened. "But the offer stands, should you have a change of mind . . . or heart."

Luke held the king's gaze, not sure whether he was supposed to or not, but the king seemed to have a deeper intention behind his words. Surely he couldn't mean what Luke was a little afraid to believe he might mean.

"Thank you, sir."

"Now," the king said as he stood and Luke followed. "I would like to get your thoughts on a few of these properties Gordon and I have discussed, so let's move to the desk."

The king called in his secretary, who took notes while Luke offered suggestions on a few of the sites the king presented, all the while fighting an inward battle over whether he'd made the right decision about the job offer . . . and whether he even *could* choose differently.

And all at once he realized his dilemma matched Ellie's exactly, except on a smaller scale. Family expectations versus the heart.

And for better or worse, they both chose the former.

For all the right reasons.

And broken hearts healed.

Eventually.

CHAPTER 18

Ellie paused before her father's office door. He'd called her a few days ago to ask her to join him at Carlstern, but she needed to finish a few meetings in Mara as well as the final updates to her own study at the cottage, so several days had passed.

Perhaps she'd wanted the distance too.

Her last conversation with her parents had been a study in their trying to contain their disappointment, along with a clear message that her reputation couldn't weather any hint of scandal at present.

Give her another year, and she'd have shown her new track record.

But before she'd even been officially reinstated as a working royal? Not the right time.

Father clearly respected Luke, which softened him to her situation, but Mother held to her pensiveness and long-held expectations that the royal family should come first. Of course it should. It was a choice Ellie made, even as her heart pulled toward picking up her mobile and texting Luke again. Her parents had made it clear that her future should focus on finding a man who understood their culture and history, who could bring a love for the country into their marriage. A Skymarian.

And Mother pushed against finding a spouse among the commoners, in contrast to her own past. All the expectations, failures, and embarrassments she'd had to overcome to finally find her place among the royals had stiffened her resolve not only to keep as far above reproach as possible but also to try to protect her children from the long years of adjusting to a life so different from her childhood.

Perhaps over time, as Ellie proved herself, Mother would soften to a broader array of romantic choices instead of a narrow wish list of candidates from the aristocracy. If not, Ellie might have to choose never to marry at all. An ache branched through her chest.

But, oh, how she wanted a family.

After spending so much time at Cambric Hall with those children, the desire to build her own home and family settled deeper. Images of Luke flipped through her mind like a movie montage of his good-natured teasing of the workers, his focus on his craft, his easy laugh and patience in teaching the boys, the way he focused on her when she spoke and found ways to show he cared. Her eyes drifted closed. The feel of his arms, his kiss. The rough patches of his hands as they caressed her cheeks.

Warmth pooled beneath her lashes, threatening to turn into another session of silent crying, but she had to stop.

Move forward.

She'd made her choice, and so had he.

She drew in a breath and dashed the tears away, righting herself before giving the door a quick knock.

At her father's summons, she entered. He sat behind his desk, poring over some papers, a familiar silhouette. His smile brightened his eyes as she entered, and he stood, gesturing her forward. With a brief kiss to each cheek, he moved with her to one of his couches, settling himself down beside her.

"How was all your business up north?"

She rested against his shoulder, welcoming his affection, especially after her weak moment just outside the office door. "Very good. It seems none of the current publicity has hurt any of my connections in the North Country or Mara, and I adored getting to watch the new football team of Kae defeat Hartington."

"Now, now, be nice, my dear. Your uncle is quite proud of his footballing days at Hartington."

Ellie chuckled, releasing a long sigh at the comfort of being with her da.

"I saw your numbers from the Board Luncheon. Dozens of new donors," Father said. "You've doubled the giving from last year."

"Lots of hard work and good people," she said. "I've loved getting to know them and show them what we can all do together for our communities. It feels right and good."

Father nodded. "You're stepping into what you're meant to do, my girl."

"The more I spend time there, the more I want to know about these places for which I am patron. And I think it would be good to become more acquainted with their histories. Knowing where someone or something has come from can make a difference in planning for its future."

"Very well said." He nodded, bestowing on her one of his proud looks.

"It would explain why I feel such a connection to that part of Skymar, I think." She smiled. "That and this journal I found at Cambric."

"A journal?"

She pulled it from her bag, glad to have the opportunity to show it to her father. "It was written by a scullery maid who had been an orphan and later took up employment there."

Father took the book and opened to the first page where the owner's name was scrawled across the front.

"Blair MacKee." His gaze rose to hers. "Dear girl, I believe this may be linked to the MacKees who own one of the largest textile businesses on the island and provide some of the greatest charitable donations to many places across Skymar, including Cambric."

Ellie relaxed back against the couch, shaking her head. "Uncle Roth married into that family?"

"Aye." Father grinned, offering her back the book. "'Tis not wise to disregard the power and influence of small beginnings to make the greatest changes, is it?"

She raised the book. "It's a simple, beautiful story about a sweet yet powerful romance that shows how the right person makes us stronger and braver and more hopeful. No matter their origin. In fact, sometimes what we need most comes in the most unexpected ways, and I think that includes royalty too."

"Aye." He studied her. "I can't imagine life without your mother. And I know she's been harder on you throughout all of this, but it's because she's trying to ease the hurt she experienced coming into this way of life. Pairing yourself with someone who understands our world makes it easier on the both of you."

"But sometimes the easiest way isn't the best."

Her father chuckled. "Well said again. Most of the time, it's not." She basked in another of his tender looks and then he nodded. "You are doing so well, Ellie, despite the recent situation. You are on your feet and I have every faith in you."

"I appreciate your confidence in me, but I need to know that you and Mother will continue to trust me, even when unfortunate headlines appear. I was not capable of making good choices three years ago, but because of your love for me and the support of this family, I am not who I was."

His eyes narrowed. "And I suppose part of this stems from the desire to make your own choices in partners without our interference?"

"I want your opinions because I know you have my best interest at heart, but it is also *my* future. I'm not under the same microscope or expectations as Stellan or even Rosalyn as the Crown Prince and Princess Royal. My path can remain more to the shadows, as I would wish it. And over the past months, I've come to realize I *am* capable of making my own choices, both publicly and privately."

Father winced in a good-natured way and then dipped his chin. "You are right. It is your life, and your mother and I have seen you step into a confidence you've never had."

"Thank you." A sudden weight lifted from her shoulders.

He raised a brow and then sighed. "Speaking of lists and a certain American carpenter . . ."

She'd not said anything about Luke!

Her father stood from the couch and stepped over to his desk, gesturing for Ellie to follow. "Luke left a gift for you when he met with me Saturday."

"You met with him?" Ellie moved to her father's side as he reached for a rectangular gift box on the shelf behind his desk. "Was it about the photograph?"

"No, no." He waved her words away. "He's the good sort—both Cameron and Gordon Frasier say so, as well as the staff at Cambric. No, I wanted to discuss some other building sites with him." Her father turned toward her, offering the gift. "But he brought this and asked me to deliver it to you when next I saw you."

She searched her father's face for a clue to the contents, but he merely shook his head with a shrug. With careful hands, she placed the box down on the desk, the pale blue bow atop lined with gold to complement the color of the box. It was an unusual shape. A little longer than a boot box. Narrower as well.

With a grip to the sides of the lid, she slowly lifted the top. Inside waited a . . .

What was it? It took a few seconds to scan the words and make out the gift.

A fishing rod?

A laugh escaped her and she slid her fingers over the box, her shoulders shaking as she looked up at her father. "He bought me a fishing rod."

"Not the usual romantic gift and, you are well aware, we have great stores of fishing rods handed down from my father, so I feel there is a special story behind this one." Her father's brows rose expectantly.

She rested her hip against his desk and smiled down at the gift.

Loyally, Luke

How on earth a fishing rod proved one of the most romantic gifts in her life, she couldn't exactly explain, but somewhere during this more candid conversation with her father, and sharing with him how she'd found and connected with the journal of a cherished love story, she decided perhaps Maeve had been right.

"I'd like to hear the reason behind the gift, my dear girl. If you're willing to share."

Ellie met her father's gaze—her wish list fresh in her mind as she cradled Luke's gift in her arms. She nodded and returned with her father to the couch.

If she could spend one more day with Luke Edgewood, she would find a way to do it. And since she had to be back in Crieff in two days for the Donors' Banquet, she knew exactly what she would do.

Pete was a great guy, but on the weekends he spent either at home in Scotland or with friends in New Inswythe, Luke always seemed to sleep a little better. The night sounds didn't have to compete with Pete's sleep talking or late-night gaming.

The scent of fresh coffee and a wood-burning fire warmed the air, giving the day a little brighter outlook than the previous one. He only had a few open shelves to hang before giving the cabin a quick check, and then, after the banquet tonight, he could leave in the morning for Skern.

He poured some coffee and walked to the new sitting room to stare out over the view. But before he flew back to the States, he'd return to Crieff to visit Cambric Hall and the Frasiers. Take those moments while he could, at least.

The sun barely rose above the distant mountains, its light filtered through a view of low-lying clouds. Darker ones hovered in the far distance and the weather app hinted at cooler temps for the afternoon and evening. Nothing frigid, especially for this part of the world, but below freezing.

He'd checked the news, and even some of the meteorologists weren't too happy about the longer-lasting cold temperatures. "The coldest May in thirty years."

Luke grinned. Just to his liking.

Down below, the lake showcased a patchwork of frozen and thawed spots thanks to the warmer weather of last week, but these mountains didn't let go of winter very easily. Kind of like home, only the North Country's grip held much tighter than the Blue Ridge Mountains'.

The sound of a car door closing pulled his attention back toward the front of the house where the front door stood. He glanced down at his phone—7:00 a.m.? Who would be up here at this hour? He peered out the side window only to see a gray car leaving down the gravel drive and back through the forest.

The car looked vaguely familiar.

Strange.

And then a knock sounded at the door.

Luke froze.

The knock came again.

With slow steps, he set his cup down on the kitchen counter and approached the door, his body on alert. Contemplating the type of individual who would unexpectedly visit a secluded cabin an easy half hour away from town left him wary.

Running a hand through his morning hair and unbolting the lock, he pulled the door open to find the last person he imagined seeing, especially at the cabin.

Princess Elliana St. Clare.

He blinked a few times, trying to make sure his eyes worked.

"Good morning."

Well, his ears heard her voice and his eyes saw her beautiful face, and she looked especially nice wearing a blue puffer jacket and matching toboggan. Made the color of her eyes deeper.

But she wasn't supposed to be here. Had he hit his head in the shower this morning?

"I . . . I know it's early."

He nodded, comprehension dawning by degrees.

"But I brought scones and cream from Bree's." She held up a white paper bag.

He slowly moved his attention from the bag back to her face, thoughts coming much too slowly. He needed another sip—or cup—of coffee to take all this in at an adult rate.

"But since I have to be in Crieff tonight for the banquet, I thought . . . well, I thought we could mark off some more things from my list, as you'd suggested a few weeks ago."

His gaze dropped to the box beneath her arm, the gift box he'd left with her father. She hadn't even taken it out of the box yet?

He flipped his focus back to her face, still trying to figure out if he'd really woken up yet. He'd spent the good part of a week trying to reconcile himself with the fact that they weren't going to have any more sweet moments.

"You always said you were an early riser, and I thought if I showed up early, it would give us more time together." Her gaze searched his. "Because everything ends tonight. Us being at Cambric Hall and . . . you being here."

She wanted to spend this last day together? The two of them? Alone?

The reality of the situation finally sank in and he sent a look toward the neighboring woods. Maybe there should be a more responsible adult available, because being alone with her . . . sounded wonderfully dangerous. "Ellie, are you sure this is a good idea for you? I don't want anything to happen where you get hurt or you think I've not respected your—"

"Luke, you can say no. Of course." She offered a wobbly grin. "But then you'll have to drive me down to the Frasiers' because Nessa's left me here with you."

He stared back toward the narrow road through the woods. It was Nessa's car!

"I've made this choice and take full responsibility for it, but only if you are amenable." Various expressions made a small wrestling contest across her face, almost like she was trying to figure out which emotion to embrace. "There are a lot of things I missed in life, and I know I'll miss more in the future." She held his attention. "But we have now, and I don't want to miss this last day with you, because I would rather have a memory than only have the wish of one."

Everything in him softened and he gave his head a shake, pushing the door back fully and ushering her inside. "Who all knows you're here?"

"Gordon and Nessa, of course." She pulled off her toboggan and her hair curled in various directions, almost inspiring his grin. "If Father can't find me, he'll probably have an excellent idea where to look. And, of course, Maeve."

"Your best friend who likes my shoulders?"

She paused in removing her jacket to offer him an impish smile. And he nearly lost his train of thought. "You do have very nice shoulders."

Maybe he *should* wish Pete were here.

But he didn't.

"What about Cameron?" He assisted her with the jacket removal, and daggone it if she hadn't worn a baggy, soft green sweater and black leggings with some sort of fuzzy boots. Thoughts of snuggling her close by a fire started jumping around in his head.

He tried to squelch them.

Those thoughts tended to slide right into a rascally direction awful quick. And being alone with her in a remote cabin by a cozy fire tempted all sorts of those.

"He thinks I'm with Nessa and Gordon." She squinted up at him. "I failed to correct his assumption, so he plans to collect me from there to escort me to the banquet this evening."

He stared at her as he went to hang her coat on a hook by the door, and completely missed the hook. Stupid brain. "So . . . we really do have the whole day."

She held his gaze. "Yeah, we do."

His grin rushed onto his face so fast, he didn't have time to catch it. "All right then. Let's make a few memories, Princess."

"Thank you, Luke." Pink crept into her cheeks and she looked away, lowering the bag of scones and the gift onto the nearby counter. "I also want to thank you for my gift. It left my father somewhat befuddled at first, but after I explained the reason, well, I don't know. He seemed touched and pensive about it all. I don't think he realized how much the past truly impacted me."

"I'm sure he wishes you'd have told him your hurts a long time ago."

"Yes." She sighed. "But I don't plan to keep those sorts of things from my parents anymore. I just felt as if . . . well, with my mother, I've always felt as if the privileges of my station warranted no complaints. She made so many missteps along the way to finding her place among the royals, small things which I feel seemed much larger to her than they actually were, and then she had to bear the brunt of some harsh media opinions about Father's choice of a commoner bride. I think all those difficulties, the hurtful press, and the struggle to constantly prove herself permeated the way she parented us."

"She didn't want you to have to struggle the same way." He nodded. "Sounds about right for a parent."

"And, as an imperfect creature, she may not have always enacted those desires in the best ways."

He folded his arms across his chest and studied her. She sure was beautiful with all that long hair and those big eyes and her pretty lips. But more than that, she glowed with an inner determination to do

good. It was real hard not to like her a whole lot. Even if she was a princess. "So it's a bit early to go fishing just yet. Have you had breakfast?"

"I brought breakfast." She grabbed the bag and shook it in front
of him.

"Scones and cream?"

"Yes."

"No." He gave his head a slow shake and heaved a sigh. "Scones
and cream are a side to breakfast. If there's no meat involved, it can't
count as breakfast."

Her smile flared. "Is that so?"

"It's the rule where I'm from, so it's the rule in this cabin." He
waved toward the room. "Why don't you take a look around and I'll
cook us up some real breakfast to go with your fancy muffins."

"Scones." She sent him a mock glare. "I smell coffee. Would there
be enough to share?"

"There's always coffee to share." He nodded toward the coffeepot.
"And lucky for you, Pete likes to drink perfume too, so we have all
that frou-frou stuff in the fridge for you to contaminate your coffee
to your heart's delight."

The cabin looked even better in person than the photos Luke had
shown her. In the new mantel, he'd carved delicate shapes of mountains across the top, the design matching the two paintings she'd
encouraged him to purchase and place on either side of the fireplace.

The little tips she'd mentioned to him at his request had come
to life. He'd taken every suggestion, as if her ideas mattered enough to
place faith in them.

In her.

The views proved some of the best she'd seen in the Crieff area, but
Cairn Haar was one of the tallest mountains in the North Country,

so almost anywhere gave a stunning vista. Well, likely a much better vista when the clouds weren't rolling in from the east.

Her coffee mug warmed her palms as she toured the three bedrooms, one used as an office and living space. A loft offered additional sleeping areas and showcased a little more of Luke's handiwork with some built-in bookcases.

"I don't know what type of fishing we'll have since it's so cold out," Luke announced from the kitchen as she made her way down the winding wooden staircase.

She sidled into the kitchen and rested a hip against the counter, watching him work. He looked great in those black slacks at the luncheon, but sweatpants fit him just fine too. She took another sip of her coffee and ogled like one of the greatest oglers on the planet.

He turned, plate in one hand and bowl in the other, with a towel tossed over his shoulder. "But if we can get the lines deep enough, we may catch some luck."

Her brain said, *"You are one of the hottest men I've ever seen."* However, her lips said, "Thank you so much for the gift. I can't wait to use it."

His grin broadened and he gestured with the plate toward the two barstools at the counter. "I'm glad you like it. Probably not what most girls want, but it seemed to fit . . . you and me."

She slid down on the stool. "You're right, but I'm not sure how."

He chuckled and placed the items before them on the counter, then took the spot beside her. As she'd expected from their previous meals together, he offered to say "grace," as he called it. At her nod, and without ceremony, he wrapped his big hand over hers on the counter and offered a sweet, simple prayer of thanksgiving.

He ended by asking God to bless Ellie's future and her hard work, so that others would be encouraged and helped by her innovative thinking and kindness.

She looked over at him while he finished the prayer, emotions growing so large within her, she thought they may burst her heart wide open. After all her failings and stupid mistakes, she'd learned to rely on the faith of her childhood in a way she'd never understood before her prodigal life, but to catch a glimpse of what life could look like from a man who understood that faith—and the very sweetness of such a love—it humbled her and renewed the ache of their impending goodbyes.

She pushed the thought away. *Do not ruin this memory by thinking too far ahead. Just enjoy being with him.*

"You really are such a good man, Luke Edgewood."

He looked over at her, those deep brown eyes examining her face. "And you're a good woman, Ellie St. Clare."

She drew truth from his words and his gaze. If he saw the best in her, even when he knew so much of her past, then maybe the one most holding her back was . . . herself.

They delved into their breakfast, her praising his work on the cabin and him accepting with a simple nod and turning the conversation by asking about her siblings. She responded in kind, learning more about Izzy and Penelope, the siblings closest to him emotionally, and then Josephine, the eldest, who was the mother of his niece and nephew.

At one point, when she started sharing some stories from her college experience, Luke's attention dropped to her lips. Her words slid to a stop at the intensity in his gaze. Would he kiss her? She certainly wouldn't mind.

"You have some cream on your cheek." He gestured toward his own mouth. "Right there."

"Ah." She released a nervous laugh. Of course he wasn't thinking of kissing her. Silly. The man knew they had to part ways—why would he want to add more kissing to the complexity of things? She took a serviette and wiped at her face.

He shook his head. "No, up a bit."

Her grin quivered. "You could just complete the entire Hallmark moment and remove it yourself."

He searched her eyes and then leaned close, snatching her breath as he did. "Ellie, if we were in a serious dating relationship, I'd find a way to remove that cream in a much more enjoyable way than *any* movie."

Her jaw loosed and heat rushed from her shoulders all the way up to her scalp. With a little hitch in her breath, she shakily recovered. "I would dare you to make good on that plan, Luke Edgewood, but I'm not certain I would recover."

His attention dropped to her lips again, his body shifting a little closer as if he wanted to make the scene in their heads a reality, but then he rocked back and drew in a breath. "Maybe we ought to try some of that fishing." His gaze moved back to her lips, and then he gave his head a shake and pushed back from the counter. "The cold air might do us both good."

"You're probably right." She took another bite of the scone just to have something else to do besides breach the gap between them.

"I'm gonna go back here and change into something warmer, then we can put together that rod of yours, stoke up the fire, and make the walk down to the lake."

"Mm-hmm," she murmured, taking another bite to keep from saying anything about stoking fires and kisses in a cabin. She pushed down a hard swallow. "I'll . . . I'll clean up."

He narrowed his eyes at her, creating more distance, maybe for the same reasons she kept taking too-large bites of the scone. "Princesses know how to do that kind of stuff?"

She nearly choked. "What?" She reached for the nearby hand cloth to throw at him, but he disappeared down the hall, leaving a wink in his wake.

Almost two hours later, they came to the lake after walking down the hillside from the cabin. Ellie looked back behind them, the porch of the cabin visible above the tree line and promising a leg-aching climb to return, but she didn't care.

She'd already enjoyed herself more in the past few hours with Luke, doing simple things like eating breakfast, putting a fishing rod together, and having excellent conversations, than she had all week doing other things. She'd take what she could get and hold on to the sweetness as long as possible.

A few times during their walk, the hairs on the back of her neck rose as if someone watched her. In her world, the paranoia of the paparazzi permeated private or secluded experiences, especially with her history, but the surrounding forest gave no hint of anyone except her, Luke, and the pervading wildlife.

She pulled her jacket more tightly around her and tucked her hat more closely around her ears. Luke walked with his jean jacket open to reveal a layered flannel shirt and undershirt, as if the air bounced off his body like bullets. The thought sent her right back into ogling like a fool. He turned to offer his hand as they stepped close to the lake's edge, his gaze catching hers.

"What?"

"I can't believe you're not freezing. Your ball cap isn't even covering your ears."

His brows crashed together. "I wore my jacket."

"But I think the temperature is dropping even since we left the house." She shook her head. "And here I am covered from toes to head like some snow monster."

"You're not a monster. Maybe more like a snow . . . bunny?"

"Bunny?" She laughed and took his hand, allowing the touch a special place in her mind. So secure. Strong yet gentle, just like the man himself. He paused at the edge of the icy water. "Okay, there are a few larger places where the ice has thawed and we can cast your line in that direction." He gestured out to the deeper part of the lake where the water shone in parts surrounded by the ice.

"Let's practice a few casts first, all right?"

She'd watched a few clips online to get an idea of what to do while fishing, but when he came up behind her and covered her arm with his, she forgot everything she'd viewed. One of his hands rested on her waist and the other guided the arm that held the rod.

She pressed back into him, his beard tickling her ear.

"I don't think you're paying attention, Princess."

"Oh, I'm paying attention, just not to the casting lesson."

"All right." He drew out the word so long she got a whiff of the peppermint on his breath from brushing his teeth. "We just need to get this out of the way." Without hesitation, he spun her around to face him, and giving her only a second to prepare herself, he pulled her forward and caught her gasp with his mouth. He caressed her lips with his own as one of his palms cradled her face and the other pressed against her back. She nearly dropped the fishing rod, but managed to hold it aloft while gripping his jean jacket with her free hand.

All the tension from the morning, and the ache from the past week, burst through her, finding some sort of sweet balm in his touch. His fingers took a little detour over her ears and into her hair, moving to hold the back of her head as they kept enjoying making a belter of a memory.

She pulled back but kept her hold on his jacket.

"Your kiss is dangerous, Mr. Edgewood." Her breath came shallow, gaze roaming from his lips back to his eyes. "Not at all like one of the good guys."

"You need more practice then, Princess." His hand tightened on her back, tugging her back toward him. "All good guys have a little bit of rogue for the right woman."

He kissed her again, thoroughly taking her breath away and leaving her warm from the forehead down. Heaven and earth, she'd never been kissed like this . . . but those kisses had all been from the wrong men.

He drew back this time and put her at arm's length. "Now let's focus on fishing."

She narrowed her eyes at him. "You know, you could have done that a lot earlier and saved us both the extra agony."

He narrowed his eyes back at her. "It's less likely to cause us as much trouble while we're out here in freezing temperatures as it would in that nice cozy cabin, Princess."

She cringed a little, half at the truth of his statement and half at the fact of how much she wanted to head right back up to the cozy cabin and practice a little less self-control than she ought.

Thankfully, the past three years had given her a better perspective and longer-term goal than she'd had before. The right man was worth the wait.

She paused on the thought. And maybe, whether in months or years, she and Luke could find a way to be together?

"Well, good news. I'm feeling much warmer now."

He dipped his head as if bowing. "Glad to be of assistance, my lady."

"Oh, stop!" She waved him away and returned her attention to the rod. "All right, let's do this and then return to the cozy cabin."

After a few tries, the cast landed in a large open spot of the lake. The quiet of the day should have calmed her, but the sense of being watched resurfaced again and again. She didn't want to mention it to Luke and appear paranoid. He seemed oblivious to any such disturbance.

They'd been waiting for one bite from a fish when she spotted the first snowflake. Nothing too concerning, as snow stayed in the higher elevations as late as mid-May during some years. But the added chill started to deepen her concern.

She glanced up at the sky. Those dark clouds from earlier crowded overhead and moved much more quickly than usual. As if to make a point, the breeze picked up, misting her face with snow and dampness.

"I think we might want to head back to the cabin." Luke studied the sky. "Maybe you can try again another day."

"I think you're right. Let me just reel it in."

She shifted closer to the edge, looking out toward the nearest bank, something green moving into view. Green?

Her line jerked just then, and she turned to Luke. "I . . . I think I have something."

"Well, don't just stand there with that pretty mouth of yours hanging open." He grinned. "Reel it in."

"But . . . but will you record it so I can show Father?" The line jerked with such force she stumbled a step forward. "And have it for my own memories."

"Sure." He looked over at her, as if waiting for direction. "With my phone or yours?"

"I can't give you my phone right now or I'm afraid I'll lose hold of the rod."

"All right, I got it." He pulled his phone from his pocket and stepped back to capture a better view, she supposed.

Ellie shot him a grin, turned back to the task at hand, and began reeling in the fish. It tugged and pulled, and she tried to dig her feet into the damp ground but couldn't get a steady footing.

The green came back into view and then . . . was that a flash?

A camera flash.

She looked up and caught sight of a man in a green hat and coat poised just across from them on the narrower portion of the lake, but in the distraction of the moment, several things happened at once. The fish pulled her forward while another flash caused her to turn back in his direction, making her feet slip forward from the wet, grassy embankment onto the ice.

A horrible noise groaned beneath her feet, and she knew what would follow. In synchrony, she released the rod and turned toward Luke, making eye contact with him just before the ice gave way beneath her with a loud *crack*.

With a scream and a flailing of arms, she was swallowed by the frigid lake water.

CHAPTER 19

Getting the kisses out of the way hadn't helped Luke's rascally thoughts as much as he'd hoped. In fact, even looking at Ellie through a phone screen made him want to kiss her breathless a few hundred more times.

And maybe the heat of those kisses distracted him from paying better attention to the weather. In fact, from the time she'd shown up on his doorstep to now, his brain hadn't been working its best, despite the fact that he'd had three cups of coffee. And with the desire to cuddle up with her on the couch and kiss her until they both forgot about tomorrow, getting out into the cold seemed a good idea.

Until now.

But the grin on her face as she began reeling in the catch made his mental instability and the unpredictability of the weather worth every moment.

The kiss probably helped too.

Lord, help him. No wonder men in stories went around kissing princesses!

Ellie stumbled from the effort to reel in the fish, likely from lack of experience paired with the damp ground, becoming a little wetter with each second.

Flurries floated around her, framing in the moment, and he smiled. Maybe he couldn't be with her, but knowing he'd given her these few memories helped ease a little of the pain in his chest.

A little.

She jerked again, but this time, her smile disappeared. Was she even looking in the direction of the fish? What was she doing? He followed her line of sight with the camera but didn't see anything, and then he turned back to her when she tripped forward onto the ice.

A sickening sound groaned beneath her feet and she looked up at him, eyes wide. His blood ran cold just before the ice gave way and she went down, the water catching her scream.

Luke shoved the phone in his pocket and rushed forward, sliding to his stomach as he neared the hole where she disappeared. She resurfaced.

"Can you swim?" he called, stretching out for her, but she was just out of reach.

"Not in winter wear," she shot back, her hat gone. At least her humor was intact. That was a good sign. "I . . . I can't get a hold." She grappled for a grasp on something, only to slip back under.

She reemerged, taking in another breath, reaching for his hands. "I . . . I lost the fishing rod."

The fishing rod? Crazy woman! "Fishing rods are a dime a dozen. Princesses aren't." He almost caught her fingers, but they slipped through his hold and she went beneath the surface again.

She couldn't maintain this, not with her soaked clothes weighing her down and the chill of the water slowing her movements. He slid a little farther out, shoulders on the ice but the rest of him on solid ground. Having both of them in the water wouldn't save anybody, but he wasn't going to let her drown.

She didn't emerge as quickly this time and he couldn't see her. He edged a little closer. "Come on back up to me, Ellie!"

Blonde hair swirled into view just before she broke through the water again, and this time he grabbed a flailing arm. With a strong tug, he drew her close enough to take her other arm. The ice creaked beneath them, so with another heave, he rolled to the side, bringing her with them and landing them both on dry ground.

Her body shivered against him, trembling like a leaf in a

windstorm. The snow came thicker and the wind began to gust, bending the trees. What on earth was happening?

"It's . . . it's . . . a snow feirge." He helped her to a stand. "Squall? Is th-that the English word?"

"I know what *squall* means, but I don't know what *feirge* means." He pulled off his jean jacket.

"Fury. Appropriate for a sudden and unexpected sno—" Her attention shifted to his fingers as he unbuttoned his flannel shirt. "Wh-what are you doing?"

"You need to get dry." He kept unbuttoning. "This shirt is dryer than my jacket, so we're going to start with this until we can get you to the cabin."

"All right." She pulled off her drenched jacket and he slipped the flannel around her, followed by his jean jacket.

"Let's walk to get your body warm from the inside, okay?" He placed an arm around her shoulder and guided her forward, rubbing his hand against her arm as they walked. "We'll go as slow as you need, but we need to get to the cabin, Ellie."

She nodded and then whimpered, turning to him. "S-someone was out there, Luke. H-he distracted me and . . . I . . . fell."

He turned her back around, moving a bit faster at the sight of her pale lips. "Somebody? What do you mean?" She hadn't been in the water long, so delirium from hypothermia shouldn't have set in yet. And if he could get her out of the cold, she may not have to worry about it at all. His gaze flipped to the cabin on the ridge.

It was a good thirty-minute walk. Snow swirled and the wind picked up as if challenging him.

"A . . . a reporter. I think. I saw a flash."

Luke looked across the lake, scanning the area, but the snow blew heavier, and whoever had been there easily could have hidden within the low visibility and forest at this point.

"I'd say whoever it was is going to have a doozy of a time getting any photos out to the world right now." He rubbed his hands down her arms to add friction.

Her hair fell in damp ringlets around her head, likely only adding to her chill. The knot in his stomach unbraided a little with a good dose of gratitude. It could have been worse. Much worse.

"Well, at least I'll still be able to attend the banquet, even if I look like an ice cream cone."

"No worries, Princess." He cooed the words, taking another glance behind them. "We'll get you up to the cabin and dried off in plenty of time to make the banquet. We just need to get you out of this cold as soon as we can, so let's walk a little faster, if you're able."

She shivered, but he had to get her out of the wind. He pulled her close, trying to push his body heat into her side, and increased their pace a little more. "I have to say, Princess, you're awfully good at being efficient, aren't you?"

"Efficient?" She looked over at him, her eyes even brighter when framed by her pale face.

"You can check off fishing and swimming in a lake from your list all at the same time."

Her laugh shook from her. "Nice." She shuddered. "I guess we shouldn't add s-sleeping under the s-stars for tonight? Might be a bad idea."

He glanced up at the sky, another gust of wind barreling through the forest with such force, the trees creaked their displeasure. He pulled Ellie as close as possible, attempting to shield her as best he could. "I doubt we'd get to see them anyway."

"How . . . how did he know where to find me? How do they always know?" Her voice broke a little and he shook his head. The last thing she needed was tears making her face even colder.

"Come on now, Ellie. What do you think he captured?" He urged her forward, each step a little faster. "Those amazing kisses or your poor princess-on-ice moves?"

Her smile failed to respond. "I don't know." Her gaze met his. "But I don't regret the kisses."

"I'm glad, because I sure don't."

She squeezed her eyes closed, her jaw tightening with another tremble. "I don't want to think about the possibilities of him being here, Luke, so I'm not."

"Good call. Let's think about a nice warm fire and how many social rules I'll break at the banquet tonight."

All the way up the hill, he kept her talking, paying attention to her speech, her clarity, looking for any signs of second-stage hypothermia. Near the last leg of the climb, she misspoke a few words and then slipped on the soft layer of snow beneath them, so he took the opportunity to catch her in his arms and carry her the rest of the way.

Despite her weak protests to set her down, he marched through the house to his room and placed her feet down on the floor. She nearly collapsed from shaking.

"You need to get out of those clothes." Under any other circumstances, the company and that sentence would have set his whole body on fire, but right now, concern eclipsed wishful thinking for his future.

He pulled open a drawer and tossed a pair of drawstring sweats on the bed. "Put these on quick, okay, Ellie?"

She nodded.

He tossed a long sweatshirt next to the pants. "I'm going into the kitchen to get you something warm to drink and eat. As soon as you're dressed, join me, all right? We need to get you burning calories, as well as warm."

She slid his jacket and flannel shirt from her shoulders, stumbling down on the bed.

"Ellie."

His voice jerked her attention to his face.

"No going to sleep, you understand?"

She blinked up at him. "I understand."

"If you're not in the kitchen in five minutes, I'm coming back in here after you." His throat constricted at the idea of finding her in some sort of state of undress in his bed. He shook the image clear. Mostly.

"Is that supposed to be a threat?"

Why did she have to go and get all sultry voiced and delirious right now? "How 'bout I promise to snuggle with you by the fire if you hurry up and"—he waved toward the clothes—"change."

She rewarded—or tortured—him with a sleepy smile. He closed the door and nearly dashed to the kitchen to put distance between them, brewing another pot of coffee and warming up some leftover potato soup. Just as he added a few logs to the fire, the lights flickered.

At least the soup was warm and they had the fireplace for heat in case . . .

And off went the power completely.

He sighed. How long did snow furies last?

Well, once Ellie was fit to travel, he'd load them up in the car and drive to the Frasiers'. Likely, the weather at the bottom of the mountain proved better than the top.

"What happened t-to the lights?"

He turned to find Ellie standing in the doorway to his bedroom, looking much better in his clothes than he ever did.

"Looks like we've lost power for a bit." He moved to the couch and picked up a large blanket. "Come on over and get wrapped up. I'll bring you some soup."

She obeyed and he tucked the blanket in around her, then brought her the soup.

She shook while she ate a few bites. "Th-that helps." She looked up at him as he replaced the bowl with a cup of coffee. "You're better than any servant at the castle."

"Aww, you're just saying that because you're delirious."

She chuckled and took a sip of the coffee. "And you even per-fumed up my c-coffee?" Her smile quivered. "Hidden talents?"

"Desperate times." He took the cup from her and placed it on the side table. "I couldn't let you die from drinking my petrol after you'd survived freezing to death."

"Your charm and valor know no bounds."

Yeah, she just needed a little time. She'd be okay. His grin broad-ened as he stared down at her. Better than okay. "Don't get any fancy ideas about me. I'm a plain and simple kind of guy."

She shook her head and shuddered again. "Not true." Her gaze held his. "You're not simple, and you are certainly not plain."

He almost breached the gap between them to kiss her again, but if that started up, it may be a long time coming to a stop. And he needed to make sure she was perfectly fine. "Stop trying to flatter me and take a few more bites of that soup." He stepped back. "I'm going to change into warm clothes so both of us don't end up teeth-chattering together."

Within minutes he was back and knew exactly what do to do next. With her body still trembling and her skin still cold, he took the bowl from her, pulled back the blanket, tugged her against his warmth, and cocooned them up together.

"Oh my goodness, you're so wonderfully warm." She nestled in close, her damp hair pressing in against his chin, the coolness of her skin still evident even through their dry clothes. Not cold, though, so that was definitely progress.

He tightened his arms around her as her body shuddered into his, but the shivering was subsiding.

"I think I'll just st-stay here the rest of the day." She yawned. "Or the rest of my life."

"Well, that sounds nice to me too, but I think we both have an engagement to make this evening, so we'll have to take a rain check on the rest-of-our-lives scenario."

And the rest of their lives wasn't an option.

A truth neither needed to voice. He certainly didn't want to break the sweetness of the moment by doing so.

She burrowed her face into his shoulder. "Can we just rest a little while before we have to think about what's happening outside this cabin?"

"Sure, Ellie. We have another hour or so before we need to get you down the mountain." He ran a hand over her hair, tucking the blanket back close.

"I love moments like this," she whispered, her breath warming his neck.

"Falling in a frozen lake and nearly freezing to death gives you a high, does it?"

She chuckled and then sighed. "I meant moments with you. Everything feels s-so safe and real."

The fire flickered in the dim room as the wind howled just beyond the walls. He kept her talking a little longer, until he felt sure she was beyond harm, and then allowed her to fall asleep against him.

In a perfect world, he knew the next steps.

Be with her. For as long as she'd have him.

But they didn't live in a perfect world.

And no matter how charming she thought him, Luke wasn't a prince.

⌕

A buzzing sound pulled Luke awake. He blinked the room into view. A weight on his shoulder turned his attention to find his dream turned into a reality. Princess Elliana St. Clare lay beautifully asleep against him, her hair falling in tangled curls around her face.

All dry.

He touched a hand to her cheek, all warm and pink.

Loyally, Luke

No wonder a guy would feel compelled to kiss a sleeping princess, especially if they looked anything like her.

And he didn't even cringe at the thought as it invaded his brain. He kind of liked it.

The buzzing happened again, and he looked over at the side table where his phone lay. A series of texts lit the screen. Careful to keep his movements to a minimum so as not to wake Ellie, he reached for the phone.

Five unread messages?

From Gordon?

> **Gordon:** You can't go runnin' off with a princess, lad. Nessa's been trying to contact Ellie for the past hour with no response.

Luke looked up at the window. Pale light shone a later hour than he expected. How long had he slept? He checked his phone and pinched his eyes closed. He should have had Ellie on the way to Crieff a half hour ago.

He read down the other messages.

> **Gordon:** We can't get to you. Trees are down all over the mountain.

Luke shifted a little and sent a text.

> **Luke:** I'm just seeing this, Gordon. Sorry. A situation happened that I'll explain later. What do you need me to do?
>
> **Gordon:** There you are, lad. Are you and the princess all right?
>
> **Luke:** We are, but the cabin's power is out. We're safe and warm otherwise, though.
>
> **Gordon:** I'll let Cam know. He's a wee bit furious at us for

taking her up the mountain, but he'll be happy to hear
you're all fine.

Ellie stirred at his side and her eyelids fluttered . . . and he forgot what he was going to text next.

"Hey." She pushed her hair back from her face.

"Hey," he murmured, watching the way all those curls fell right back into place.

"You make a really nice pillow."

"I've been called worse things, so I'll take that."

She smiled and looked around the room.

Luke hated to ruin the moment, but waiting would only make it worse. "I just got a few texts from Gordon that Nessa has been trying to contact you."

Ellie's eyes widened and she looked up at the window, probably making the same assessment he'd made a minute earlier. She pushed back the quilt and stood, stumbling as she did, so he steadied her.

"The banquet. Luke. I can't miss it. It's imperative that I show my support to this."

"I know." He showed her his phone. "We're trying to figure it out."

Her gaze came back to his. "My phone. Where is it?" She rushed back to the bedroom and came back a moment later, phone in hand. "It's dead. The water."

"All right." He nodded. "We'll figure this out. Do you know Cameron's number?"

"Not from memory."

He looked back down at his phone and began texting. "Gordon can get it for us."

Within a few minutes, Luke had Cameron on the phone and was explaining what had happened and trying to sort out a plan. But as Cameron detailed the extent of the storm damage, the truth became clearer.

She wouldn't make it.

"Holton is going to share the news about the storm keeping you, Ellie." Luke repeated Cameron's words from the other side of the phone for Ellie's benefit. "The people will understand. Cameron said a good number of folks have had to cancel their trips due to the weather, so you won't be the only one."

"And what is the plan?"

Luke turned the phone on speaker. "Ellie asked what is the plan, Cam?"

"I'll be there in less than two hours."

Luke's brows rose as he met Ellie's gaze. Ellie gave a one-shouldered shrug.

"With the storm damage, you think you can do that?" Luke asked.

"I work for the king, Mr. Edgewood," came Cameron's pedantic response. "He has the power to make the impossible happen."

"Well, I'm sure the princess is all for the impossible right now, so I'm glad to hear it."

Not even a chuckle. Sigh.

Luke gave Ellie his phone to contact whoever she needed, so while she retired to the bedroom for some privacy, he worked to get her clothes dry without electricity.

After a while, she walked back into the room, still rocking his clothes. "Cameron just called. He said he should be here in ten minutes."

Luke looked down at the clock. True to his word. He'd even managed to make it up the mountain in about an hour and a half. "I think everyone needs a Cameron in their lives."

"By the time we drive down the mountain, I still won't make it to the banquet. And this was my opportunity to show everyone in this very visible way how I followed through with a task close to my heart." She sighed. "And I bungled it like I do all the time."

"Hey, hey." He moved to her side and touched her arm. "You

may be royalty, but I don't think you have the power to control the weather."

"But it's my patronage, Luke." She sank down onto the couch. "And now it's my fault all over again. And whatever photos the reporter took will only capitalize on the fact that I chose my heart over my duty."

"You did not." He took her by the shoulders. "Ellie, I'm glad to hear that I reside somewhere in your heart, but the truth is, you had every intention of fulfilling your duties. Not telling Cam the truth might have been a bit reckless, but you never meant to forgo the banquet. Everyone at Cambric knows that those kids live in your heart too."

He gave her shoulders a squeeze, drawing her attention back to him. "Don't let them jerk you around. You're stronger than that. We can spend a lot of time living a lie when we give people the power of our identities, but they don't really have that power. They're pretending to have power over you because it's been working for so long."

Her brows crinkled as she listened.

"Do you doubt your dad's going to love you even when you mess up?"

"No, he's been so gracious to me with all of my brokenness."

"Right, so he's not going to just toss up his hands and say, 'Nope. Ellie's not my daughter anymore because she screwed up one too many times,' right?"

"No." She grinned, blinking up with those watery eyes. "He'd never do that."

"You'll still be his daughter." He smiled down at her. "Keep that truth close and embrace what God says about you. Who He says you are." He ran a palm down her arm, wishing he could infuse strength. "Then those reporters and naysayers and Monster Maxims . . . they won't have any hold on you anymore. Because you'll know your real worth and you can walk with your head high."

"My head knows you're right. My heart is struggling with the consequences of my choices and people's reactions." Her perfect posture deflated. "It's so hard not to let their words beat at my insecurities, Luke."

"I can't even imagine what life is like for you, but the woman I've come to know is compassionate, kind, funny, determined, creative." He gave her shoulders another squeeze. "And you have a whole lot of strength inside of you too."

"Do I?" She frowned. Not a pretty look on such a pretty face.

"You have a track record that shows it. Over and over again, folks have tried to keep you down, and you've stood right back up and moved forward. Just like what Rocky says."

"*Rocky*?" Her smile improved upon that frown very nicely. "The old boxer movie?"

He nodded. "Goes like this: 'Nobody is gonna hit as hard as life. But it ain't about how hard ya hit. It's about how hard you can get hit and keep moving forward. How much you can take and keep moving forward. That's how winning is done!'"

"You remember that whole quote." Humor danced in her eyes.

"I've got a whole lot of information in here." He tapped his temple. "But most of it is useless. That quote, however, is not. Focus on who you are, really, at the soul level and how many people love who you are. And do what you can, when you can, to make right the wrongs. That's all any of us can do. You're only going to stumble if you keep looking back when you're trying to step forward."

Her smile softened. "I feel as though I should start calling you Obi-Wan for some reason."

"Well, at least you chose a good character. Though I'm partial to Yoda."

Her lips tipped into a broader grin and she opened her mouth to speak, but the sound of a loud engine broke into their quiet. Cam was here.

Luke blinked to attention and took her clothes from the couch. "Here, go get these on real quick so you won't have even more to explain."

She rocked up on tiptoe and pressed a kiss to his lips as she took the clothes. "Thank you, Luke."

Within minutes, he'd opened the door to Cameron, and Ellie met him on the threshold.

Cam looked as serious as ever. "The power should be restored within the next few hours. Will you be fine until then?"

"I should be fine." Luke dipped his chin. "Wood is stocked and I have a solar-powered emergency charger for any electronics."

Cam nodded and turned to Ellie. "We are ready for you, Your Highness."

Luke shifted forward a step, drawn toward her. But he knew, they both knew . . . this had to be the end.

Ellie started to walk and then paused, turning back to Luke, the door closing off Cam. Stepping close, she lowered her voice, holding his gaze with those sapphire eyes of hers. "Just so you know, I don't regret choosing you today. And you are wonderful just as you are, Luke. More wonderful than I ever imagined anyone could be. If things could be different—" Her fingers wrapped around his, squeezing for a second. "No matter what happens, I loved choosing you." She stepped back and pressed a fist to her chest. "I'll *never* regret it."

CHAPTER 20

Text from Maeve to Ellie: I'm still trying to process your phone call.

Ellie: It's all quite the story, one I hope doesn't make it into tomorrow's headlines.

Maeve: How did the donors respond?

Ellie: Holton announced that I'd been hindered from arriving at the banquet due to the weather, which was true. And Holton relayed that the donors only sang my praises and were proud to have me as their patron. Even Mrs. Kershaw spoke highly of my work and care for the children. All of it could be ruined if that reporter took any photos worth publishing, though.

Maeve: Maybe the reporter didn't make it out of the storm alive.

Ellie: Maeve!

Maeve: Just saying what you're hoping.

Ellie: I am not! Though I wouldn't mind if his camera fell in the lake or he slipped and fell in the lake holding his camera.

Maeve: Like I said . . . didn't make it out alive.

Ellie: But HE made it out. Not the camera.

Maeve: Details.

Maeve: I suppose Taugen House is on alert for any unhappy headlines.

Ellie: As usual. So far there's been nothing, so perhaps the camera did fall into the lake.

Maeve: Or the photos were too blurred for recognition.

Ellie: Right. Or they're waiting for the weekend edition.

Maeve: Or the news of the storm damage and lives lost are taking up airspace, so they're waiting until they can get everyone's attention?

Ellie: That's so horrible it might actually be true.

Maeve: El, whatever happens, I'm in agreement with Lifesaver Luke. You are strong and you will get through this. And the people who really know you, KNOW you.

Maeve: As a reminder, I'm fine with hand-me-downs from princesses, especially when they wear flannel, save lives, and are excellent snugglers.

Ellie: Maeve, I have never experienced anything so absolutely wonderful in all my life (not the falling in the lake part, to be clear). But just being with him. It makes me imagine what private life could be like. I think I could handle any public disaster or media catastrophe with him to come home to.

Maeve: You need to tell your parents, El. They need to know the truth of your feelings. Maybe there is a way . . .

Ellie: I can't imagine one where one of us wouldn't have to give up our family and our responsibilities to be together.

Maeve: Your parents still need to know.

Maeve: How did your parents respond to everything?

Ellie: So far, they've been too busy to have a proper conversation. Or perhaps they're on edge about the possible headline too. Father intimated that he planned to phone Luke to thank him for his quick thinking and care of me.

Maeve: And what happens with Luke now?

Ellie: He's already gone to Skern to spend the last few weeks making small renovations on a cottage for Lewis Gray. Then he has his cousin's wedding. Then he returns to the U.S.

Maeve: So the cabin was goodbye. Oh, El.

Ellie: We didn't say goodbye.

Loyally, Luke

Luke's phone buzzed to life on the table beside him as he finished up a few final emails to Mrs. Kershaw and Mr. Holton.

Unknown number? He shrugged off the curiosity and went back to the email, giving a detailed account of all the finalized pieces of the kitchen remodel.

His phone buzzed again. Same number.

He tapped on the icon and two messages appeared.

> **Ellie:** I don't think I properly thanked you for rescuing me yesterday.
>
> **Ellie:** So, thank you for being my hero.

Familiar warmth filled his chest, and he couldn't suppress his rising grin. After she'd left the cabin yesterday, he wasn't too sure he'd get another chance to connect with her. And after her last words—the fact she'd chosen him no matter the consequences—well, something in him broke and fit right back together all at once.

She chose *him.*

Just as he was.

She didn't want him any other way.

His eyes stung, so he took a long drink of coffee.

> **Luke: I don't usually respond to unfamiliar phone numbers unless they refer to my hero skills.**
>
> **Ellie:** I'll make sure to remember that for future correspondence.
>
> **Ellie:** In all seriousness, Luke, thank you. You can't know how much it meant to just . . . be with you yesterday.

His chest twinged in response. Just being with her fit too. Much like the crazy emotions slamming together inside him. But how could he fix this? How could he bridge the impossible gap between their lives? The more time he spent with her, the more he wanted to rearrange everything about his life and convince a king to let a pauper take care of his daughter for the rest of their days.

A renewed sting pricked at his eyes and tingled at the bridge of his nose.

Nope.

And he took another gulp of coffee.

Luke: **Besides the near-death experience, the simple cabin seemed to suit a certain princess well enough.**

He could almost envision the subtle tip of those lovely lips of hers.

Ellie: The princess would call it an almost perfect fit.
Luke: **Breakfast wasn't fancy enough for Your Highness?**
Ellie: Breakfast was lovely, especially the classy scones.

A chuckle shot out of him as another message popped onto his screen.

Ellie: Though scones paired fairly excellently with eggs and bacon.
Luke: **Some things can fit together surprisingly well. Class and common?**
Ellie: Perhaps the best kind of combination. And the surroundings were nearly perfect too.
Luke: **Did I need to add a few more animal heads on the walls, or were the frou-frou coffee fixings not to your liking?**
Ellie: Well, you could always increase the coffee fixings, but I

think the cabin would be simply perfect if it were a little
bigger to fit a dog or two.

Luke: True. The perfect cabin needs a dog or two.

Ellie: And a couple extra bedrooms in case the class and
common needed to add a few wee bairns.

Bairns? Children? His breath lodged in his throat, both of them
tiptoeing around a dream. His throat tightened.

Luke: Seems reasonable to me.

Ellie: And maybe the children wouldn't mind occasional travel
back and forth across the ocean.

God, how could this work? If Luke could turn the world upside
down to be with her, even swallow a life as a royal, at this moment,
he'd choose it all to be with her.

And the very idea of making that choice hit him like bricks in the
chest. Could he ever convince her dad to take him on as more than
an advisor for forestry and building, but a man who would take care
of his daughter's heart? The possibility seemed . . . truly impossible.

Her family wanted a native Skymarian.

And an aristocrat.

And Luke was neither.

But with each additional text or conversation or kiss, the grip on
his former life and desires loosened. He felt like his chest was being
ripped wide open.

**Luke: Well, I reckon if it started getting unwieldy for them,
their parents could figure out a different plan.**

Ellie: Perhaps the princess could take a sabbatical to cozy up
next to a cabin dweller.

Would she even contemplate such a sacrifice? Didn't seem fair to ask.

> **Luke:** Or the country boy could take up residence in a castle
> for a while.

A pause followed, almost as if Ellie felt the same impossible desire too. Luke's body bent, deflated from the pull and push of wanting something he couldn't have. He closed his eyes, a prayer pooling through him for guidance . . . wisdom . . . miracles . . . anything.

> **Ellie:** I want you to know that I am so grateful we met. You
> can't know how much your kindness and authenticity have
> meant to me. You are wonderful just as you are, and I hope
> you know that. And I'm grateful to call you my friend.

Pain sliced through him. He knew what was happening. This was the end. Her way of saying goodbye. He'd convinced himself he'd accept it, but now, now when he had to . . .

> **Luke:** I'm honored to be your friend.
> **Luke:** Ellie, you are amazing. Remember that. It takes a strong
> person to come back from what you have to try again.
> Over and over. So don't let your past dictate your future.
> Don't settle, if you can help it. You are braver than you
> think and your heart is full of compassion. And you're
> funny. It's an underrated life skill, so just think how much
> more prepared you are because you have a sense of humor.

A pause. He'd already typed so much, but . . . to his own surprise, he needed to say more. If this was the last time she heard from him, he needed her to hear the truth.

Loyally, Luke

Luke: I don't know all the protocols and rules you have to live by, but I do know you have so much to give to the people around you and the ones you serve. I'm proud to know you, and will watch from afar as you show Skymar who you really are.

He paused. Trying to sort out what to say next.

Ellie: I don't want to type goodbye.
Luke: Then don't. Good night, Ellie.
Ellie: Good night, Luke.
Luke: Keep checking things off your list, all right?
Ellie: I will.

Text from Penelope to Izzy and Luke: I know you explained things on your video call, but I still wasn't prepared for today's headlines, Luke. Have you seen the photo?
Luke: You're up either really early or really late.
Penelope: Late. I'm working on some last-minute prep stuff for our first performance at the Ashby since reopening. Matt is picking me up in a few minutes, so I'm waiting by the theater door with my umbrella. Maybe he'll sing in the rain to me.
Luke: Gross.
Penelope: He's done it before. It's swoony. Maybe not as swoony as saving someone from drowning in icy water, but still noteworthy.
Izzy: Oh my goodness! I just saw the headlines when I read Penelope's text. What exactly is happening in that photo? She's lying on top of you in the snow!

Luke: That picture is actually of us right after I pulled her out of the water. But the jerk reporters put their own spin on it, didn't they?

Penelope: Of course—she's wet! You can easily tell from her hair if you know what to look for.

Luke: Well, whatever the papers say, it's not true.

Penelope: Of course it's not true. Izzy and I have actually watched the movies I sent you to prepare you for this very moment.

Luke: I don't watch those kinds of movies.

Penelope: Not even Princess Diaries 2?

Luke: I refuse to watch that one on principle.

Penelope: What? But it has Julie Andrews in it!

Luke: It also has Chris Pine in it, and after suffering through listening to you girls talk about him ALL THE TIME when we were younger, I refuse to watch him.

Luke: Except in Star Trek. But also on principle.

Izzy: You may act like it's not a big deal, but you can't really be as nonchalant about the whole media thing as you're pretending to be.

Luke: Nope. I'm not. But after chopping a load of wood at daybreak, I'm feeling a little less like threatening people's lives.

Izzy: And Brodie's mom will be so grateful for your hard work to stock her wood supply while curbing your inner Braveheart.

Penelope: Speaking of movie references, I would try to predict your future again, but Hallmark movies don't usually include lifesaving moments followed by nasty paparazzi. Thus the reason I sent Princess Diaries 2. I know what I WANT to happen next for your life, but my confidence level in my accuracy has dropped.

Loyally, Luke

Luke: I know what I'd prefer to happen too, Penny-girl, but it
would be selfish and not what Ellie wants or what Skymar
needs.

Penelope: For her to give up the crown and move to the States?

Luke: But then I think of what she loves and how great she's
going to be at making a difference in Skymar and it
doesn't hurt as bad. I'm so proud to know her.

Luke's phone buzzed to life in his hand and Penelope's name
flashed on the screen. He pinched his eyes closed and raised the phone
to his ear.

"You know you're totally worthy of a princess, right? This is nothing at all like Clara."

Her voice shook, likely from trying to keep her tears in check. "I
know she's not Clara, Penny-girl."

"But you have to know, Luke, that she can't do better than you.
Ever. I'm being serious right now. Not only are you the best guy I
know, only equal to Matt—"

The highest praise.

"—but you're a perfect match for a princess. You've shown that my
whole life. You don't mind urging other people out in the spotlight to
see them shine. You actually love it. It's a gift of yours too." She sniffled.
"I can't tell you how many times your presence behind the scenes in my
life made me brave because I knew you were there. Cheering me on
in your gruff, sometimes needlessly sarcastic way." She sniffled again.
"Everyone needs a safe set of arms to find strength and comfort and
courage. You may not even know it, but you *are* that person. You always
have been for me."

He lowered his head and released a long breath to steady himself.
His baby sister tended toward the dramatic, but her words hit home
in her attempt to cheer his heart and ground him.

"Thanks, sis."

"Don't lose heart, Luke. I don't know what's going to happen with Ellie, but I just can't believe the story is over yet. She's too smart to let someone like you out of her life."

"I appreciate your unending optimism, but sometimes stories don't have a perfect ending and we learn to live with that anyway. I'll be okay, sis."

Though his heart didn't seem to agree. At all.

They talked for a little longer, with Penelope finally sobbing into the phone how much she loved him and then saying her goodbyes.

He leaned his head back against the couch and tried to quell the ache in his chest.

Text from Matt to Luke: Thanks for having Penelope in tears when I came to collect her from the theater.

Luke: I'm sure it wasn't the first time.

Matt: True. But she's less consolable than usual.

Luke: I had to tell her a hard truth about not getting what I want but hoping that a certain princess gets exactly what she needs.

Matt: Definitely not the ending Penelope prefers, but you're a good man, Luke. I feel certain, even if you never know it, you've made a good difference in Princess Elliana's life.

Luke: Thanks, Matt. I'm sure that will make me feel better in the long run.

Matt: Yeah, right now everything just sucks.

Luke: Pretty much.

Matt: I'm here if you need to talk.

Luke: Thanks. I appreciate it.

Luke sat by the small table in the cottage, sipping his coffee and staring down at the screen of his phone. The headline inspired a bout of nausea.

Loyally, Luke

Prodigal Princess at it again.

He skimmed the first paragraph, detailing how Ellie skipped out on the Donors' Banquet in order to spend time with her secret boyfriend behind the Duke of Styles's back.

Just enough truth in there to make it feel real.

They even spun it to imply that she'd been shirking her other duties to spend time with him in secret. But who would believe they actually had a kissing match on the ground in a snowstorm?

He looked back at the photos. One was of her lying on top of him, her face turned toward the cameraman, which only helped with identification. The second was a photo of them removing their jackets. Nothing explicit, but enough to spur all sorts of innuendos.

He ran a hand over his face.

How was Ellie? Should he text her? Would she want that or would it just make things worse for her?

He closed the site and growled, taking another sip of his coffee.

Oh, how he wanted to fix this, but what could he do? Nothing. No wonder the press infuriated people so much. They had the power to spout off whatever and people just had to deal with it.

Or ignore it.

Which was what Luke preferred.

With a moan, he shook his head and tapped on the photo icon, skimming through a few photos of his recent reno to send to Lewis Gray, when a photo within the collection caught his attention.

Ellie with a fishing rod?

He opened it.

But it wasn't a photo at all. It was a video. His pulse skittered into a faster pace. The video he'd been taking when Ellie fell in the lake. He tapped the Play button and grinned as she cast the line, then looked back at him with a proud grin. Yep, he was keeping this video as long as he could. Just to see her looking back at him every now and then.

Then she looked back again, but this time she looked worried. Was that when she'd seen the reporter?

The line tightened and she called out that she had something. He heard his own voice encouraging her to reel it in. Then the event played out before him. Her pulling on the line, her attention looking out across the lake, the stumble, and then the fall through the ice.

He paused the video and rewound it a little, then zoomed in to the area where Ellie had looked. A figure became visible, almost hidden in the trees. Then in the next frame, he came out from his position, camera in hand.

Luke allowed the video to continue playing, but it didn't stop after Ellie fell through the ice. No, the screen went somewhat black, but he could still hear the voices. His and Ellie's.

He must have pushed the phone into his pocket without turning off the recording.

Their conversation, his intentions, her response came through loud and clear. But was it important for any reason?

Text from Luke to Penelope and Izzy: I have an idea. It may take some of your magic to work, but right now, I'm banking on some. I'll even take a bit of pixie dust too, if you have some to spare.

Penelope: Channel Julie Andrews. That's even more reliable.

Izzy: And praying would probably be a good choice (you two heathens).

Luke: Well, I started with that.

Izzy: Nice. I'm glad to hear your priorities are in order. Not sure about Penelope's sometimes.

Penelope: Hey now. Matt and I prayed for Luke and Ellie as soon as I stopped crying.

Luke: Well, keep 'em coming. I'm not sure how this will help and I get nauseous at the very idea of what I might have

to do, but I think I know someone who can give me some direction.

↟

"I don't know how we can repair this, Elliana." Her mother pressed her fingers into her forehead as she sat in a chair across from her in their parents' sitting room. "And after you'd made such progress with your public reputation." The weariness in her mother's voice pricked at Ellie's spine, but she attempted to maintain her composure.

She was not sorry for being with Luke.

She only hated another reason for her parents to have to fight for her public credibility.

"Oh, Elliana. I never wanted this for you, darling." Her mother's tender response drew Ellie's attention. "Why did you go?"

Ellie paused. Myriad answers swarmed through her, all right and good, but how could she fully explain so her mother would hear her? She caught her father's look and the idea emerged. "Because I love him and I wanted to spend one more day with him."

"Love him?" Mother glanced over at Father as if he'd provide some help. "You barely know him."

"I know him well enough to realize that I feel at home when I'm with him. That he makes me a better version of myself because I don't have to pretend to be anyone else. And I love—" Air burst out in a voiceless laugh. "I love loving him. So yes, I wanted to capture whatever memories I could for whatever time I had, at whatever cost. And I'm sorry to have placed you and Father in this situation, but I am not sorry for choosing to be with him."

"Life is hard for two people of such different backgrounds, Elliana. The sacrifices . . . the choices . . . the ridicule."

"Would you have become the strong, confident woman you are right now if the road had been easy, Mother?"

Her mother's expression softened and something close to a smile gentled her concern. "No, likely I would not, but I also would not wish such hardship on you—on any of my children, especially with all you've already borne."

And then Ellie understood the stubbornness, saw it for what it really was. A mother's protection. An act of love. Ellie moved forward and lowered to her knees, taking her mother's hands in hers. "One of the best women I know was refined by love and hardship, and I hope to be half the woman she is."

Ellie could count on one hand the times she'd seen her mother cry, but the regal woman's eyes filled and overflowed down her cheeks. "Perhaps there are some things I can learn from *you*?" She sniffled through her light laugh.

"I think every royal house needs a thorough commoner thrown into it now and again." Ellie stood and took the seat next to her mother. "Look at the excellent perspective you brought to Father's life and this country. Your view on education reform has been the bedrock of so many healthy educational changes here, and it stems from your history. A history"—Ellie looked over at Father with a smile—"of which you should be extremely proud."

Ellie reached for her bag and brought out the journal. "I found this journal at Cambric. It's the beautiful story of simple people experiencing hardship, falling in love, and then becoming people who brought positive change to those around them. People from your town in Crieff." She pressed the journal into her mother's hands. "The regular people of Skymar want their royals to marry those who will support Skymar and bring good change to our country, no matter where that person is from. Because when we're loved well, it is no matter whether that person be a king"—she gestured toward her father—"or a commoner. That type of love makes us stronger, better versions of ourselves so we can serve others out of the overflow."

Mother's palm pressed against her chest. "That's . . . lovely."

"It is." Ellie smiled, tapping the journal. "And I think you'd like this story because it will remind you of the good of who you were, even as a commoner." She gestured toward Father. "But also of the greatness of what being in love has done, even despite, and sometimes because of, the hardships."

Mother looked over at Father, her pale eyes watery and tender. He smiled in a way that communicated his love for her.

"And this is how you feel for Mr. Edgewood?" Mother wiped at a tear beneath her eye.

"I do."

"He's worthy of a princess then?" Father chimed in, a smile in his voice.

Ellie looked from her mother to her father, her smile growing at the idea of Luke trying to fit into her world. "Worthy? Oh yes, but . . . while he may not be the sort of man you would choose for your princess, he is certainly the sort of man you should choose for your daughter. I would choose him, because he would make me a better person."

"You could choose to go with him, you know." Mother held her gaze. "This royal life doesn't have to be yours."

"The past three years, I've realized how much I love this country and the ability to serve our people. Before, I resented my station and my responsibilities, but now I see the honor and privilege of being an agent of change for good in a way few other people have the power or influence to do. I choose this family first, this calling as a royal."

Her mother's eyes filled with tears again. "And . . . and he won't stay for you?"

The question stabbed her heart, but she raised her chin to face the reality head-on. "Should his love for his life and his people prove any less influential or important than mine?" The memory of how he'd wrapped his arms around her on the cabin couch and just let her rest against him came to mind, and she almost smiled. "If . . . if he thought I *needed* him to stay, I believe he would, because that's who he is, but that isn't fair to him." She sat taller. "Or to me."

"What do you mean?" Her father came and sat across from her.

"He should stay first and foremost because he chooses this life, not because he thinks I need him to stay." She blinked back the tears, refusing them exit. "We both have made a choice to move forward with our lives separately because he knows I love this place, these people, and I will not betray your trust in me again, but he cannot spend all of his life in a royal world." A sad sort of chuckle emerged at the thought of him in a world of constant balls and royal responsibilities. "He would try. I know he would, but having to live in this life all the time . . . well, I think a part of him would fade and I . . . I love him much more than to ask him to give up his world entirely for mine." She drew in a breath, attempting to brace her heart against the ache. "And since there is not a world in between, then we've made this choice. Together."

CHAPTER 21

The Daily Edge: Social Tattle from
One Edge of Skymar to the Other

Our Prodigal Princess Elliana has taken another hard fall
this week. Only two days before the most illustrious social
event of the season, the Wild Hyacinth Ball, the Earl of
Tallon has been taken to hospital and will no longer attend.
Appendicitis appears to be the culprit, but some sources
say that the princess's most recent snowy escapade with her
"American country boy" forced Tallon's hand and he doesn't
wish to have his reputation at risk by her behavior.

With the ball only two days away, will the King and Queen
still continue with their plans to give our scandalous princess
back her royal duties? And if so, who will be her plus-one for
this notoriously coupled ball? Our tattlers want to know.

• •

Text from Maeve to Ellie: I hate The Edge. Not only are they
    doubting poor Timid Timothy's health report, but they're
    digging at you again.

Maeve: You have access to a whole host of torture devices in
    the archives of the castle. Maybe it's time to see if they
    still work.

Ellie: I think you may need to stop watching medieval
    documentaries or cut back on the caffeine.

Maeve: Seriously, they're trying to hit your reputation
    wherever they can. Do they even consider how you

feel? No! You don't have a date for the BIGGEST ROYAL
EVENT OF THE YEAR! Jerks! Plus, I'm calling them a few
very creatively nasty names in my mind.

Ellie: Putting things in capitalizations doesn't help my
nerves, Maeve. I'm fully aware of the importance of this
occasion. Not only as a highly anticipated event but as a
night for me, in particular.

Maeve: And your parents are still going to restore you? After
everything?

Ellie: Yes. In fact, my mother even said something about
growing from her own mistakes to stand by the woman
they know I am, regardless of what the world may say.

Maeve: Your mom said that?

Ellie: The journal really impacted her. Grounded her, I think,
in her past and the value of being loved well. She even
said that being loved makes us stronger, but loving well
does too. And she wants to love me well in this moment
and in the future.

Maeve: I'm not crying, you're crying. Wow. Ellie. That's
amazing.

Ellie: There was something different in both of them today. I
can't explain it. It was almost like they were attempting to
contain their excitement for me, despite everything.

Maeve: I'm so glad to hear it. You ARE ready for this moment,
friend.

Maeve: So do you need me to be your plus-one for the ball?
I am willing to drop the total ten I'm bringing if you need
me. I just want you to know how much I love you.

Ellie: Your willingness to sacrifice humbles me, but I just had a
talk with my parents and . . . I've decided to go alone.

Maeve: Is there even a precedent for that? The Hyacinth has been around for two centuries, and I've never heard of anyone, especially royalty, showing up alone.

Ellie: I admit I'm terrified, but I've been living in the fear of what people think for much too long, and I think it's time to set a new precedent. At least to show the skeptics I'm not afraid of them anymore.

Maeve: I am so proud of you, my friend.

Maeve: But if you do get extra nervous, look my way. Or take my arm. Or whatever you need to do. I'm here for you.

Ellie: Just pray I don't stumble down the stairs along with walking alone. If I'm going to enter on my own, I would love for it to be grand, glorious, and accident-free.

This was crazy.

Luke pulled at the collar of his button-down as he waited for the door in front of him to open.

Ridiculous. Probably the craziest thing, outside of college, he'd ever done.

He looked over at Jackson, the PR person for the king. He'd been good enough to give Luke a thorough review of what would happen during the press conference. Once Taugen House released a part of the video of Ellie breaking through the ice to their trusted news sources, then every other network would snatch it up like chocolate at a junior high girls' sleepover. He shuddered. He'd been witness to too many of those in his lifetime.

"We will permit a few questions," Jackson relayed, dipping his head in Luke's direction. "But only a few. Enough for the reporters to feel somewhat engaged, and then we will finish."

"Ten minutes at most, you said," Luke repeated back to the man from their earlier conversation.

Jackson dipped his head again. "Keep to your script and our conversation. You will be fine."

Luke swallowed the lemon-sized lump in his throat and rubbed a sweaty palm down the side of his slacks. He hated speaking in front of people. And right now, he was getting ready to speak to the press. What sort of idiot was he?

He squeezed his eyes closed and Ellie's face came to mind.

An idiot in love, it seemed.

Love. Bah.

And yet even his internal Mr. Scrooge gave way to a sweet sort of warmth at the memory of Ellie in his arms. Her laugh. Her humor and conversation.

He was a sap.

A stupid, sentimental, ridiculous sap.

And he'd never been happier than when he spent time with her.

His shoulders slumped.

A stupid, sentimental, ridiculous sap who was giving his first press conference and then leaving Skymar with a broken heart and some of the best memories of his life. Who wrote this story? He looked heavenward with a raised brow.

"One minute," Jackson said, touching his earpiece and meeting Luke's gaze for a second.

Luke took a deep breath to help calm the nerves, but it was just a stupid trick that never worked.

In an attempt to prepare himself, he'd spent a good half hour looking up press conferences on YouTube before arriving at Taugen House. Even—his stomach twinged at the mental admission—watching the scene from *Notting Hill* since it involved a commoner and a famous person.

A truth he was NEVER revealing to his youngest sister.

"It's time," Jackson said, leading the way forward.

Mr. Erikson—another advisor—followed behind Luke and held the door.

The paper in Luke's hands crinkled in time with the mild squeak of the door, and then Luke crossed the threshold.

A few flashes greeted him from the dozen reporters in the room. A smile or two maybe, which took him off guard. He wasn't quite expecting people to be foaming at the mouth and shouting, "Off with his head," but a sense of welcome certainly hadn't been in the mental script.

Luke waited by the door as Jackson approached the lectern. The poised man greeted the room and then continued with his introduction.

"As many of you are aware, a video was released earlier today giving evidence of Her Highness Princess Elliana's near-death experience in a frozen lake in the North Country. This incident was instigated by the presence of paparazzi on private property within the Yarrow Fell. It is an unusual step for the royal family to respond to recent allegations related to the princess's private life, but since these false allegations include a private citizen who is a guest in our country"—he gestured toward Luke—"Taugen House has called this press conference. The private citizen, Mr. Edgewood, has offered to take a few questions in the interest of truth."

Jackson's steely gaze roamed over the audience, the pause creating a palpable discomfort. "Keep in mind, Mr. Edgewood's courtesy will only last as long as you are polite."

Jackson stepped back from the lectern, giving way for Luke to approach.

Luke swallowed through his dry throat and took his position, giving the room a quick sweep before flattening the paper in his hand against the lectern. His own words, culled by Jackson and his team, blurred back at him.

"Good afternoon," Luke's voice came back at him, louder than he'd expected, so he backed up a step and cleared his throat. "My name is Luke Edgewood, as I imagine most of y'all know." He flinched. "Y'all" wasn't in the notes. "And I'm here to speak to the situation that led to the recent allegations in some media outlets related to Princess Elliana and myself."

He gave a quick look up at the group of reporters and another flash blinked in his periphery. Luke looked back down at the paper.

"I was hired to work at Cambric Hall as the lead of a construction team to renovate a part of the orphanage to better serve the children and staff and provide a safer environment. As patron of Cambric, Her Highness is the patron of the orphanage and overseer of the renovation project. We worked closely together and became friends. She came to the cabin on Yarrow Fell in order to express her gratitude for my work and to say goodbye." All true. He didn't have to include their particular style of showing gratitude. "Princess Elliana had every intention of leaving the cabin to arrive at Cambric's gala and would have been able to reach her destination if the lake accident hadn't occurred. After measures were taken to ensure her health and safety, the hour had grown late and the roads had become obstructed. I'm grateful to say the princess was not more hurt than she was." The image of her staring at him from the lake water, the fear of how long she could continue to fight through the water before she didn't have the strength anymore, flashed back to his mind and he looked up from his paper. "Things could have ended much worse than they did. Much worse than even the allegations proposed."

A long quiet filled the room at Luke's ending, and he waited for the next part Jackson had reviewed with him.

"Mr. Edgewood has agreed to take a few questions," Jackson announced into the silence, which seemed to give the reporters the jolt they needed.

Hands rose into the air, along with the sound of voices competing for attention.

"Dawson," came Jackson's response as a middle-aged man with bright blue eyes stood.

"Did you know about the princess's past when you started developing your . . . friendship?" Skepticism laced the man's words and Luke pressed his palm down on the lectern in an attempt to steady himself. What was the old adage his grandpa used to say—"*You catch more flies with honey than vinegar*"?

"Truth be told, I didn't even know she was a princess when we first became friends." He pushed up a smile as a murmur bled through the crowd. "Asking if someone is royalty isn't a typical conversation starter in the States, so the notion didn't even cross my mind."

Another dozen hands rose in the crowd. A woman with curly, strawberry-blonde hair stood.

"She's part of the royal family. How did you *not* know who she was?" she asked. "And what was your response when you found out?"

"I'm pretty simple as far as technology goes and I've never been what my youngest sister would refer to as a royal watcher. In fact, I usually have enough trouble keeping track of my dogs—the last thing I need is to worry about what's happening in the lives of folks who don't even live in my town, so I'd never had any reason to know who she was before now." He shrugged a shoulder, watching as some of the faces in the crowd responded to his grin with their own. "I was surprised, of course, but we all have histories. The woman I'd come to know as my friend was the one who mattered to me more than the one who'd made some poor choices in the past."

The woman placed her palm over her heart and wilted down into her chair with something like a sigh.

Hands rose again.

"Larson?"

A young fellow with dark eyes zeroed in on Luke, the tilt of his lips and brows giving off an air of arrogance. "Mr. Edgewood, the video released shows the princess's fall into the lake while fishing."

His brow rose high, a hint of doubt in his words. "Fishing? It seems a bit far-fetched to me and possibly staged."

Jackson stepped forward as if to intervene, but Luke shook his head. Jackson tipped a brow in question, but Luke just turned back toward the reporter. Holding the man's gaze, Luke took his time formulating a response. If someone started questioning his own words and intentions, he wanted to sort it out himself.

"I'd given her a fishing rod as a kind of parting gift, thinking I wouldn't see her again. Fishing was something she'd always wanted to experience. She brought it with her so I could help her put it together and teach her how to use it." Luke shrugged a shoulder, keeping his tone calm while never breaking eye contact with Larson. "Any fishermen in the room can vouch for the comfort and clarity a little bit of fishing can provide when regular life gets messy. And I'd say, with the intense scrutiny and pressure inherent in royal life, even a princess could do with the benefits of fishing every once in a while. Wouldn't you?"

A few chuckles bubbled from the crowd and Larson returned to his seat.

"Ms. St. Charles?"

A blonde in a pink dress offered a coy smile before beginning. "Elaine St. Charles from *The Daily Edge*." She paused as if expecting him to respond to her declaration, but Luke wasn't sure why. "Mr. Edgewood, how friendly would you say your relationship with Her Highness is? Should her current suitors be threatened by you?"

Jackson cleared his throat. "Mr. Edgewood has already spoken to the nature of their friendship, Ms. St. Charles. Do you have another question?"

Her smile dropped for a second before returning with a bit less potency. "I'll rephrase." She looked back at Luke. "Do you have plans to stay in Skymar long-term?"

"No, ma'am. I return to the States next month."

"We have time for one more question." Jackson interrupted Elaine from adding something else. "Mr. Pool?"

"Darien Pool, the *Morning Gazette*." The older gentleman dipped his head in greeting and squinted toward Luke. "As a longtime reporter of the royal family, I am curious to your thoughts, Mr. Edgewood. Since you consider yourself a friend of the princess, are you concerned about her past sabotaging her future choices as she potentially steps back into life as a working royal?"

This question carried so much intention behind it. Luke paused, considering how to address it. "Mr. Pool, are you a hunting man?"

The older gentleman's gray brows rose. "Pardon?"

"Skymar, especially the North Country, has some great places for outdoorsmen. I was just wondering if you ever did any hunting?"

Mr. Pool cleared his throat. "I have, more so in my younger days than now. It's a valued pastime of Skymar."

"And rightly so. I'm not highly familiar with the royal family of Skymar and their history. To be honest, I'm more of a face-value sort of guy, so I'll give you my opinion from that simple perspective." He scanned the crowd. "When I've been hunting, the tracks tell you a lot about what you're looking for, right? Follow the wrong tracks, get the wrong animal. People leave tracks too. Their reputations and actions. Any solid Google search can give plenty of details of what sort of tracks Her Highness had three or four years ago, but the same online search can also show how those tracks have changed in recent history. Any good reporter worth his or her salt can follow the accounts of accurate news and see how Princess Elliana has made a good and real difference to the people she's served in the North Country. I don't know about you, but I'd much rather people look at the track record I've left behind since I've grown from my mistakes rather than the one I left before then."

Luke nodded toward the older man and then turned to Jackson, who wore an odd expression of . . . almost a smile? The latter gentleman gestured toward Luke and Luke followed him from the room as the calls of competing reporters clamoring with more questions resounded behind them. The awareness that he'd made it through the press conference suddenly weakened him. Kind of like the feeling of nearly falling off a roof, the few times that had happened.

All right. He'd survived. Maybe hadn't sounded too stupid. And hopefully helped Ellie out, at least a little, in the process.

Jackson turned to Luke as the door closed behind them. "Well done, Mr. Edgewood."

"Thanks, Jackson." Luke released a long breath and tugged off his suit jacket to cool down. "I don't think it would have turned out so well without you."

"It is what I do, sir." Jackson offered a deferential nod before adding, "Though I have no doubt you could hold your own, if necessary."

Luke shot him a grin. "I wouldn't wish for another opportunity anytime soon, but it was the right thing to do for El—for the princess." He looked away as heat rose up his neck at his near-blunder. "And, well, we muster up the courage to do a lot of crazy things for the people we—for those who need it, don't we?"

"Indeed, sir." A glint lit Jackson's eyes. "Indeed we do."

Text from Izzy to Luke: YOU. WERE. AMAZING! No one would have known you were nervous at all.

Luke: I had to change my shirt afterward because I'd sweated through it.

Izzy: Well, you couldn't tell from the television screen. Truly. You seemed pretty calm, except that one time you stared down some guy. No one else probably knew that look, but I did and it's terrifying. I loved it when you used it on Arnold Cramer during my senior year. Nobody tried to break into my locker after that.

Loyally, Luke

Luke: Why hasn't it ever worked on Penelope?

Izzy: She knows you have a soft heart, so she's immune to the Rambo "kill you" look.

Luke: I hope meeting with the press helps people see the truth. That's all that matters to me.

Izzy: I wish you could see her again. Just one more time maybe.

Luke: Yeah. I'd like that too. I hate the feeling of not being able to fix this. I'm not a native. I'm not on the "princess list," so to speak. So . . . I just have to let go.

Izzy: One of the hardest things for a fixer to ever do.

Luke: Now stop worrying about me and finish all those wedding plans. You've only got a little over a week left. I may not be a fan of Hallmark movies, but I sure am a fan of happily ever after for the people I love.

Izzy: Aww, that may be one of the sweetest and non-Luke-ish things you've ever said.

Luke: Thus the reason I said it to you and not Penelope. I don't think I could handle the reminders.

Luke: Or the dozens of movie links, quotes, or memes she'd send me afterward.

Izzy: Do you want to head down to Fiacla with Brodie and me this afternoon? Penelope, Matt, and Iris are set to arrive at the airport in the next hour and we were planning to go out to dinner before they crashed. We can celebrate your media success!

Luke: I'd love to, but I can't. Gordon messaged me last night and said that he found a few unfinished things he wanted me to check back in Crieff today. He suggested I just stay the night over there. Could we meet another night this week?

Izzy: Sure. But I can't imagine you leaving anything unfinished. Unless it's a certain relationship with a princess.

Luke: Touché. But I'd like to say we both came to a mutual understanding that made sense for both of us and our futures.

Izzy: Yeah, sounds like there's a whole lot of "unfinished" in the middle of that sentence.

Luke: I'd love to continue to rehash my love life, but Gordon wanted me in Crieff by four, and I'm already running a little late because of just getting back from the press conference. Need to get a quick shower and be off. In fact, I might even use the excuse of trimming my beard to get out of this conversation.

Izzy: You're hilarious. We won't know you're getting married until the day before it happens from the amount of information you share.

Luke: Not true. Mostly. Now get back to your own love life and wedding planning and leave me alone.

Izzy: Fine, but one more thing . . . are you still planning to pick up Josephine and the fam from the airport on Tuesday? I have my last dress fitting.

Luke: Yep. On my calendar.

Izzy: You have a calendar now?

Luke: The one I keep in my head.

Izzy: Right. Fantastic. I feel so much better now.

Luke: Have I ever failed you with it?

Izzy: Touché right back atcha. Wednesday is still when we're all getting together to make wedding decorations. Don't forget.

Luke: It's my favorite date of the week.

Loyally, Luke

Izzy: You are a horrible liar. Talk to you later. Have fun in
Crieff. I know you love the people and place.

Luke: It's always an adventure. :)

Luke pulled into the back of the Frasiers' shop where their residence connected to the antique store. The house part of the building spread out into an L shape from the shop, allowing space for Gordon to build a front porch for his bride—a fact she bragged about often and Gordon, in typical fashion, gave a gruff nod. Then changed the subject.

But there was no mistaking the slight hint of a grin on his face at the story.

Luke felt a kinship with the man all the more when he saw moments like those. The soft side of the burly builder. Luke sighed. He knew his own weaknesses. Having been raised around girls, he'd learned real quick that his quiet, tough exterior was no match for a person in need, especially children and women.

In particular, those he cared about.

And Luke's heart had turned to putty in Ellie's hands, plain and simple.

A fact slicing right through his chest every time he contemplated never seeing her again. He wouldn't say he was sad that Earl what's-his-name decided not to go to the dance . . . or party . . . or whatever it was with Ellie, though he hoped she'd find another partner. Just not one she liked a whole lot.

He gave his head a strong shake and stepped out of the car. No use dwelling on things he had no power to control or change. They'd both made the best right decision for the people in their lives, and that was what mattered.

Even if it was rotten.

The weather had turned nice enough that Luke left his jean jacket in the car with his toolbox and took the front steps two at a time to the door. Why Gordon decided to meet at his house instead of Cambric Hall didn't make sense, but maybe the man wanted to walk on a fine spring afternoon like today.

That might do Luke some good too.

After giving a knock, he adjusted his cap and waited.

A sudden commotion exploded within the house. Something sounded like it crashed, then a man's loud voice—likely Gordon's—exclaimed something in Gaelic. Probably not a word his wife would have appreciated.

Luke's lips twitched. Sounded kind of like his uncle.

Another round of scuffling erupted from behind the door and then—

Was that a child's voice shouting, "He's here"?

Were his grandkids in town? Luke didn't think they were old enough to talk in sentences yet.

The door flew open to reveal Nessa Frasier's wide smile and dancing eyes. "Oh, thank heaven, you've finally arrived."

Faye's little face peeked out from around Nessa.

"Well, lookie who's visiting y'all." Luke leaned down. "Hey, pretty lady."

She giggled and waved, the necklace he'd given her dangling from her neck.

"Gordon and I are considering a long-term agreement for Jamie and Faye." Nessa's smile widened and she leaned close to Luke. "We've started the initial paperwork for adoption. Gordon's even mentioned adding Cade to the list."

"That's some of the best news I've ever heard, Nessa." Luke's laugh burst out and he pulled the woman into a hug. "Can't think of any kids finding a better home than right here with you." He shrugged. "And even grumpy ol' Gordon too."

"What ya say, lad?" He lumbered forward, a frown in place as he gestured toward his wife. "You're standing around here haverin' on like we have all day to dally. We're already late as it is."

Luke looked from Nessa to Faye to Gordon, and even to Jamie, who'd just entered the foyer with everyone else. "Late?"

"You dinna tell him why he needed to hurry?" Nessa rolled her eyes heavenward. "Did you think he might need to know?"

"I was trying to keep it a surprise."

"A surprise? We're already going to be a half hour late, and you thought to keep it a surprise? Why on earth did you think that was a good idea? It's the king!"

"I was trying to be blinkin' romantic," Gordon roared back.

"Were you now?" Nessa's voice dropped into a coo and she leaned up and kissed the man on his cheek. "Well, a few minutes won't hurt, will it?"

Nothing, except the love between Gordon and Nessa, made sense at the moment.

And the fact they'd decided to adopt Faye and Jamie.

Everything else reminded him of a scene from a Monty Python movie.

"What are you two talking about?"

"You're going to a ball!" Faye shouted, her hands outstretched like something Penelope would do. "A real ball! Just like a princess."

Even though Luke didn't understand anything about what Faye just said, a knot started developing in his stomach.

"Och, lass. You kinna say it like that." Gordon shook his head and reached for a garment bag hanging on a closet door nearby. "Go on in that room and put these on. You kinna go looking like you just finished working a job."

Luke stared down at the garment bag in his hand. "I don't quite understand what—"

"The king sent a special invitation to you for tonight's Wild Hyacinth Ball." Nessa's voice grew in volume and pitch to the point Luke took a step back. "Isn't it marvelous? We were given orders to get you there, if you're willing."

Nope. Still not fully comprehending. Ball? As in . . . really? Luke blinked a few times as he tried to make sense of the situation. "The king invited me to a ball?"

Even saying it made him feel a little queasy. And ridiculous. And like he'd stepped into one of Penelope's daydreams. A shiver ran through his body.

"That's right." Nessa took him by the shoulders and guided him to the next room. "And we're going to get you there." She laughed. "Like regular fairy godparents."

The Penelope daydream reference died a death in his brain.

"Fairy godparents?" Gordon groaned. "Do I look like a fairy to you?"

"At the moment, you look more like an ogre," Nessa shot back, brow raised.

He huffed.

Nessa turned back to Luke and nudged him into the room before whispering, "Skymarian godparents then. Every story needs one or two, you know?" She laughed again. "So get yourself ready, my boy, so we can take you to your princess."

Another unrecognizable Gaelic word sounded from Gordon as the door closed, followed by some giggling and another thud or two.

Luke stared at the closed door. Why did he feel like he'd stepped back in time to one of Izzy or Penelope's sleepovers? An ache pulsed over his left eyebrow.

What was happening? He looked down at the garment bag in his hand and unzipped it to reveal—the knot moved from his stomach to his throat—a tux?

A sudden chill spilled ice through his body. No, he couldn't do this. He wasn't made for something like this. A ball? A royal ball?

He had a hard enough time not wanting to run for his life from a friendly meeting with the king in his private apartments. And if he sweated like a cow in a slaughterhouse over a structured and somewhat brief press conference, how on earth would he make it through an entire evening of dancing and small talk with rich people?

He reached for the door handle and paused. But one more night with Ellie?

He rocked back from the door and placed the tux on the nearby chair, staring down at it as if it held some answers. If her dad had invited him, then he knew he at least liked Luke enough to be seen in public with him, let alone to allow his daughter to be seen with him.

A ballroom, though? And dancing . . . in front of other people?

His hands grew sweaty just thinking about it.

Memories of spending time with her over the last month flooded through him and his chest responded with a strange contradiction of expanding and contracting, like a fight or flight between pain and sweetness. Love was hard.

Achingly hard.

High-risk hard.

But also worth-it hard. He stood a little taller. Fighting hard.

He caught his reflection in a mirror across the room and stared back at himself. His body straightened, his own eyes challenging him. His jaw stiffened.

He may not have to fight a dragon, but he could fight against his own fears enough to show up for her.

To be there for her.

Tonight.

He shrugged off his flannel shirt and stared down at the tux again, and then, like any good warrior worth his salt, he accepted the mission head-on.

When he finally emerged from the room, feeling as uncomfortable as a man could feel in a tux he hadn't planned to wear to a ball he'd never even contemplated attending, Nessa rushed forward.

"Aw, don't you look class." She patted his shoulders and grinned. "A bit tight in the shoulders, isn't it?" Her eyes gleamed. "Not that anyone who matters will mind at all."

Heat exploded in his face, behind his eyes, inside his ear canals. He hated being on display.

"Aye." Nessa studied him to the point he wanted to squirm. "Rather fetching if you ask me."

He raised the bow tie to her to redirect her praise. "I can't get this to work. It's . . . too tight."

"Well, let me see what I can do." She took the item from him and began working with some piece of the cloth on the strap, and then Gordon emerged with Faye and Jamie on his heels.

"Come on now, woman, if we're goin' ta get anywhere before the night is done, we need to leave now."

"Then stop your bletherin' and let's get in the car." She frowned over at her husband but donned another smile for Luke.

This was crazy.

Gordon opened the door and gestured with his head for the children to climb in. Nessa grabbed her purse and followed.

Luke started to move, but Gordon stopped him. "Mind this, lad. You look as decent as any of the lot who'll be there." He narrowed his eyes. "And you're worth more than most of them because you'll do right by Ellie. I think she'll need you before the night's out, mate." He tapped his head. "Mind what matters and you'll be fine."

Gordon waved his hand to Nessa, who was in the passenger side of the car. "Give Luke the front. He'll have more room."

"But what about his tie?" Jamie interjected from the back seat, a little hesitantly.

"Och," Gordon growled, studying the situation. "Jamie, my boy, up front. Nessa and Luke in the back with Faye. Now let's be off."

All the cars in Skymar looked small.

And piling five people into one only proved it. Besides the fact that Luke was a tall, fairly average-sized man wearing a monkey suit, he also sat between Nessa, who attempted to strangle him with a bow tie, and Faye, who kept singing princess songs while Gordon drove like a maniac down roads too small to be two-lane.

He was, possibly, living one of his worst nightmares.

"Do you think you'll marry Princess Ellie?" This from Faye, who'd stopped singing long enough to become curious.

"Take Reddling Way, luv. It'll be shorter," Nessa called from the back.

"I don't think we can get married, Faye." Luke tried to keep his voice low. "I'm not a royal or even from Skymar."

"But that doesna matter, does it? Amara is from Nigeria and I'm from Skymar and we're still friends forever."

"Reddling Way will be too congested this time of day," Gordon shot back. "Route 45 is faster."

"Marrying a princess is a little different than just being friends, I think." Luke pinched his eyes closed as the car swerved. "She has responsibilities here and I have responsibilities back at my home."

"What are responsibilities?" Faye tilted her head and studied him.

Nessa gave the bow tie another jerk and then smiled. "You look braw, my boy." Then she turned to the front. "Route 45 will have work traffic from Kelmer and you know how that is."

"Responsibilities are things that are important to each of us that we need to do. That other people expect us to do." Maybe he preferred being in the back seat, because watching Gordon drive from the front seat would probably look more like a *Mario Kart* race.

"You're going to miss the exit, Gordie." Nessa's voice rose. "There it is."

"Och!" Gordon growled and swung the car over two lanes to take the exit.

Faye didn't seem fazed at all. Jamie held on to the side door with a white-knuckled grip.

"But she's a princess. That makes it special," came Faye's voice through the madness.

"It does, which means she deserves someone special to help her meet those responsibilities, and I live too far away." The statement hurt because it felt so true.

"We've gained at least ten minutes on our time." Nessa looked over at him, her eyes glistening. "Oh, it's so exciting, Luke." She glanced around the car expectantly. "Does anyone else feel like Cinderella?"

A few of his man points died inside him.

Faye gave a rousing clapped response, but every male in the car failed to be amused.

"Cinderella, woman?" Gordon gave his head a strong shake. "Right now, I feel like we're in a blooming Jason Bourne car chase."

And the men gave their hearty approval.

Man points restored. Mostly.

"Can't you and Princess Ellie just live in the middle?" Faye asked.

Gordon scoffed. "If they were merfolk."

"There's an ocean in the middle, Faye," Luke clarified.

The car swerved again, and Faye nearly landed in his lap.

"We're not far now," Nessa announced, patting Luke on the arm. "I can't wait for you to tell us all about it."

"We'll collect you at midnight," Gordon said. "Text us when you're ready."

Loyally, Luke

"Midnight is when Cinderella's magic ran out too," Faye added with a smile.

Luke wasn't even sure if his smile still worked. Was it possible that his little sister was writing this scene of his life and cackling from her place of omniscience?

"Do you think midnight will give you plenty of time?" This from Nessa.

"You don't have to wait for me." Luke shook his head. "I can rent a car and get back to Crieff."

"And allow us to miss the story?" Nessa gasped. "You kinna do that. Gordon and I will take Jamie and Faye back to Cambric and return for you later." Nessa sent Faye a wink. "And I'll share all of it with you tomorrow, Faye. Don't you worry."

The car swerved again and Luke braced himself with his knees as the tires screeched through a turn.

Maybe God was using this car ride to make him grateful to finally put his feet on steady ground again. Even if that steady ground started at the bottom of a staircase to a castle to meet a princess.

Yep. Still sounded weird.

And completely impossible.

CHAPTER 22

Three years ago, Ellie attended her last Wild Hyacinth Ball. Three years ago, she'd been a very different woman than the one staring back at her from the mirror in the royal attendance room, where she waited to step out onto the grand staircase as one of the attendants announced her presence.

Her parents would enter first.

Then the Crown Prince and his wife, followed by Prince Kurt and his fiancée. Then Rosalyn, the Princess Royal.

Then Ellie.

Alone. In front of hundreds to walk down the grand staircase.

She stared back at her reflection in the mirror as the rest of the family moved to the holding room to begin their entrance into the Great Hall.

Her eyes, so large and vulnerable, stared back at her, mocking her decision.

There would be no barriers. No one else to share the attention or on whom to lean.

Only her.

She closed her eyes and breathed out a silent prayer, and Luke's words came to mind. *"Embrace what God says about you."*

Blessed.

Secure.

Worthy.

Rescued. Her palm pressed over her heart as she recalled Luke pulling her from the icy water.

Restored. She smiled on the thought as she considered her own story over the past three years and the significance of this evening in her royal life. And then, an hour ago, Father sent her a video of the surprise press conference Luke held. Tears warmed beneath her closed eyelids. He'd done that for her, to fight a veritable reputation dragon in the only way he could.

Why?

She pinched her eyes tighter, smile stretching against her cheeks. *Beloved.*

She raised her chin as she drew in a deep breath. Those eyes staring back at her didn't look as vulnerable as they had a moment before. She turned toward the holding room as Rosalyn and her guest, Lord Devlin Westby, exited into the Great Hall.

Arran should have followed her, but in usual fashion, he failed to arrive with the family.

Collins, one of the royal attendants, dipped his head as she passed, his uniform displaying the national colors of dark green and pale blue. "Happy to have you back, Your Highness."

Ellie stood a little taller and smiled. "Happy and *honored* to be back, Collins. Thank you."

She stepped forward, each pronouncement drawing her closer to the top of the grand staircase until Rosalyn and her guest disappeared through the doors. A quote filtered into her mind from a childhood movie. What was it? She almost grinned. Cinderella? *"This is, perhaps, the greatest risk any of us will ever take: to be seen as we truly are."*

With a deep breath, she stepped out onto the grand staircase to a ballroom filled with the elegant and important. A hush fell over the room.

"Princess Elliana St. Clare, Duchess of Mara and the North Country."

She sent a look over the room, pausing for only a second longer, and then . . . into the fray she went. Each step gave way to more courage and confidence. Each movement forward, she reminded herself of who she was. Truly. Flaws and all.

Beloved and all.

Without one misstep, she reached the bottom of the staircase and joined her family, breathing a sigh of relief.

The hardest part was over.

At least, she hoped.

Father welcomed everyone, thanked all who helped make the evening possible, and then waved his hand for the music to begin. The sound of strings filled the space with a sense of magic. Lights glowed down on the golden floor. Pale blue banners brought a cele-bratory air, and slowly, led by her parents, couples filled the dance floor.

She closed her mind off to the fact that she stood alone. Other people chose not to join in and they framed the dance floor, speak-ing to each other and apparently enjoying the luxury and elegance of Carlstern Castle's finest.

"You look stellar, of course."

Ellie turned to find Maeve walking forward, her deep green gown a perfect complement to her dark hair and unique green eyes. A defi-nite ten walked beside her. Dark hair. Dark eyes. Skin the color of dark bronze. Where did she find him? On a beach in Italy?

"As do you."

"And this is Marco." Maeve braided her arm through his. "We met while watching a performance of *The Barber of Seville* last week." Maeve leaned forward, her brows giving a little shake. "He doesn't speak a lot of English, but we've managed to communicate in other ways."

Ellie caught her laugh with her hand. "He certainly increases the visual value of the room."

"Doesn't he?" She sighed and looked up at him. Even the lost and somewhat overwhelmed look on the man's face failed to mar his near perfection. Maeve smiled. "I am so proud of you. Walking down those steps on your own with the confidence of a queen. You stole the air in the room."

"I know my ability to breathe was certainly coming in short supply."

"You were amazing. You are amazing." Maeve's expression turned uncharacteristically somber. "And you're a wonderful princess on your own too. You've proven that already."

"I know I'll be fine on my own, but I don't *want* it to remain so." Ellie pinched her hands together in front of her, wishing so hard her knight-in-fuzzy-flannel would toss all care aside and sweep her off her feet. "And right now the idea of being on my own for the next several hours isn't appealing at all, especially with a dance floor."

Maeve opened her mouth to respond when her attention fixed on something just over Ellie's shoulder. A slow smile curved her lips. "I don't think you're going to have to worry about that."

Ellie stared at Maeve for a second and then turned.

A wave of warmth rushed through her, yet her body froze to the spot.

Standing at the top of the stairs, looking every bit the part of a gentleman, stood Luke Edgewood. Gone was the flannel, and she couldn't really say she was sorry, because Luke Edgewood in a tux left her dazzled. He'd shaved his beard close, giving off more of a five-o'clock shadow look, and the cut of the suit highlighted those exemplary shoulders of his.

"Whew," Maeve muttered. "There ain't nothing wrong with that view."

Ellie gave her head a little shake in response, her attention fixed on Luke like he'd stepped right out of her daydream into reality. Because, in a manner of speaking, he had.

He tugged at the sleeve of his jacket and scanned the room, the slight movement and deep breath he took the only hints of his discomfort.

A gasp of air burst from her in disbelief and she stepped forward, drawn to him.

The motion caught his attention and his gaze flitted to hers, then held. His focus moved from the crown on her head all the way down her gown and back up, a wonderfully crooked tip to his lips spreading in time with the appreciation in those eyes. Without another moment's hesitation, he descended, his focus never wavering.

She felt like the only person in the room, and in this case, she didn't mind at all. Being the center of *his* attention placed her in one of the best seats in the house.

The closer he came, the more his body relaxed and his smile grew . . . and the more she started to believe it was actually happening.

"I think Marco and I will leave the two of you to"—Maeve waved a hand—"stare?"

Ellie spared Maeve a look as her friend moved to the dance floor, and then Luke was standing in front of her, real and smiling and wonderfully dashing.

Oh, he looked even more attractive up close.

"Hi." The word trembled out on a whisper.

He dipped his head, never breaking eye contact. "Hey." His simple response, uttered low and slow, sent a delightful tingle up her neck. Paired with his hooded look, she nearly melted to the floor in a heap of blue satin and happiness.

"You're here."

He nodded. "I can't say I fought a horde of monsters to get here, but I did see my life flash before my eyes a few times."

Her laugh burst out. No, she wasn't dreaming, because his response proved classic Luke. "Sounds like there's a story attached to that statement."

He shook his head slowly, his smile growing wider. "Let's just say I'm certainly going to need another reward after the car ride I just survived to be here."

Oh . . . heavens. She drew on all of her practice as a royal to keep her expression steady. "So . . . is this a real date?"

"I don't wear a tux for fake ones."

She pulled in a shaky breath. "I must say, Mr. Edgewood, I think we should invest in a great many real dates in the future if I can see you wear a tux on occasion."

He stepped closer, the heat from his eyes sending warmth to her cheeks. "It's not so bad to wear it if you keep looking at me like you are."

"Believe me, it is no hardship on my part at all."

"I'd say the feeling is mutual on that score." His gaze trailed down her again, leaving a lovely trail of tingles in its wake. "You're—" His breath caught. "Breathtaking."

The power it took within her not to breach every protocol and kiss him proved she'd developed a great deal of self-control in the last few years. "I'm so glad you're here."

His entire expression grew tender, except for the quirk in those lovely lips. "It seemed a shame not to get the full Skymarian experience."

And though his words teased, his eyes told her much more. He came for her. And only her.

She stepped closer to him, almost afraid to touch him for fear he might disappear. "It would be a shame to leave without a royal ball, a harrowing car ride, a snowstorm, and your name in the gossip columns."

He studied her a moment and then looked around the room, one brow rising in unison with the crook of his lips. "Well, while I was watching my life flash before my eyes on the way here, I realized there is *one* Skymarian opportunity I have yet to experience."

"What is that?" She barely voiced the question, her pulse beating in her ears.

He drew in a deep breath, as if preparing for some challenge, and then offered his hand. "Dancing with a princess."

"Oh, you really are dangerously charming when you put your mind to it."

"Seems I just need the proper inspiration." Her hand slipped into his, those ridges and calluses a wonderfully familiar touch.

"I feel as though you're showering me with your particular brand of chivalry, Luke. A press conference, showing up to a royal ball, and now you offer to dance with me?" She stepped into his arms, and the warm scent of spice and coffee filled her senses. "I could get used to this."

"I'd do about anything, Princess Elliana, if it meant one more date with you."

Luke almost turned around three times once he crossed the threshold into the castle. Every step on the plush carpet or glistening marble, every glimpse of the ornate chandeliers and intricate tapestries, practically screamed how out of place this country boy was.

But then he saw Ellie, looking every bit the part of a princess in her silky blue gown that fell to the floor. One of her shoulders showcased a bow of some sort and the other side revealed her beautiful bare shoulder.

He promised himself right then and there that he'd embrace this night like the fairy tale it felt like, complete with a midnight curfew.

With her in his arms on the dance floor, he didn't care how ridiculous he looked in a tux or how much the guys back home would tease him about attending a royal ball. In fact, nothing outside the look Ellie gave him mattered.

Being with her mattered.

Maybe the royal gig wasn't *so* bad.

Parts of it, anyway.

The Ellie parts.

And the service parts.

And the ability to plan for good change as well as the power to make it happen.

"I had no idea you knew how to dance." She smiled up at him, the blue of her gown making her eyes almost glow. "But from what you've told me about your sisters, this sounds as if it may be a Penelope adventure of some sort."

"Our dad couldn't carry a tune in a bucket, so I was volunteered to be her dance partner."

"The dancing carpenter?" She blinked up at him with faux innocence. "Your friends must stand in awe."

He narrowed his eyes in a mock glare. "Now why would you go and ruin a perfectly fine conversation with an image like that? It's almost as bad as mentioning certain Christmas chime movies."

Her quiet laugh inspired his smile. He loved her laugh. "How did you get here? It's a rather exclusive invitation list."

Exclusive list? Luke paused on the thought. "Your dad sent an invitation by way of the Frasiers, and they sort of . . . encouraged me to accept."

Her dad had invited him. Could that mean he made an even more exclusive list? A list grand enough to win Ellie's heart for good? Or was it just a "thanks for the press conference" kind of list?

He didn't even know how to process this possible change in his plans.

He'd set his mind and his heart on having to end things with her forever.

"I'm so glad they did." She searched his face, her smile softening. "So very glad." She squeezed his hand. "It seems you are more adept at performing in the public eye when necessary than even you realize. The press conference was remarkable, Luke."

"'When necessary' being the key phrase," Luke said with a shudder. "But I wanted to disappear from the world for a good week after that. It was exhausting."

"It's not my favorite either, unless I can point the attention to someone else."

She looked at him with such admiration, he felt pretty sure his chest expanded to Superman proportions. "And I must say, you certainly know how to enter a room like a royal, catching everyone's attention."

He tipped his head a little closer, gathering in a deep breath of oranges and Ellie. "I wasn't here for anyone else but you."

The dance blended into a second and a third before Ellie, thankfully, offered to have them take a break. The muscles used in dancing and in building weren't the same. Both hard work in their own way, but one was much less familiar to him than the other.

Gratefully.

"Luke!"

Luke looked over, wondering who in the world would know him in a place like this, and found Lewis Gray approaching. The older man personified class from his gray tux and matching streaks in his hair to his excellent posture.

"Mr. Gray." Luke took his outstretched hand. "A pleasure to see you here, sir."

"Lewis, lad." Lewis Gray shook his head. "Call me Lewis. We are on friendship terms now, I believe."

Luke always had a hard time calling older men by their first names. Maybe it stemmed from the "respect your elders" mantra of his youth or just the fact he felt they usually knew a whole lot more than him, but he would try to comply with Lewis's request. At least in his head.

Lewis offered a bow to Ellie. "Your Highness, it is a pleasure to see you again."

"Thank you, Mr. Gray. I'm so glad to have you here this year."

Loyally, Luke

"It is an honor to be invited." His eyes lit. "And I am especially glad for your return as a working royal. My hope is that your courage and hard work toward a second chance will inspire many other people to incorporate such virtues within their daily lives."

"I haven't thought about it that way, but I like the idea of inspiring people in a positive direction instead of how I am often portrayed."

He chuckled, sending Luke a wink. "I think we have the news duly pointed in a positive direction from what I hear about a certain press conference today. You may very well fall out of the tabloids altogether if you stay as wholesome as this."

"From your lips to the heavens, Mr. Gray." Ellie smiled, slowly entwining her arm around Luke's. Nice feeling. Good fit. Right beside him.

"And, Luke, your work on my cabin has been remarkable. I hope you'll consider coming back to Skymar for a few more jobs." Lewis's attention flitted to Ellie and back. "I'm sure we can provide plenty of inducements for your return."

Ellie straightened by his side. "Will you excuse me a moment? Father is calling for me." She gave Luke's arm a squeeze, sending him another smile before moving across the room to meet other members of the royal family.

The gown she wore fell over her body like water, and he had to reexamine his thoughts about sweaters and leggings as her sexiest fashion. Satin and heels worked really well for her too. His throat tightened. Really well.

"Would you be interested in coming back to Skymar, Luke?"

Luke pulled his attention back to Lewis Gray, the amusement on the man's face as apparent as the twinkle in his eyes. "I think I'm warming up to the idea." Luke's gaze moved back across the room.

Definitely.

"Your Mr. Edgewood proved himself quite capable today during the press conference, didn't he?"

Ellie smiled up at her father, the memory of Luke's defense of her still fresh and sweet and wonderful. "Diplomatic, even."

"I think his quaintness may have charmed a few of the reporters in the process." A sudden glint in her father's eyes caused Ellie to study him more thoroughly. "An excellent skill to have for anyone special in your life."

"Anyone special in my life?" she repeated slowly, attempting to sort out his meaning.

"Showing up tonight proved the final test, really." Her father's grin turned apologetic. "More of a final answer I needed to enact a plan your mother and I have been composing."

"A plan?" Her pulse took a steady upswing and she looked nearby to find her mother watching them, as if she knew exactly what sort of conversation they were having. "Involving Luke?"

"Aye. And I'd like to meet with the both of you this week to discuss it further. Something with more of a happily-ever-after ring to it, I believe." He tipped his head and studied her face. "Would you speak with him about the meeting? I think it may come off better from you than me."

Happily ever after? For her and Luke? Was it even possible? What would she have to give up? What would he?

"Y-yes. Of course." For the first time in this entire scenario, hope swirled to life in her chest. Was there a way to have both her royal life and her private one . . . with Luke? Nothing came to mind. No real solution to meet all the requirements from both sides, but a king often had a much greater vision.

And power.

"Though I'm not certain how free his time will be this week, Father." Her smile fell a little. "He's flying back to the States next Wednesday, and this week is filled with responsibilities related to his work for Lewis Gray and in preparation for his cousin's wedding on Friday evening."

Father nodded, his grin never faltering. "I think once you hear of the plan, we can sort out something. The decision will ultimately be his."

Ellie's gaze flew back to Luke, who now conversed with a small crowd of men, his newfound popularity and everyone's natural curiosity leading them toward him. If he despised it all, she couldn't tell from his welcome smile and poise, but this was only one night. A few hours of "royal life." Luke wouldn't want this forever, even for her.

Father's confident grin brimmed as the music stopped. How could her parents' proposal solve the very real problem of two people shouldering two separate responsibilities and living in two very different worlds?

Father winked. "We are in need of a liaison to the United States, you know. To build our relationship with them and encourage more tourism."

Her eyes widened. "What . . . what do you mean?"

The guards took their position for Father's entrance, so he merely shrugged and offered his hand to her. "Are you ready for the announcement of your return as a working royal?" He gestured with his head toward the crowd. "It's what they are all waiting for."

Ellie smiled up at her father, his question giving her one last chance to step back away from it all and embrace a life out of the spotlight. Even with the promise of some kind of future with Luke glimmering in the recesses of her mind, she knew her father wouldn't have encouraged her to go through with her reinstatement if that hadn't been considered.

She belonged here and she had to embrace it all—the good and the bad.

And maybe even . . . the impossible.

"I am."

Father dipped his head in assent and took his place on the grand staircase. Luke came to her side, his presence the perfect pinnacle to this night and her new life.

The announcement began and her smile widened with her deep certainty of her choice. Despite her past and even her present stumblings, she still possessed the heart of a princess.

She gave Luke's arm a quick squeeze before stepping forward to Father's summons.

And perhaps she'd found her prince too.

CHAPTER 23

<u>Text from Penelope to Luke:</u> YOU WENT TO THE BALL????

<u>Luke:</u> Oh great, how did YOU find out, of all people.

<u>Penelope:</u> Grandpa Gray said he saw you there. And he told me ALL about it. The way Ellie walked down the stairs alone, and then you showed up and the room went quiet for a whole new reason. And then the dances and the announcement and how you and Ellie spent the whole evening together until you had to leave. AHHH!! Luke!!!

<u>Luke:</u> You could have just waited to talk to me today since you're back in Skymar, instead of blowing up my phone with your book-long messages.

<u>Penelope:</u> Oh my goodness, Luke! It's that scene in all the royal romance movies where the woman stands at the top of the stairs and the guy sees her and is totally amazed at her beauty. Except you're her. You ARE the Hallmark heroine!

<u>Luke:</u> You've been waiting to type that paragraph all morning, haven't you?

<u>Penelope:</u> I thought it looked really spontaneous. And now we have it in writing! See? I can be really funny.

<u>Luke:</u> Semantics.

<u>Penelope:</u> So . . . how did things end with you and Ellie? Was it really goodbye this time? Please say no! It will disprove all of my happily-ever-after movies AND break your heart.

<u>Penelope:</u> Okay, so the priority is not in that order. Your heartbreak is much more important than my obsession with HEAs.

Luke: Thanks for clarifying. I might have lost sleep over that.

Luke: It was a weird goodbye to be honest. She said something about trying to see me before I leave, but my week is crazy through Friday. I hope we'll find a time, but I'm not sure what else there is to say or do. She mentioned something about another option.

Penelope: Are you open to another option? I mean, you did survive a fancy luncheon, a press conference, tabloids, and a ball! I think you've proven you are somewhat adaptable to change of the most mind-boggling kind.

Penelope: Mind-boggling for you. I've planned to live moments like that my whole life, so I feel prepared.

Luke: I don't know, Penny-girl. I can't imagine what option she can offer. I'm a background guy. She's a princess.

Penelope: Which is exactly what Ellie might need most, Luke. Someone who keeps her grounded and doesn't mind staying in the background. I know you've always been that person for me.

Luke: You're trying to make up for the Hallmark heroine comment, aren't you?

Penelope: No! I mean it. I can't imagine having a better brother, but even more than that, you're a great person. You don't always know it, but you are because of how you change other people's lives by living yours so well. You're good at loving.

Luke: The romantic vibes of wedding week are sending you over the edge, aren't they?

Penelope: I know you appreciated what I said because you deflected. :) I've thought a lot about your situation after nearly breaking down on the phone with you last week. Maybe your brand of care is exactly what a whole country needs! Sounds like something your stalwart,

testosterone-loving heart could handle. You know?
Saving a family, or a country, or a PLANET!

Luke: Don't get carried away there, Penny-girl. Oh wait,
that's your MO. Never mind.

Penelope: I'm just saying, I think you'd make a great consort
to a princess. Ooh, just the idea gives me lovely tingles.

Luke: Sounds like you might need to see a doctor about those.

Penelope: I'm rolling my eyes, just so you know.

Penelope: But I also wanted you to be the first to hear a
secret. Matt asked me to marry him last night on the
Darling House theater stage!!! It was super romantic and
sweet and I just can't wait to be his wife and Iris's mom!!!

Luke: Congrats, Penn! I'm really happy for you. And the only
thing people will be surprised about is that you kept it a
secret! Why aren't you proclaiming this from the social
media mountaintop?

Penelope: Because I don't want to distract from Izzy's week
at all. I plan to tell her in private too, because it's so
wonderful to just celebrate her and Brodie right now.

Luke: That's sweet of you. Mature.

Penelope: Well, I'm going to be a mom! I'd better garner a
little more maturity. Good moms can be silly too, though,
and that can be just as wonderful.

Luke: Then you'll be all set on that part.

Penelope: (Ignoring.) Anyway, I really am in love with a
wonderful guy, and I want you to be happy too, Luke.

Luke: Penn, I will be. Just like you've told me so many
times before, I can choose joy. That might be tough
right now, but that doesn't stop me from still trying to
choose joy, because there's so much to celebrate right
now for you and Izzy, and even with Josephine and the
twins.

Penelope: Well, choose joy but don't close off possibilities. Remember: "Impossible things are happening every day."

†

Weddings were hard-core.

Or maybe just this wedding since it happened in a different country than home?

And . . . it was *his* family.

Luke couldn't have known ahead of time, but between getting family members settled in—especially those with twins and a bad case of jet lag—navigating the last parts of his reno job for Mr. Gray . . . er . . . Lewis, and helping repair a broken wedding arch two days before the ceremony, he needed a vacation from his vacation.

The calmest people of the bunch were the bride and groom.

In fact, Brodie and Izzy rolled with all the difficulties like they were floating through a lovestruck cartoon and nothing could dampen the anticipation.

Even the stag party for Brodie kept a low profile, with steaks and drinks and talk about life and books and hunting. After a ball—an unusually good night with his lovely princess—and a week of wedding prep, a little bit of testosterone-driven time talking about nothing related to romance fit the mental health bill.

Except, Luke kind of wanted to talk about romance.

With one person. And *only* one person.

He grinned as he waited in the foyer of the beautiful stone church, dressed to the nines for a second time in less than a week. Though at least this monkey suit proved to be a sleek-looking gray suit and tie instead of a tux.

Brodie and Izzy wanted a simple affair. Close family with a larger reception afterward, and Luke was honored Brodie asked him to be a groomsman. Him and Matt, with Anders as best man. Of course, Izzy had Penelope as her maid of honor and Josephine as matron of honor. Brodie's two sisters were included as well—the youngest, Fiona, guided by her elder sister down the aisle. Izzy had even been thoughtful enough to include Matt's daughter, Iris, in the festivities as a flower girl.

He sighed. Everyone he loved best in the world was right here.

Except one person.

The music began and Luke took turns with Matt escorting guests to their seats down the stone aisle. Roses decorated various places in the room, the soft red color a nice contrast to the gray stone walls and floor.

But just before the ceremony was about to start, Matt met him at the beginning of the aisle with a strange sort of grin on his face. "I think you ought to escort the next guest, mate."

Luke frowned and turned toward the foyer.

Standing in a simple light pink dress, golden hair spun up in some twist on her head, stood Princess Elliana St. Clare, Duchess of Mara and the North Country. Luke's brain stopped working altogether and he blinked.

She was still there.

Luke looked back over at Matt just to make sure they both were seeing the same thing, and with a reassuring nod from the latter, he shifted forward a step. Then another. Until he came close enough to breathe in the scent of oranges.

"What are you doing here?"

Her smile faltered. "Well, I've been trying to meet with you all week, so I took whatever advantage I could to get your attention."

He gave his head a firm shake, just to make sure he saw straight. "You've definitely done that." He lowered his voice and offered his arm to her. "But . . . even as a princess, don't you need an invitation to a wedding?"

Her grin returned. "Well, I received a rather humorous and exuberant message from your sister Penelope through Lewis Gray."

Luke cast a look behind him to find Penelope peering around the back entrance to the church, her grin as wide as ever. His chest tightened. What was happening?

"And with a little bit of inventive thinking, I worked my way onto the guest list as your plus-one." Ellie raised a brow, her arm squeezing into his as they started walking down the aisle. "Assuming you're fine with having me as your date?"

He peered down at her, forcing words through his throat. "My date for today, then?"

Her gaze held his, some secret message within those blue depths. "Well, let's *start* with today."

He froze, waiting for her to expound on that little hint, but all she did was take her seat with the other guests and leave him standing in the aisle dumbfounded, like one of the church statues at the four corners of the room.

If the *Lord of the Rings* theme hadn't started playing from the string quartet in the corner, Luke would have joined Ellie in the pew to get the rest of the story, but that particular song was his cue to make it back to the foyer for the bridal party's entrance.

All throughout the ceremony, his gaze kept straying back to Ellie's, and each time, he found her looking right back.

Even when Brodie and Izzy spoke their vows.

And just before the prayer.

And once during the reading of the love chapter in Corinthians.

And definitely as he escorted Brodie's sister back down the aisle during the recessional.

But it wasn't until the transition from the wedding to the reception that he had a chance to locate Ellie and pull her into one of the small alcoves in the back of the church for some privacy.

"Blast it all, Princess. Your eyes kept saying something the whole service that your lips didn't clarify back there, so I'm not waiting another minute to get resolution."

Without hesitation, she wrapped her fingers around the lapel of his suit and rocked up on tiptoe to press her lips to his. His body stilled for half a second before he pulled her into his arms and finished what she so sweetly started.

He wouldn't have referred to his side of the kissing as sweet.

Powerful? Hungry? Grateful?

Definitely the latter. And maybe a little of the middle. Because she tasted so good.

"How was that for a little more clarification?" she asked, stepping back, her cheeks as pink as her dress and her breath a little shaky.

"Ellie, though I appreciate the nonverbal answer, I'm a man. I need direct and clear, because you're sending off messages I'd like to be able to answer in the affirmative, but—"

"How would you feel if I flew back with you to the U.S. on Wednesday?" She kept her hands on his jacket, her gaze searching his, her lips close and smiling.

He tilted his head, studying her as if one of them had gone crazy. "What did you say?"

"My parents have offered me a proposal." Her eyes fairly glowed with words she hadn't said yet, and his entire body tensed in anticipation. "In light of my affection for you, but also my desire to serve Skymar as a working royal, they have offered a compromise. A way to hopefully meet halfway."

"Meet halfway?" Luke's brain didn't compute. "We're not merfolk, Ellie."

"Merfolk?" A laugh burst from her. "No, we're not. We *are*, however, two people who I believe make a better pair together than apart, and my parents see that too. Especially after the press conference and the ball."

The halfway part still tangled in his thoughts.

"Since most of the duties and meetings that require my physical presence happen between January and June every year, I've been given the opportunity to join you in the U.S. from June to December. I can work as a liaison between Skymar and the U.S., which is something Father has been hoping to enact for a while now."

He blinked. What was she saying?

"I can't work a paying job due to royal restrictions, but I thought my interior design skills could benefit your business." She kept searching his face and saying words, but they couldn't be real. "Assuming our relationship continues to move forward in the way I hope."

"Wait a minute." He didn't even believe the words getting ready to come out of his mouth. "You'd move to the U.S. for half a year to be with *me*?"

"If you want me to, I will." A sliver of uncertainty flickered across her face.

"Want you to?"

"And if you were willing to return with me to Skymar for the rest of the year, Father has hopes that you would be willing to take on some responsibilities that I believe he has discussed with you already."

Luke looked away, the pieces of it all starting to click together. Help with building and orphans and forestry . . . and be with Ellie, but also learn the royal world?

"As a younger sibling in the royal family, I have more freedom to live a quieter life, which is what I would prefer." She looked down, focusing on where her hands held his jacket. "But being with me would require certain social and public responsibilities. A sacrifice on your part."

"You'd move to the U.S. to be with *me*?" He still couldn't quite comprehend it.

"Of course I would."

"Ellie, you're a princess and I'm just some country carpenter who lives in a really small town in the Blue Ridge Mountains. People in my world name their *cats* Princess. They don't expect to meet one."

She laughed. "I can handle that."

"My life is simple." He needed her to understand so she would straighten out this crazy story he kept hearing, but not believing.

"I like simple whenever I can get it. But the real draw is you." A flicker lit her eyes and a playful grin tipped her lips. "Don't forget, Luke—most importantly, I am . . . just a girl . . ."

Warning alarms started blaring in his head. "What?"

"Standing in front of a boy . . ."

He began to recognize the quote from one of Penelope's ridiculous rom-coms. "Don't you dare say it."

"Asking him to—"

He captured her lips before she could finish the disgustingly sweet quote. She tasted of cinnamon and pastry and forever. He'd have groaned at his own thoughts, if he didn't feel them with such certainty. But thinking them didn't mean he had to say them out loud, so at least he could hold on to a little pride while he gave his heart completely to this amazing woman in his arms.

She kissed him back, wrapping her arms around his neck and giving with as much thoroughness as he did. He breathed in her scent. All right, maybe he could work up saying the words too. If he had to. And maybe that was why all those silly movies ended up sticking with people. Deep down they communicated something everyone wanted. Everyone hoped to find.

Being worthy of someone's love just as you were. Being enough.

His chest squeezed. She thought he was worth it, and he'd spend however long it took to convince her she'd made the right choice, from one side of the ocean to the other.

He drew back first, his gaze roaming her face. She'd leave her world for him. No one did that. Definitely not a princess. But she would? His thumb skimmed over her chin. "You don't have to ask me to love you, Ellie." Emotion pressed his words into a rasp. "I already do. I think I have since the first moment I saw you."

She laughed and cupped his face with her palms, her smile so close. "I'm so glad, because it would be horribly inconvenient for this to be one-sided."

"No, ma'am. I'm all in. On both sides of the sea." He snuck a kiss. "You can be my country girl princess."

She chuckled. "And you can be my flannel-wearing knight?"

He groaned. "Naw, let's stop right there. It's starting to sound way too much like a really bad country music song."

"Or the makings of a sappy, dramatic, unbelievable, and wonderful happily ever after?"

"I'll take the unbelievable and wonderful parts, but let's leave the sap and drama out of the planning, okay?"

She raised a brow and he sighed. "All right, sap and drama are bound to come, but we'll keep those to a minimum."

She pulled him into another kiss, leaving him ready to go in search of the preacher to make things official. "All right, a little sap may not be bad either."

Her expression sobered a little, but the tenderness in her eyes stayed the same. "I love you, Luke. I want you in my future, no matter where that future takes place."

He kissed her again, because he could. Because she'd not only chosen them but fought for their future when the easy thing would have been to give up. And if she was willing to meet him halfway, merfolk or not, he'd match her.

And they did match.

Loyally, Luke

An unlikely, unusual, unexpected match.

But perfect.

Above them, the sound of church bells rang through the evening air.

A chime? He rolled his gaze heavenward, making sure God knew he got the humor of the moment. Then he drew in a deep breath of Ellie's sweet citrusy scent and pressed a kiss to her forehead, like the romantic he was trying to hide. Maybe this happily-ever-after gig wasn't so bad after all.

But he didn't have to admit that to Penelope.

Ever.

Text from Izzy to Penelope, Luke, and Josephine: Brodie just showed me our plane tickets and itinerary after keeping the location of our honeymoon secret!! NEW ZEALAND!! He is taking me to NEW ZEALAND!! I am going to live my lifelong dream of being a hobbit! Move over, Samwise and Rosie. Here come Brodie and Izzy!

Izzy: Penelope, I thought you'd appreciate the capitalizations and exclamation marks.

Izzy: Luke, I thought you'd just appreciate Brodie's perfect honeymoon destination choice.

Luke: For you, it's stellar. He ran it by me a few months ago.

Izzy: You knew? Why are you so good at secrets and I end up telling everything?

Luke: I just like to have things to hold over people. It gives me a sense of superiority.

Izzy: Truer words have never been spoken . . . texted?

Penelope: Proof positive he's meant for royalty.

Luke: Nope. Stop with the royal jokes. You've already exhausted them in person. Let's not contaminate our texts too.

Penelope: But why not, when you're such a Prince Charming?

Luke: You're gross, Penny-girl.

Penelope: I'm wonderfully romantic. It's my crowning achievement.

Penelope: And you should see them together, Iz. Ellie and Luke are sitting on the couch across from me in Grandpa Gray's house and Luke looks so smitten. I can't stop grinning. It's adorable.

Luke: Never use the word "adorable" about a grown man. It makes me want to beat my head against a wall.

Josephine: New Zealand? Oh, Izzy, the scenery is magnificent. I don't know if you remember that I visited there once. It was the only time I ever rode horses bareback across the plains with those glorious mountains on every side. Unforgettable.

Izzy: . . .

Luke: . . .

Penelope: Oh, Josephine. That's . . . amazing.

Josephine: I was on a strictly fish diet at the time. For some reason, besides it giving me very oily hair, I often felt a sense of euphoria. It was where I met Patrick, if you remember. He was interning to provide foot care to poor communities.

Izzy: Josephine, you have completely altered my image of you in my mind.

Luke: So . . . let's change the subject from the clear paradox Josephine has set up for the rest of us, because I don't think any of us are prepared to process everything that unfolded there.

Loyally, Luke

Luke: Mission: Impossible and The Last Samurai were filmed in New Zealand too. Hobbits, bioterrorists, spies, and samurai. Sounds like a place everyone should visit.

Penelope: Ew, clearly your romance gene is severely underdeveloped, Luke. Bioterrorists and spies for a honeymoon? Ugh. Though I'm not sure how well hobbits fit in with that either, but it will make Izzy happy and that's all that matters.

Izzy: Speaking of secrets and romance . . . I'm so happy for you, Penelope. Engaged!!

Penelope: I'm in love with a wonderful guy! What can I say?

Josephine: And Matt has assured me he and Iris plan to remain in the U.S. with Penelope. He's even started applying for citizenship. What a comfort!

Izzy: Luke will be there part-time, Josie! ("Josie" seems to better fit an adventurous bareback rider.)

Penelope: Because the other part of the time he has to go fulfill princely duties. AHHH!!

Luke: Whoa there, y'all. Ellie and I haven't even gotten on the plane to the U.S. yet. There are still a lot of things to work out.

Izzy: We know you, Luke. If you love her, you'll find a way.

Penelope: And we'll all have each other to help us get through all the craziness of life, no matter what side of the world we're on.

Luke: The real question is . . . what will Josephine do with all her free matchmaking time now that we are all happily matched?

Josephine: Don't you all worry about me. There is always the next generation.

Izzy: I'm sure Luke will have a whole lot to say about that.

Penelope: Not right now! He just took Ellie by the hand

and disappeared out on the terrace. For someone who doesn't like to talk about romance, he sure doesn't mind it too much when he's been sprinkled with his own fairy dust. I don't think we're going to get a text back from him for a long time. *sigh* I love happily ever afters.

Izzy: So do I, Penn. So do I.

And they all lived . . . happily ever after.

THE END

Acknowledgments

This story was one of the most difficult and enjoyable to write. Why? Well, the enjoyable part was due to the Edgewood family and how much I've grown to ADORE them, especially Luke. The difficult part was the fact that this was the last book my dad and I brainstormed together before he unexpectedly passed away, so bringing this story to a close felt like another little goodbye within a year of goodbyes to him. However, I'm so proud of this story because in Luke there are glimpses of my dad's personality and his ferocious love for his family.

But, apart from those things, there were some AMAZING people who helped support me while writing this story too.

I cannot thank the wonderful author Debb Hackett enough! She became my very own "royal watcher" and British support person to ensure I kept my Skymarian royal family as believable as a fictional royal family can be. ☺ Her enthusiasm for this story was a definite encouragement along the way of writing it too!

On the note of research, I cannot thank Becky Young and her husband, Chris, enough for all their encouragement and guidance. Chris was great at helping me solidify some of my building research and Becky kept helping brainstorm little ideas to bring to the story.

My bestie, Jennifer Boice, who has followed the Edgewood stories from conception to revision to final, is a constant sounding board and encourager for all my crazy ideas. The best friends can handle a little crazy.

There is such a lovely group of ladies who are first readers and truly

ACKNOWLEDGMENTS

encourage me every step of the way through all my challenges and pro-crastinations and self-doubt! Thank you so much to Joy Tiffany, Beth Erin, Andrette Herron, Michelle Lunsford, and Alissa Peppo!

I'm so grateful to my agent and friend, Rachel McMillan, who not only continues to be a brilliant agent with an amazing grasp of the publishing world, but she's a top-notch cheerleader too!

My daughter, Lydia, has been a brilliant team player by shar-ing her creativity and encouragement for all three of these Edgewood books. Those maps at the beginning of each book are her work! Plus, she's just fantastic at cheering on these bookish dreams of mine.

I am so grateful for my family. We've weathered a lot of different types of rough patches together, and every time I'm completely amazed at how God, in His kindness, continues to bring us closer. Some of the inspiration for the Edgewood siblings comes from my own expe-rience with my brother and cousins, but also from living life with the Basham five.

I'm thankful for my mom. She's been such an example of God's grace through a long, tough season. She and Dad have always dreamed big for me, and I'm so grateful they've both had the chance to see God take that little girl who liked to make up stories become a woman who still likes to make them up for His glory.

Lastly, I am so glad I got to dedicate this book to my dad! He would have LOVED it, and I know a piece of him will find its way into every book I write in the future. He was my loudest, proudest, and most ardent cheerleader, and I know I have enough amazing memories and love packed into the almost five decades of life with him to last me until heaven. I'm so grateful that, because of his love and example, my dad led me to the Great Storyteller. And because my dad exemplified such a strong, faithful, and constant love, it helped me better understand the even stronger, more faithful, and eternal love of God.

Discussion Questions

1. The Edgewoods have close family ties. What are some things that let you know how close they are in words and in actions?
2. Luke and Ellie both have pasts that have shaped their current thinking patterns. How are each of them struggling with the impact of past choices/hurts in being able to think about future relationships?
3. Ellie's and Luke's worlds are very different, but what are some characteristics of the two of them that are the same?
4. Physical attraction is certainly a part of Ellie and Luke's relationship, but what are the more enduring things that attract the two of them to each other? What specifically draws Ellie to Luke and vice versa?
5. Is there a scene or two that you really enjoyed? What about those scenes really stood out to you?
6. How are Ellie's and Luke's relationships with their families similar? What about those relationships may have influenced each of them for the good?
7. Both Ellie and Luke must remind themselves of where their identity truly lies. How does this awareness help them when they are facing difficulties? How would it help you?
8. Luke makes a statement about how sometimes life offers two right choices. Have you ever been at a crossroads between two "right" choices? How did you come to your answer? What is Luke's advice on dealing with this dilemma?

From the Publisher

GREAT BOOKS

ARE EVEN BETTER WHEN THEY'RE SHARED!

Help other readers find this one:

- Post a review at your favorite online bookseller

- Post a picture on a social media account and share why you enjoyed it

- Send a note to a friend who would also love it—or better yet, give them a copy

Thanks for reading!

AVAILABLE IN PRINT, E-BOOK, AND AUDIO

Penelope takes the stage in
Positively, Penelope

About the Author

Michael Kaal @ Michael Kaal Photography

Pepper Basham is an award-winning author who writes romance "peppered" with grace and humor. Writing both historical and contemporary novels, she loves to incorporate her native Appalachian culture and/or her unabashed adoration of the UK into her stories. She currently resides in the lovely mountains of Asheville, NC, where she is the wife of a fantastic pastor, mom of five great kids, a speech-language pathologist, and a lover of chocolate, jazz, hats, and Jesus.

You can learn more about Pepper and her books on her website at www.pepperdbasham.com.
Facebook: @pepperbasham
Instagram: @pepperbasham
Twitter: @pepperbasham
BookBub: @pepperbasham